LITTLE SISTER

22. 9. 16

Vince Fernandez

Manor House

Library and Archives Canada Cataloguing in Publication

Fernandez, Vince, author
    Little Sister : a novel / Vince Fernandez.

ISBN 978-1-988058-10-8 (hardback),

ISBN 978-1-988058-09-2 (paperback)

    I. Title.

PS8611.E7495L58 2016   C813'.6   C2016-904809-8

Printed and bound in Canada / First Edition.
Editor: Susan Crossman, Crossman Communications
Interior layout-edit: Michael Davie
Cover Design-layout: Jessica Heald, Dig It Design, 416-238-0985
384 pages. All rights reserved.
Published September 15, 2016
Manor House Publishing Inc.
452 Cottingham Crescent, Ancaster, ON, L9G 3V6
www.manor-house.biz (905) 648-2193

This project has been made possible (in part) by the Government of
Canada/ Ce projet a ete rendu possible (en partie) grace au gouvernement
du Canada. Funding by the Government of Canada / Finance par le
gouvernement du Canada

To my parents, Brigitta and Xavier, who taught me perseverance.

To all those who helped chase away the paper tigers.

Acknowledgements

This novel could never have been realized without the help and encouragement of many people.

First and foremost, to my Anne: You gave up and offered much to allow me to reach my goal. My courage came from you. Words are insufficient to express my gratitude. To my Nadia and my Sonya, thank you for your constant hope and encouragement. You gave me the tenacity to see this through.

Many people suffered through early drafts. Thank you and sorry. I am indebted to my mom, Brigitta, my sister, Christina, Alison Doyle, Angela and Jay Bhutani, Anne-Clotilde Picot, Catherine Bergman, David Neale, Inez Costa Arslanian, Joanne Bergman, Karin Treiberg, Rani Cruz, Susan Fulford, and Tracey Methven.

To Susan Crossman, my amazing editor, how often did you steer me back on course when I strayed? Your mighty, metaphorical red pen purged clutter and added "Louboutin's" of wisdom. Your assistance cannot be understated.

A big thank you to Jessica Heald of Dig It Design for such a wonderful and evocative cover.

To Norb Vonnegut, who spoke to me at the right time, offering wise advice on being a writer. Your knowledge and experience helped me navigate murky waters and seize the opportunities.

To Michael Davie at Manor House Publishing, thank you for taking a risk on an unknown author. You shared my vision and guided Little Sister to its publication.

Finally, to those not mentioned who played a role, thank you all.

Vince

Foreword

Two trends scared Vince while he was working as a portfolio manager at top Canadian investment firms. One was the use of wireless technology in medical devices. The other was the secondary market for life insurance policies which, simply put, can now be traded like stocks, bonds, and other investment securities.

When we discussed his concerns over lunch in the summer of 2014, I was intrigued — not only as an author of financial thrillers but also as a veteran of the financial services industry. Vince found it terrifying that personal data about one's heart rate, blood glucose and other biological functions can circulate in the hackosphere; that medical devices can be hijacked with a few keystrokes. This alarming reality, he explained, is why he wrote *Little Sister,* his chilling debut novel.

Owning someone else's life insurance was a topic I had tackled in *The Gods of Greenwich,* and I was curious about how Vince would handle the subject. Trading life insurance polices, or "life settlements" as they are known among US hedge funds, is a practice that began as the AIDS epidemic emerged in the 1980s.

Early victims of the disease sometimes depleted their savings while searching for cures. Many had no choice but to sell their life insurance policies to investors who patiently waited for the inevitable, a relationship between buyers and sellers that gave new meaning to the simple inquiry, "How are you feeling today?"

Fortunately, medical research delivered huge breakthroughs in the treatment of AIDS.

But once started, the secondary market for life insurance continued to grow, evolving beyond the needs of those with terminal illnesses and gaining traction with money managers, even though there is something profoundly uncomfortable about betting on mortality. That is, the sooner the deaths of the insured, the better the financial returns of investors.

This is the background for *Little Sister*, a story set in the financial district of Toronto and one that puts a new spin on an old question: How far will you go to get what you want? Mila Mirkin is a young psychology student, ambitious and fiercely independent, determined to get what she wants, even if it means making personal compromises with the financial elite, compromises that isolate her from the one person she truly loves.

John Lister is a big part of her life. He is a philanthropist, financier, and a hedonist you'll love to hate. He is desperate to resurrect a failing hedge fund and find pleasure (however and wherever possible) in a life that has grown joyless.

His wife is distant and disinterested. His surviving twin daughter is hateful and bitter. And what looks like John's personal compassion is really... well... it's better you find out for yourself by disappearing into the sinister and frighteningly real world Vince has woven for us.

It was Lord Bacon who said, "Great men are almost always bad men." No matter his keen insight, which continues to withstand the test of time, I find few things more riveting than a good story that peels back the professional veneer of financial power brokers and exposes the underbelly of their corruption, greed, sexual predation, and revenge. With *Little Sister,* Vince succeeds in doing just that.

- **Norb Vonnegut** is an American writer of Wall Street Thrillers (*Top Producer, Gods of Greenwich Village, Mr. President* and *The Trust*) and contributing columnist to the Wall Street Journal online (WSJ.com).

1

Little sister, can't you find another way?
No more living life behind a shadow.

John Homme, Queens of the Stone Age

"You bastard," Adriana wailed. "How could you?"

He caught her hand before she could slap him again.

"I was trying to get out before you came back," Connor said, slinging his overnight bag over his shoulder.

"After five years?"

"You gonna come in? You gonna make a scene in the hallway."

Adriana held up her keys between her fingers, ready to gouge at his face.

"Put your hands down. You know you'll never do it."

Adriana raised her fist to his eyes before lowering her hands to her side, pocketing her keys. She stood unmoving on the threshold of the apartment.

"I gotta go," said Connor as he tried to walk around her.

"That's it? You gotta go?"

"Jesus!"

"After all I did for your Dad before he died."

"You wanna do this? You wanna do this now? Okay. Let's go."

"What?"

"What? You're kidding, right?"

Adriana said nothing.

"You want me to begin? Do you? Okay. You work too hard."

"I do not."

"You're never around and even when you are, you're still working."

"I schedule time for you."

"Schedule time? For me? Do you hear yourself?"

"I cleared this weekend ... for us."

"Bullshit. Your office called earlier. They moved the meeting to eight a.m. tomorrow."

Adriana looked down at her salt-stained boots.

"I'm your partner," Connor continued. "I'm supposed to be your lover. You don't schedule time with me. You be with me."

"I'm bogged down at work."

"No, you keep yourself busy. You leave early. You're always home late."

"I'm working on..."

"The biggest case of your life," he mocked. "I know. Like the one before. Christ, we haven't had sex in three months."

"Connor..."

"Who's the big bad wolf this time?"

"You know I can't..."

"Tell me. Won't tell me. Great. You can't trust me to keep my mouth shut. I'm so outta here."

"John Lister!" she blurted.

Connor stopped on the threshold.

"Lister? The hedge fund manager?"

"You know him?"

"Of course. Everybody does. I covered his firm in derivative sales. Bumped into him at a few industry functions. You're gonna take him down?"

She nodded. "I'm gonna try."

"There is no try. He takes no prisoners. You better do it."

"Or what?"

"Or you're done."

"I know. That's why I ..."

"You ignore me."

"Honey ..."

"I get it, but it doesn't change anything. I gotta go. I gotta think."

"Bullshit! You think I don't know about her?"

Connor gave no response, then finally said: "I'm going to the cottage, alone. I'll get back in a few days."

Adriana held up a small canvas bag from Connor's favourite clothing boutique.

"What's this?"

"Happy Fuckin' Christmas."

"Uh, thanks." He set the bag down on the bench in the foyer. "I gotta go," he repeated, shaking his head.

She watched his face for something, anything, as he brushed past her. Its emptiness told her what she needed to know. She let the door shut quietly behind him. Her cat brushed up against her leg.

"Hey Gus," Adriana said bending down and scratching his chin. "Just you and me kiddo." Gus purred with delight. "I bet he didn't even feed you, did he?"

Gus chirruped more loudly.

"I'll look after you in a moment."

She sat down on the wooden bench in the foyer, tugged at her black knee high leather boots and placed them by the door.

She hung her coat in the hallway closet, brushing off the remnants of snow melting into beads, cursing as she caught her finger on the sharp silver broach Connor had given her at Thanksgiving. She had never liked it. She sucked her finger and tasted of copper.

"C'mon Gus, let's go fill your bowl."

Adriana picked up her bags and made her way to the kitchen in her stocking feet, sliding on the polished hardwood floors, Gus at her heels.

She set down her bags and filled a clean dish with kibble that he crunched hungrily.

The glow of the city illuminated the room through the windows she had never bothered to cover. She caught her reflection and turned away from the tired face looking back at her.

From deep within her purse, her phone pinged an alert. She sauntered to the washroom, Gus in tow.

From the top drawer of her vanity, she took a black silk bag containing the paraphernalia necessary for controlling her disease. She marvelled at how much riskier managing it used to be.

Recently, she had resisted her doctor's advice to get an integrated blood glucose monitor and insulin pump.

She refused to abdicate responsibility for her health to a machine. The telltale bulge of the device at her hip would not be flattering either. She had compromised, opting for a glucose monitor from a new company called Glucosure.

The tiny lancet exacted a pinprick of blood and began its work.

She sat on the edge of the bathtub as Gus brushed up against her legs.

"Come here big guy," she said as she picked him up and rubbed his tummy. "You like that don't you? You know, your Papa Connor's a bastard."

The machine beeped three descending notes.

"Bloody barrista. I told him sugar free. Damn it!" she said out loud to Gus. "Down you go," she added, setting the cat down.

In any case, the treatment was beyond rote. She walked back to the kitchen, pulled some leftovers out of the fridge, put them in the microwave and pushed the reheat button.

From the fridge door, she removed a new vial of insulin. She returned to the bathroom and placed the required items on the vanity: syringe, vial, alcohol wipe.

She popped the safety cap and pushed the needle through the top of the vial and drew 40 units into the barrel. She withdrew the needle and pushed the plunger to remove the inevitable air bubbles.

With her free hand, she untucked her blouse, swabbed the skin above her hip bone and then inserted the needle. Her skin yielded as she applied gentle pressure to the plunger. The hormone would do its work in a few minutes.

She returned to the kitchen and felt instantly cold. Snow floated in front of her. Her knees gave out and her head struck the counter as she fell. There was no pain.

She landed with her cheek resting on the cool tiles, her arms twisted underneath her. She tried to move but could not.

The vial of insulin rolled to a stop in a grout line in front of her face.

"Oh shit! He's not back 'till Sunday," she said out loud, her word slurring, her tongue thick in her mouth. "Connor! Oh God!"

She screamed. A whisper left her lips.

All she could hear was the whirl of the microwave fan and Gus purring in her ear.

Her eyes closed and her world went red. Then all faded to black.

Vince Fernandez

2

"So, everything is in order Mrs. Babiak?" asked Tom. "It's just like last time."

"Yes, Mr. Tournimenko. It appears to be," replied Edna.

"Please, call me Tom."

"Wally and I just needed time to think."

"I understand. I do."

He glanced at his Rolex, a knockoff his sister had picked up when she was in Manhattan. He was late for his next appointment. "I'm just going to go outside and stretch my legs while you talk.

"Thank you. We won't take long."

Tom got up slowly from the dining table. He had forgotten how uncomfortable the chairs were. Wally muttered something unintelligible. His hands quivered and his wedding ring now rapped out a confused beat on the scratched surface of the table.

"No pressure," said Tom. "Take your time. It's a big decision. By the way Mrs. Babiak, I like your shawl. My grandmother used to have one just like it."

Edna smiled as Tom left the room. Outside, his cigarette tasted better than he expected. As his shoulders relaxed, he dialled his sister. "Isabella, it's Tom."

"Well, hello to you too little brother. Pleasantries, remember. They makes the world go round."

"Hello. How are you? Better?"

"Much. How's the scalping going?"

"You should know. I'm sure Mr. Lister and Val update you."

"Apart from me getting them to consider hiring you, I'm not involved. Anyway, you didn't answer my question."

"It's slow but it's better than that shitty broker I worked for."

"Need a hand?"

Tom stiffened. "No sis," he said slowly. "I'm fine. Are they going to allocate more money to the strategy?"

"I think so. For now, all I know is that Val and John want every life insurance policy you can get your hands on. Remember, the sicker the better."

"Yeah, yeah, I got it. I'm just closing one right now. Should get me on track for the month. Just giving them some time to stew."

"You're still meeting target?"

"Don't sound so surprised. I said it was slow, not dead. Should be close this month. With this one and a little luck, I should be there. People love getting their hands on the cash."

"Some do good things with the money, right?"

"Don't know really. Don't care. They talk of medical procedures but I think most of them blow it. Anyhow, it'd be better if Val reviewed the files faster. People get antsy. I do have some competition out here. Can you pass that on to Val?"

"Doubt he'll listen but I will. So how many more congregations will you be joining?"

"Best places to meet old people."

"Mom would be pissed if she knew how you've become a religious slut."

"Hey, it works. Dress my best, pour some watered down lemonade, hand out pinwheel sandwiches after the service. First they tell me it's a shame that there's no ring on my finger and then they set me up with their granddaughters."

"You really are a skank."

"All part of the job."

"Yeah, right."

"It's so easy to I.D. the targets. They're always complaining about the speed of the health care system and that they have to wait and wait. Sis, I gotta go. They've stewed long enough. Love ya."

"You too."

Tom glanced at his watch. "Ten minutes. Perfect."

When he sat down at the dining table, Edna and Wally were still reading the document, talking quietly. Tom smiled. With his kitchen Russian, he understood the gist. He knew what would come next. Edna squeezed Wally's hand, the pressure halting the tremors.

"We'll sign," said Edna.

"Wonderful. Just a little paperwork and we're done."

"When will the money come?" Edna asked. "We've booked our tickets to the Cleveland Clinic for eight weeks from now. We'll need to send the deposit in two weeks."

Tom placed his hand on top of Edna's and looked at Wally.

"It never takes longer than that. I can see you're nervous. I'll ask my group to make your case a priority, okay?"

Edna handed over Wally's medical file, five inches thick with detailed reports of his illness. Tom placed it all in a brown paper accordion folder.

The insurance policy face value of $2-million meant Val would expedite the review. He'd already told Tom that based on the preliminary information, they'd receive $1.1-million, with half to arrive next week. It was Tom's largest contract to date.

"Thank you Mr. and Mrs. Babiak. You've made the right decision. I wish you good health. I'm sure the surgery will make all the difference in the world. I'll be praying for a speedy recovery."

Tom left them and climbed into his rented Lexus. It was a free upgrade and it instilled more confidence than the lime green rust bucket parked at his apartment.

Edna came to the window, parted the yellowing lace curtains and waved.

Tom looked up, smiled back meekly and checked his watch again and hit speed dial on his phone.

"I'll be twenty-five minutes. Don't start passing out the sandwiches without me."

He was an hour and fifteen minutes behind schedule. He had two more churches to visit today, one Catholic and the other United. He preferred the United. The congregation was older.

3

"Mr. Lister, you've a ten o'clock with the Montreal Pension Plan and Mr. Bhutani-Singh insisted he see you at 4 pm."

"Jargit's coming? He isn't scheduled till next week."

"He said it was urgent. He didn't like last week numbers. I can tell him you're not available."

"That will never work. Shit."

"I'll make sure to interrupt before 5 pm. That should leave you enough time to get to the dinner with the Superintendent for Financial Services. Mike will drive you."

"Thank you Yvonne. Man, can you do something for me? See if Benny Figueredo is around this week?

"The insurance analyst at Richmond Capital? What day do you want me to book him?"

"No, no, don't schedule anything. I want to see how long he waits after the tonight's conference to come to me."

"Yes, sir. I'll see what I find out. Do you need anything for today's meetings?"

"I assume the presentations are ready."

"Of course. Have I ever failed you?"

"No, of course not. Not you. The rest of these schmucks around me, yes, but you, never."

"You're too kind. Want do you want for the Montreal team?"

"Tea and cookies."

"Okay and for Jargit?"

"Nothing will placate him."

"He's tough?"

"He never lets up once he's got you down."

"Sounds familiar."

"I just..."

"You kinda admire him. How bad is it?"

"Oh, the numbers are horrible," said a voice from over a bank of monitors.

"Tim, shut up. You may be the best trader I've ever had but you're still a prick."

"I'm working at trying to get us out of this mess. You're yakking. But yeah, Jargit's a hard ass."

"I've heard rumours," said Yvonne. "Did he really bury a someone under bitumen?"

"I don't know and I don't want to find out. Get him a fifth of Johnny Walker Blue. And, oh, send a gift certificate to his wife for that spa place she likes so much."

"The Elmwood or the Stillwater?"

"Do I care?"

"No. Not really. For how much?"

"How much last year?"

"$400."

"Double it."

Yvonne handed him a folded note and left.

"What's this?"

"I think you know. AA meeting today at noon at St. Andrews. Don't miss this one. You'll get another chip!"

As Yvonne walked away, John unfolded the note. There was a stick figure with a medal around its neck and seven concentric circles about its head. It looked like a halo.

Congratulations! Eight years. I'm proud of you!

"If you're done making kissy, kissy with Yvonne, can you get back to work please?" asked Tim.

"Tim, it's only because you're the best that I don't rip..."

"Rip me a new one. Idle threats, John. So unbecoming of a master of the universe."

Tim eased his bulk out of his chair, his hips squeezing through the arm rests, groaning as he did. He adjusted his pants and tucked in his shirt and looked at John.

"Jesus. You dressed like boring Brooks Brothers bitch. Great suit, but the tie."

"What? What's wrong with it?"

"First, you're wearing one. You'll get no street cred if you dress like a muppet. Second, pink, green and burgundy. Good God, did you dress in the dark? Did Lily give you that for father's day? Or it was Alison?"

"Tim..."

"Okay, over the top I know. Sorry."

"Tim, three things: Sit down. Shut up. Make me money."

Tim returned to his seat, dialled a number and barked a trade. John sat back down as well.

"How bad is it?" came a quiet voice no one else could hear.

John sat motionless, staring at the crude, hand-painted wooden frame on the desk in front of him. It was a photo of his girls, Alison and Lily, when they were six years old, the year Alison first fell ill. She had followed him everywhere like a beagle. She had always run to him instead of his wife when she had been scared by lightning or had scraped her knee. The glass was smudged where he'd caressed her forehead. Twelve years had passed since that photo. Six years since she had succumbed. The ache was ever present.

"It's bad Honey," he whispered, "but Papa's gonna be okay."

John's Blackberry rang. He looked at the screen and cursed quietly.

"Hello Joan. What do you want?"

"Oh John. No hello Dear, Honey, Love of my life. None of those pleasantries for your wife."

"Yes, Dear, Honey, what is it?"

"The gals from the club and I thought we'd beat the Christmas rush to North Palm. We're heading down tomorrow. Be a dear and instruct Esmeralda to stock the fridge."

"The usual?"

"Evian, Greek yoghurt and champagne. Oh, and for God's sake, no Veuve Cliquot. I'm so bored of it."

"Yes, Dear, but of course. As you wish. Anything else?"

His computer pinged.

John jumped to his personal email account, reading through the inbox. It was the seventh time he had checked since he had arrived this morning at 5:30 am.

"No," said Joan. "When will you be arriving?"

"Sure, anytime."

"No John, pay attention. When are you in Palm Beach, dearest?"

"So you know when to get rid of your boy toy?"

"Ernesto is not around right now."

"I fly in the same day as Lily. Goodbye Joan."

John ended the call, put his phone down and refreshed his browser. His muse had not responded. With four fingers, he pounded out a message but hesitated.

"Just a school boy. Stop being so needy," he said out loud to no one, drawing a look from a junior trader next to him. John scowled.

His screen chirped again. He deleted his draft but stayed logged in, hoping that she might respond.

John shifted his attention to his other screens. They were all a sea of red. A face flickered above the trading desk on one of the four flat TV screens.

"Christ, not the frog again! I thought he was dead."

"Just back to administer grief," said Tim. "Fucker's never even tried to run dough."

"Why hasn't he been fired? He's a fuckin' retard. Tim... Isabella...Who's got the fuckin' remote? Anyone... Turn it up!"

Tim held the remote up and the volume increased.

"Monsieur Laroque, welcome back. It's good to see you," said the host of the Money Hour.

"Thanks Bill. I've missed the day-to-day of the markets. So exhilarating," Pierre began. "Great to be back. I'm feeling much better. It's amazing what those cutters can do. I want to thank my surgeon Dr. Marc-Phillipe Hallet and my cardiologist, Dr. Rudie Gelt. The ticker's a metronome again. Those electronic gizmos are great."

John made a note in his diary: Call Rudie.

Laroque turned to the camera.

"Thank you to all you viewers who kept me in their prayers. You sped my recovery. God bless you all."

"Well, Pierre, you've had some time to think, what do you have for us today?"

"Bill, thanks. This week, well..." began Pierre rubbing his hands together. "This manager could do no wrong. He has made his clients millions the past. He's the king of the cocktail circuit, but this morning even my taxi driver was recommending I stay away. I think his crayons might be a little bit dull."

The screen faded from Pierre to the logo for John's firm. It then dissolved to an image of John's face superimposed onto the body of a preschooler. A cartoon graphic indicated his diaper was soiled. An analyst let out a muffled laugh. John stiffened.

"Oh no, he's has done a number two," said Pierre, "and now he's just sitting in his mess."

Pierre's co-host chuckled.

"It's a disaster," Pierre continued. "Lister Asset Management and your Golden boy John Lister will be delivering nothing but coal this Christmas. No holiday cheer at all."

Pierre leaned forward in his chair as the camera zoomed in till only his face was in the screen.

"December's just beginning. Can't wait to see what LAM brings to the table in the New Year! For Christmas Mr. Lister, I send you a box of crayons."

Pierre opened up the box lying on the desk in front of him.

"Oh, they're all red. Seems appropriate. Happy Holidays, Johnny!"

Mouths were agape. Everyone's eyes were downcast.

John stood up and pulled out his bill fold from his pant pocket, peeling off ten new hundred dollar bills. He held them aloft.

"The first of you shits to make a yard today, net, gets it. The second place, steak knives. The lowest on the pole is gone. Gone! Now go make me some fuckin' money!"

All hands grabbed for receivers looking for trades.

John sat down opposite Tim, hidden behind a bank of screens.

Tim cleared his throat.

"Yes, Tim."

"You fuckin' quote Mamet poorly, ya know?"

22

"No one here has a clue anyhow."

"Glengarry Glen Ross. Love the flick. You gonna can someone?"

"Maybe, but not today. They need to squirm. They're too fuckin' complacent." John paused and let out a sigh.

"Hey John, you gonna offer Benny a job. It'll drive Val nuts, you know?"

"Yeah, it would be fun to watch wouldn't it? Nah, I just want to check his loyalty. See if he is as straight as his aura."

"The guy's bright."

"Yeah, he'd be an asset. Tim, let's clean this up."

"Who's your first victim?"

"A surprise."

"Happy hunting."

John looked down at the thirty pre-programmed numbers on his phone. He needed a sucker.

The first two numbers he dialled offered John safety scissors to go with the crayons.

He reconsidered and started scrolling through his second-tier relationships on his computer. He dialled the third on the list.

"KWE Bankgesellshaft. Martin Rotfeld."

"Where's Bertie?"

"Bertie... Mr. Bertelsmann's away on vacation."

"Can you trade?"

"Who's this?"

"JL."

"The John Lister?"

"Yes, Marty, I'm from LAM. Pleased to meet ya. It's a yard sale here. Got a buck of Cedar Resources to go, want 'em? A dime under quote and they're all yours."

"Please, one moment. Just need to get some colour on this."

The phone clicked to mute. John imagined the young man looking over the football field of a trading floor in New York City, searching for a senior trader to get approval.

The pause meant he was either being scolded for considering buying a block from LAM or the pup was screwing up his courage to take down the million shares.

John bit his nails as he waited.

The line clicked live.

"50 cents below, I'll take it."

"Fifty? You're scalping me! That's five percent under market. A quarter under and I'm putting a quarter million in your pocket. You could buy your girl something beautiful. Bertie always said you're a tough nut. We done?"

There was silence.

"Martin, are we done? John asked slowly, pausing between each word. "Two dimes and a nickel. You're cleaning me out," he lied.

He had another four-million shares to dump right after the call. He was going to swamp Martin.

"Done and thank you Mr. Lister. Merry Christmas."

"Frohe Weihnachten, Marty."

John hung up and screamed over his screens to Tim.

"Tim, Sold, a yard of Cedar at ten bucks, twenty-five cents, to KWE to trader Rotstein, Rotman... Rotweiler... whatever at KWE."

"Not Rotfeld!" shouted Tim. "Shit John, I just stuffed the kid with 500 large of Birchriver. Bertie's gonna to kill you. You know, Martin's the chairman's nephew, right?

"Tim, sounds like you care."

"Fuck John..."

"Martin needs adult supervision."

Tim slammed his phone down on the cradle, stood and waving his index finger at John. John chuckled.

"You find this amusing. Don't screw around. We need 'em. We've already lost a third of our credit lines. I'm meeting KWE later this week. We're on thin ice, man."

John knew that the prime brokers who had lent LAM money were itching to pull the credit lines they had outstanding. If they did, his fund would collapse.

"If we fuck the dweebs," Tim continued, "where do you think I'll find the credit to fund all the insurance you're buying..."

"Tim!" John barked.

Tim fell quiet for a moment.

"Damn it John, if he survives, he'll never go back in the water again with us. I wanted to see if he was swimming naked."

"Gotcha. You done?"

"Yes."

"Okay."

John took a deep breath.

"Okay, fix it with the Rotweiler."

Tim picked up his receiver and dialled. John could hear him give a gift trade even an incompetent like Martin could not screw up.

John knew Tim was right. Martin was a potential gusher. He could be milked for a lot more, just not in one day.

John's personal Gmail address pinged him an alert. He glanced across the four screens on his desk to the one dedicated to messages. The other three screens flashed movements across foreign exchange, commodities, rates and equities. Green was up and red, down.

The screen was a sea of blood. At the bottom of the third screen, was a small yellow box, the live profit or loss of the portfolio.

"Tim, is the P and L right? Are we really down $10-million today?"

"Feels right, but I'll have Val run the numbers again."

John's secretary tapped his shoulder. He smiled and nodded.

"Be there in a sec. You know what, grab that bottle of single malt from Val's desk, the one I gave him from my trip to Scotland. He'll never drink it anyhow. Put a bow on it and leave it on the table in the board room with the cookies. The frogs will love it and it's better than the case of Export we drank the last time I saw them."

"Seem to remember a large bill from the Canadian ballet," piped in Tim.

"Tim, do you ever keep your mouth shut?"

"How do you think I became so svelte and trim?" he said patting his ample belly.

John took one last look at the funds tally.

Next to that was his own personal account. He had lost personally over $2-million dollars on the day, $7.5-million for the month.

John's consolation was that he knew that Tim had lost more in his personal account, and it was a third the size of John's.

"Hey Tim, I'm down over seven bucks on the month. You?"

"Screw you."

"Come on. Tell me. I could just get compliance to let me know."

Tim sighed. "Probably eight large."

"Ooh, feel the burn."

"Like I said, screw you."

John's personal email pinged again. It was not Tatiana.

"Tim, message from Sean O'Malley."

"Another cop fund raiser? The last one was so boring."

"I know. There wasn't even any blow. Come on, what's it say?"

"SUGAR."

A big grin broke across John's face.

Tim stopped talking mid-sentence and dropped his phone, the handset clattering with a sharp crack on the concrete floor.

The hum of the desk stopped for a beat and then resumed.

Tim, still standing, turned to his junior.

"Short another 300 large of Glucosure."

"Now?"

"No, in three hours. Yes, now!"

"Dollars or shares?"

"Ya think I care about $300k, you putz! Shares Goddammit!"

"We're stopped out!" said the trader.

"Holy fuck, just do it. Now! Half for my p.a. I'll deal with Graham later. Got it?"

John and Tim both sat down, hidden from each other by the computer screens.

"Honey, ah, sugar, sugar!" Tim sang quietly.

"You are my candy girl," John continued. "The month might not be so bad after all."

"And a monkey off our back."

4

"Tatiana, do you have to leave already?"

"Yes, it's time," replied Mila, still not used to her sobriquet even after four years.

"Stay. The bed's warm. Come under the sheets with me. I'll make it worth your while."

"Tempting, I'd love to hun, but I really can't. I'm having dinner with my parents. I've stayed longer than I should have."

"I want to thank you for listening. I do appreciate it."

"My pleasure."

"Not many people I can share with."

"Anytime. Just be direct okay. No fuzziness."

"Okay. I will be. I just get overwhelmed sometimes."

"We all do. It means you're not a robot."

The man's eyes watered and his bottom lip quivered.

"Tears are okay too," she continued. "We're just human. We all need to share."

"And you, who do you talk to?"

"I've got someone."

"I hope you do."

"They're a little distant right now."

"Why?" he asked.

She didn't answer.

"Oh, I'm sorry. None of my business."

"That's okay. I reacted poorly to something they did. I've been trying to find a way back since," she said taking a deep breath. "Maybe someday."

"I hope so for you. You saw the envelope?"

"Right next to the lovely Tag Heuer you left me. My God, so beautiful. You'll spoil me, you know."

"You're worth it."

"You're too kind."

"It'll look better on you than me, anyhow."

"It'll swim on my wrist."

"I had a number of links removed from the band. Guess it was not enough."

"I can easily adjust it. It's sweet of you. Thanks so much."

"When will I see you again?"

"You know how to reach me. I hope you have fun watching your nieces at their recital."

"I will. But it's you I'd rather see dance. When's your next ballet performance? I'd love to come. I could bring my girls to watch you."

"First, no. No mixing business with pleasure. And second, might it not get a little bit awkward?"

"I only..."

"Just no. Is our time together like this not sublime enough? Do you really want to change any of this? I don't. I love it this way."

As she went around the hotel suite gathering her apparel, her client sat up in the bed and looked serious.

"Tatiana and I know that's not your real name, but Tatiana, what's next for you?"

"I told you before: Life, liberty and the pursuit of happiness."

"Inalienable rights?"

"All I need."

"Does it make you happy though?"

"What do you think?"

"So there's a goal behind all of this?"

"So direct."

"A raw nerve?"

"Really? You sure you want to play this game?"

"Ya, I do."

"What about your daughters and the Mrs.?"

What?"

"Aren't they waiting for you? Waiting on the doting father and husband?

"First, ouch. That I have a family, you knew that already. This isn't about me. Right now, it's about you. I'm sure you have a play beyond acquiring Louboutin's and Chanel handbags. You're extraordinary."

"Aw, thank you."

"No really. You could do whatever you want."

"Hmm, I don't know."

"You're the epitome of the girl next door, a beautiful punk, with tattoos and piercings. If you were six inches taller, you could have been a model. Your alabaster skin, your dimples, your heart shaped face, your fucking blue eyes. Your locks. The blue streak. Men must melt when you flash your smile."

"And..."

"I'm not sure the world sees it very much."

She smiled, straining to keep it genuine.

"See. All men would fall under your spell. You're not of this world, or at least not of mine. You're energetic and without cynicism. Direct, brutal, honest."

"Why wouldn't I be? Is there any other way?"

"I suppose there shouldn't be, but there is."

"I've been seeing you for four years. You've kept it fresh and incendiary. You leave me utterly fulfilled and gutted."

"I'm sorry."

"Not your fault. Just my foibles. I know this is just physical for you."

She began to open her mouth but stopped as he held up his hand.

"I know I have no right, but I need to know, what's lurking below?"

"I've got plans."

"I'm listening."

"Grad school. Psychology. In the US. Columbia. NYC."

"That'll cost a penny."

"Uh, yeah."

"Are you close?"

"Pretty close. Another year or so. I'll be finished undergrad by then. With a teaching assistant's position, it'll all be good. I'm focused. Not like other girls. No drugs, no parties. There's a bike I'm looking at."

"Bike?"

"Yeah, my Dad gave me his old Suzuki. It's fine, but it's not a Ducati."

"I rode a Ducati as a kid."

"My bike won't be like yours. Guaranteed."

"Whatever? You're being evasive."

"I've got a few rules and your treading all over them. Nothing personal."

"After all this time."

"Yes, even after all this time."

31

A buzzing came from her purse.

"Sorry," she said as pulled out her phone. "Shit. I really gotta go. I'm late."

She move in to give him a peck on the cheek. He turned at the last moment so his lips met hers. She pulled back immediately.

"Juvenile but cute."

She moved forward and pressed her lips against his, flicking her tongue for a moment. She pushed back and stood. She zipped her shoulder bag closed and shrugged on her floor length, fitted leather jacket over her shoulders, cinching the belt, showing off her frame.

Mila blew him a final kiss and headed out into the hotel corridor, moving as fast as her thigh high boots would allow.

She bowled over a haggard-looking housekeeper as she rounded the narrow corner, upending the towels and toiletries stacked on her cart.

"I'm so sorry," Mila said, crouching to help pick up the mess she had made.

Under the fluorescent lights of the hallway, Mila saw that the woman was about her age. Her skin was waxy, her hands rough and her nails unadorned.

"I'm so sorry," Mila repeated.

Mila knew the woman endured ten-hour days of hard, monotonous labour as she emptied garbage, tucked corners, and ran through a mind-numbingly long check list to ensure the room was to the hotel's standards. She would not earn in a day what Mila made in an hour.

Mind you, the housekeeper did not have to subject herself to what Mila had just endured; welts on her buttocks from a lash, a reddening hand print around her throat concealed beneath a black turtle neck sweater and the lingering scent of the latex that seemed to take longer and longer to scrub away.

The housekeeper stared at Mila without a smile.

"You don't have to do this, Miss."

"It was my fault. I need to fix it."

"No. It's okay," she said sternly. "I'm always cleaning up after you anyhow."

"Pardon?"

"I hate the cleaning suites with the Privacy Please signs on the door handles in the afternoon."

Mila lifted the last of the towels onto the cart and hurried to the elevators, stabbing at the button.

She looked back for the housekeeper, but she had moved on. Mila popped a piece of gum in her mouth to chase away a bitter, lingering taste. She reminded herself not to come back for a while. There was no need to test the hotel management's ire.

She pushed the down button again and stopped. Her hand remained outstretched and she admired her new Middle-Eastern inspired tattoo, the skin was still raw and raised. The intricate lace of ink ran from her wrist down her middle finger ending at the battered and scratched three-banded silver wedding ring. Her grandmother had placed on her middle finger as she lay at the foot of the stairs where Mila had found her.

"Only move it for your one true love," she had said.

Mila played the rings as she waited for the elevator, pulling one over the other, back and forth along the digit. Her phone rang the tone she had assigned to her brother Vitaly.

She reached into her bag, ignored the call and checked her text messages. There were none from her friends.

Vitaly had fired off two text missives regarding tonight's dinner, reminding her to arrive ahead of her parents.

She toggled over to "Tatiana's" email account. There were ten messages from John. She did not bother opening any of them.

She listened for the elevator to come.

5

Mila burst through the doors of Biff's Bistro on Front Street and looked around for her parents and her brother.

From the street, she had seen that they were not sitting in their usual corner by the window.

She was searching the diners' faces when a stern voice interrupted her.

"May I be of assistance?"

It was Caroline, her Miss Caroline, Caroline, the one who loved her, who confused her, who had made her cry.

Mila turned and threw her arms around her and squeezed her hard. Caroline hugged her back. Mila broke-off and re-established a cool, serene demeanour.

"How are you Ms. Mila?" Caroline said in a prim and proper voice.

"So kind of you to inquire. I'm quite splendid," Mila responded with an equal affectation. "And yourself?"

Both broke into laughter.

"They've been waiting for..," Caroline said as she glanced at her watch, "sixteen minutes."

"Great. Under Dad's threshold. Quick, where are they?"

"I'll tell you only if you'll promise to come back and have lunch on me. Tomorrow?"

"Sure."

"Promise?"

"Cross my heart."

"We must catch up."

Caroline caressed the blue lock of Mila's hair.

"Your mom's gonna freak."

Mila smiled.

"Since you liked the hair, you might fancy this too."

Mila unbuckled her coat, slid it off her shoulders and lifted her hair off her nape. The back of her head was shaved.

"Wow!" exclaimed Caroline. "Gorgeous!"

A Phoenix tattoo in green, gold and red, raising from the flames graced her skin.

Caroline ran her fingers over the fine stubble that was growing over the bird. Chills ran up Mila's spine and goose bumps spread across her neck and scalp.

"Oh, I'm sorry," Caroline blushed.

Mila turned and smiled.

"Come back tomorrow and tell me everything. I've missed you so, Rabbit. It's been too long."

"How's Marc?" Mila asked as Caroline escorted her through the tables.

"Uh, well, not so good. We're having a hard time."

Mila's heart jumped.

"Oh, I'm so sorry," Mila said, trying to sound sincere. She was not sure if she was.

"Thanks Rabbit. We're dealing with it. I'll tell you all when you come back."

"I'll come. Now, where are they?"

Her parents and brother were hidden at the rear of the bistro behind a drawn velour curtain.

Drinks were on the table but as of yet, no food. As Mila walked, she adjusted the shawl of her collar and pulled her sleeves over her hands.

Caroline pulled back the curtain with a flourish.

"Mr. and Mrs. Mirkin, Mr. Vitaly, may I present Ms. Mila Petrovna Mirkin?"

Then, looking at her watch, she added, "And she's only 19 minutes late."

"Caroline, protecting my little one?" said Petr. "I count 21, but my watch might be fast."

"Petr, you have too much patience," Zoya scolded.

"It's good to see you all again," said Caroline. "Unfortunately, I must go. Have a good evening."

"Zoya," began Petr, "How can Mila grow without patience?"

"How will she learn discipline if indulged? She always late."

"But today, she was a minute ahead. It's an improvement."

"Vitaly wanted to order," said Zoya. "So did I."

"I knew you'd be late," said Vitaly.

"I knew that you'd be just in time," said Petr.

"What is with blue hair?" Zoya said, confirming what Mila had anticipated.

Mila was glad she was wearing the turtleneck. The new tattoos and studs on her arms would not go over well. The marks on her wrists from the restraints would be unexplainable. Mila hugged Vitaly, his spidery arms holding her tight.

"Great hair, sis."

"I could dye yours too."

"Oh, the judges would love that."

"I thought justice was blind.'

"More like visually impaired."

Mila sat down opposite Petr and Zoya with her brother at her side.

"So Vitaly, what dates are you not telling me about?"

Vitaly had known it was coming.

"Oh, do tell!" said Mila, turning towards him.

"Mom, I know you think I'm working too hard, but I do have a life. There's someone... It's just..."

"I can't screw up my courage to ask her out," said Mila, dropping her voice an octave and sounding rather mopey.

"No, it's... well nothing."

"If you cannot say, leave note like Papa," said Zoya. "He wooed me with poetry."

"What?" cackled Mila. "With fifty verses waxing about your cheeks as rosy as borscht, your eyes grey as the winter's steppe."

"Or maybe," added Vitaly, "there once was a lady from Vilnius..."

"Whose body was shaped like a..." chirped Mila. "Hey, that doesn't rhyme. Venus! Venus!"

"Do not tease Papa," said Zoya, rubbing her husband's back.

"Or maybe she was from Regina?" pondered Mila aloud.

"Enough. Can't you see how sweet he was? No, not borscht or cold winter plains. I was Matryoshka doll, woman of many layers of beauty. How could girl resist?"

Her parents kissed.

"And you sis, it's been like four years since you had a steady, what's up with that?"

"That's because she scares all good boys away with wild hair and tattoos."

Zoya reached out across to Mila, a silent command for her to take her hands from her lap and place them in hers. Mila did so reluctantly. Zoya held her palm in hers and traced her finger tips over the new lace tattoo a few times, admiring the intricate detail, appreciating its beauty. She stiffened as she remembered her role.

"See Petr, I told you. More ink! When will stop?"

Zoya moved to slide Mila's sweater up her arm, to see where the ink ended. Mila grabbed Zoya's hand brusquely before the four studs that ran up her forearm. She returned her hands to their place underneath the table.

"A girl's gotta have secrets," she said.

"Even from Mama?" Zoya asked.

"The ink, doesn't it hurt?" asked Vitaly.

"Well, when you dance with Mary-Jane, there's no pain."

Zoya looked perplexed, clearly lost. Mila held her thumb and finger to her lips as if holding a roach. Zoya's eyes widened.

"Petr! Mary-Jane!" she said exasperated. "Well, you still have ring."

"Mama, the ring will never leave my hand. I promise."

"I know, I know. You good girl."

"Please, order food?" asked Petr.

They glanced over the menu but they all knew what they were going to order. Biff's was their home restaurant, the family having long abandoned the mile of cheap delis on Roncesvalles Avenue. When Petr had been out of work, they could not even afford them. It was then that Mila developed her aversion to kielbasa.

Vitaly looked preoccupied, even though Mila knew he ordered the same each time.

"Mila, how was trip out west?"

"Good, Papa. Dr. Simintov's research is fascinating. I'm learning so much about how addicts rationalize their behaviour."

"So why'd he send you, a third year?" Vitaly asked scornfully.

"Dr. Simintov asked me to analyse a new cohort out west," Mila said ignoring her brother. "He just received a grant so we can expand on the paper we co-authored last semester. The working title is *The Simintov Displacement*."

"What is that?" asked Zoya.

"It's a theory that explains how people develop new addictions when they enter recovery programs for a primary vector. The new addiction masks the underlying pathology."

"Like when I quit smoking," said Petr, his voice still raspy from years of cheap Russian cigarettes.

"Yes, he gained ten kilos from candies he sucked in taxi."

"I got that under control, but only when I realized we would survive in new country. Cigarettes and candy were masking stress."

"Well, the research I'm doing is a follow-up to the baseline work. I presented an abstract of our upcoming paper in *American Psychologist* at the conference in Calgary."

"No way, sis, wow!"

"The original theory was mine but Zablon helped a lot. Without him, it would have gone no where. Still I think *The Mirkin-Simintov Displacement* sounds so much better."

"You are out west so often. You rarely come by house," said her father.

"Lots of research Dad," she lied.

What Mila of course did not tell her family was that the trips for Zablon only covered about a third of her travels. Her alter ego took the rest. It had been two years since Mila had dropped the escort agency where she had started, inspired by an article of a courtesan in Toronto Life magazine.

Being independent was convenient, felt oddly glamourous and allowed her to be selective about her clientele. Also, she kept the entire amount of the donation instead of handing 30 per cent over to the booker. That was the practical reason.

The impetus for leaving the agency was the outing of her friend Olga, a beautiful girl with sparkling green eyes, straight, waist-length blonde hair and an arresting constellation of three beauty marks on her right cheek. Her referral agency had published photos on their website that had revealed, along with her curves, a little too much of her face.

At the start of Olga's second year at the University of Toronto, her physics professor turned out to be a client she had seen a few times over the course of the summer. Two days later, she received a summons from the Provost. An application of ethical misconduct had been filed against her. Olga was expelled: conduct unbecoming a student, purveyor of a corrupting influence. The consumer was not to blame.

Olga's withdrawal from campus life was swift. Mila had lost touch with her, but she did receive sporadic email dispatches from Calgary.

"The research not affecting marks, is it?" asked Zoya.

"Mom, I'll never be as good a Vitaly," said Mila.

"That is not what I say."

"I have a life. He didn't, graduating summa cum whatever."

"I worried trips might be too much," said Zoya.

"I'm still getting good marks. Still good enough for grad school Mom. Don't worry."

"You smart cookie. I know. I worried."

"And you Vitaly," asked Zoya, "what is new?"

"Not much. Just work."

Everyone waited for more. There was none. Mila broke the silence.

"Well, there you go. Sharing again."

"Mila!" said Petr. "Let him talk."

Vitaly began and Mila tuned out.

From her seat, she could see only a sliver of the restaurant but it was the part she cared for. Caroline was at the hostess station for a few seconds at a time as she wrote a note or looked up a reservation.

Caroline always greeted the waiting patron with a beaming smile. Its radiance surpassed her memory. Mila imagined she was speaking to her.

"How beautiful you look tonight! I've missed you so... Happy you could join us... Don't be a stranger."

The invitation to return from lunch weighed. When Caroline was close, Mila felt empowered and weak, elated and fearful. Could anything ever change?

Her infatuation began at the barre. After one very long session four years ago, Mila entered the women's change room just as Caroline took off her leotard and removed her tights. Instead of hiding herself, Caroline continued undressing.

Mila just watched her, admiring the lines of her hips, the grace of her limbs and the form of her breasts.

She caught a glimpse of the bright shock of red hair. Caroline saw Mila gazing and smiled.

Mila had hurriedly dressed, pulling her pants on over her tights, a sweater and jacket over her leotard and slung her bag over her shoulder.

She scooped up her battered, salt-stained boots, stopping only at the foyer to slip them on, not bothering with her socks.

Mila ran out of the school, crossed a small parking lot and slipped through a break in the chain-link fence that led to the railway tracks.

She walked north along them and came to her favourite spot beneath a large willow tree whose graceful boughs reached down to the ground, providing a wall to hide behind.

She sat in the mottled light of the sun streaming through the branches, fished out her cigarettes, and extracted the one she had hand-rolled. She breathed in its oily smoke and held it, waiting for the calm to overwhelm her.

It was then that Mila noticed Caroline was standing there, waiting for permission to join her. Mila's smile was enough for Caroline. She sat down, pulling her knees tight against her chest, her shoulders just rubbing against Mila's. She passed the joint to Caroline who breathed in deeply, exhaling slowly through her nose.

Caroline turned and kissed Mila gently on the cheek, placing her palm where her lips just were. She drew Mila to her and kissed Mila on the lips, gently. The hair on Mila's neck tingled. Mila shifted forward, eyes wide at first, and then allowing them to close.

Caroline's tongue flicked her lips. She followed her forward as Caroline pulled away, almost losing her balance. Mila slowly opened her eyes, got up and ran. It was still the most passionate kiss of her life.

Zoya kicked Mila under the table.

"Pay attention to brother. Learn something proper."

Vitaly was still droning on.

"Just another secondment. I'm going to work for the Ontario Securities Commission for a while. Regulation Services. Started a few weeks ago."

"What? Again?" said Mila. "Stop getting kicked around. Your boss is just stringing you along."

"No Mila, he just finding way," said Zoya.

"He's not, Mom. Vitaly's the guy you call when you need a get out of a jail free card."

Vitaly was silent.

"How many of the schmucks he defended should be in jail instead of garden leave in the Muskokas? No offense, but most of those guys should be behind bars and you know it."

"Just doing my job."

"A little too well sometimes, no?"

"He does good job," said Zoya.

"Yeah Mama, I know, but the sooner he grows some, the better off he'll be. He's not a kid anymore. He's fuckin' brilliant."

"Mila, language!" Petr said.

"Papa, he is and you know it," she continued turning to Vitaly. "You've gotta take charge."

"Like you have."

"I'm still in school and I'm a research assistant."

"We are proud of you both," said Petr, "Right Zoya?"

Zoya nodded.

"V!"

"I know, I know," said Vitaly quietly.

Mila grabbed his hand in hers and looked him in the eye.

"Then do it. Do it."

"So what you do at OSC?" asked Zoya

"I'm heading up a team in the only part of the OSC that has any teeth. Not enough as my new boss made clear during my interview. Their senior litigator died about three weeks ago from an insulin overdose. My team's still stunned. She'd worked there for five years. My boss made it clear that she'd be a hard act to follow. I've three baby lawyers, Derek, Paul and Maiwen. They do mostly research. If they get overwhelmed, we've the occasional law student and, when we need him, I've got access to a cop from the RCMP. He's the muscle. I've little idea of how to use him. He said he'd rather be looking for bodies than cash."

"So, how's new boss?" asked Zoya.

"Wallace? Horrible. I can't wait to get back to the old shop."

"Why?" asked Petr.

"He's an egotistical megalomaniac."

"Just like everyone else on Bay Street," Mila chirped.

"Yeah sis. He's not really the role model I was hoping for. He starts meetings the same way every time. He reminisces about the past, trumpeting his prowess and spouting all sorts of garbage. He brags that this is his public penance, that the position's really quite straightforward and that the three-year commitment he made to the Minister of Finance was costing him a bundle, given what he earned in civilian life."

"Sounds like fun."

"Sometimes I wish I had your favourite temporary condition."

"Ha! Situational Tourette's? Like now, where I'd scream - Boring, boring!"

Vitaly ignored Mila.

"Most of the time," Vitaly continued, "I want to yell 'Bullshit, Bullshit, Bullshit!' I've no idea how my old boss got hooked up with Wallace. He promised me my purgatory would be limited, that I'd be welcomed back into the fold once I did my time."

"Cannot be that bad?" said Zoya. "Can he?"

"Our last meeting was a disaster. He's losing patience with me already."

"But you have only been there few weeks," said Petr.

"He wants high profile results, with the credit going to him, you know, front page, above-the-fold headline kind of stuff. It pissed, excuse me, it upset him when I was given credit for a settlement in the Globe. I just finished Adriana's work and I told him that. He wouldn't hear it."

"It is wonderful photo of you," said Zoya.

"Just happened I was the only person in focus in the photo. I can't control what the papers print.

"You were handsome. I sent photo to family in Vilnius."

"Mama, no! Who are you setting me up with?"

"No one," his mother smirked. "Just answer phone politely if girl named Vika calls."

"No!" cried Petr.

"Vika?" snickered Mila. "Your best friend's daughter?" She laughs like a donkey. Oh God, Mama. V. and Vika sitting in a tree. K.I.S.S.I.N.G. "

"She is fine young woman. Just finished Master's in economic history of Soviet Union."

"Mom, I wish you wouldn't."

"Just be polite."

"Yes, Mama. Anyhow, I was just following Adriana's lead. I'd have liked to have met her. She seemed bright. Anyhow, Donald let me know that if I didn't make him shine in the next few cases, I'd be gone. My old boss says he's not sure I'd be back if that happens."

"Oh, I'm so sorry," Mila said.

"Yeah, great way to start, eh? At least my team's starting to come around. They were stubborn at first. The memories of Adriana trickled through every conversations. Someone even left a size 17 shoe on my desk."

"Cute," said Mila.

"I was going to throw it out but instead, I nailed it to the wall. There's no hiding from it. Adriana will be hard to replace. Slowly, they're accepting me, but it's been in fleeting steps. The one exception's been the cop. He supported me right away."

"Quite a transition," said Mila. "Going to the bright side."

"Sort of. I shouldn't talk about it, but my next case could be big or a waste of time. Brian, the cop, interviewed the complainant. He said she's a bit of a nut-bar, but we'll see. You'll never guess who's involved!"

Vitaly looked around the table at blank faces.

"Come on, guess!"

"Just tell us!" said Mila.

"Promise you won't tell?" Vitaly warned.

"Cross hearts," said Zoya.

"Of course," said Petr.

They leaned in closer. Vitaly lowered his voice.

"John Lister."

"No way," said Mila. "The hedge fund manager?"

They all turned to her.

"What? I read the business section of the paper sometimes, for Dilbert. From what I've read about him, he seems kind of boring."

"He is guy who do fundraising for cancer care," said Zoya. "We just volunteered. What was it called, in Annex? Oh, ah... Alison's House."

"There was a big photo of Mr. Lister with some teenaged girl," continued Petr. "He charitable."

"Mama, Papa, don't be deceived," said Vitaly. "It's not charity, it's philanthropy."

They looked at him perplexed.

"I thought they same thing," said Petr.

"In the donor's mind they are. In reality, private foundations are just tax planning. Instead of paying the government on some windfall earned on an investment, they donate money to their own private foundation and then they pay out the assets slowly over time. A minimum of three and a half per cent of its value each year."

"That's all?"

"Yeah, and that's lower than it used to be."

"Three and a half percent," said Zoya. "We donate more of income."

"Yes, Mama, so do I," Vitaly agreed.

"Essentially, the government is allowing the rich not to pay their taxes and to dribble that money back into the economy on things they deem to be important. All the while the recipients fawn over them, desperate to get money that should have been circulated a long time ago," he explained.

"Oh, and I looked into the Lister Foundation. Lister hasn't made a contribution to his foundation in five years."

"So, what'd he do?" asked Mila.

"Well, he's accused of steering good stock trades to his firm's account and the bad ones to the funds that he ran for other people."

"And that's a big no-no?" asked Mila.

"Yeah, a big one."

"Come on," said Petr. "He is one of good guys! He help peoples."

Vitaly knew that his father did not approve of his earlier successes. His son had done his job, but that job had meant that guilty men had not paid a price for their actions.

"Papa, I'm one good guys now."

"A new sheriff?" Petr joked.

"Sounds like great opportunity," Zoya declared. "You do right thing, won't you?"

6

Vitaly hugged his parents goodbye outside the bistro. Zoya looked up at her son and held his shoulders.

"You have done good Vitaly," she said. "We are proud of you."

Vitaly gave Mila a playful shot in the arm, a gesture she returned with enough force to make him wince.

"Mila," he said, "close your eyes and hold out your hands."

Vitaly placed a handful of clear amber-coloured candies wrapped in cellophane in her upturned palms.

"I love these," she exclaimed with the glee of a six year old, hopping up and down. "I'm such a sucker for maple," she said.

"I snagged them from a conference a few weeks ago."

Mila pocketed all but four and distributed them amongst her family. She popped one in her mouth and wrapped her arms around her brother again.

"Thanks. You're the best."

She gave him a peck on the cheek, leaving a slight smear of red lipstick, which she rubbed off with her thumb.

"Okay, we are off," said Petr. "You are still coming home, right Mila?"

"You making blintzes for breakfast?"

"For you, of course."

"I have baking for you too," said Zoya.

"Vitaly, come. Spend the night," said Mila.

"Nah, I'm just gonna walk home. Early start tomorrow, though the blintzes do sound good."

"This weekend then?" asked Petr.

"Of course. As always."

Vitaly had lied about going home. Even if he was now working for the government, he did not intend to change his routine. He walked to Starbucks. He needed fuel for the next few hours. The coffee shop was one of the few refuges still open downtown that was not a bar. Young men were typing madly at their laptops. Women sat in groups warding off the cold with lattes and hot chocolates.

"That will be four dollars, sixty-two cents," said the barista.

"I haven't even ordered yet."

"Triple, tall, skinny latte, right?"

Vitaly smiled, thought of changing his order, but nodded. He had placed the order so many times but he had never considered why it was ready so quickly.

"So much caffeine, so late at night. Not good for you, ya know," the woman teased.

"This coming from a barista."

He smiled and wished he could ask her for her number. He had noticed her two weeks earlier, but could never summon the courage. Despite his ability to argue before the greatest legal minds in the country, battling on esoteric points of the law, his sister was right. He was petrified of talking to women.

She waited to catch his eye again.

"I'm Martha," pointing to herself as Jane would have when meeting Tarzan.

"V...V," he stammered, "Vitaly."

"Ya sure?"

"Vitaly," he repeated with more confidence, "Vitaly Mirkin."

She smiled. "Vitaly, pleasure to meet you. Sorry to rush. Other people to serve. Your latte will be on the corner," Martha said with a wink. "Next?"

Vitaly watched Martha from the end of the counter while another barista prepared his drink. He admired her offbeat choice of clothes; nothing matched but the muddle of fabrics and colours worked. It was endearing and a stylistic change from the sharpness of suits.

Cup in hand, Vitaly headed back to his office on the tenth floor at Queen and Yonge. As he walked, he noticed a scribble on the sleeve of the coffee cup.

Come back soon. Martha ☺

Her scrawl was followed by a happy face.

In ten minutes, Vitaly was at the office. To his surprise, his team was still working. Vitaly could hear Derek and Maiwen in Paul's office, a gentle banter emerging. Paul stopped mid-sentence when Vitaly popped his head in.

"What are you up to?"

"Just finishing up some work."

"You're all dismissed. We've been scrambling since I arrived. I need some time to figure out our priorities."

"And Wallace?"

"Let me get through the dockets. We'll talk tomorrow."

The three shrugged, grabbed their coats and shuffled off. Vitaly went to his desk and studied the large painting that hung from the wall. His secretary popped her head in to let Vitaly know she was leaving. She caught him staring at the canvas.

"Maintenance can take it down in the morning. I'll see if the family wants it."

"No, no. Leave it for now. I understand Adriana niece painted it. I love the sense of discovery, the playfulness of the colour."

Vitaly went through his email. It was a mix of administrative notices and RSS feeds sent from various business sources. He was struck by the number of articles highlighting the deaths and injuries from wireless glucose monitors, mostly from a new company called Glucosure. He looked up the stock price; it was off over 40% in the last five trading sessions. Most of the rest of the emails were from the IT department making sure that everything was in order and that service was going to be disrupted over the weekend. He deleted those and replied to a few notes of congratulations that still straggled in. There was also note from Donald Wallace addressed to all staff.

My Dear Colleagues:

We are all saddened by the sudden passing of Adriana Pollen on December 6th of this year. She was a long-time, dedicated employee. I had the privilege of participating in a memorial in her honour yesterday. The family has permitted me to share with you all the words I spoke this afternoon. I wish to extend a warm welcome to Vitaly Mirkin. He recently joined the Regulation Services Group and his introduction is overdue. He will be heading up Adriana's team. I am sure he will make a fine addition and we all look forward to working with him.

Sincerely,

Donald Wallace

Vitaly opened the attachment and shifted in his chair.

To Adriana's parents, Benjamin and Jennifer, her sister Muriel and her brothers Jeffrey and Jeremy, on behalf of the Adriana's colleagues at the OSC, please permit me to express our deepest sympathies. To Adriana's nieces, Natasha and Sandrine, your aunt often mentioned her joy in watching you learn to appreciate the arts as she did. The paintings that she hung in her office were the envy of the staff.

Adriana exemplified all that is good about our profession. She worked tirelessly on behalf of the people of Ontario, indeed the people of Canada, to help make the financial industry fairer and just. She was a visionary for setting the agenda for future regulation.

While her work took up so much of her time, perhaps too much of her time, she spoke fondly of her family and friends. She also led us forward as a group through her volunteer work with Renewal Foundation, a group dedicated to the treatment and support of addicts and their families in the Greater Toronto Area. The organization has historically catered mostly to men in the corporate world. Recognizing the circumstances of women who are bedevilled by addiction, the way they suffer alone and the differentiated path to their recovery, Adriana pushed to have a greater balance between the genders. She changed the way women are treated as they enter recovery. In honour of Adriana's memory, and with your permission, I am proud to announce that the Ontario Securities Commission will establish an endowment to help women without means access addictions treatment.

My thoughts are with you. To you Adriana, my colleague and my dear friend, we, I will miss you.

Vitaly closed his email account. He picked up one of the twenty-two cases that she had left behind. It was going to be a long night.

7

John entered the main boardroom at Trinity Asset Management, his hedge fund's parent. He hated this weekly ritual, an obligation of subservience. He despised his colleagues here. To John, they were feeble-minded, dogmatically following an ill conceived and poorly executed program.

He always arrived first for the weekly investment meeting, and took his preferred seat by the window. He never sat at the rectangular dark oak conference table capable of seating 40 people comfortably.

As he sat by window looking out the 39th floor at the view of Lake Ontario, John rubbed his hands together after the walk over from his office. For the first time in a century, Toronto had shivered under a week of minus 30 temperatures in December. John hated the cold.

Tim, and only Tim, knew that John had almost died from hypothermia late one January night before John had started LAM. *John was at the back of a parking lot on Front and Parliament, hidden behind delivery trucks, his seat reclined, revelling as a sweet cocktail of alcohol and Vicodin coursed though his veins. His eyes were closed and he could see his Alison smiling at him. She whispered that she was so alone and she missed her Daddy. She urged him to join her. He was ready to do so.*

A blast of cold air and glass bit his face as the baton of a cop smashed the window to unlock the door. His forehead bore the marks of that evening; a small skin graft to look after his frostbitten temple and some tiny scars on his cheek. John still thought the officer had overreacted, having taken perverse pleasure breaking into his Porsche.

John's attention was split between the messages on his smartphone and the ferry nudging the ice floes as it crossed the harbour to the Toronto Islands. Jargit had sent a text warning that

John had three months to show improved numbers, otherwise there would be consequences. He left those unspecified. Given that Jargit's capital had declined by over $100-million dollars in the past year, John was sure it was worse than not receiving Christmas fruitcake. He wondered how heavy hot bitumen felt. Did it soothe or scald? John assured Jargit that the numbers would be turning. He had a number of things in the bag. With luck, it would be less than three months.

Eugene Shagass, the Chief Investment Officer of the Trinity Asset Management always arrived only after the room was full.

"Welcome John. A little nippy out there today, isn't it?"

John just smiled politely, declining to engage. Eugene plunked down the foot thick sheaf of handouts in the middle of the table.

"Now, I have a little presentation to go through with you all."

A collective groan went around the room.

"I'm sure you will all enjoy it."

As Eugene's assistant distributed the materials, she apologized under her breath as she gave John a USB key. He turned over the first page of the package, which had been annotated in a pre-schooler's scrawl using a red crayon.

Sorry to hear about yesterday's meetings. If you need help selling down the portfolio, my traders can liquidate it. E.

John seethed but smiled at Eugene and started to flip through the presentation. Eugene called the meeting to order.

"Okay, we're all here. I'm going to pre-empt the usual 'round the world talk and just present my conclusions. Okay?"

The junior analysts held their pens at the ready, hoping to glean something to help improve their individual, if not their collective, performance.

"Earnings are starting to revert to normal levels for this stage of the cycle in North America. I recommend we add to equities and reduce fixed income and cash. The new ratio will be 70% equities,

27% bonds and 3% cash. I expect to see the balanced fund reflect these changes in the next few days. Does anyone disagree?"

Eugene paused for long enough for the silence to become uncomfortable. John smiled. Eugene had seen John use the tactic many times. Mimicry is the sincerest form of flattery.

The heads of the various teams stared at each other but kept quiet. John looked out the window. The assets he managed at LAM were a side show to all of this, totalling less than a fifteenth of Eugene's responsibilities.

Baiting the group, Eugene continued, "Com' on, someone's got something to say. Anyone?"

John sat up a little straighter in his chair. He had spoken to the portfolio managers earlier in the week. He knew their views were the opposite to Eugene's, but Eugene would be dolling out the profit sharing pool shortly. He watched Sharon Pooles, the head of fixed income, frantically recalibrating what she was going to say.

"Sure Eugene. Your conclusions are sound. Perhaps some prudence in the pace..."

"Grow some," was all Eugene said.

John let out a stifled laugh. Some turned towards him. Most dared not look.

"Okay," continued Sharon, "Of course we can implement the changes, Eugene."

She then trailed off, recapping the trades she had placed in the last week. Erica, the head of US equities, looked at her counterpart. She was stuck. She knew the path Eugene was advocating was wrong. The numbers from her group were terrible and her own personal contribution to the portfolio lagged her analysts. But she wasn't worried. Eugene had her back. Their prep school days had been spent solidifying their relationship. Two members of her team had left in disgust. Erica kept quiet and just listened to her team gripe.

"Eugene... your material supports my conclusions as well."

John closed his eyes at the lie.

After the meeting adjourned, John walked back to LAM below ground, picked up a latte for Tim, and rode the elevator back up to the office. The doors opened onto a marble tiled floor and a brushed steel door, with a window like that of a prison cell and a single phone on the wall. Three people had the code that opened it outside of the firm's normal 12-hour days: John, Tim and Val.

John punched in his code and placed his hand on the glass panel next to the door that read his palm. He listened for the dull thud as the magnetic locks released and the door swung inward. The hallway led to the trading floor.

"Oh Snap. I can't believe you," yelled Tim before banging the headset on the top of the desk. "No, wrong price, you, you..."

"Yvonne caught you again?" asked John.

"Shit, I mean shit, I'm already out four hundred bucks to your fine piece of ass secretary from last fuckin' week. If I can't swear, I can't get my fuckin' point across."

John held out his hand and Tim pealed off two $50 bills and put them in John's palm.

"How will they know I serious if I can't rip them a new one every now and then. John, it's hampering my productivity."

"Well, the street might just think you're civilized."

"You want that? I'm the best John because I'm modest and humble. I never forget my "pleases" and "thank yous" and I clear the dishes without even someone asking. This is bullshit!"

"It's just two more weeks. You'll be fine."

John's secretary had left a brown lunch paper bag up on his chair. John felt its weight, satisfied that he knew what was inside. John pulled out his wallet, counted off four crisp new fifties and stuffed them in the swear jar and winked at Tim.

"Okay my little analists," he screamed, "my little salad tossers, into the boardroom, now!"

The din in the room did not die.

"Sodomites! Stop talking and get walking!"

As the analysts scurried to the board room, the lone female, Isabella Tournimenko, ignored John, finished her conversation and handed a note to Tim. Only then did she saunter after the others. Isabella was always the last one in. Boomer, as she was known, was a tall, attractive brunette with high, Slavic cheek bones. Her beauty was evident to all. Her heterochromia was disconcerting and kept everyone on edge, their eyes never knowing where to rest.

Long ago she had given up trying to mask her sensuality. She played to the lowest common denominator. When she was hired, everyone thought that she was a sweater girl. In short order, she proved her worth. Her contributions to the funds topped all other analysts year after year. Her former colleagues at RX Wireless and Qualcomm continuously tried to woo her back. They could not compete. She earned multiples of her old bosses.

After everyone was seated at the round, birch table, John shut the doors.

"So, I just came back from a meeting with Shagass. He's predicting a strong equity market. He also gave me this USB to show me what a smart boy he is. For all of you, I have this bag."

John inverted it, scattering the contents across the table.

"Go on! Pick 'em up."

Red crayons were piled like pickup sticks. The last came to rest in front of Isabella. Nobody moved.

"Pick them the fuck up, you fucking pricks," John seethed.

No one reached for a single one. John pounded his fist on the table.

"Pick 'em up!"

Spittle flew from his mouth.

The crayons jumped at the impact. The message was clear. The shame was shared. Reluctant hands reached out but Isabella crossed her arms and stared John down. She moved no further. He broke off with a smirk.

John inserted the USB key into the computer and the overhead screen came to life as John ran through a jumble of spaghetti graphs without a narrative, signifying anything. Shagass had been working with the same charts for so long, and believed so completely in his own rhetoric, that he failed to notice that rather than repeat, the markets were evolving.

"Okay, let's run the gauntlet," said John. "Top ideas, let's hear 'em."

"Short banks on expected higher rates."

"Nope, already done. Next."

"Long the new Longmarch IPO. Management have brought three companies public in the past, all successes."

"We're already in on the deal."

"Spread trade – Long Cisco and Short Juniper."

"No, c'mon. Somebody give me something!"

"Long credit default swaps on Glucosure," said Isabella.

"Yes," said John clearly intrigued "Continue."

"We shorted the stock already. The security software is shit. We know that. What was not in the initial analysis is the extent of the potential lawsuits."

"Continue."

"The cash on the balance sheet is the base value but that now is going go the settlements and the lawyers. The liabilities will be greater than the remaining assets. The debt worthless. That's why you go long the CDS."

"Good. Position size."

"Up to you boss, but four per cent of the fund seems reasonable."

"Okay. Tell Val."

"Next? Wilson. How about you?"

"Uh, nothing this week boss."

"Wee Willy, that's three weeks in a row."

"Sorry."

"Go easy on..." began one of the junior analyst.

"Willy, baby? What do you have for me?"

"Nothing."

"Hmm. Do our clients pay us to do nothing? Do you think they care as we sit here earning fees off of their hard earned assets that we do nothing?"

"No boss."

"I know you've have a hard time these last three week. Your wife losing one of the twins and all. I know. It was terrible."

"Thanks boss."

"But do you think our clients give a fuck? They don't give a flying rat's ass that you and the missus are grieving. They really fuckin' don't. So why should I? We get paid for returns. You get paid for generating ideas. Get the fuck out!"

Wilson just sat, tears forming in his eyes.

"Does it sound like I'm fuckin' around? Get out now. Leave the door open."

The analyst left everything on the table and hurried out.

"Lesson over, my precious ones. Any questions? No? Now get out and don't fuck up. Everyone but Boomer."

The guys rolled their eyes as they left. Isabella hated it when John did this. After the last of them left, John shut the door.

"Don't worry Boomer. I'll stay on this side."

John had once made a very public pass at her at the first Christmas party she had attended. She chalked it up to his sick daughter and stress. She knew he was in recovery. She admired him for his resolve.

"Little harsh John, no?"

"Should I have gone easier? Would you have like that?"

"Yes and no. Wilson was always a dead weight."

John spun in his chair like a child sitting in a swivel chair for the first time, rotating in full circles. She waited till he came to a halt.

"Am I making partner or what? Headhunters are calling. Eugene even approached me."

"Shagass, approached you? You wanna join him? *Him?*"

Isabella leaned forward on the table, hands clasped together, not breaking her eye contact with John. He averted his gaze.

"We'll discuss bonuses soon," John whispered. "You won't be disappointed. The rest of your colleagues might be, but you won't. Okay?

"I need to know John."

"Boomer, you're good."

"For now."

"Yes, for now. So, how's part two of the wireless project?" John asked.

"Progressing. Almost ready."

"Almost?"

"Almost. I did a test run, a hide and seek of sorts, to see if we'd be detected. It appears we might've been successful."

"Bullshit, Boomer! I saw the results. The run was fantastic."

"It may have been a one-off."

"You need to complete the hack. I need to grind Glucosure down further. I agree the bonds are worthless. Let's make sure there is nothing for a white knight to come and save.

"John, legal approved this, right?"

"We're not breaking any laws. We're just pointing out a flaw in their software. That we profit from it... well, we've done the work. All this needs to happen next week."

"You don't want to have the cost of re-buying the February put options."

"If we've got to do that, we will, but there's always information leakage and the trade will get crowded."

"Okay," she said. "The backdoor's almost open."

"More like falling off the hinges."

"As you suspected, health care companies don't know shit about security."

"The device will get yanked off the market once the FDA is made aware of the deficiencies."

"And you will inform them?"

John whistled three descending notes.

"It'll crush them."

"Let's hope," he said with a devilish grin.

"I've something new for you. I think you'll like the challenge."

John slid a file across the table. She began to leaf through it.

"This is way bigger."

"I know. You'll work with Matt."

"No. Anyone but Murphy!"

"Why?"

"Uh, let's see, maybe because he's fuckin' nuts."

"That was a long time ago. He'll allow you to work much faster."

"Fine. I'll do it."

"Good. Murphy's on hardware. You're on security again. Heartwave's trying to get ahead of St Jude and Medtronic with a new wireless system for their implantable defibrillator."

"It makes sense. Cardiologists can monitor patients from anywhere and adjust as needed."

"I need a solution in a month."

Isabella shook her head.

"It'll take way longer."

"A month."

"You're a vampire! You know that."

"Yup."

John got up and left.

Isabella sat at the table and reread the file. John's timeline meant a month of not seeing anyone, except maybe her trainer at the gym.

8

"Dolores," Benny called out.

His secretary opened his door a moment later. "You bellowed, my lord and master?"

"A guy from the OSC sent me an email. Figure out what Vitaly Mirkin wants, would ya?"

"An acquaintance of yours? Should I be worried?"

"I only know one Vitaly. He's the only guy ever to knock me down boxing. That was a long time ago. All's good. Dismissed."

Benedicto Figueredo Aguero de Silva Costa was simply known as Benny to anyone on the Street. He was the highest ranked insurance analyst on Bay Street.

His professional pedigree was impeccable: MSc in Finance from MIT, highest mark for his year on the Chartered Accountants exam, Chartered Financial Analyst. He'd worked for the Office of the Superintendent for Financial Services where he had written many of the policies implemented in Canada for the past decade.

Eleven years ago, the lucre of Bay Street called and he crossed over to Richmond Capital where he wrote research for portfolio and hedge fund managers in the hope they would bring their trading business to his firm.

He had developed a loyal following eager to pay for his brain. He knew how insurance companies were run and where the secrets were buried.

A minute later there was a knock and Dolores entered.

"That was fast."

"I'm no miracle worker. I forgot to give you these," she said as she handed him a sheaf of phone messages. Important people and those who wanted to be discreet, never use email. It left a trail.

"When did Lister call?" Benny asked, holding up a chit.

"Around 11 this morning."

"And he wants me at 2:30 pm today. You didn't think you should have started with that?"

"I just..."

"Cancel the rest of my afternoon ... please."

"Are you being summoned?"

"Wipe that smirk off your face. I gotta go." Benny hated being summoned to meetings. He hated John even more.

****

Benny arrived at the LAM offices 10 minutes early. Just as he approached the door, it buzzed open.

John's personal assistant, Yvonne, led him down to a large board room. It was stark, finished with contemporary furniture and abstract art. A round silver tray sat on the table with a pitcher of ice water and three tall cylindrical glasses.

The assistant poured a glass and left. Benny stood at the window and looked south along York Street.

The woman returned two minutes later.

"I took the liberty of contacting your secretary earlier. I hope you don't mind. She mentioned you like a cappuccino after lunch. Mr. Lister and Mr. Kozak will be just a moment."

She placed the cup on the table without a sound and then closed the glass door behind her.

Benny was not sure why he was there. Why John spoke to Bay Street analysts at all was a mystery. He and his team normally knew more than he did. Benny knew he was there for one of two reasons: either John needed information or he had discovered something and wanted to gloat.

John and Val entered at the same time.

"Benny, still a pussy?"

"John, still a prick?" thought Benny. He just smiled politely.

"Val, did I ever tell you about the first time I met Benny?"

"Yes, John."

"Let me refresh your memory. 9/11. 12th floor at 8:30 am at Banker's Trust building if I recall. Benny, you remember, right?"

"How could I forget?"

"Indeed. We've never discussed it, you and me. Quite a scene to be looking over the World Trade Center Plaza, no?"

Benny looked off, stiff.

"The main thing I still remember is watching you running away like a little girl."

"Two planes hit the towers."

"There was money to be made, blood in the streets and all that Baron Rothchilds' nonsense."

"They broke all the trades that day. How'd you make any money?"

"They broke the equity trades, not the FX nor the credit default swaps, especially offshore. Made out like a banshee buying bond protection. And you ran away."

"Good for you John. I was just happy to get off Manhattan."

"Let's sit, shall we? Enough chit-chat. I asked Val to join us today as he might be able to articulate a few things better than me. You know me, I don't usually admit to not knowing something, but this time, Val and I have a wager."

"What's that?"

"Well, it's kind of a secret," John smirked. "You're a smart guy. You might figure it out over time."

"Anyhow, business," John added. "All of us girls around the table know the insurance companies are screwed. The financial crisis wasn't the real problem. The aftermath is. Rates have been kept way too low, way below what they ever contemplated. They're not earning what they thought they would. Not even close."

"All investors face the same problem," said Benny. "I see where you're going."

"Do you?" asked Val.

"Yeah, the regulators are worried that they'll not have enough capital to support the annuities they sold. They need to either raise more capital or restructure their balance sheets."

"What do you think they'll do?"

Benny took a deep breath.

"A bit of both, I guess. The capital structures are all messed up. The assets are all worth less than the insurance policies they've written. If interest rates stay much lower for a long time, maturing bonds will be replaced at ever-lower rates. They won't be able to meet their obligations. When the regulators come knocking, they'll force them to raise equity. To get me interested, they'll have to lower the price a lot; ten per cent lower, maybe even fifteen per cent. They won't be happy. You might be. You'll get to buy the stock at a great price."

"That's what we are hoping for."

"Corinne Graham, the Superintendent for Financial Services," Benny said redundantly, "had spoken about this at a conference in Cambridge a while ago. Low interest rates may have saved the markets..."

"But, it's heroin."

"Easy to get hooked on and tough to get off."

"Anyway, I know all this. I was there."

Benny paused for a moment.

"I was at the dinner. I saw you biding your time, trying not to interact with anyone at your table. And that you got a kiss from the prettiest girl in the room."

Benny remained silent.

"You and Corinne both went to Western, didn't you? My buddies tell me you use to grind the sheets a fair bit."

"Pardon?"

"The Street's a small place, Benny, you know that."

"Getting smaller everyday apparently."

"Okay," continued John, "So Corinne had some interesting things to say about the need to raise capital and excluding us hedge funds, interlopers I think she called us, from playing in the sandbox."

"She was just doing what regulators do, you know, protecting the establishment."

"Protecting the guilty more like. What I want to know is why you didn't call anyone about this? You sat on intel from that evening.

Benny squirmed in his seat.

"Did the investment bankers buy your silence while they collected their fat fees?" asked John. "I hope they share."

"I do okay."

"Benny, they're stealin' your thunder. Come work for me. You'll be rewarded."

"Thanks, but no."

"We could use another connected mind, couldn't we Val?"

"Well, only if you really, really want to come," Val said.

"Thanks for the offer. I'll consider it."

"That's all I can ask. Okay, where were we?"

"Shareholders," Benny continued, "do not want to be diluted down by the managements that got them into the trouble."

"And?"

"They've got two choices. Raise more equity at depressed prices or sell their liabilities."

"But which ones?" asked John. "What can they move without a loss?"

"If you were the CFO," Val prodded, "what would you shed?"

"Annuities but they would take a blood bath. No one who owns one would sell it. Term life is their next valuable asset because they collect premiums and don't have to pay out until people die."

"Continue," said John.

"About ten per cent of the policies lapse each year because people forget to pay or they can't afford to. Either way, the companies love it. They could, I guess, try to persuade more people to surrender their policies, paying them next to nothing. If people don't lapse, the insurance companies are screwed. Their pricing assumes an eight per cent lapse rate. If that rate goes down to say six per cent, they'll lose a ton of money."

A slow smile slid across John's face.

"They will, won't they? I want to own those."

"What? Why?"

"The payoff's good."

"You're willing to pay the premiums? Waiting for people to die? Could take years."

"Yeah, but we all know the actuaries are wrong. For your physical, you're on your best behaviour, right? You know, no salt diets, eating lettuce to lower your weigh, no booze, maybe a colon cleanse. Once you get the policy though, it's back to super-sizing those fries, a pack of smokes a day, maybe some blow or oxy.

Secure Life Assurance produced a chart recently. The average age at death had gone down, not up for the past ten years. Walk around outside of Toronto. Half the population is obese and the other half is trying to be. Were the policies underwritten correctly? When I buy the policies, I'm just hoping people die sooner. I don't know 'em, so what do I care?"

John laughed.

"Bit of a death pool," said Benny, "betting on people dying."

"Look at what I give 'em."

"Give 'em?"

"Everyone starts life at Point A; young and dumb, with no money and if you're are lucky, a job, an education. You want to get to Point B, a comfortable retirement, the occasional golf game, the odd trip to Casino Rama. You'll spoil the grandkids and take an annual trip to the Caribbean at some all-inclusive resort with your spouse, lining up at the buffet for dinner at a quarter to five in the afternoon. It sounds horrible to me, but whatever. With rates so low, what most investors face now is Point C; renting a draughty apartment in a crumbling tenement in Scarborough, waiting for a meagre, government pension cheque, watching TV with the volume cranked up because you can't afford batteries for your hearing aid. Soon, you can no longer taste the difference between canned tuna and cat food."

"That's a little extreme!"

"The Hell it is. At the big banks, the median retirement account is what, two-hundred-and-twenty-five grand. That's it. Not much. They're sixty-two. They better die by seventy-five or they'll run out of cash."

"Okay, so what do you give 'em?" said Benny.

"Hope!"

"Hope?"

"Most people have two large assets: their house and their life insurance policy. Shelter they need. Most can live in something smaller. What they don't need is life insurance. Their dependents are grown and look after themselves. Given the way most kids treat their parents, they don't deserve a dime of inheritance."

"John, I'm not following."

"Benny, I want their term life policies. They get money and I get their asset. I'll offer them way more than what the insurance company ever would. Look, the insurance company will give them maybe five cents per dollar of face value. I'll give them sixty, maybe sixty-five. Take a policy we just underwrote. Mildred's a widow, sixty-five years old. Melvin, her recently deceased spouse, bought the policy when he was in his twenties. It's the wrong policy. It pays out to their asshole child who only calls at Christmas and Easter. Mildred's stuck with bills that piled up after Melvin's stroke. They burned through all their liquid assets caring for him at home and in a private hospice and now Mildred is cash flow poor and is about to have to sell her house."

"I think Benny gets the picture," said Val, clearly perturbed.

"Say I buy the policy from her for six-hundred grand, ten, maybe eleven times over the surrender value. The annual premium is two-thousand. Her life expectancy is seventy-seven years. I'd carry twelve years of premiums, at twenty-four grand. At death, I net three-hundred-and-sexty-six thousand – one-million, less the premiums I paid and what I shelled out to her. Mildred's happy, tucks into filet mignon every now and then and goes to Atlantic City with her blue-haired darlings to forget Melvin. It's a win-win. I generate a return that's independent of the stock market, and she gets cash to do whatever."

"I thought you didn't want underwriting risk?"

"I don't. Val will crunch the numbers and we have a team finding new angles."

Val laughed. John's team consisted of a kid who couldn't find his shoes if they were on his feet, Tom Tournimenko.

"You're going to outsmart the actuaries? C'mon John, be realistic."

"Let me worry about that. You see why this is so attractive, right? I get asymmetrical risk, payouts that favour us."

"The math's not compelling. It would generate, what, a return of four per cent per annum on the capital committed. That's way below your historic returns, way less than your investors would expect. Maybe with some leverage? Val, you'd need differentiated information, that our Mildred would die sooner than expected. How could you know that?"

"Let me worry about the underwriting."

"The insurance companies would hate it but there's not a lot they could do," Benny said. "It wasn't contemplated and therefore never prohibited. You could execute the strategy in Canada, the US and Europe. So, what do you want from me? You've done all the talking."

"So, what am I missing?" asked John.

"Okay, say you can do it, how do you mass the policies you need to make a difference to LAM? The only thing I can think that would be similar is the Canadian reverse mortgage program. It took them a decade to build a critical mass. You've got what, two-billion under management?"

"More or less," said John.

"If you put in ten per cent of the fund at six-hundred-thousand invested per policy, how would you build your book? You need…"

"Three hundred and thirty-four," said Val.

"Three hundred and thirty-four," repeated Benny.

"Let me worry about that," said John.

"Commissioned sales," blurted out Benny. "Of course, pay those guys enough and they'll sell their daughters as courtesans."

"We're counting on it."

"Clever," said Benny. "No overhead."

"Okay," said John. "I think we're done."

"Why tell me this?"

"I've got what I needed," John said.

"But I didn't tell you anything you didn't already know."

"Benny, I needn't remind you that our conversation's been taped."

"We're counting on your discretion," said Val. "Wouldn't want to let anyone else in on our game, now would we?"

"Never crossed my mind," Benny lied.

"Oh and welcome to the club," said John.

"Sorry, what club?"

"How's that OSC investigation going? You didn't do anything wrong, did ya?"

Benny's mind raced. He had been reassured that all the discussions were in camera.

"Just a misunderstanding," Benny replied. "It'll be cleared up soon."

"Good to hear, eh Val? Come. Let me walk you out," said John. "Hey, I'm serious about the offer. Consider it? And ah, your new wife? Joan bumped into her in Yorkville. The girls, they like to chat."

As Benny walked back to his office, he was convinced that John was the most conniving man on Bay Street. As he entered his office, Dolores was just leaving for the day.

"How did it go?"

"I have no idea," Benny said as he sat down at this desk. A new sheaf of messages waiting to be answered. "You're off?"

"Generally what I do at 6 pm."

"Oh, right. Go catch your train."

Benny knew John had not revealed all. He considered John's threat. If he disclosed anything, even internally at Richmond and

John got a whiff, he would be cut off. Commissions at Richmond would plummet and he'd be off the Street, canned and disgraced.

As well, his wife would be "disincluded" from the ladies who lunch. Benny was sure she would find another man to finance her lifestyle once his social capital evaporated. He might have to sell his collection of Porsches.

He was not sure what would be worse, losing her or the cars.

Benny began a search on life insurance settlements. A number of Canadian funds came up with glossy marketing pitches and illustrations.

He skimmed through them: attractive returns, no market risk, no write-downs or impairments, limited credit risk, comprehensive protection.

It was legal to buy the policies from another person in a few provinces. Would a hedge fund qualify as a person?

Benny made a note to contact Corinne. Given her statement as the conference, he was not sure how much longer Ontario would allow the program.

He read on only realizing it was after 9:00 p.m. as the cleaning staff came through the office.

His wife had not bothered to call.

He put on his coat, felt for his car keys in his pocket and took the elevator to the ground floor. His wife had not missed him for the past two hours, what is one more, he thought to himself.

Benny walked over to Vertical, the resto-bar across from his office.

He ordered an Old Fashioned and the bartender allowed him to flirt with her.

She said her name was Gwen.

9

It was the beginning of February and Mila was ten hours and two months late as she snuck into the kitchen of Biff's through the back door. She had called ahead to check that Caroline was working. She had promised Caroline that she'd return to see her the day after her Christmas dinner. Life had intervened.

No, that was the lie she told herself. It was easier than the truth. Since Christmas, Mila had withdrawn from her friends and could not remember the last time she had racked a pool table or downed a pint while throwing darts. Her sole outlet had been the choreography she was preparing on for her audition. It distracted her from her studies, but she felt compelled to try. It was honest work that was progressing slowly.

"You're too wound up," her teacher had admonished. "Too controlled, not free. Let emotion flow."

They had worked on many exercises but Mila was at a standstill. Nothing had worked. Since Christmas however, her teacher had seen tremendous progress. Seeing Caroline had broken the seal on her soul.

"Why the change Milaska?" her teacher asked. "You are now the movement. Where does it come from?"

"I'm just thinking of a friend," she said shyly.

"No, you're not," she replied with a broad smile. "You're no longer suppressing fear. Your desires are... how do you say, touchable, your love vulnerable. You're venturing through a dark world where vile secrets are revealed. But you risk exile."

She held her gaze on Mila's blue eyes.

"Don't hold back your tears. It's okay. You're communicating with the one you who loves you as you are. Continue. Let it flow."

****

Mila found Caroline sitting alone at the bar in the lounge. She was reading a fat textbook, a yellow highlighter in hand, going over passages, the marker squeaking under the pressure. She watched Caroline in silence, wondering how her friend had wandered so far away from her passion. This was not the vibrant soul she remembered, the woman she had envied for her strength and grace. Caroline shuddered, slammed the book shut and launched the highlighter towards at the wall of bottles in front of her. Mila stepped forward and hugged Caroline from behind.

"It's okay. It's okay, my Caroline."

Caroline melted into Mila's embrace. She shrugged, and turned around. Mila buried herself fully into Caroline's arms, her cheek against her chest, the faint drumming of her heart resonating in her ear.

"I'm sorry I'm late," said Mila. "I truly am."

"You've a strange way of telling time," said Caroline, forcing Mila to take a step back. "Look at you. You look like the blue superhero."

It was true. While winter had been started out unseasonably cold, February had been incredibly warm, so much so that Mila had ridden the motorcycle to the restaurant.

"I love the leathers," Caroline said, feeling the dyed skin with her fingers. "Your hair! Great cut! I could never get away with a bob. I'd need your heart shaped face."

Mila held a small paper bag in front of her.

"No? You didn't?" asked Caroline.

Mila just raised her eyebrows. Caroline immediately snatched it from her, reached in and took out a charred, roasted chestnut.

"Oh, they're still warm."

She cracked the papery shell, soot spreading across her fingers. She extracted the meat, offered half to Mila and they both chewed slowly.

"Where'd you get 'em?"

"The same old rickety cart at Nathan Phillips Square."

"Where I took you figure skating once upon a time?"

"You wanted to show the link between ballet and movement. You made me put on skates!"

"I remember," Caroline giggled.

"Never had a swan lead such an ugly duckling across a frozen pond. The only good part was the chestnuts."

"Thank you," Caroline said as she gazed into Mila's eyes, chewing slowing.

Mila's eyes smiled back.

"Studying?" asked Mila.

"Trying to. I'm so far behind."

"Can't be that bad."

"Uh, yeah. I need a biz diploma to move into management. Apparently my time at Juilliard doesn't qualify for anything. If I don't pass, they'll give the position to someone else and I'll be stuck at the host station."

"Can I help?"

"This time, I'm on my own," she said, closing the text. "But I'm done for the night. Can't cram any more in. Thirsty?"

"I thought you'd never ask."

Caroline moved around behind the bar, retrieved her marker and tucked it into her apron pocket.

"You like tequila?"

"A bit odd for a French place, no?"

"You're right. The stuff here sucks anyhow. Calva!"

Caroline took two brandy snifters down from the rack over hanging the bar. She poured a finger of the golden liquid into each glass. Mila inhaled: fresh apples, wet soil, spice and heat. Caroline walked around the bar and bent in close as Mila picked up the paper bag.

"Come," Caroline beckoned, motioning to the corner booth. "We can talk over here."

Mila shuddered at the whisper of Caroline's breath on her ear. Her body followed Caroline while her mind raced. Mila took off her jacket and slid into the semicircular booth next to Caroline, their thighs touching underneath the table. Neither moved away.

"So, apart from being, oh what, two months late, what the Hell have you been up to?"

"Knitting."

"Knitting? You?

"My babushka taught when I was small. She wanted to give me a way to help me slow down, you know, when I need to think.

"Knitting, eh? It's been two months. That must be one long scarf."

"Not too long I hope. Close your eyes and hold out your hands."

Mila unzipped her satchel and placed a small parcel wrapped in golden tissue paper held in place by a simple silver ribbon in open palms.

"For me?" Caroline asked.

"Of course. Open."

Caroline carefully unwrapped the present.

"Mila...It's beautiful. The colours...and so soft."

"Alpaca. I thought the crimson and hunter green would go great with your hair."

"Thank you, thank you."

Caroline wound the scarf around her neck twice and hugged her friend. Mila relished the softness against her face. It was the safest place in her world. They sat for a few moments until Mila broke the silence.

"A toast. To you...my teacher, my friend..."

"And to you. It's so good to catch up."

"What are you doing here?" Mila asked.

She had practiced the conversation forever, telling herself to be brave and to ask about Marc first. The rest was secondary. She bit her lip. Caroline smiled meekly.

"Age caught up to me."

"What? You're the most beautiful woman I know."

"You're sweet. You know the 10,000 hour rule?"

"Yeah, takes that long to master anything. Sometimes, when I'm at the barre, I'm still in my pink body suit."

"Well, my ankles only had that many hours in them. Now, I can only stand and walk around. Can't hold poses. You know my teaching style."

"You always lead. Oh Caroline."

"I miss my students, especially the little ones. I loved watching 'em grow. I miss helping them with their first choreography for the Dance! Dance! Festival."

"I was a snowflake."

"I remember. Too cute."

"I think my Dad still has a picture of me from that performance at his office."

"I miss the way they'd hug my legs at the end of class and the drawings they'd bring me. My fridge was covered with them. They were my kids."

Caroline looked away and wiped the back of her hand across her eyes.

"You know when you were here in December? You asked about Marc?"

"You guys good? Did he stay on? At the ballet school I mean? I don't mean to sound cruel... He's so cute and all but he kind of creeped me out."

"Slow down. Too many questions. Creeped you out?"

"A man looking at me in a leotard. Ya know, teenage angst, a changing body, nowhere where to hide."

"He had to watch you. He didn't just bang the music out on those crappy pianos. He adjusted the meter if you were ahead or when you fell behind... Anyway, we are... He was so despondent when I couldn't continue, that he left the school as well. He said he was empty working there without me."

"How long have you two been together?"

"Seven years."

"I'd have thought you'd have pushed out a puppy by now."

A pall came over Caroline's face.

"We tried."

"I didn't mean to make light."

"I can't... I can't keep 'em."

"Oh Caroline. I so sorry. You'd have made a great mom."

"I would, you know."

Caroline drained her glass.

"Me," Caroline continued, "I only wanted to dance and a babe of my own. Teaching was going to keep me close to 'em but that's gone now too."

Her voice trailed off.

"So you ended up here," said Mila, trying to sound positive.

"Marc says I've abandoned my art. He accused me of whoring my talents for a pay cheque."

"I'm sure he's just disappointed..."

There was a silence that neither felt the need to fill. Eventually, Caroline walked to the bar to poured another round. She sat down just as close as she had before.

"And you, what have you been up to?"

Mila held Caroline's gaze for a long time and played with her grandmother's ring, slipping one band over the other. She began at the place that felt comfortable.

"Umm, mostly school. The psych's easy. The stats is brutal. It'd help if I attended more classes though."

"Why don't you?"

Mila paused again. The ring was nearly off her finger.

Caroline reached out tentatively and traced the intricate tattoo on the back of Mila's hand. The hair on the nape of Mila's neck tingled again. She did not dare move, fearful that Caroline might retreat. Caroline's finger glided to rest intertwined with Mila's. It was warm and comforting and proper. Caroline turned Mila's hand over so their palms were touching. She stared at the tattoo on the inside of Mila's wrist. It was written in Cyrillic - Храбрым.

"What's it read?"

"Brave," Mila whispered.

"Are you? Are you brave?"

"I don't know."

"You are, Mila. You've always been. You're one of the bravest people I know. You may not feel it. I've always seen it in you."

"Thanks. I am. I guess."

Mila took a sip of Calvados.

"So why do I miss class? I travel a lot, doing research for a prof. I was just in Calgary, presenting an article I just co-authored with my professor."

"What! You're published? As a third year?"

Mila sat a little straighter.

"Not yet but soon. The paper discussed drug addiction and the different modalities to dependence. The research pays a small stipend. Helps make ends meet. Apart from that, I...Caroline, I'm ready for a change... ready..."

"Whatta yous talkin' about?" demanded a waitress who had entered the bar.

Mila completed her sentence in silence. "For you."

"Oh snap," muttered Caroline as she turned to the woman.

The woman's skirt was a little askew, her shirt untucked. She sat down, picked up Caroline's drink and took a sniff.

"I fuckin' love calva," she proclaimed before downing what was left of the glass.

"Olive meet Mila. Mila, this is my intoxicated friend who has certainly been busy in the kitchen."

"Tell us, what's good tonight?" asked Mila.

Olive looked at Mila, sizing her up. She burst into tears.

"Federico, little bastard. After all I've done."

"I've bet you've done a lot," said Mila. "For him, I mean."

Caroline chuckled, trying to look concerned. Olive stared at Mila, snorted, and turned to Caroline.

"I don't like her at all," she slurred. "She wouldn't understand men. Not like you and me."

Olive hiccupped once and placed her hand over her mouth, the smallest amount of vomit squeezing through her fingers.

"Mila, time for you to go! I gotta deal with this... this shituation,"

Caroline shoved Olive off the bench and grabbed her by her shoulders.

"C'mon Buttercup. Time to make you feel better."

"No, Caroline, I don't wanna throw-up again," she whimpered as she wiped her hands on her skirt. "It got in my hair last time."

Caroline walked behind Olive, guiding her to the washroom.

They almost made it around the corner before Caroline turned and called.

"I'm so sorry. I'm not done with you, Rabbit. You never told me what you're ready for. I need to know."

"It's okay. You can reach me here," Mila said as she held up a card as she walked by the hostess station.

"I still don't know anything," called Caroline. "It'd better not be two months!"

Caroline's voice trailed off. Mila could hear retching.

"Goddammit, Olive, in the toilet!"

"I hope not!" said Mila to herself as she left Biff's through the kitchen. "I can't wait that long."

Mila found her way back to her bike. It was now 10:30 p.m. She had classes in the morning.

It would take her ten minutes to ride to the house on Queen Street West where she an apartment with four other people.

She would be drinking warm milk three minutes after that and then asleep in her bed.

Her bike sputtered to life with a low growl. As beaten up as it was, the old ride still sounded good and throaty.

She straddled it, letting the engine warm, when she felt buzzing in her shoulder bag.

She took out her phone. It was John. She let it go to voicemail.

Balancing the bike, she revelled in its soothing hum. Her phone buzzed again. This time it was a text.

U downtown. Here late. Office. Please come.

Need distraction.

She had no desire to see him nor go to his office. Last time, they had been interrupted by the cleaning staff.

Busy Hun XOX

It was his fifteenth message of the day.

"Hey loser," she said to herself. "I've seen you three times this month. Your stipend's covered."

Come. Now!!

"Or what?" she said aloud. "Cut me off."

Nite, nite!

She turned her phone off and tucked it into her bag and he swung the satchel around and shifted into first. She released the clutch and left the downtown core.

****

After listening to Olive retch as she held most of her hair out of the toilet, Caroline finally exited the washroom.

The air of the bar felt fresh, but the stench of the vomit clung to her clothes.

She had left Olive resting her head on the cool porcelain of the vessel.

Caroline headed to the utility room behind the kitchen for the mop and pail. Her better angels had had enough of covering for Olive. There was no way she was leaving this for the cleaners.

Caroline walked down the hall and stopped, remembering Mila's last action.

She went to the host station to find the reservation book closed.

Caroline turned to the day and found nothing but the scribbles of the table assignments.

She thumbed her way forward page by page, until, she got to May 15th, her birthday. A business card had been placed in the crease of the page with a kiss of lipstick on it. She was perplexed. It read:

Tatiana Nikoleavna

tatiania1xox@gmail.com

10

It felt like she had cheated winter. It was mid-March and Mila had ridden her bike everyday for the past week. She cruised the streets of John's neighbourhood, getting increasingly disoriented. None of the winding roads ever met at right angles.

"Shit!" she said driving up another street she did not recognize, "You've been here enough times. Damn it."

It was Wednesday afternoon, the time of her usual appointment. It always seemed odd to meet mid-week, but who was she to complain. It meant she was done at a decent hour and the location, being far away from downtown, meant that the envelope was usually padded to compensate for the commute.

Mila kicked the engine down a gear and slowly applied the front brakes. Despite the work her roommate Mickey had done over the winter, the callipers still complained as she slowed to a stop. She unslung her leather shoulder bag, stuffed full with the items John had requested and pulled out her iPhone. Her GPS immediately showed her where she had gone wrong. It was the same place every time. She was three streets away.

In November, she and John had entered into an arrangement. He'd started with sporadic 30-minute bookings that soon extended to two and three hour blocks. These longer appointments proved to be exhausting. His appetite was insatiable. Mila knew that he must have been munching some little blue pills. She had to encourage him to, no, *demand* that he finish. When these sessions were no longer enough, he added evenings or overnights, mostly on weekends and the occasional trip to New York, Boston or a hook up in Calgary.

Her mind wandered. "How bad are you John? What would Vitaly find on you?"

She knew he was an investment manager. Sure there were rules, but how far could he go? Vitaly had only handled really nasty people at his old firm. Perhaps his new role was more of a parking enforcer than a cop. She shook her head. He was wasting his talent again. It was typical of Vitaly. Smart guy run over by the social side.

A matte black BMW sedan with three teens pulled up slowly beside her, windows lowered.

"What now?" she said to herself, flipping her bag back across her shoulder.

"Hey there," said a kid in the front seat, wearing an Upper Canada baseball cap and aviator glasses. "Did you fall from Heaven?"

"Sorry?"

"Because you have the face of an angel."

"Oh, cute. Great line. Does that work with all the chicks?"

"Uh."

"Articulate too. You guys happy. Got a good look at my ass?" Mila said, shifting into first gear.

"Hey Babe, you lost or something? Can we help?"

"Thanks. I'm good. Gotta go."

Mila double checked to make sure her satchel was in the right spot. The car inched forward, blocking her.

"C'mon, we know where you really want to go," said the front seat passenger.

"Excuse me?"

"Wouldn't you rather ride on this?" said the smallest of the three from the backseat, thrusting his hips up and down.

Mr. Sunglasses grabbed Mila's wrist. The bike leaned over as she struggled to retain her balance.

"Come with us," he said with a lopsided smile. "Leave your crappy bike and we'll show you a good time."

In a swift motion, she rotated her arm free and brought her fist down hard knocking his cap off and his glasses with it, nearly tipping over on the bike, the mirror scraping the paint of the car.

"I don't straddle Twinkies," she bellowed. She spat in his face, spittle landing on his nose and in his open mouth. She gunned the throttle. The scree that had accumulated on the shoulder of the road during winter shot out from under her tire, spraying the side of the car and cracking the rear window. It took the boys a few seconds to process, with Mr. Sunglasses screaming that she had spit on him.

"Get the bitch!"

Mila was already around the corner but she could hear the growl of the BMW as the driver strained to get into gear. Her bike was no match for the sedan in straight lines. She jigged through streets, leaning the bike over hard in the corners, praying the treads would hold their grip. She could feel them gaining. Her heart raced and her breath fogged up the visor. She flipped it open and her eyes instantly teared up and her blinked repeated to clear them. She caught sight of John's place, sped up the driveway, dumped the bike at the steps and sprinted for the front door, banging with her clenched fist. The BMW slid to a stop, the front wheel banging hard against the curb.

The boys jumped out and raced up the driveway. Mila turned to face them, her back against the door, ready for a fight. She jammed her left hand into the satchel feeling for her pepper spray.

"Wait," she reminded herself out loud. "No point in just scaring them. Need to hurt..."

She fell backwards and landed hard on the marbled floor of the foyer. John stood over her, staring at the approaching boys. He reached to the right, and pulled an umbrella from the corner. With this left hand, he detached the handle, revealing a long triangular blade that tapered to a fearsome point. Mr. Sunglasses stopped on the top step as John thrust it forward just shy of his forehead.

Mila could hear the boy panting.

"Hello lads. Come to do a man's job?"

John pushed the blade forward. It made a hard tink as the point scratched the lens. He flicked the glasses away and returned the point to the right eyebrow of the boy. He pushed gently and then drove it upwards. Blood streamed into his eye.

"Gotcha!" said John.

The boy fell back without moving his legs, trying to get away from the blade. His feet followed and he tumbled down the steps onto the first crocuses peaking through the snow in the flower box. His friends picked him up tentatively, not wanting to getting any blood on their clothes. The three bolted for the car. John mouthed out the license plate.

He calmly stepped down the stairs, picked up Mila's bike and disappeared for a moment as he pushed it inside the garage. John returned to the house and the electronic lock engaged as the front door shut.

"You okay?"

"Just some kids."

"Alright, then get changed."

John walked away down the hall to his office.

"Okay, John."

He stopped, turned and stared.

"Pardon?"

"I mean, yes, Sir."

"Better. Now get ready."

"Yes, Sir," she repeated quietly and followed him down the hall lined with wood block prints. John entered his office, shutting the door behind him. That was her cue. She stopped outside the bathroom and examined one of the prints. It was a still life, a bouquet of lilies. She marvelled at how a knife through contrast and shadow had created softness and beauty.

Mila entered the bathroom and shut the door quietly. Her monthly payment was on the counter it always was. She had ceased counting it. The sum was always correct, if not a little more. John had stopped leaving little love notes; familiarity had set in.

Mila's hands trembled and her lips quivered. She surveyed her reflection in the mirror, shook her hands and then ran her fingers through her hair, massaging her scalp. She followed the orb of her skull, feeling the transition from her natural hair to the extensions to just above the nape of her neck. That was freshly shaven.

Mila slipped off her riding boots and stretched. She took a few slow breaths, exhaling deeply each time, clearing the carbon dioxide from her lungs and the adrenaline from her blood. She undressed, folding her clothes, leaving everything stacked neatly on the vanity. Her boots she tucked under the sink, side by each. She dressed in the clothing John had requested. She removed all of her jewellery except for her grandmothers wedding band and from her satchel, she removed a small silk sachet, loosening the drawstring and poured its contents into her hands. It was a Celtic pendant on a thin silver chain that John had given her a year and a half ago. It was something you would give a young teenager, not a courtesan. Mila wore it for him on occasion. She applied crimson lipstick, checking to make sure she did not get any on her teeth. Before leaving the bathroom, she tied her hair in a loose bun, revealing the ink on the back of her neck. He liked her tattoos and though he had seen it before, she knew he would be excited to see it again.

The heels of her thigh high black leather boots clicked on the wooden floor. The office door was still closed. She knocked lightly and waited. She heard John talking, presumably on the phone. He paused. "Come."

John was seated behind his ornate, oversized, walnut desk, a bluetooth headpiece hanging off his ear as he typed on his laptop. After a brief pause to take her in, he resumed talking.

"What? Jargit called? What'd you tell him?...God...Good...I gave him a bottle of Walker Blue and he's still a pain in the ass...Okay...On Brainstim and Heartwave, make sure Val has all the structures in place...Okay...Yes, I've a guest over...None of your business...Short it and a couple of the other medical device names just in smaller amounts...Isabella did good work...Say a five-to-one. I know we're behind. Isabella will be ready...Yes, if you do it right, it'll look like a sector short...Thanks Tim, see you tomorrow. Can you put me though to Tournimenko? Not Isabella, Tom...I don't have his number handy."

There were two glasses on the table, a highball full of sparkling water with a twist of lime for John and a crystal flute. The cork was still in the demi bottle of Asti Martini as it always was. He knew she would not touch it if it had been removed. He loved the ceremony of the unwrapping of the foil, four turns to remove the muselet, the gentle pop as the cork eased out. He never partook. Mila had never asked why.

The desk was not where John usually waited for her. More often than not, Mila would find him on the couch pretending to read some financial magazine and she would have to rip it away so he pay attention to her in her cut-off jeans and white tank-top or school girl uniform. Today, she stood in the door wearing a red bustier, trimmed with black silk, a matching mini skirt, and boots that rose nearly to the skirt. She stood on the threshold, still quivering with an empty feeling in her stomach. John dialled another number.

"Hi Tom, it's John. Val tells me that you're making progress."

John held up a finger to Mila. She looked around the room. Nothing had changed. The space was sparsely furnished: two overstuffed, antique lounge chairs, a large piece of contemporary art on the wall and four analog clocks. None labelled but the one of the left was Toronto. The second hands ticked in unison, marking time precisely around the globe.

"Ahem," she said, toying with her pendant coquettishly.

He repeated his gesture. Mila raised one eyebrow, sighed and slumped against the wall.

"I understand Tom...You gotta move faster. Val told you a half truth when you started. You're our most recent hire, but don't worry, you have the Greater Toronto Area to yourself...The other guy didn't perform...We're prepared for whatever you send...Yes, any size is good, but bigger is better...Tell me about your new strategy...The churches... How many congregations? Five!... Uh huh. You're a religious bastard, aren't ya? How did you get into the Korean Baptist?... Oh never mind... Seniors... How do you know about their medical devices?... Focused on recent surgeries... Good... Canada or the US?... Both? Excellent. Sounds good. I gotta let you go. I have a friend I need to...tend to...You're on the right track. Let's talk next week... Yes, I'll get Val to process the recent stuff faster... No worries... Your sister was wrong about you. You're doing just fine. Cheers."

John hung up, taking his earpiece out and putting into the desk drawer. He pushed his chair back from the desk. "Come here."

Mila strutted around the room, taking a circuitous path, pretending to find interest in the few books on the shelves.

She paused at the French doors that overlooked the backyard so he could take her all in.

"Here! Now! You minx."

She moved sensually, exaggerating her hip movements and attempting to make her 5'3" frame taller than she was. John was clearly enjoying the show. She moved over to him, walking around the desk, her fingers feathering the surface till she stood in front of him. She raised one foot and placed on the seat between his legs, the point of her boot dangerously close to his inseam.

His finger tips caressed her calf. She wobbled a little and giggled at her lack of grace. She lowered her heel to the floor and bent forward, readying to give him a kiss and then pushed him back in the chair.

Rather than let her straddle him, he swung her around brusquely and sat her down in his lap like a child. The desk chair tipped back at the sudden movement, nearly toppling them over, their arms flailing to regain their balance. The casters squeaked wildly under them.

Composure restored, John returned his focus his computer, his arms reaching around her as he typed.

"You wanna know who those pricks in the Bimmer were?"

"I guess..."

"Close your eyes. Keep 'em shut now."

Mila turned on his lap, her chin resting on his shoulder, her breath in his ear.

"Good?" she whispered.

"Um... Great."

John typed in a few commands.

"There. Turn around."

On screen was the website for the Ontario Ministry of Transportation. John typed clicked on the login button, entered username and password.

"How the hell?"

"We do many things at the shop. We need information from many sources. Sometimes from sources that don't like sharing. The real secret's not getting caught."

"Like most things in life."

"Right," he said letting his eyes descend from the tattoo on the nape of her neck to the small of her back. "Shall we? With any luck...," John's voice trailed off. "ATVW 756. Here you go. The car's registered to Tobias Denoon, age nineteen."

A photo came up of a smug-looking kid.

"The driver," said Mila pointing at the screen.

"Not the guy I cut, but I'd bet they're classmates. 1780 Wychwood Park. A little far from home, aren't you Toby?"

John dropped the address into Google Maps. Immediately a map of the neighbourhood came up, followed by a street view image of the front of a yellow stuccoed house with blue shutters and well-manicured lawn and hedge. Mila made a mental note.

"Okay Toby, let's see if you're really an old boy."

John opened up another pane in Internet Explorer.

"There are a few advantages to being a board member."

John moved to the Upper Canada College website, and entered Toby's full name.

"Ah, there you are."

A photo of the graduating class appeared on screen. Tobias was standing in the second row, third from the left. Next to him was a taller teenager with a crooked smile.

"That's Mr. Sunglasses," Mila said pointing at the screen. John zoomed in on the caption below.

"Evan Quick," said John. "Let's see about your marks, shall we? We'll get to Toby's afterwards. Now, I can't mess up his life forever but we can make him sweat. Looks like he's a straight A student. Not for long."

John lowered his mark in each subject by twelve to twenty-five percent. He entered no round numbers. Each mark looked plausible.

"If there are any infractions, I'll make sure that they're recorded. Good?"

"Ah, yeah," was all she could muster.

"My pleasure."

She turned and planted a kiss on his cheek. Then she stroked his ears the way he liked, her other hand slowly sliding down his chest, coming to rest on his thigh.

"Thank you," she said breathlessly in his ear, kissing it gently, nibbling on the lobe.

11

"Vitaly, you sure you can do this?"

"What? Why not?"

"Because you hate crowds," said Paul.

"No offence bro," added Derek, "but you're the most awkward person I know,"

"Thanks for the peptalk," said Vitaly.

"Derek, way to build him up," said Maiwen. "Don't listen to him. You'll do fine."

"I gotta go," said Vitaly. "Got ten minutes to get to Vertical.

"We've got one chance to get into John's inner circle. Do you really want to send him?" asked Paul to Brian. "Why don't you do it?"

"He'll do fine," said Brian. "You can handle this right?"

"I'm just meeting Benny."

"In a bar," said Derek. "With loud music and people, people you don't know. When was the last time you were in a bar?"

"Does Starbucks count?"

"No!" hollered Derek and Paul at the same time.

"He's going to do great," said Maiwen wrapping Vitaly's scarf around his neck. "It's cold out there. You got something to calm you down."

Vitaly tucked his hands deep into his overcoat pockets, finding loose change, keys and a stray maple sugar candy. He unwrapped the confection and popped it into his mouth, and savouring its smoky sweetness. He smiled at how happy Mila was at his little gift before Christmas. He reminded himself to pocket more the next time he could.

"You all need to relax," said Vitaly. "Benny's easy."

The Lister docket he had inherited intrigued him. The case should be simple and Vitaly was surprised no-one had brought the issues forward before. The complaint lodged was by an investor in the Sunquest Insurance Canadian Equity Fund, a fund sub-advised by Lister Asset Management.

That was the sales pitch: buy Sunquest's fund and you get performance that should mirror John's Flagship fund. Except, that is not what had happened. The Sunquest fund had trailed John's by 10% points per year. That was a difference was 1.5 times over the decade. John Lister was the lead manager on both funds. The performance should have been the same.

Earlier in the week, Vitaly and his team combed over their options.

He could barge into the offices of LAM and demand an explanation but Brian wondered if there were the other cockroaches hiding.

Something was obviously going on. Vitaly and his team had agreed on a different approach.

Vitaly had called Benny Figueredo, an old acquaintance with deep connections on Bay Street. Vitaly had followed Benny's career from afar. The sentiment about him was that he was smart, imaginative and straight shooter.

What surprised Vitaly was how nervous Benny had been on the phone. He came out directly and asked if Vitaly might be investigating him as he had received a summons from the OSC. Before the call, Vitaly had checked the database. There was a minor infraction for an incomplete registration. Vitaly assured Benny he would look into his issue, maybe even make it go away, if Benny was cooperative.

He pressed Benny on how to get into John's firm.

Simple, Benny replied: talk to the most embittered person there. They always talked too much when given the chance to feel important. Vitaly drew a blank on how he would do that. Benny said he would set it up. He told him to meet at Vertical for drinks and he would make an introduction. The rest was up to Vitaly.

****

The glass door of Vertical was covered in a thin film of condensation. Through its translucence, Vitaly could see the room was teeming. His chest clenched.

The volume rose dramatically as he opened the door.

The warmth and humidity of cologne, alcohol and perspiration stunned him.

He pushed through the loose outer throngs of drinkers and caught sight of Benny holding court in the middle of the room, his back against the wooden bar. There were two others with him. The three clinked their shooters together and downed some brown liquid, cursing each other afterwards.

Benny waved Vitaly over, pulled him in for a hug, whispering in his ear.

"Is it taken care of?"

"All cleared up."

"Good, good," Benny said moving back, releasing Vitaly's hand and patting him on the shoulder, sizing him up. "Still boxing?"

"Nah. All done. Don't like seeing stars anymore. You?"

"Only for fun now," he said. "You and me, we should go sometime. Maybe knock me down again."

"Get my bell rung by you again? No thanks."

"Poor you. Did I hit too hard?"

Vitaly just laughed. Benny was the only person to ever scare him in the ring. He hit hard. He hit to hurt. Benny made the introductions without pointing to either of the guys.

"Graham, Jimmy, meet Vitaly."

"Pleased to meet you," said the taller, lankier man. "I'm Graham Kent."

"Jimmy Leering," said the other.

Vitaly looked at Benny with a half-cocked eyebrow. He gave a nearly imperceptible shrug. An additional person had not been part of the plan.

"So what do you boys do?"

"Is he always this serious?" said Jimmy. "Doesn't even have a drink in his hand and he's talking shop. Benny, c'mon. Fix this."

Benny spun Vitaly around, facing the bar.

"Vitaly, what the...play it cool, man."

The waitress came over immediately. They never did that for him.

"Gwen, meet the Big V.," he said, patting Vitaly on the chest playfully. "You'll look after him, right?"

"I'm Vitaly."

"Lovely to meet you. What'll you have?"

"Stoly straight, lime twist."

"One Vitaly special, coming right up. Single or double, Hun?" asked Gwen, her cleavage revealed ever so carefully from beneath a black, skin-tight shirt.

"Single. I like to start slowly."

"I'm sure you do," Gwen purred.

Vitaly turned beat red.

Gwen turned to the rows of bottles on shelves behind the bar, pausing so all could take in her view from behind. In the mirror, she caught Vitaly looking, and she smiled with a wink.

He shifted his gaze quickly, his feet suddenly garnering his complete attention. He turned to Jimmy.

"So, how do you know Graham?"

"Work. I'm sorry. I'm horrible with names. Vitaly, right?"

"Yes, Vitaly."

"Vitaly..."

"Mirkin."

"Okay, Vitaly."

Vitaly recognized the memorization technique. Say the name enough times and it might stick.

"Oh, Graham and I work...Oh shit, excuse me," as he reached into his pocket and looked at the screen. "My girlfriend..."

Jimmy unlocked his phone and Vitaly turned away, providing Jimmy with a bit of privacy as he dialled a number.

"Hi Honey. Got your message. Can't leave just now. Who'm I with? Graham and a couple of buddies, Benny and Vitaly Mirkin. Okay, fine. When will you be there? Okay, I'll leave in five. Just finishing my drink...You want me to bring someone? Okay. I'll do my best."

He hung up.

"Gotta go," said Jimmy turning to Graham. "Heading over to the Soho House to meet Heidi."

Graham looked at him blankly.

"My girlfriend! Graham, come with me. It's just a few blocks. You'll have a drink in your hand in no time. She really wants to meet you."

"Thanks. I'll stay here. I'll meet your gash another day."

"She brought her roommate, Anastasia. Smokin' hot. Incredible eyes."

Graham held up his left hand. His wedding band was still shiny and unmarked.

"Married, remember?"

"Just window shopping and a couple of cocktails. That's all. Come. She's not to be missed!"

"Tempting, but I'm gonna stick with Benny," said Graham putting his arm over his shoulder. "He's the man!"

"Whatever? Suit yourself. Really, you'll regret it. You don't know what you're missin'!"

"Nah, I'm good. Thanks," he said turning back to Benny.

Jimmy downed his drink and bolted out the front door and headed across the avenue. He stood at the curb, looking up and down King Street.

Two black sedans with tinted windows pulled up next to him.

The driver hopped out and opened the rear door of the first sedan. A statuesque blonde got out, eyes fixed on the bar above.

"Good evening Beate. You look as lovely as ever."

"Thank you. You were right to call security, Mr. Leering."

"At the Art Gallery again?"

She turned and looked at him quizzically.

"Your lapel pin."

She pulled it off her coat and dropped it on the ground.

"Hope I didn't take you away from any of that Modern Art shit."

"Contemporary. It is contemporary art shit. Modern Art is from 1860s to the 1970s. Contemporary is now."

Jimmy's eyes glazed over. Beate sighed heavily.

"You're sure it's Mirkin?" she asked.

"Absolutely. It's him. Graham's still there."

"You tried to get Mr. Kent to come?"

"Yes, but he wouldn't."

"Okay, I will let Mr. Lister know. Go. The car will take you wherever you want."

"Uh, Okay."

Jimmy hopped into the car and shut the door. It idled next to her while Beate remained on the sidewalk, staring up at Vertical. She took her phone out of the holster on her hip and dialled a number. It rang four times.

"Yes Beate?"

"Hello Mr. Lister. Sorry to disturb you, Sir."

"What is it?"

"How is your evening, sir?"

"Is that why you're calling? To ask me about my evening."

"No, Sir. Of course not, Sir. We've a security incident reported by Mr. Leering... Understood... Will investigate... Good night."

She hung up, entered a new phone number and spoke rapidly giving instructions to the person on the other end.

"Yes, now. four cars, eight people, King between Bay and York. Vertical. Two couples inside. Four others in cars. Ready to ten minutes. Understood? Execute."

She tapped the roof of the car twice and the sedan did a U-turn on and headed west at great speed.

****

Gwen came back with Vitaly's cocktail.

"Your regular tipple, eh? Really, you should try something new."

Vitaly reached for his wallet, but before he could, Benny was handing Gwen a twenty. He closed his hand around hers for a moment and gave her a wink. She leaned in close.

"Ah, thanks Benny. Now my mom can have that operation!"

She laughed and turned away. The suit next to them desperately tried to flag her down. She stared right through him.

"Not a bad tip for an $11 drink," said Vitaly.

"Worth every penny. You'll see."

Benny turned to Graham and picked up their conversation about their old rugby team.

Vitaly listened distractedly; the topic held no interest. He was amused by the primping and preening going on all around him. The men were peacocks, their plumes Tag Heuer watches and their loosely knotted Ferragamo ties.

The women ignored the fluff and focused instead on finding the mate who would listen to their sweet song and buy unconditional drinks.

After about ten minutes, Vitaly left the two, saying he was going to get something to eat.

Benny waved him off and said they would be over shortly.

As he left, Gwen set down four large shooters in front of the two men. They toasted each other before slamming the glasses on the counter top, picked up their seconds and did the same. Benny ordered another round.

Vitaly made his way to the hostess' desk, pressing through the crowd.

"Table for one?" the hostess said the saccharin smile.

It was almost a statement.

"Sort of," Vitaly said. "I'm waiting for my friends to get hungry. Might be a while. Still thirsty," he added as he saw Benny lean over the bar to put another bill into Gwen's hands.

"How many will you be?"

"Three and somewhere quiet please. We don't want to embarrass ourselves."

She led him down a hallway, past the kitchen and into the main dining room to a crescent shaped booth near in the corner where he could have a view of the room. It was not ideally located, a little close to other tables for Vitaly's liking, but it would do.

"May I get you started with a drink, Sir?"

"Water, cold, neat."

The waitress smiled awkwardly and left.

Vitaly drank nearly four glasses of water before Benny finally poured Graham into the booth, sandwiched between them.

"Sorry I didn't stick around," said Vitaly. "My ex was around and last time...well..."

"Nasty, eh?" slurred Graham eyeing the two glasses in front of Vitaly. "Which one's vodka?"

Vitaly didn't respond.

"Graham and I were discussing old times. Figured out that I was the last one to make two-hundred-grand," said Benny. "Well, my take-home was better than most."

"Do tell!" said Graham.

"Well, let's just my boss showed me how to make my tax returns so incomprehensible that the CRA pukes give up. By the time they figure it out, most of my money is in Panama, at least as a first stop."

Vitaly knew it was a lie. Benny was as straight as they come and if he was not, he wouldn't be so careless as to tell his old friend. Graham took the bait.

"Bad teachers turn out bad students."

"Sorry?" said Vitaly.

"Uh, nothing."

"What's it you do anyway?" asked Vitaly.

Graham looked at Benny quizzically.

"Didn't Benny tell you? I work for a hedge fund," said Graham, almost puffing out his chest.

"Oh? Which one?"

"John Lister's of course. Best there is."

"No shit."

"Yup."

"Wish I had the coin to get in."

Graham looked Vitaly up and down. Vitaly knew that Graham had easily judged that he would never have qualified for the $10-million minimum.

"Not many people do, and most of them shouldn't anyway."

"What's that mean?"

"Nothing really"

"You must be one of the portfolio managers then?"

"You'd think by now given my background. Nah, I'm just an allocater. Can't even crack the bloody analyst pool! You've got to be psycho or a skirt to get in."

"So, what's it you do all day?"

"Not much, play solitaire and allocate trades. We got all sorts of compliance regs we're supposed to follow. Boring as all get out."

"Long days I guess. What rules?"

"Trade priority and allocations. We run some strategies on a third-party basis that mirror the core fund."

"Must be complicated, keeping it straight."

"Nah, the male lion eats first, right?"

"What?"

"How do you think we do so well?

"No idea."

"Buy me some vino and grub and I'll spill. First, I gotta leak."

As Graham left, two couples came into the restaurant. The hostess lead them to far corner away from Vitaly when the man stopped her and motioned to the booth closest to him. They looked like trophy wives and their hockey player husbands.

The women stood out with their obviously dyed blonde hair and excessively plucked eyebrows. They were pretty, their silhouettes stunning and they were admired by the men in the restaurant, and a few of the women too.

The husbands glared at anyone who dared take a peek. They were muscular, dressed in open-collared shirts and sport coats that were too tight on their frame. Their noses had seen straighter days.

"Why are we here? Can't you take us somewhere fancier?" complained one of the women to her partner.

"Please," he said to the taller of the two women, "Sit. Enjoy."

She sat down in the booth, evidently not pleased with her companion and began speaking in Russian to the other woman.

The shorter of the two men caught Vitaly watching. He shrugged with a smile that did not show his teeth. Vitaly could overhear their conversation. It was banal and he ignored it. Benny waved to the waitress who came over straight away.

"Yes, Mr. Figueredo."

"Stop calling me that Jennifer. It's Benny."

He beckoned her to come closer. She crouched down beside him, her skirt riding up her thighs. Benny eyes did not meet hers as he whispered.

"Yes, Mr. Figueredo. I'll let her know. Back in a moment."

She returned a few minutes later with a bottle of 2003 Opus One and three fresh wine glasses. She stood next to the table in silence and waited as Graham swayed back to the table.

Benny got up to allow him to slip into the booth. Jennifer presented the bottle, opened it and handed him the cork.

She poured the wine. Benny passed his glass to Graham. He swirled the liquid, examining the legs, sipped and swallowed.

"So? How is it?" Benny said.

"Awfully good!"

Jennifer poured the glasses for the other two.

"Is there anything else for the moment, Mr. Figueredo?"

"Thank you, Jennifer, no."

Graham turned back to Vitaly.

"So...where were we?" asked Vitaly, "You were explaining how LAM does so bloody well"

"Huh? There's a big team but I keep track of the trades for John," Graham explained.

"He'll reallocate the stock to a different fund before the trade settles. If the stock price goes up, it goes to LAM. If it goes down, one of the sub-advised gets it."

"Like Sunquest or Trinity," said Benny.

"Poof, no bad trades for John. Everyone else takes the pain."

"I thought you had to pre-allocate these days," said Benny.

"Well, that's what's supposed to happen. Between trade date and settlement date, John and I watch."

"Why doesn't Trinity do something about it?" ventured Vitaly.

"Are you that dim? John's got 'em by the short 'n curlies. You don't want him to tug, do you? You know Trinity owns a third of LAM, right? We pay them a dividend to each quarter." Graham said.

"Before our performance crapped out, the dividends dwarfed what Trinity earned on its core business. Sure they're happy with the money but it drove Shagass nuts. He kept quiet though. Money is his master. His share of the profit just paid for the cottage that was featured in *Toronto Life*."

"I saw that spread," said Benny. "My wife's all over me to get something like that."

"Anyways," Graham continued, "that's nothing compared to the new stuff."

Vitaly had heard enough. It was time.

"Graham, did Benny tell you what I do?"

"Uh... Compliance or something. You're in town for a conference...."

"Sort of."

"Private wealth op, no? Ottawa Secured Capital."

Vitaly chuckled.

"Smooth Benny. Close. My firm has the same acronym. OSC, Regulation Services."

"Oh shit!"

"Oh shit indeed."

Vitaly made a gesture to a table across the room. Brian put his fork down made his way over to the table, just as Benny got up to excuse himself. Brian slid onto the bench, moving tight next to Graham, still chewing.

Without a word to Graham but a nod to Vitaly and Brian, Benny walked towards the exit.

One of the two hockey players left at the same time.

Benny paused at the end of the small corridor next to the hostess station. Gwen was waiting for him. She kissed him on the cheek and took his arm before continuing out of Vitaly's sight.

The man exited the restaurant, not stopping for a coat.

He took the stairs out to King Street and walked directly to Beate who was standing at the bottom of the stairs, beside a park bench in the plaza, her foot on the armrest.

She was wiping something off her shoes as he walked up. She straightened and he kissed her on both cheeks.

She listened to him for a moment, reached into her coat pocket and dialled a number on her phone.

Two large black SUVs appeared quickly from the East and stopped.

Beate and the man crossed the street and each got into the rear of separate vehicles.

The woman's car sped away when the passenger door shut. The second SUV idled in place.

****

Graham sat slack-jawed.

"Graham Kent," said Vitaly, "allow me to introduce Detective Brian Cranston, Commercial Crimes Unit, RCMP."

Graham moved to get up but Brian put a gentle hand on his shoulder.

"You don't want to go anywhere, Graham. Believe me."

"I want immunity."

Vitaly reached into his suit jacket pocket and pulled out his iPhone. He went to the video camera and hit play. The screen was black but the audio was clear. Graham heard his voice.

"There's so much more I can share," Graham pleaded. "Don't you want my help? C'mon guys, I've got a wife and twins."

"We've enough for now," replied Vitaly. "This is what we're going to do. You, me and Brian are going to enjoy a lovely meal and finish this bottle that I have no idea how I'm going to expense."

"Benny recommended the wild boar ragu. I took the liberty of ordering three before you sat down," Vitaly said.

"No allergies? Good. You're going to tell Brian exactly what you have just told me," he added.

"By the way, I don't give a shit about you. There are bigger roaches to squash."

12

Mila and John lay on the leather couch, their skin stuck to the cushions beneath them, their clothes strewn around the room.

John gently stroked Mila's body with the back of his hand: her shoulders, her hips, her thighs. He reached around from the small of her back and placed the palm of his hand on her flank, his fingers resting into the hollow of her ribs. He paused and felt the rise and fall of her breath. He cupped her breast briefly and then slid his hand down and tickled her flat belly.

"Hey, that's my pudge," she said, playfully slapping his hand, "Source of my ultimate power. Hands off!"

He held her wrist and with his free hand rubbed the three bands of her ring. She tugged her hand away, putting the ring back its rightful place.

"That's a Russian wedding band, no? Why's it on your middle finger?"

"A promise made to my Babushka. Wear it on my right until I've found my true love. I keep my promises."

"I'm sure you do."

He moved his hand back below her bellybutton and rested his palm on her pubic bone. Mila had no idea what he was thinking about—love, lust, a child? She quickly took John's hand in hers, massaging the flesh between his thumb and index finger, feeling the tension of the muscles that lay beneath.

"I've been meaning to ask, you've got a lot of scars for a desk jockey."

"Well, I'm clumsy I guess," he replied.

"Tell me."

"This one," he said pointing to a small circular scar, "was when I was building a bird house for my mom for Mother's Day and thought it'd be faster to use a nail gun. Went all the way through."

She turned his hand over to look for the exit wound. He pointed to a small raised star on the back of his left hand.

"This one here was when I was nine and Murray Toth, my next door neighbour growing up, thought it would be good fun if we chased each other with hockey sticks. I dislocated his pinkie. He broke mine with a really good, two-handed slash. Two screws held it in place for a month. Still can't make a full fist."

He contracted his hand but the tip of his little finger never quite reached his palm, the digit resting flaccidly. Mila pointed to a large, angry scar about the size of a quarter on the top of his wrist.

"This is where my father extinguished his cigars."

Mila looked at him in horror.

"Don't worry, he was blind drunk at the time. First time drinking for me too. We were on a fishin' trip up north and it rained and rained and when it didn't rain, it poured. We alleviated the boredom with cribbage and scotch. I was only sixteen. Threw up for the first time. He nearly burnt down the cottage. He'd knocked over a kerosene lantern and as we both dove for it, he landed on me with the cigar and fractured his wrist. Thank God it didn't break the skin. I drove the country roads back to the nearest town more than two hours away. I only had my learner's permit. His arm was swollen like a football when I pulled into the clinic parking lot. I was so stressed. My hands were cramped around the wheel. I don't know what I'd have done if the car had been a standard. Taught me a lesson though. Watch out for drunk men and cigars!"

Mila chuckled.

"That's why I never partake. I inherited his problem, with the drink."

"Me too, too much goes to my head."

"No, Tatiana, I'm a... I'm a recovering alcoholic and prescription drug abuser. I'm telling you this because I wanna be open with you."

"Okay," said Mila, unsure of where this would go.

"It started with my Dad. The cottage was not a one-time occurrence. He drank because it was expected of him. He'd have to entertain clients. That meant taking them out, dinners, wine, cigars, strippers. He'd be piss drunk when he came home and if I looked at him the wrong way, well, let's just say I walked into a lot of doors. Mom got it worse. One day, she up and left."

"I'm so sorry."

"I started drinking after school, during school, before school. In subtle ways. I'd steal my mom's syringes, she was a diabetic, and I'd inject oranges with vodka or gin. Instant Screwdrivers and no one was the wiser. My wife, you knew there was a Mrs. Lister, right? We're not really together anymore, not really. My wife and I, we'd drink too and more. That's how we hooked up, pissed at a Christmas party. It was fun at first. I was making good money. She had her trust fund. The cash flowed and so did everything: pills, coke, eight balls. Eventually, it got in the way. We both needed rehab. Went to a clinic in Miami. Great place to dry out. Sun, salt water, blue skies. It was hard adjusting to sober life. We had to ditch our old friends. Slowly we made new ones."

John chuckled to himself.

"What?" asked Mila.

"Well, one afternoon while we were prepping to have people over for the first time, Joan looked at me in panic.

"We don't have anything to drink," she said. "They're not drunks like us."

"In recovery dear."

"Drunks! Recovery, whatever. Stop watching the game, get your arse down to the store and buy something wonderful."

"That was the first time I went to the liquor store in a year. I wandered the aisles, eventually found something and went home without cracking the bottle."

"Good for you."

"Man, it was tempting.

"But it wouldn't be just a sip, would it?"

"It wouldn't. Anyhow, that night we sat down for dinner and Joan asked me to pour something for our guests. I went to the kitchen, brought it back in a paper bag and plonked a fifth of Chivas on the table. I pop the cork and threw it in the corner. Old habits die hard I suppose. Whiskey goes with everything, right? The drink of champions. Our guests were too polite to say anything. I didn't touch a drop that night and haven't since. Our guest laughed at how well the rye went with the poached salmon. Joan fell off the wagon again six years ago and never got back on."

"John. I'm impressed. Overcoming your demons. Good for you."

"I've even got a medal each year," he said as he opened the desk drawer and pulled out seven of the them. "Each December, I get another one. I'm proud of them all, but the last one always feels the best."

You're ahead of the curve. Staying clean for so long, amazing!"

She rubbed his hands in hers and kissed his wrist.

"Tatiana, I... I.. .care about you...That you're safe... I know that you probably get into situations... some beyond your control... I'm... I, uh, don't want anything bad to happen to you."

"Thank you, John."

"Tatiana, I guess... I just don't want you to come to any harm."

"You're a sweetie. But I'm a smart cookie. I don't get into trouble."

"Like this afternoon?"

"Just overactive kids. I was ready for them."

"Overactive? Tatiana... you are safe?"

"Yes, John, I am."

She caressed the back of his hand gently, brushing the jagged scar with her fingertips and her lips. It was obviously a many years old but it was still purple, raggedly healed.

"Tell me about this one here?" she said pointing to his right hand.

John turned serious, the smile sliding off his face.

"That.. .that came about when somebody I love disappointed me. I lost my temper. And I lost her. I regret it to this day." He paused. "You won't disappoint me, will you?"

"Have I ever?"

Mila got on her knees and reached under the blanket that covered him from his waist down, parting his legs and letting her hands run up his thighs.

"I won't."

Mila glanced up at the four clocks on the wall, remembering that the one on the far left was Toronto. It had been four hours since he had rescued her from the teens. The room was dark as neither of them had bothered to turn on the lights. The windows creaked as they were buffeted by the wind, the clouds whipping past, glowing faintly with the energy of the city. She shivered at the thought her ride home.

They had lain there, exhausted and spent, under plush grey throw that was usually draped over the back of the couch. John turned in his sleep, his arm slipping around her waist. Mila glanced around the room. The office was an exercise in control. It stood in stark contrast to the entrance way with the large bouquet of flowers and the floral prints on the wallpaper.

Mila only ever saw John in his office. To the North, the office overlooked the street. Mila had looked out the window a few times in the past as she waited for John to stir post coitus. He never shut the drapes when she visited. At first, she felt uneasy. He seemed not to care about how she might feel about being exposed. Now, so seldom did anyone pass by, that she could stand uncovered without fear.

Everything in the room was white save for the desk and the antique chairs. The ceiling was adorned with elaborate cornices and a grand, blown-glass chandelier. The walls were lined with built-in bookshelves, but few books sat on them. Attached to them were oversized, white hooks, the kind used for hanging coats. There was a single closet with a lock in the handle. Mila had tested it once. It did not open.

There were only two photos in the room, both on the same shelf. One was a black and white photo in a painted white frame showing a stern-looking man holding a young boy's wrist. Mila presumed it was John and his father. The other was of John as a young man on a mountain somewhere with four or five days of stubble on his face, smiling back at the camera. Prayer flags were fluttering in the background. He looked relaxed and happy, pleased with whatever the photographer was bringing to the moment. She had turned the frame over but there were no revealing marks or notes.

The remainder of the house, apart from the office and the hallway, was a mystery. Mila never dared wander around while he slept and hadn't even stepped onto the deck that led to the garden. Once, as he slept, she had padded down the hall to the entrance, studying the black and white wood blocks that hung along the wall, careful to keep within sprinting distance of the office should she ever hear keys in the door. This had only happened once. Mila had beaten a naked retreat to the office and slammed the door shut, giggling at the near-miss. John awoke from his sleep, stormed out, nude as well and hurled expletives as the poor housekeeper cowered and ran off to the kitchen.

John slowly stirred, pulled Mila closer and kissed her shoulder. He propped himself up on an elbow, looking into her eyes.

"You clearly have a question. Ask away."

"So how does this work? How come you're off in the afternoon in the middle of the week?"

"A man has to relieve his stress, no?"

"No seriously."

"Well, it's quite simple. I own the place with two partners. When you came in, you heard me talking to Val. He's the brains. My other partner's Tim. Who knows, maybe you'll meet them someday. Real gents."

"Okay, but what's you do exactly?" asked Mila looking around the room. "I was at the office but as you remember I only saw your boardroom. You're obviously doing great, whatever it is. Why so much stress?"

"Ah, we're having a bit of a rough patch. The trades aren't gong as anticipated. Clients are climbing all over my back. I should be at the office but sometimes when you know you're right, you've just gotta wait."

"So tell me more about your biz. You always just say you're in investments."

"I own a hedge fund. John Lister Asset Management. We invest money for people with over $10 million in assets. For the most part, they're straightforward. Some, though, are real asses. I've one client that I'm been trying to get rid of for two years but can't."

"Just hand back the money."

"No can do. They're my first clients and when my lawyer drew up the investment agreement with them, he, okay me, neglected to include an exit clause. They can leave anytime, but I can't fire 'em."

"You can't be their slave?"

"Short of shutting down the fund completely, I am."

"So even the rich can be serfs."

"Yup, of a sort."

"Okay, but you still haven't told me what you do."

"We invest in equities, bonds, forex, that's foreign exchange, derivatives and some private investments. Anything that we think we can make money on. We do research and want to see all the angles. We don't ever want to get stuck with an investment no one else wants."

"Makes sense. You need to sell to someone else later on."

"You just learned what it takes my fresh hires months to understand. Anything we buy, we need to able sell for a profit. We need to see the other side of the trade."

"But how do you know the other side? Can't there be many different outcomes?"

"I'm going hire you when you graduate."

"Wouldn't that be a little bit awkward?"

"You're right. I'd have to fire the current in-house courtesan."

"John!"

"It'd be convenient. I could write you off as a business expense. Maybe as a consultant?"

"The other side?" said Mila exasperated.

"We figure stuff out. You heard about the problems with the US mortgages?"

"I don't live under a rock."

"Sorry."

"People buying places they couldn't afford."

"Exactly, tons of people got dragged down when the market tanked. You know how they say a fool and his money are soon parted. I think a fool and his money were lucky enough to get together in the first place. Half the people shouldn't have had a mortgage at all. Their banks roped them in with the lure of cheap cash. Most didn't have the income to support it. So many lost everything."

"Sounds like you feel for them."

"Yes and no. It was a rich hunting ground for Val. As everyone was panicking, Val did his homework and figured out which mortgages had value and which didn't stand a chance of ever being paid off. His process was brilliant. He bought a database of all the mortgages in the US that were ever packaged into bond pools. From the data, he could see the individual mortgages that made up the bond. Most of these originated in the mid-two-thousands, years when housing was booming."

"Okay, I think I get it. Val's seeing if the sum is really the addition of the parts."

"He had more information than the individual filings ever provided and his view was way more accurate than the Street. He did this every month and instead of having just a snapshot, he created a film of sorts. We could see the plot unfold."

"So why didn't everyone do this?" Mila asked.

"It took time to figure out the structure."

"And you get paid for doing your homework."

"Exactly. You've got to do the right work. You've got to see things from all sides."

****

Mila woke up with a start, still on the cushions on the floor. She was alone. It was often this way. John rarely slept, even when they travelled together. She didn't mind. This was all act after all. She didn't know what he did when he left, but he was rarely at ease when he returned. She would have to calm him down.

She was not looking forward to the ride home. She cringed at the thought that the boys in the BMW might still be lurking out there somewhere but convinced herself that they would not be back, at least not tonight. At a minimum, Mr. Sunglasses would need a few stitches to close the gash through his eyebrow. Then, he would need to rest his ego.

Mila stood at the French doors that opened onto the garden, naked but for the grey throw draped around like a cloak. She watched the bare trees against the amethyst sky, and listened to the whistling of the wind through the crowns of the oaks that marked the perimeter of the property. Countless twigs were scattered across the lawn, broken and black against the melting snow. She touched a pane in the door, feeling the warmth of her hand dissipate into the glass, leaving a handprint that lingered. John's reflection was beside her own.

"Shit, you scared the Hell of out me. I didn't hear you come in."

He reached out and put his right hand where hers had been, his digits extending beyond hers. The condensation reappeared. She moved to face to him, but he stopped her and kept her facing away. His hand slipped under the throw and descended to the crest of her hip. He exhaled, his breath against the nape of her neck. His gaze was not on her but the outside world.

"What does the future hold for you? Why do you...where are you going?"

"John, please..."

"Tatiana, why this? You're bright, intelligent, vivacious. You're at the threshold of your future. You need only cross..."

"There's a ticket taker and he's looking for... well could you spare two-hundred-thousand? I need it for grad school. After I finish here in Toronto, I want to go to Columbia like my mentor did."

"Why, only two-hundred-thousand? I'll write you a cheque right now."

John bent forward and breathed on the cold window. In the condensation he scrawled: *To Tatiana, $300K, JL*

"That's more than I need."

"Girl needs some spending money, doesn't she?"

"You forgot to date it," said Mila as it faded slowly.

Mila considered asking to stay the night. She imagined herself on the couch, John somewhere else in the house. Then she thought of the feminine touches she had seen: the bouquet of flowers at the entrance, the patterned umbrella in the stand where the blade was close at hand. She scolded herself. This was business and it involved her pretending physical contact carried emotional attraction. She drew upon what she had learned from her high school drama teacher. Do not think about how one would portray the person; be the character. Her character right now was a university student, a stunning punk who kept the company of a much older man, but the time for her to leave was now.

Mila gathered her clothes and headed for the shower, preparing for the cold ride home. After she had dried herself, she repacked her shoulder bag quickly, but carefully, and she walked back to the office. She stood in the doorway and waited again for John to notice to her. He was on the phone again and his voice was quiet.

"Yes, Beate... Uh, huh... Damn...Yes... Jimmy did the right thing... Benny... but he left... How serious? You heard... The table next to them... Who was the other guy? OSC... Okay... okay... Ah shit... Fuckin' idiot... Clean it up... Yes, clean it up... By morning... Yes. For good!... I understand... I understand... Thank you. Good night."

He hung up, let out a deep sigh and rubbed his eyes.

The rubber soles of her riding boots squeaked on the polished parquet floor as she shifted from one foot to another.

He looked up. His pained face turned into a smile. He got up, walked over to the couch and pulled his pants on not bothering with underwear and slipped his shirt on but did not button it. He walked to Mila and kissed her hard.

John took Mila's hand and walked her to the door that led to the garage from inside the house. Mila could do nothing but follow. She knew where the garage was but did not know the pass code for the exterior doors. She descended three wooden stairs to her bike. It was standing next to his Porsche, parked where another car usually sat.

John stayed at the top of the stairs. She straddled the bike and put on her helmet, but left the visor up. He punched in a code on the panel and the door opened. She backed out into the dark, instantly chilled. She kicked the starter over twice before it caught. She turned on the light, spotlighting John on the steps. He held his hand to his eyes.

Mila turned the handlebars and rolled down the driveway before shifting into first gear. The garage door was already closing. She drove away into the night, passing a large black SUV parked at the corner. Two faces illuminated dimly in the violet light of the dashboard followed her as she drove past.

Mila found her way through the neighbourhood to Yonge Street. She drove south quickly, arriving home faster than she would have thought as the traffic was light and she hit almost every green.

She turned down the small alleyway and coasted to the house's graffiti-covered garage where she parked her bike. She climbed the rusty steel fire escape two steps at a time and unlocked the back door.

Mila saw the flickering light of the TV emanating from the living room and hear the staccato of machine gun fire. Her four roommates were sprawled on the couch, intertwined like a giant beast watching "Aliens" again. Mila stood in the doorway for a few moments waiting for one of them to notice her.

"There are roses in your room. Who's JL?"

Mila froze.

"We figured they're for you. The card's addressed to the Girl in Blue. They're on your bed."

"The vehicle database," she thought. "Shit, of course. He'd have run my plates. Probably had long ago."

"Arrived around seven this evening," Mickey said, taking a swig from his beer. He was the only one who looked at her.

Mila crossed the living room as nonchalantly as she could and scurried down the hall to her room. On her bed, wrapped in cellophane, were three-dozen blood-red, long-stemmed roses.

She shut the door. The click of the latch was deafening.

She placed her helmet on her desk and let all of her clothes fall to the floor. She slid under her comforter without disturbing the flowers. She carefully lifted the card off the cellophane that enveloped the bouquet, tore it open, and held it up to the light from the alleyway peaking through the threadbare curtains.

Sorry 'Tatiana', I couldn't resist. Please be safe. JL.

The day drained from her. Her hand lay on the comforter, inches from the plastic, her ring was tight around her finger. Mila shut her eyes. A wet, sweet scent seeped out of the wrapper and enveloped her.

She was chilled and alone. The lump in her throat was suffocating. Her mind raced. She needed more than this. She needed change. She sobbed until she could no more and slept.

13

"Graham, you okay", asked Vitaly. "Hooshang here is going to drive you home."

"Here, let me help you in," said Brian.

"Don't, you fuckin' touch me. I'll puke."

"Might've been the shooters," said Vitaly.

"He doesn't have the guts to handle pressure," said Brian.

Vitaly took a quick look at his watch. It was nearly 12:30am.

"Graham, take your time, said Hooshang. "You just sit there. Keep your feet on the ground and lean over the gutter. You soil this car and you get the bill. Got it?"

"Graham?" asked Brian.

Graham sat, breathing heavily. His phone rang and he reached into his suit pocket, looked at the screen.

"Oh Christ!" he said as he fumbled with the receive button. "Hello Honey," he croaked. "I'll be home soon. I was out with Jimmy and bumped into some old friends... I'm just getting into a car now... No, I'm not driving... A limo... Yes, a service.. .Don't worry, I'm not paying for it... H & something... Honey... I don't know... Can I stop for diapers?"

Graham looked up at Vitaly who shook his head slowly.

"No, Love. Can't. I'll be home soon. Promise. Love you."

"Stupid witch. Fooled her," Graham said looking up at Vitaly. "She doesn't even think I've had anything to drink."

He resumed his bent over position.

"Graham," said Vitaly handing him the scarf he had left behind in the restaurant. "This can two ways. You want immunity?

You want to protect your family? Cooperate. Come to the office at nine a.m. tomorrow. I'm putting my card in your pocket."

"Yeah, Yeah."

"Graham, if you don't cooperate, if you tell a soul, well, there's no need to threaten, is there? See you at nine a.m. sharp. Not a word to anyone, you hear. Not even to your wife. Understood?"

"Got it. Not a word."

Graham smiled weakly, heaved once and then vomited all over his black suede brogues.

"What a waste of good ragu," said Brian.

The driver sighed, shaking his head. Vitaly knew him well. Hooshang Askari had shared a cab with his father when Vitaly's parents first immigrated to Canada.

"That's why my son usually drives the nightshift," said Hooshang.

"Mr. Askari...," Vitaly began.

"Vitaly, call me Hooshang. I've known you long enough."

"I'll pay for any cleaning."

"Yes. Yes, you will."

Hooshang reached into the car behind Graham, grabbed a box of tissues and passed them to him. Then he opened the front door, and pulled from the glove box two air sickness bags. Graham continued to stare at his feet, breathing deeply, before emptying what was surely the remainder of his stomach. Hooshang jumped back, avoiding the splatter. He glared at Vitaly. Graham hung his head again.

He took a few more breaths and bent over to blot his shoes, smearing the smaller chunks into the patterned holes of the toe cap before giving up. He looked around to see where to put the soiled tissues before dropping them in the gutter.

Hooshang stood in front of him, feet spread wide and snapping his fingers.

"Hey you! Hey! You done?"

"Yeah, I'm good."

"Here," said Hooshang handing over the bags, "you know what to do with these, right?"

"Don't worry. I'm...Good to go."

Hooshang opened one of the motion sickness bags and placed it in his lap as Graham lifted his feet into the car. He reached over him to secure his seatbelt. The stench of vomit permeated the vehicle. He shut the door.

"Goodnight Hooshang and thank you," said Vitaly. "Send me the bill."

"Don't worry about that. You'll get one. Brian, good to see you again."

Hooshang rounded the car and got in. He pulled a quick U-turn across King Street to head east, narrowly avoiding a black SUV parked on the South side. It pulled away just after Hooshang passed.

"That's got to be awful," said Vitaly.

"My happiest day was I when no longer had to drive a squad car," said Brian. "Smelt it way too many times. Anyway, I'm grabbing a cab home. Share it with me. I'm driving past your place anyhow."

"Nah, I need to walk. I've some digesting of my own to do. See you at seven a.m., bright and early, okay? I'll text the rest of the team."

Vitaly began walking down King Street West towards his loft. He knew that putting the case together wouldn't be easy. Most of what Graham had disclosed was likely inadmissible. 'You got the informant inebriated,' Donald would reprimand him. 'The defence counsel's gonna tear you up.' Vitaly smiled to himself as he heard his old boss' voice in his head. 'Cases aren't built in a day. Never, ever rush.'

Graham's words were those of a drunk. How much was truth and how much was bitter bravado? How much was frustration over the utter failure of his career? Vitaly would have to tease that out tomorrow. He doubted Graham would say the same things again, let alone give a sworn statement. What Vitaly had was a case for breach of trust. The case would mar Lister's reputation and that of Trinity Asset Management and it would correct the complaint. Surely it would lead to civil proceedings but he knew there was something more, something Graham alluded to near the end of their conversation. As he walked, Vitaly texted his team:

At the office at 7 a.m. Lead in Lister case. Lots to do. V

Vitaly looked up from his Blackberry just as he stumbled over a woman who was waiting at the crosswalk in front of him, nearly pushing her in front of a passing cab. He grabbed her collar and pulled her back off her feet. She clattered to the ground. Vitaly lost his balance too, and landed on top of her. He got up quickly, helping her to her feet.

"Oh! Martha? I'm so sorry. You okay?"

"Yeah... I guess," she said, rubbing her hip.

Vitaly steadied her on her feet. She looked down.

"Oh my... my boots, she whimpered, "The heel."

It was nearly shorn off the right boot. She swung it under her to keep an even platform.

"My stockings are torn too," she sighed.

He noticed a run starting at knee and disappearing above the hemline of her green and red plaid miniskirt. Blood was beginning to trickle down her leg.

"Permit me," Vitaly said as he took his handkerchief from his coat pocket, stooped down and he applied pressure to the wound. His right hand supported the back of her leg. The blood stopped flowing after a few minutes.

"Let me walk you home. Where do you live? I mean, do you live near here?"

"Yes, a few blocks away."

He extended his arm as he had seen his father do many times for his mother. Martha looked at him, unsure what to do. She took a step and stumbled as the heel came out from under her. She caught herself on Vitaly.

"I guess I do need you after all," she laughed, reached down and ripped the heel from the sole and pocketed it.

She kept her hand in the crook of Vitaly's arm as they walked down the sidewalk, her gait that of a peg-legged pirate. She held his arm tight, tighter than she needed to. They strolled along King Street in silence. Finally, Martha spoke.

"Where were you going when you bumped into me?"

"On my way home."

"Why are you always in so late? You on a graveyard shift or something?"

"No, I'm a lawyer. I start at 8:00 a.m. usually, tomorrow an hour earlier. Criminals never rest!"

"Vitaly, that's lame."

His heart jumped. She had remembered his name.

"I know. Just a busy night."

"It's 12:45p.m."

"That's my life, apart from running people over."

"Work, work, work. When do you play?" she asked coyly.

"Well, once a week I fence! Good workout, like running and playing chess at the same time."

"Okay....right," she said. "That's not really what I meant."

"Oh."

Vitaly was at a loss for words. They turned south onto Portland and in half a block reached her duplex. She reached into her coat pocket for her keys, drawing them out slowly, hoping he might take the hint. She dropped her keys

"Oops," she said as she bent down to pick them up.

Predictably, he pounced. Their heads collided gently. His hand was on the keys. She placed her gloved hand on top of his. She looked into his eyes for a moment and closed them. Vitaly had the good sense to stay kneeling, moved forward and warmed her lips with his. After a few moments, she moved her gloved hand to his cheek, the soft leather palm caressing his face. She broke the embrace and rose uneasily on her broken heel. Vitaly, somewhat bewildered, followed her and stood. She put the key in her door, unbolted the lock and crossed the threshold. A sweet smile radiated from her face.

"Can't invite you in. My roommates..."

"Goodnight Martha," he said.

"Goodnight. See you tomorrow?"

"Yes. Good bumping into you."

She laughed, reached out and grabbed his coat lapels and pulled him in. She kissed him hard, with an open mouth, her tongue caressing his. After about ten-seconds, Martha pushed him back and shut the door.

Vitaly just stood as he heard the bolt lock. He walked down the pathway and tracked back to his apartment. He had overshot it by five blocks.

14

Hooshang left downtown and drove east on King Street. His phone rang and his son's faced appeared on dashboard screen.

"Hi Nico."

"Hi Baba. Where are you?"

"I'm on Vitaly's run. Should be home soon. While I have you, I wanna double check the address. Going to...,"

The address had been programmed into the on-board GPS, but he liked to make sure.

"347 Glenrose Place," said his son.

"Any other runs tonight? Should be done in twenty."

"Not much else going till tomorrow. Behrouz will pick up Miss Jane at 4 a.m. I'll pick up Dr. Marion at 6:30 a.m. for you. He lives near Jas anyhow."

Hooshang opened his mouth to scold his son, but they lived in Canada now, didn't they? His son had a western name. They were engaged and Hooshang thought the world of his future daughter-in-law.

"Oh and Nico, the car will need a cleaning. The stench is bad."

"Another drunk."

"Yup. Send the bill to Vitaly."

"Got it."

"Good night Nico. Thanks for taking the early shift. Love to Jas."

"Will do. Bye bye Baba."

Hooshang ended the call and continued east along King Street. When he arrived at the intersection with Jarvis Street, he waited in the left lane for the advanced green to flash. An imp with a piece of cardboard approached the car. He smirked as he held up his sign.

'Smile If You Masturbate!'

Hooshang could not help but smile. The imp turned over the sign.

'A Little Change Please. It's Cold Out.'

In the cup holder beside his seat, Hooshang fished for a couple of loonies and rolled down his window.

"Great sign kid. When was the last time you ate?"

"Yesterday, Sir."

Hooshang dropped the change, felt for his wallet in the front passenger seat and held out $10 dollars.

"No drugs, okay?"

"Food only, promise," said the imp with bloodshot eyes and a runny nose. "May God bless you sir."

"Thank you. May you be blessed as well."

He knew he was being naive but with the window down, he felt cold too. Hooshang glanced in the rear view mirror at his passenger. Graham was leaning against the passenger side window, eyes closed, the friction of his cheek keeping his head upright. As he slept, drool trickled down his stubbly chin. Hooshang could hear him snoring the deep sleep of the drunk.

The light flashed green. He accelerated smoothly through the intersection and began heading north, not wanting to hold up the sole car behind him.

It was clear driving all the way to the Mount Pleasant Junction where he veered east under the Bloor Street Overpass.

As he rounded the bend, a car was blocking the left lane with its hazards on. Hooshang pulled over hard into the right lane and immediately the black SUV on his bumper, its headlights blinding him in the rearview mirror. Hooshang accelerated to avoid a collision.

He was now doing over 80 clicks, too fast for the turn. His tires squealed their displeasure. The SUV stayed on his bumper. It had surged, reaching the sedan, pushing it forward.

At Elm Street, another black SUV was stationed in the middle of the intersection, its hood popped open. A tall blonde woman dressed in black stood pointing what looked like a large megaphone at Hooshang. Thick orange electrical cables ran from it under the hood of the car.

The SUV gave a final push and braked hard. Hooshang could see the headlights retreat in the rearview mirror as it skidded to a stop. Hooshang yanked the steering wheel to the right to avoid the woman. His hair tingled all over his body as the car went dead; no brakes, no power steering, no lights. Nothing.

He fought the car and crashed through the wrought iron fence that surrounded the Branksome Hall parking lot, clipping two parked cars and coming to a halt. The alarms blared shrilly.

Hooshang opened his eyes. The windshield was a spider web of cracks. There was blood all over the airbag. He could feel shards of glass in his brow and the panelling of the door cut into his hip. His vision blurred crimson as blood flowed over his eyelashes and down his nose. He felt for a gash in his forehead with his hand. His chest hurt. He looked down and saw a black metal rod two inches in diameter impaled into his torso, just below his collar bone on the right side. He was pinned.

"Shit. Shit."

He heard Graham moan. The rear passenger door swung open.

"Help!" Hooshang croaked, blood bubbling across his lips. "Help!"

A shadow reached into the backseat. Hooshang could hear someone fumbling with the seatbelt buckle.

"It's jammed," said a male.

"Let me try," said a female.

In the mirror, he caught a glimpse of a black ski mask and leather jacket, blonde hair extending below the neckline. There was the flash of a blade and the sound of the belt retracting as it gave way to a knife. He watched as Graham slumped sideways and was dragged out of the car. He made no sound. A head, also masked, appeared in the window of the front passenger door and the door opened. The person leaned in and smashed the in-dash screen with a metal object.

"Do we need to take all the electronics?" a man said. "The HERF should have done its job."

"Yes, take them," the woman answered from the rear seat. "It only disables them. It does not fry the memory."

"I won't be able to open the hood though – too bashed in."

"Grab his phone."

The man reached into the front seat and took the phone. He grabbed Hooshang's wallet too. Hooshang grasped at his wrist.

"No," said Hooshang, "photos... my son... Jas."

The man flicked out the photos out of their sleeve and pocketed the wallet. He then raised the object he had used to smash the in-dash screen to Hooshang's temple. Its coolness startled him.

"Miss, live or die?" he asked. He waited a moment. Then he cocked the trigger.

"Live," whispered Hooshang, terrified. "Please."

"Got Graham's phone," she said holding it up. "Go!"

"Live or die?" the man repeated.

"Leave him be. He will be dead soon."

That's when the gun cracked his skull. Pain radiated through his head. For good measure, he was struck again. He remembered no more.

15

"Mila's okay," said Martha. "She'll be okay."

Vitaly awoke with a start, eyes adjusting to the faint light of the city in his bedroom, his T-shirt soaked with sweat.

He shook his head. There was no sound at all.

His Blackberry buzzed and Vitaly reached and slapped at it, hoping to hit the snooze to secure ten more minutes of sleep.

Not thirty-seconds had gone by when it buzzed again.

Vitaly reached over and the light from the screen pierced his eyes. The phone read 2:03 a.m. The buzzing was not the alarm but rather two text messages from Nico Askari.

Vitaly: Dad never came home last night.

Mom's worried. Nico

Vitaly clicked the second.

Where is he? He had your friend as his last client.

I need the car for tomorrow!'

Vitaly responded.

No idea. V

Vitaly lay back on the bed for a moment. His eyes closed but his mind raced.

Vitaly's alarm rang. There was nothing more on his phone from Nico. His first thoughts were of Martha, her words and of her kiss.

He dressed, taking much more time than he normally did picking out a tie and shirt combination, leaving a collection of cast offs on his bed.

Vitaly left his condo but instead of waiting for the streetcar, he walked along to Queen Street West, the morning sun in his face, melting the frost off the sidewalk.

He tried Nico's phone but it went straight to voicemail.

After his third attempt, he did not bother any more.

When he arrived at the office, to his surprise he found everyone except for Brian waiting for him.

Brian straggled in ten minutes later looking awful.

"Sorry Boss. You mind kicking the recycling bin over. Just in case," Brian said slumping in his chair.

"Brian," asked Paul, "you and Vitaly tie one on last night?"

"It was supposed to be reconnaissance," said Derek. "How much did you have?"

"Oh man, Brian, did you bathe in it?" asked Maiwen. "Here," she said, handing him her cup from Starbucks, "you need this more than me."

He took a sip.

"Bloody Hell! Green tea."

Brian reached across Vitaly's desk and opened the top drawer.

He fumbled as he took out a large bottle of Tylenol, dropping it on the ground. They enjoyed watching as he groaned and picked it up, struggling with the safety cap.

"Here, let me," said Vitaly, opening the bottle and shaking two into his outstretched hand.

"Keep' em coming," said Brian.

Vitaly deposited two more into his palm. Brian popped them into his mouth, chewing them without a chaser, grinning as the others looked on.

"Sideshow's over," Brian growled.

"So how was last night?" asked Maiwen.

"Let's cover the rest first," said Vitaly. "Okay, team, what have we got?"

"I've got a few stale reports," began Maiwen.

"Spent the better half of the week just getting the financials I could. Our illustrious archiving corps aren't up to their usual standards. I can get all sorts of docs on Trinity but there is precious little on Lister's firm."

"Not much of a surprise really," mumbled Brian, with his head leaning against the wall, eyes closed, his hands folded on his belly.

"I'm hopeful something will turn up," Maiwen said.

"They had to have filed," said Derek.

"Okay," said Vitaly. "What are you going to do?"

"I've sent a request in to Lister's firm under an assumed name but I have not yet heard back. You know what's weird? Beyond Lister, I can't even figure out who works there. No org chart. According to our files, the chief compliance officer's position has been vacant for three years. Lister's the only person listed on any of the corporate documentation."

"Alright, do your best."

"I'll be careful. Won't spook 'em."

"Derek? Paul?"

"Well, not a lot either," said Paul.

"The street has all sorts of things to say about the ineptitude of Trinity but nobody will say boo about Lister or LAM," he added.

"There are no former portfolio managers floating around. There are a couple of analysts but we've yet to talk to them. All the traders told us that they're a bitch to trade with."

Derek chimed in.

"And when Lister calls, they know they are about to get Greeked."

Brian chuckled. Maiwen looked at Derek quizzically.

"What? Oh man, do I have to spell it out?"

Derek looked at Paul and Brian and finally at Vitaly. All were chuckling.

Vitaly sighed and nodded to Derek to go ahead.

"Uh... Maiwen, You know... intercourse... in the... behind."

Maiwen turned beet red, flushed with embarrassment but did not look away.

"The bond traders hate 'em," Paul continued. "They never know if what they bought from them was toxic or a gift. There're casualties all over the street."

"Usually," he added, "it's a young kid, fresh out of school, with a puffed out chest who is suddenly polishing his shoes on the street corner trying to figure out what the Hell went wrong."

"On the flip side, if you were anointed as worthy, you wield enormous power. A trader could be make five-six times what he would otherwise. Lister's volumes are that good.," he added.

"Half of the cottages in Muskoka are probably paid for by Lister, indirectly, maybe directly. I'm sure a few envelopes have crossed some tables to secure a first call. If you are in, you don't mess with 'em. You take your sporadic losses and drive on. If you upset John, your firm will toss you."

"You haven't talked to any former traders directly, have you?" asked Brian.

"There aren't any," replied Paul. "We've looked high and low. In 10 years, LAM has not lost anyone of substance. I've only yesterday tracked down one analyst. He was fired but he refused to speak."

"Somebody has got to be retired," said Vitaly.

"As far as we can tell, there is only one but he wasn't a trader."

Paul opened his note book and flipped back at least a dozen pages or so.

"Henry Wade. Lives in a place called... Ala. Ala... shit... Somewhere, Costa Rica. He wigged out and started bringing snakes, like boas and pythons and shit, to the office. Put one in a woman's desk drawer as a prank. Isabella Tournimenko. According to Border Services, he has not been back to Canada in five years."

"Don't think that's one to follow up," said Vitaly. "No one is vacationing there in the next few months?"

"I'll go if you want boss," Paul volunteered. "No skin off my back."

"Donald would love to see that expense. No, just follow up. Probably a dead end anyway."

Brian sat up and groaned as he adjusted his head to a new position. He awaited Vitaly's recount of the previous night's events.

Vitaly's blackberry shimmied across his desk.

He let it go to voicemail. Immediately, it shimmed again. Vitaly could see the message bar. It was from Nico.

Vitaly excused himself and clicked on the message.

V - Dad's dead. At St. Mikes. Come quick. N.

"Vitaly," asked Brian, "what is it? You've seen a ghost?"

"Hooshang's dead. St. Mike's, now!"

Brian followed Vitaly out the door like a shot.

16

Vitaly kept on Brian's heels as he wended through the maze of corridors leading to emergency at St. Mike's.

He went right to the reception desk and spoke to a short, round Filipino nurse.

"Brian, my love, what brings you back?"

"We're here on business, Rhonda. For Hooshang Askari, brought in late last night."

"Exam 12. Not good," she said shaking her head, "not good."

"Thanks, Hun. How's your mom? Good?"

Rhonda shooed him away.

Brian ran over to room 12.

He could see beneath the grey curtain the legs and shoes belonging to a man and a woman.

Brian coughed.

"Mrs. Askari? May we?"

Nico opened the curtain. His face was wet with tears.

Maria did not turn around. She held Hooshang's hand, tracing the lines of his palm, her mouth moving without sound.

Hooshang lay on a gurney. His shoes were still on. The top button of his pants was undone.

His shirt had been cut away in strips, his arms still covered in his dirtied sleeves. Blood drenched a dressing across draped his chest.

The left side of his torso was sunken, stuffed with what were once white bandages. His eyes were swollen shut.

Vitaly reached out to Nico who collapsed into his arms, barely remaining on his feet. Vitaly just held him.

"Mrs. Askari, Nico, I'm so sorry for your loss," said Brian. "Will you excuse me please. Vitaly, stay!"

He ran into Rhonda as he snaked through the corridors on his way back to reception.

"What the Hell happened?"

"Single MVA, around midnight. The EMS had a hell of a time getting him out of the car. They worked on him for four hours. No I.D. on him. Took awhile for the constable in charge to circle back to the car company to get to next of kin, just a couple of photos. Couldn't even get him stable enough to move upstairs. So much blood. Too much blood."

"Who's the officer on the file?"

"O'Malley."

"Ah shit!"

"You know him."

"My sister's ex. He beat her up real bad one night and me and the boys, well we look after ours, you know. You know if he's still here?"

"He's still chatting up one of the nurses."

"Rhonda, where?"

"Check the lounge. Better knock first."

The constable and a nurse were straightening their clothing when Brian barged into the lounge not thirty seconds later.

"O'Malley!" Brian announced, "Still a shithead beat-cop, I see."

"You... Brian," said O'Malley, raising a finger and backing until he hit the wall, "I gots a restraining order on you."

Brian turned to the woman.

"Uh, Hun, missed a bit," he said pointing to her cheek.

She glanced towards the mirror over the sink and brushed the back of her hand across her lips.

"Made you look!"

The nurse finished smoothing her greens, picked up a clipboard and paused at the door.

"You'd better call me this time."

"Sure. Of course."

She left without looking at Brian.

"Zip up and shut up," Brian said pointing at O'Malley's crotch. "Conduct unbecoming of a member of the service. I know a few people who'd love to hear about this."

Without breaking eye contact, he closed his fly.

"I don't give a shit where you get your rocks off," Brian said holding out his hand. "Gimme your notes on Askari."

"Who?"

"The MVA!"

O'Malley reached into his chest pocket and pulled out a small rectangular note book. He thumbed his way about half way through. Brian was tempted to rip it from his hands.

"Single MVA. Called in at one-oh-five a.m. Lost control on Mount Pleasant Parkway heading north at a high rate of speed, ninety-plus kph. Slammed through the fence at Branksome Hall. Caught a post in the chest. Bad shape."

"Bad shape! Hey, shit-for-brains, he's dead, you fucking prick."

Brian took a breath.

"What else?"

O'Malley continued:

"Well, best I could tell there as probably at least one other car involved. The front end and driver's side were all banged up. He might've clipped someone. No paint left behind, but the limo was black and if it was hit by another black vehicle, we couldn't tell." He said.

"After the firefighters got done with it, cutting him out and all, the car was a real mess. It's down in forensics now. Take a few days I reckon," he added.

"Why do you care?"

Brian ignored the question.

"Was there anyone else... I know there was a fare on board. No one else but the driver, right?"

O'Malley hesitated for a moment.

"Well... Ah, found a scarf at the scene, elegant one too, silk blend, a male's. Not the kind of thing the driver would wear, if you know what I mean. High-end. It's at 53 Division with the other stuff we scraped up."

O'Malley stopped. He had seen the same look on Brian's face when he was investigating violent crimes and was trying to recreate a scene.

"Can I go?"

"Go."

O'Malley moved for the door, staying as far away as possible.

"Sean," said Brian, "Thanks! And, ah... good job."

"Yup, okay," he said as he walked off down the hall.

Brian followed him out and went to find Vitaly.

17

"Vitaly, it means so much to me that you're here."

"Not a word, Nico. It's the least I can do."

They stood next to a stainless steel table as the staff wheeled in a gurney on which a shrouded body lay. As the staff of the York Region Islamic Center hovered around, they carefully transferred Hooshang's corpse to the table. An older man dressed in a long, white tunic approached Nico, taking his hands in both of his.

"Mr. Askari, I am so sorry for your loss. Your father was a great man. I will miss him."

"Thank you."

"We are ready to begin."

"Okay," Nico said. "Please."

The staff pulled back the shroud revealing a naked body. The man in the tunic began recanting a poem in Farsi, as the others poured warm water over his limbs first, his head and then his torso. The wounds wept the translucent maroon rivulets. Once the water ran pure, the staff wrapped Hooshang in white bands of cloth and finally Nico and Vitaly lifted a pure white linen sheet over Hooshang.

"Come Vitaly, we must travel with him and never lose sight."

The staff transferred to the body to a waiting hearse, behind which two town cars were idling. Vitaly's parents and Nico's mother Maria were already seated in one. Vitaly and Nico joined Mila in the other. Nico was the first to break the silence.

"What happened last night? Who was the passenger?"

"I can't tell you much."

Mila glared.

"Vitaly," she said, "it's Nico. You can trust him."

"I'll tell you, but you can't say anything, not even your mom. Okay, Nico? Mila? Understood?"

"Of course," they answered in unison.

"Okay, last night, Brian and I had dinner with one of John Lister's employees. I'm investigating his fund company."

"I know him!" Nico interrupted. "His firm's been a client for a few years. I drive his wife to the airport all the time.

"The employee was Graham Kent," Vitaly continued. "He gave us some inside info about shady stuff going on at LAM. I've no idea what happened last night after your Dad picked him up, but the employee's gone and I know my conversation had something to do with it. Nico, I promise I'll let you know as soon as I find out what happened. We've already got a theory but it's too early. I don't want to give you any false hope."

The procession entered the cemetery and slowed in front of a small gathering of friends who had come to pay their respects and to offer up forgiveness for Hooshang's soul. Having known him for more than twenty-five years, Vitaly could not think of a single reason why he might need such a prayer. He was not perfect, but he was a good man. All present knew that.

A group of pallbearers, all livery drivers, carried Hooshang from the hearse to the gathered crowd. Nico climbed down into the grave and Vitaly, his father and a few of the men lowered the shrouded body. Nico oriented his father towards Mecca, eased him onto his right side and, with his hands, re-formed the three small balls of soil that the gravediggers had left to support his shoulder, chin and head. Vitaly helped Nico back out.

Maria stoically threw three handfuls of soil into the grave as she prayed aloud in unaccented Farsi,

"We created You from It and return You into I,, and from It, We will raise You a second time."

Nico repeated his mother's word, his voice breaking, letting the earth pour from his hands. Petr and Zoya dropped small, paper

Canadian flags and stepped back as Mila followed, watching for a moment as it fluttered to rest in the dirt. She stood next to Maria and held her papery hand. Their adopted homeland had treated both families well. Petr and Hooshang had often spoken of how much they loved their lives in Toronto and how much they appreciated the opportunities presented to them. Nico urged Vitaly to come forward. He did so in silence. Vitaly raised his hand over the grave and let the dirt, cold and clammy, slide between his fingers in a steady stream. As the other mourners followed, Nico and Maria stood in silence, hand in hand, their faces wet with tears.Vitaly stood still, watching in silence as the mourners covered the shroud in soil.

Brian, who was standing apart from the gathering, motioned to Vitaly to join him. He was agitated and his fists were clenched. As Vitaly approached, he gestured aggressively toward the rear of the procession. There was John, looking solemn, slowly making his way towards Maria and Nico.

After yesterday morning's debrief from O'Malley, Brian and Vitaly had sat for a long time, trying to figure out what had happened.

"How long 'til we get the forensics back?" asked Vitaly.

"Couple of days, three maybe."

"Why wasn't Graham in the car? Where'd he go?"

"I don't know but no way would Hooshang sped without reason," said Brian. "Graham was loaded and had already vomited. Hooshang treasured his cars."

"I know. They were always spotless. He would have giving Graham the smoothest ride possible. There was no reason to speed, not unless he was forced."

"And the impact with a fence on a dry night, it was like he was evading something."

"Where's Graham?"

"Anything weird at the bar?" Brian had asked, "Before you sat down."

"Shit Brian, it's all weird to me. There was just me, Benny and Graham. Benny's cool. He wouldn't tip anyone off."

"Anyone else? Take your time."

"Just Kent, Benny, met the bartender, Gwen. Oh and one other guy. There for a couple of minutes. James...James...Fuck, what's his last name? James, no Kent called him Jimmy, Jimmy Leering. He left just after I arrived. He got a call, or a text or something, from his girlfriend. Said he needed to leave, to meet her. Tried to get Kent to go. He was insistent. Said his girlfriend wanted to meet him. Going to the Fifth, no the Soho Club."

"Did Benny know him?"

"Don't think so, not from school, industry, maybe."

"Anything else?

"That couple, no, the two couples when we were eating. They were speaking Russian? One of the men left just as you sat down. He never returned. Big guy, hockey player type. Forties?"

"Vitaly," said Brian. "You were made."

'Made?"

"Your photo in the paper?"

"Fuck."

"Given how little we've have been able to dig up, Lister keeps stuff tight. Graham's a weak link. He knew shit, loads of shit, stuff that gives all of you prosecutors wood. Wild guess?"

"Shoot."

"Jimmy tipped off Lister. His security was ready by the time we left the restaurant. Someone was watching the bar, watching us. The couples that sat near us. They were close enough to hear."

Vitaly shook his head.

"Too far-fetched."

Brian continued:

"They wait for Graham to leave. Someone that drunk isn't gonna drive, not getting on the subway. You'd need eight, maybe ten guys, four cars, two in front on King, two on Adelaide, four inside in the restaurant. The longer we talked to Graham, the antsier they got. They wait and follow. They know where Graham lives so they have few places to get him. Could be at home, but the wife and kids are there. They're not gonna get him while we're around. Graham lives in Leaside. Mount Pleasant only makes sense. A staged accident. A trap. It's not that hard."

"Too complicated. All those loose ends."

"No, just options. The ideal is an intercept en route, easiest to execute and the cleanest if you do it right. Maybe they did. If they missed him, Plan B would probably be a home invasion."

"I don't like it but until we get the forensics, it'll have to do."

****

Mila watched her brother join Brian, surprised that he had left Nico's side. She held Nico's his arm, hoping to reassure him. Her gaze followed Vitaly, scanning the crowd and settling on the end of the queue. John! Vitaly motioned to Brian to stay put as he turned to get to John before he could approach Maria or Nico. Her eyes widened.

"What the Hell?" she said to herself. "What the...?"

John looked towards the larger gathering. Mila quickly turned away and buried her head in Nico's shoulder, her face obscured by his frame.

"Nico, I'm so sorry," Mila sobbed, "so, so sorry."

Nico put his arms around her and looked at Jas dumbfounded. Nico tried to comfort her but Mila kept her head against his chest, her hair hiding her face. Meanwhile, Brian followed Vitaly, staying a few paces behind him as they approached John.

"Mr. Lister, may I help you?"

"Oh. Such a sad day. I've come to pay my respects. My company's a client of H&N."

"This is a private event."

"They were, I mean, are, superb. Hooshang always drove me. Been with them, well so long I can't remember. Always reliable. Such a shame, a pity, really."

"Please leave," Vitaly said, ready to do something, anything to keep him, away from Maria and Nico.

"I'm sorry?"

"No need to apologise. Please don't make a scene."

"Like you are?"

"Leave. Now."

"Vitaly Mirkin right? By the way, one of their cars was driving an employee of mine home two nights ago. He never made it. His wife gave me a call yesterday morning wondering where he was. Strange. I wonder what could have happened."

John then turned away from Vitaly and faced the rest of the mourners. They shuffled forward. John followed. Brian stepped in close.

"Mr. Lister," he said, "the list of mourners has been restricted to family and close friends. Thank you for your consideration. I'll let Mrs. Askari know that you paid your respects but it's time to leave."

Brian reached into his back pocket, took out his wallet and flipped his badge.

"Okay, Detective Cranston," he said reading, "I never..."

"Well, you do now. Leave. Quietly."

Brian smiled and held his ground. John turned and walked away nonchalantly towards his car some thirty yards away, parked discreetly away from the others. He got in and gave a curt nod to Brian and Vitaly. He pushed the ignition button and the engine purred to life. He put it into first gear and promptly stalled the car.

John looked around frantically. He pushed the start button again and sped off, squealing his tires, driving far too quickly for a solemn place. The congregation turned towards the sound. Brian looked at Vitaly. Mila briefly lifted her head out of Nico's chest.

"That was a little brazen," said Brian.

"I know," said Vitaly. "I know."

Once outside the cemetery walls, John slowed down to the pace of the traffic. He headed south on Avenue Road back towards downtown and his office. He continued on in silence for about twenty minutes as he collected his thoughts.

"Call Beate," John said to his iPhone.

"Yes, Mr. Lister. Sir, how may I help you?"

"Beate, look up Brian Cranston, RCMP badge number 8537. Background data, citations and disciplinary notes. Send notes to my home account."

"Got it. I'll have it for you within an hour."

18

When Mila awoke, her room was filled with light. She was exhausted. The last two days with Hooshang's funeral and reception at the Askari house had been such a whirlwind that she had spent barely an hour at her own apartment.

Tears welled up constantly. Hooshang had been an uncle to the family, helping her out whenever he could. Nico was her age. She could not imagine losing her Dad now. She was still his little girl.

Her head swam. Could John really be involved? Was it just a conjecture of Vitaly's? She had convinced herself that John was benign. He knew stuff and his hacking the various databases was illegal, of course, but to be involved in a death? He did deal with the UCC boys swiftly and more violently than she'd have thought.

The bouquet John had sent still lay on her bed but the roses now gave off nothing but decay. Mila rolled out of bed and looked in the mirror. She looked tired but she admired her skin art; multicoloured, Yakuza style, harsh and striking forms. Hooshang had always marvelled at her ink. On her left flank was a snow covered scene of playful giant panda, sitting on its haunches, munching on bamboo overlooking of a serene frozen pool. Its reflection was a rabid polar bear, its teeth bared, its claws scraping at the underside of the ice. Across her back, wrapping around to her side, she had inked in Cyrillic, Никогда не сдаваться: Never Give Up.

Mila grabbed her worn silk robe from the hook behind the door before unlocking it and listened for her roommates. She had no desire to see any of them.

Her stomach growled, reminding her that she had not eaten since lunch the previous day. Cinching the robe tight, she padded down the hall to the kitchen, grateful to be alone. Her behaviour of late, and the flowers in particular, would, in time, require an explanation. She was not up for it today.

Despite the alternative appearance of her roommates, most were not adventuresome outside of their routine. All worked in the service industry, comfortable only behind a counter of a bar or an independent music store. If it did not involve piercings, punk rock and getting drunk, it did not interest them. The exception was Mickey. He was an innocent of sorts, slowly finding his way.

Mila opened the fridge, cringing at what she might find. She took the milk out of the fridge, sniffed it and then examined the best before date. Three days grace. Cereal and milk were the only communal foods in the kitchen.

She grabbed one of the few clean bowls still in the cupboard, retrieved a spoon out of the drawer and sat down at the small blue painted wooden table she had found in the garbage last spring. Her stomach mollified, she looked up at the clock and froze.

"Oh fuck! Course the apartment's empty, you idiot. It's eleven a.m."

She took one more spoonful raced down the hall to her room. She got dressed in two minutes and was on her bike in four. She was going to be late for Zablon's class on the psychology of addiction. No doubt she would miss the first half entirely. She hoped she could get there before he resumed after the break.

Zablon had a habit of keeping irregular lecture hours. He always started on time and never exceeded the three hours allotted but he would often cut the class short if he had covered everything that he wanted to. If a lecture only took two hours, why stretch it to three? The students loved him for it.

Once the formal part of the lecture was over, those who wanted to leave could. A discussion would always ensue with the students seeking greater clarity though it often veered off course. Near exam time, he would often tell jokes, trying to ease the students' stress. Great debates would rear up, with Zablon playing the proponent of a particular point, sometimes the antagonist. Occasionally, he would arbitrate competing views, maintaining a balance.

As Mila entered the hall, she knew it was one of the shorter lectures as most of the most class had dispersed. Zablon was holding court at the front with students clustered around him, some seated, others standing. He looked up.

"Ah, the North star returns to my constellation! Why, you shine so bright! Ms. Mirkin, kind of you to grace us with your presence. Join us, won't you? Since you missed my earlier pearls of wisdom, you might pick up something of value now. Enlighten us all, will you: why is it, after a night of drinking, no matter what you ate for dinner, you'll always throw up carrots?"

"Because you don't fully..."

Everyone burst into laughter. Mila flushed.

"Ladies and Laddies, tune in next week when Mila may answer another rhetorical question. Unfortunately, I need to leave you kind hearts and gentle people. Ms. Mirkin, would you walk with me?"

A number of the female students glared at Mila. She ignored them and followed Zablon, smug with the attention he paid her.

Mila slowed her normal pace to match his shuffling gait.

"Is your knee hurting more than usual today? The weather can't be helping."

He did not respond.

"Zablon, why are you..."

"I think it's best I keep my mouth shut until we are at my office. Okay?"

They walked in silence the rest of the way as they took the elevator up to the fifth floor and made their way down to the end of the hall. A couple of students were waiting outside his door.

"Wait," he said to Mila. "This will only take a moment."

She slumped against the wall and sat on her motorcycle helmet. She stared at the room number, 543. The last 48 hours washed over her and she shut her eyes. After about five minutes, the door opened and the other students left.

"Mila, come. Please sit."

He motioned her toward the only arm chair in the office, then offered her a candy from the bowl that always sat on his desk.

"No thanks."

Zablon took one, unwrapped it carefully, popped it in his mouth and crunched it between his teeth. He flattened the wrapper and slid it into an envelope on his desk.

"What's up Zablon?"

Zablon went to the window and opened it a crack. The stale air of the office began to dissipate.

He sat on the couch opposite Mila. Zablon reached over to his desk and after shuffling through a few papers, pulled one out and handed it to her. It was her independent mid-term assignment.

Mila leafed through the paper, looking at the notes in the margin. The red were made by Zablon's T.A and the green by Zablon himself. She skipped to the end, eager to read the paragraph of suggested improvement he wrote on every paper and, of course her mark. The page was blank.

"Why were you late today?"

"I, ah," Mila began, choked up, "I was at a..."

"While you're conjuring up an answer, where've you been for three out of the last four lectures?"

Mila pursed her lips but said nothing.

"In first year, you were always on time if not early. You stayed late after class in the jam sessions and your rhetoric always swayed the discourse. That's why I hired you as a research assistant. I turned down applications from grad students who were desperate for practical work. Your paper on the Statistical Methods for Measuring Bi-polar Disorders in the Indigent was exemplary. Professor Schmidt said that your work exceeded all expectations.

He showed your assignment to his engineering colleagues as an example of what a bird-brain psychology major could do."

Mila smiled, but she remained silent.

"I've been doing this for fifteen years. I've never had one as bright."

Zablon shifted a few papers that were on his cluttered desk and opened a file folder. He took out a paper.

"I looked at your file. Mila, of your five courses this semester, you're the top student in two, second in two others and fifth in the last one. Mine. I know why. You've missed too many classes. Your answers on the quizzes reflect the material in the text and those classes you have attended. You're missing only the information I've provided in the lectures you skipped. So, I'm going to ask you again, where've you been?"

Mila rolled her paper into a tube and patted her palm with it, ready to bolt.

"That paper you're holding, it goes beyond what an undergrad would do, could do. I'm not sure what to do with it. It's too good. That's my problem. Where'd you get the data?"

She stared at the ground as she wound the tube tighter.

"Mila, look a me. You don't cite any secondary sources beyond the few obvious ones on the Madonna/Whore complex. You took Freud's basic tenants and Tuch's extensions and turned them on their head. Let me see if I remember your phrasing...'Men don't despise the Whore as much as they are unable to unite the solitudes of love and lust'... Your work's a breakthrough."

"So you want me to cite it, to work with you on it, so that you can steal the credit. Like you did with the "Simintov Displacement."

"No!"

"Get your name in *Psych Today* again. Is that it? Been a while since you published anything."

"Don't flatter yourself! This isn't about me. It's about you and your big, complex brain. Your work is solid, not just in understanding the sex trade worker/client relationship but you extended it to every relationship, to the struggle between the physical and the emotional links in our sexual lives."

"Like Hitchcock in Vertigo?" she said. "It not complicated. I'm not sure why you men make it so."

"Don't you dare diminish the value of your work! This is not some pseudo-analysis that you lifted from a late-night film. Don't demean your intellect!"

Zablon eased his mass back down into the chair and looked out the window.

"I was going to volunteer to be your supervisor on your fourth year thesis, maybe even fast track you to grad school. Now I'm not so sure. If you're not honest with me, if you can't see your own worth, why should I bother?"

The hole in her stomach grew.

"The material is rich but there's so much un-referenced data. My T.A. doesn't want me to believe you did this on your own. How'd you collect all this? It's important work. Who'd you talk to? I need to see your raw material, your notes!"

The paper was now as stiff as a truncheon.

Mila remained silent.

"Since you're not going to respond, I've no choice. I'm obligated to report you for academic dishonesty."

Zablon paused, letting his words hang.

"My T.A. wants you to fail. He argues you'd have to have interviewed at least fifty subjects to get this data or you'd have to be a prostitute yourself. I know it's not the latter. Mila, you'll be censored, maybe even expelled for plagiarism."

"That's because I understand the material better than he does, than he ever will," she said quietly. "How could a man ever understand such relationship?"

"Ah, she speaks! Mila, did you plagiarize? He can't find it on Turnitin nor Plagscan."

"Those are lousy programs and you know it."

"You need to reveal your sources or I'll have to agree with him. You'll leave me no choice."

"There's always a choice," she whispered.

"Pardon?"

"I said, there's always a choice."

She had stopped wringing her hands and looked him in the eye. Her irises had gone cold and grey. The whites were red and tears began to form.

Zablon looked out the window.

"For God's sake, Tell me! How the Hell did you get the data?"

"I didn't cheat," she whispered, her voice cracking.

A tear left the inside corner of her right eye. She tasted its saltiness as it ran over her lips.

"I didn't cheat Zablon. I didn't."

"Then why wont you tell me?"

"I can't! I know there needs to be sources and citations. I know. The people I spoke to asked for anonymity. I respect their request. I could have labelled it subject one, two and three, but that would be meaningless, wouldn't it? I mean, who would believe that a third year could do primary research? I took a risk. You're telling us, telling me all the time to take risks. Here's mine."

She let the paper from fall from her hand and to the ground. It rolled around as the pages unravelled, straining to return to flat.

"I'm not going to write about... I just can't tell you how I got to it. The research is real and trust me, one day you'll know. "

"Not good enough!"

"Okay. Then fail me then."

"You want me to?"

"You have no choice!"

"Mila, I'm not going to. It'd screw your chance at Columbia."

"That was your dream for me, Zablon, not mine."

"Not true, and you know it. Whatever it is, it's... You say I've a choice. Well, I suppose I do. Re-submit this with proper citations or write a new one. Either way, it will be due in two weeks. That's your choice."

"Two weeks?"

"Is that going to be a problem?"

"No."

"Fine."

"Fine," she repeated and then she added barely audibly. "Thank you."

She brushed the tears from her cheeks with the back of her hands. She shouldered her bag and grabbed her helmet. Zablon moved to stand between her and the door.

"Two weeks and I want to see it fully annotated. And..."

Zablon reached into his desk and rummaged in a drawer. He held out a card.

"I think... I think you should see a friend of mine. He works here at the University. It's confidential. Whatever is turning inside," he pointed at her temple, "needs to get out. It's not worth keeping in."

"I'm okay."

"No, you're not."

"Two weeks?"

"Two weeks."

Mila took the card without reading it and headed down the hall, noticing for the first time the sound of her own foot falls as she walked.

She turned the corner, called for the elevator and forced herself to read the card.

Student Mental Health Services

Andrew Millin, Counsellor

There was a phone number and e-mail address at the bottom.

She crumpled it, let it drop to the floor and stabbed at the elevator call button repeatedly, but then headed for the stairs, taking them two at a time.

Movement felt good. She hurried for her motorcycle. It was starting to spit rain as she ran across the parking lot.

The ride home would be wet and nasty.

Two black SUVs were parked near each exit.

This struck Mila as odd. No student would be caught dead driving a Tahoe or an Escalade or whatever they were. Probably drivers for some dignitary or CEO popping in to share with the unwashed masses at Osgoode Hall.

The bike turned over after the first kick again. It had never run better.

She reminded herself to buy some salmon jerky for Mickey next time she was in Vancouver. He loved that stuff.

19

"Only ten minutes late and before Vitaly!" Petr said with a smile.

"I got here as quick as I could," she lied. "My shift ran overtime."

"That's okay, you here now," said Zoya. "I so look forward to this. So romantic."

"You do remember that young kids die because they are stupid, right?" asked Mila. "Because they couldn't communicate."

"Mila, do not ruin for Mama. I am Romeo and she my Juliet."

"Oh dear God. Please, not all night."

"Sis, you beat me for a change," said Vitaly, a lovely brunette trailing behind him. "Mama, Papa, this is Martha. Martha, my parents, Zoya and Petr. My kid sister, Mila."

"Pleased to meet you Mr. and Mrs. Mirkin," Martha said turning to Mila. "You're not the witch your brother said you were."

"Good to know you're not a figment of his imagination," replied Mila.

Leaning in close to her brother to kiss their hellos, Mila whispered, "Finally found your voice, did you brother? I like the way this one dresses. There might be promise."

"Mrs. Mirkin," said Martha, "I think it's so sweet you take your children to the opera."

"We never intended to. We had tickets one Valentine's and the babysitter fell through. They sat on our laps. It became tradition. No laps now. I am glad you could join."

Vitaly smiled. Mila approved of his friends with about the same frequency as he did of hers. A moment later, young man in his early twenties, dressed in a dark purple plaid suit, a maroon leather tie, and a black, pork pie hat strode up. With a flourish, he swept it off his brow, bowed and offered Mila a single pale, pink rose from behind his back. He stood straight and gazed off into the distance over the gathering crowd and spoke in a clear voice.

"O, she doth teach the torches to burn bright!

It seems she hangs upon the cheek of night

Like a rich jewel in an Ethiop's ear

Beauty too rich for use, for earth too dear!"

Mila blushed.

"Bravo, bravo," shouted Petr.

"Thank you, thank you," said the young man, bowing again and blowing kisses to his audience both near and far.

Mila brought the bud to her nose and breathed in. It was soothing. She appreciated the gesture, though she knew he had lifted it from a bud vase at the cafe where he worked. The colour was delicate, hopeful perhaps.

"Papa, Mama, this is Mickey, one of my roommates."

Mila stood gave him a peck on the cheek. It was his turn to blush.

"He's the one keeping the Suzuki running, Papa."

Mickey's eyes lit up. He shook Zoya's hand first and then took Petr's with both of his, shaking it with great gusto.

"It's such a wonderful ride. I've been adjusting the carburetor. Running smoother that before."

"You're watching the points?" asked Petr.

Zoya's eyes glazed over.

"Time to take seats, no?" she said. "Follow me. We on same level, just not together."

Mila followed her parents into the hall, Mickey walking with her, her arm in his, allowing him to guide her through the crowd.

157

Apart from the brief peck on her cheek, it was the only time he had ever touched her. She did not mind. Their relationship was platonic, was it not? She felt honoured.

Mickey helped Mila remove her overcoat, draping it over the back of her seat, as she settled in.

Her phone buzzed and Mila felt for it, forgetting in which pocket she had stuffed it.

Mickey was bemused as her life streamed out of the pockets: gloves, tissues wrapped in plastic, her keys and maple candies and finally her phone. She gave one of the candies to Mickey and popped the other in her mouth as she read her phone message:

It's oh so romantic.

U here?

You look radiant. Your eyes! Who's the kid?

Mila looked up from her phone and scanned the room. There was John, a dozen rows forward from her. A young blonde woman whose face she could not see was at his side. He waved as she looked right through him. He returned to his phone.

So, serious? Need I be concerned?

Mila ignored the text and murmured a few words into Mickey's ear and kissed him again on the cheek, slipping her arm under his. Her phone buzzed again.

After first act, basement level, lighting director's office.

Mila typed, hiding the screen from Mickey.

WTF U have a date!

This! Nothing compared to u

She smiled and pecked at the screen.

Sorry. Can't. Folks and friend. See you soon?

Be there. Got it. Or it's done;)

Mila glared. John shrugged.

K

As Prince Escalus banished Romeo from Verona, the curtain fell on the first act. Mila rose from her seat and excused herself, complaining of an upset stomach. She wended her way through the crowd towards the washroom, found the elevator and descended to the basement. The doors opened and a tall man in a light grey flannel suit and a fire engine red turban blocked her exit. He was talking to a muscular man with a gentle pink face with a mess of scars on his chin and the kindest of pale grey eyes. The turbaned man stuck his hand across the door and did not let Mila pass. She looked at him incredulously.

"Mike, please inform Mr. Lister that his performance had better improve or the next time I'm in Calgary, I'll pay his daughter a visit."

Mike bristled.

"Worry not my kind hearted friend. It's simply a threat. I am not a monster."

He held out his hand for Mike to shake. He did not take it.

"I admire your loyalty. I respect that, but you should come to work for the Family. I could use good man as head of security."

"Thank you Mr. Singh for the kind offer, but I must decline."

"Suit yourself. My guess is in six months you may change your mind. The offer will still stand. Please relay my message."

The Sikh turned to Mila.

"Oh my Love. My deepest apologies. I've been rude beyond measure for keeping you waiting and forcing you to listen to this banal conversation. He's all yours now. Please."

Mr. Singh stepped aside and let Mila exit. He stepped into the elevator and the doors closed.

"This way Miss Niko, Miss Nokolev... Miss Tatiana," Mike stammered.

Mila followed Mike down the dim hallway, the footfalls of her stilettos echoing off the grey concrete floor and the yellow-tinged cinder block walls. The fluorescent light was sallow. He lead her to a door with letters stenciled on it in black, knocked with two quick raps and opened it inward. John was leaning against the steel desk inside, his tuxedo jacket draped across the wooden desk chair, an empty champagne flute on the table behind him. His face was drawn and gaunt. He had lost weight since she had last seen him and the bags under his eyes were darker, his eyes bloodshot. The heavy door shut quietly, the latch finding its home.

"Who was the man?" Mila asked kissing on the cheek. "John, are you okay?"

He looked up but did not flash his usual smile. His hands trembled as he reached behind his back and undid his cummerbund. "Thank you for coming. Everything's fine."

"That man I passed in the hallway. He said something strange about Calgary."

"Everything's fine," John repeated.

She stepped forward, he lifted his hands, gently cradling her face. Still holding her, he lowered her down to the front of his pants.

Ten minutes later she found her parents with the others on the mezzanine enjoying their champagne, just as the chimes began to call the patrons back to their seats.

"Feeling better, my little one?" asked Petr.

"Yes, Papa, I'm fine now. May I?" she said, pointing to his nearly full flute.

"Your stomach?" asked Mickey.

"Bubbles always settle it."

She downed the flute in a single pour.

20

"Hey Vitaly," Mila said cradling her phone while she typed on my computer.

"Hey Sis, how's tricks?"

Mila smiled.

"Not bad. Jammed with school. I gotta rewrite a paper one of my prof didn't like. Too advanced for the course apparently."

"I had to do that once."

"Really? No kidding?"

"No, just shittin' ya."

"Thanks. Needed the encouragement. Much obliged."

"Must suck have to the rework something you did already."

"Calling to cheer me up, are you?"

"Sorry. You okay? How's work?"

"Kinda slow at the bar."

"I went by the other day. Didn't see you."

"Not too many shifts."

"Ya, they said you were out."

"Like I said, kinda a slow."

"Need a hand? You tight on cash?"

"Nah, I'm okay. How's your girl?"

"Good."

"Hey monosyllabic Neanderthal! I can see you on a date. Fun times. Okay, this is how a conversation works. I pose a question, you answer with more than a single word. Then I ask another for clarification. Then we go back and forth. Otherwise, I get bored and hang up."

"Okay. Settling in."

"Your boss is still a prick?"

"Hmm, yeah."

"Good, now you're sharing."

"Mila. I get it. It's just I deal with sensitive stuff."

"Cross my heart, hope to die. Stick a needle in my eye. Good enough?"

"Okay, but loose lips sink ships."

"Aye captain, they do."

"Brian, the cop you met, is still trying to piece together what happened to Hooshang. Papa's still devastated. He regrets not inviting Hooshang to join him at the printing company."

"Papa should't feel bad. It's not his fault Hooshang was still driving."

"I know. I told him that. I'm the one who booked him."

"It's not your fault either."

Vitaly was silent.

"Is it?

"I don't know."

"What really happened that night?"

"I've already said too much. We can't find the passenger. He gave us some really good intel. Mila, but not a word, okay!"

"Okay," she said distractedly.

"Mila, I mean it. I've already shared too much. No gossip, nothing."

"Promise. Not a word."

"Gotta go. Survive school. There's a huge world waiting for you."

"Thanks. Cheers and go get laid, okay?"

"See you, M. Love you."

"Right back at ya."

Mila hung up. She tried to process the conversation and returned to her paper. Each sentence was an exercise in frustration. Her phone buzzed. She ignored it, trying to finish her paragraph. She saved her document and shut down her Mac. She was tired and needed to pack before she tucked in for the night. It was 11 p.m. Her head pounded from caffeine and she dreaded the 4:30 a.m. wakeup call Niko had volunteered to provide.

Her phone buzzed again.

"Oh for Christ sakes."

Sitting at her desk, Mila picked up her phone and swiped it open. She went to her real Gmail account first and then to her pseudonym's. She had not checked the latter in days. Former regulars had emailed, wondering if she was still around. Mila replied with a wink and a flirt to keep them hanging on just in case things turned sour with John. There were a number of other emails, including a couple from the National Ballet of Canada ticket office. She ignored those for the time being. She would come back to them later.

Of course, John had sent his daily missives. She hesitated about opening them as she knew that he had set up read notification. His emails were about inane things he had come across that he thought might be of interest to her. In their quiet times, Mila had shared her obsession with ballet. He was more intrigued by contemporary movement and at the moment, was infatuated with the work of a Vancouver choreographer, Crystal Pite. He had once spent an entire evening trying to convey to how Pite had converted the troop into a beehive; the emotions were sinister and the relationships feral. He sent links to YouTube with interviews of the dancers and clips of the performance trying to convince her of its brilliance. Tired of his fixation, she declared all contemporary dance to be crap. She knew better but she did not care.

She clicked on the email from John entitled Calgary.

Okay sweetie. All Set. Le Germain Hotel 899 Centre Street SW, Calgary. See you Monday night for a 'sleepover'. Be there before 6pm. You'll love the suite. You can see the Rockies, Top Floor! If you're not too busy on the weekend, come to Banff. I'll send a driver. We can ski. You can do your little research project later. It'll be fun! John

She replied.

Aw. That would be awesome. Thanks for the offer Hun but school and research are really important to me. Monday night is all I can spare. xox Tatiana.

Mila rubbed her eyes and began to pack, remembering vaguely the few special requests for John's entertainment. She also made a mental note to check her baggage. The clothing and the toys John he requested would be a little hard to explain to security at the airport. Mila stripped and slid under the covers, curled up and went back up to the email from the National Ballet. A ticket for *Giselle* was waiting for her at the box office: Ring 5, Row C, Seat 12. She knew it well. She had sat in the seat before.

Come. I need to see you.

"I'll be there, ready for you," Mila typed and hesitated.

She pondered the second half of the sentence, erased it and hit send. Her clock read 11:53 p.m. Mila trembled, both elated and frightened. It was going to be a short night, shorter still as Caroline danced through her mind.

21

It was Friday night just before 9 p.m. Isabella sat at her desk in the LAM office arranging her files, deciding what to keep and what to pitch. She had blown through John's first deadline and had worked straight through weekends for months without a day off. She was now eager to catch up on her other work. Her normally organized desk was covered in reams of stock research, most of which was now useless given its short shelf life. She had already emptied her recycling bin once tonight. She was tempted to dump the lot.

John's project had taken a toll. Her fridge was bare and she was reduced to late night take-out, too tired to cook or contemplate groceries. She was embarrassed when she passed a neighbour in her condo hallway on the way to recycle a large stack of Styrofoam food containers. This was not what her hard work was supposed to buy her. She made a note in her iPhone to buy some new plants. Hers were desiccated beyond revival, having shed their last leaves two weeks earlier. She felt slovenly. Her nails were bare and bitten to the quick. Her parents had left message after message on her answering machine, both at home and at the office. Even her brother was wondering where she was.

A Skype notification popped up on her computer screen:

John Lister: Answer? Decline?

She accepted the call with video.

"Hi John. You're early. Just a sec. Just need to shut the door."

"Boomer, everyone's gone by now. No one's gonna hear."

"Habit."

"You're right. You never can be too careful."

She sat back down in front of her computer.

"You look radiant."

"I do not."

"I've pushed you too hard."

"I'm taking tomorrow off."

"Sure, if this works. By the way, tomorrow's Saturday."

Isabella started to respond but stopped. She was too exhausted to care.

"John, still wearing a tie?"

"Dinner with Joan and some Foundation guy she's sucking up to."

"Isn't Tim over as well?"

"Yup. Always a blast."

"A glass of wine? You don't drink...ever."

"Well, just a little tonight. To celebrate your impending success."

"Whatever, and I'm taking a couple of days off whether this works or not."

"If this works, take the whole fucking week. I'm ready."

"You have the materials Murphy provided?"

"Of course."

"Remember how it works?

"Indulge me."

"Really? Again? It's so easy," she said, "I punch in the code for the product and the login is routed through about a dozen countries and even more servers before ending up on the desk of one of a dozen neurosurgeons I've selected in North America. For tonight's demonstration, you are Dr. John Lister, MD, Neurology. You ready?"

John held up a jumble of wires attached to a matte grey device the size two small boxes of matches. It was the latest offering from Brainstim, designed for people with Parkinson's with the promise that with leads implanted deep within the brain, the small electrical pulses would regulate the firing of the synapses.

"Good, insert the leads into the tester. Red first, then blue. The green goes last. The tester is our brain and the current will provide the stimulation. It's on right?"

John hit the switch. The LED readout on the tester indicated normal and showed that the amperage was correct.

"Everything looks like it's within normal parameters."

"Ready?"

"Ready. So how did you get the codes?"

"Do you really want to know?"

"You're right" John paused. "This is a simulation, right?"

"You're not going to kill someone. There's no mirror product out there."

"You're sure?"

"Positive."

"Okay, enter 2343ASED//AASS658."

"Okay. Got it."

"Push enter."

"That's it?"

"Yup. Child's play. Even an idiot can do it."

John ignored the jab. He knew he had pushed her hard.

"Executing," she said.

John waited a few moments.

"It's still routing. Give it another twenty seconds."

He sighed and took two large gulps from the glass. Isabella could hear a knock through the speakers. John looked away from the screen but did not move from the desk. He made a tucking motion as he pulled the device behind the screen. Isabella kept quiet.

"For God's sake Joan! I said I'd be a moment."

"I was looking for the damn maid. Thought maybe she was blowing you."

"That would be nice."

"Your clumsy Tim just spilled the last of the Margaux all over my grandmother's tablecloth. It had better come out."

"You don't care about the linen."

"You need to reign him in. He's embarrassing himself."

"No, he's embarrassing you," John said with a laugh.

"In front of Leif. Reign him in."

"So Leif can get you on the Foundation. Why don't you just sleep with him?"

"That's Plan B."

They glared at each other.

"I'll be there in a moment. I'll bring another bottle."

"Dessert is about to be served. Bring the Chateau D'Yquem. You talkin' to your trollop, again?"

"Shut the door please."

Isabella heard the door slam.

"Okay, I'm back."

"Pleasant, isn't she?"

"Sometimes."

"Who's your trollop?"

"Don't you start... Still nothing... wait... Boomer, you're a fucking genius!"

The hack was complete. She had overridden the security protocols for Brainstim's product. They could now do it at will. John looked at his watch.

"Total time... two minutes, five seconds."

Isabella sat beaming.

"Good night Isabella. Take the rest of the night off."

Her screen went dead as Skype disconnected. She glanced at her watch. It was 9:13 p.m. Another night alone. She was going to treat herself to the French bistro around the corner from her apartment. Her mouth salivated at the thought of steak frites and a glass of Côte-Rôtie.

There was a noise outside her door. Isabella froze. She could see nothing through the glass. The cleaning staff should be long gone. She should be alone. She slipped out of her heels and grabbed the golf putter that a broker had given her from behind the door. She had never used it.

She opened the door quickly. There in front of her, sat a burly man sitting at the trading desk, feet up on another chair, leafing through the Economist magazine. He turned to face her.

"Oh, Mike. You scared the shit of me."

"Sorry about that, Miss Isabella. Mr. Lister wanted to make sure you got home safe. I've a car downstairs for you when you're ready."

"Thanks. Just a moment."

She walked back into her office, replaced the putter in its usual spot, slid on her heels, and grabbed her hand bag. She shrugged into her coat and shut her door.

John remained at his desk. He wiped his sweaty palms on his thighs, took another gulp of wine, reopened his Skype account and selected the fifth name down the list.

"Oh, hello John."

"Did you follow that?"

Matt Murphy's face appeared on the screen as he took a long drag from a hand-rolled cigarette. Based on the depth of his drag and the calmness that came over him, John knew that there was more than just tobacco in it.

"The video was a bit choppy but the audio was fine. Isabella thinks it's still theoretical, doesn't she? Ah, she is as naive as she is fuckable."

"It's not, is it? What was your read-out?"

"The amperage fluctuated wildly. Total voltage delivered... well, more than enough to poach a quail's egg. It's ready. Are you?"

John typed as Matt recited the series of letters, numbers and symbols.

"Matt, you know this is fucked up. You have one hardwired into your brain."

"I'm just not stupid enough to allow anyone to connect to it wirelessly."

Through the speakers, John could hear a child calling. Matt looked away and spoke gently before returning to John.

"Just send the money to the Cayman account."

The screen went blank as Matt hung up.

John's fingers hovered over the enter key. The code was destined for a real device, installed deep in the brain someone he knew of but had never met.

It made sense. John had funded him to live symptom free for three months. It was time to collect on Wally Babiak. Edna would be able to think back on how she had regained the man that she once knew and loved for their anniversary and her birthday.

"Cheers Wally!"

John drained the last of the wine and set the glass down on. He wished it was not empty. He wanted more.

He depressed the return key twice to make sure the signal was sent and he sat back in his chair. His temples throbbed with adrenaline.

"Was it worth it? The last three months, was Edna happy?"

He looked at his watch. Two minutes and ten seconds had passed. He opened up his email account to a draft he had begun earlier.

Dear Jargit:

I am pleased to announce that our extended investment program is working well. I look forward to showing you the improved results. I think you will be impressed. Thank you for your and the Family's ongoing support. It is a pleasure to serve you.

Sincerely,

John Lister

He hit send. He heard Joan calling him back to the dining room. He hesitated and thought of sending an email to his Tatiana, unsure of what to say but wanting to share his triumph.

John logged out of his computer and closed his laptop.

The act was complete and John was $860,000 richer. The policy was worth $2 million, the pay-out to the Babiak's $1.1 million.

Tom' commission was $30,000. Premiums paid were $10,000. He did the calculation in his head; 76% return in three months, 304% per annum.

He chuckled. It was still less than the annualized rate of a payday loan.

Only a portion would be going to the fund. He had earmarked the rest for something completely different.

21

"Good morning Mila," Nico said cheerily. "Rise and shine. I arrive in 15. Green tea?"

"Sure Nico. Sounds great. Good night," Mila said and she hung up.

Her phone rang not twenty seconds later.

"Mila, It's Nico. Get up! You're going to Calgary today."

"Of course. Shit. Sorry. Late night finishing a paper."

"No worries. See you in 15."

She jumped out of bed and turned on her computer, getting dress while it booted up. Everything else was ready.

"God dammit, run computer," she said. "Run!"

Finally her browser opened and she uploaded her assignment on Turnitin.

Mila gathered her bags and slipped out of the bedroom.

Her door squeaked wildly. She had been meaning to oil it and had even made her way down to the local hardware store for that express purpose. The oil sat on her dresser, waiting.

She had also picked up a few mousetraps which she had put in her drawers. They made good deterrents for any hands that might snoop while she was away.

Three traps guarded her dwindling stash of pot in the third drawer of her dresser and two were hidden around the base of her dresser.

Mila kept escape money taped to the underside of the bottom drawer.

Only she knew where to place a hand safely.

She had thought of using rat traps instead but had decided that wandering fingers probably needed slapping not breaking.

John had persuaded her to keep the bulk of her money in the bank rather than keep it in her room.

She hated going there to make deposits. 'Spread it around,' he told her. 'Keep them below $10,000 at a go. Shouldn't trigger the authorities' radar that way.'

She was not the bank's average client in appearance and whenever she walked into a traditional branch, she was a book judged by its cover.

The tellers had no idea that her cash flow surpassed theirs by a margin of four or five to one, all tax free.

For now however, her escape money felt far safer in her room.

She crept down the hall and out the front door to Nico's waiting sedan.

****

Mila was jolted awake by the wheels touching down.

She looked out the portal at downtown Calgary and the Rockies off in the distance.

As she exited the baggage area, Mila's heart jumped.

The same man who had guarded the lighting director's door when she had seen Romeo and Juliet was standing at the exit.

He was holding an erasable plastic sign with her pseudonym.

She tried to appear nonplussed but she knew her gait had changed slightly.

The man looked up, her motion catching his eye. He looked right at her and checked his cell phone with his free hand and smiled.

She walked past him.

Her phone buzzed. It was from a blocked number; she ignored it and kept hunting for a nearby taxi as she exited the arrivals area.

Her phone chirped. She walked behind a pillar, and stood out of sight. Mila reached into her coat pocket and took it out.

It was a message from John.

Welcome to Calgary. Mike texted. Said you walked right by.

He'll take you anywhere ;) JL

She looked up from her phone and the driver was next to her.

"Ms. Niko...? Ms. Tatiana?" he said with more confidence the second time, but still messing up the pronunciation.

"I'm Michael Brennan. We sort of met sort of at the opera. Mr. Lister asked me to deliver you to wherever you want to go. Please, come with me."

"If I don't?"

"Miss, I don't know. No one has ever said no. Of course, you can say no. I don't know what will happen if you do. Ms. Tatiana, please, it's all right."

Mila reluctantly handed Mike her carry-on bag and her suitcase and he led her towards the parking garage.

She headed to the front passenger door of the Escalade SUV but when she looked in she saw that the seat was covered in school books, texts she recognized from Grade 12.

Mike gently directed her to the back seat.

She climbed in and Mike shut the door.

In the rearview mirror, he caught Mila staring at his scarred knuckles. He was missing two segments of his ring and little fingers.

"I was helping my mom with the washing. Got my hand stuck in the machine. Lucky I didn't lose all of it. Hurt like a bitch, if you'll pardon my French. Anyway, no pain anymore."

"Sorry. Didn't mean to stare."

"It's alright. Everyone does. Wrecked my violin career. Don't look so surprised. I was good."

"Just having a hard time imagining you with a tiny bow."

"So, where will I be taking you? Mr. Lister is at Le Germain. Or are you staying somewhere else?"

"I have a choice?"

"Miss, Mr. Lister was hoping for the pleasure of your company, but..."

"Please take me to the University of Calgary's Foothills campus. I'll give you directions as we get closer."

She paused for a second.

"After you drop me off, please thank Mr. Lister for your services but I won't be needing them anymore this trip. I'll be at the hotel at five p.m. sharp on Monday as planned," Mila said.

"Have him leave a key for me at the reception," she added. "I'd like some time to prepare for him."

"He should wait till six-thirty pm before entering. I'm in Calgary to conduct research and don't want to be disturbed until then. Understood?"

"As you wish."

Mike put the car in gear and drove to the campus.

Mila texted her friend Olga along the way to see if she could couch-surf.

Being at the short-term student housing did not seem like a good idea after all.

Mila sank into the leather seat, craving a smoke, anything really to settle her nerves.

23

Vitaly walked around the office, looking for his squad.

He found them in the board room, ready to go.

Derek was reading the Report on Business.

Vitaly caught a headline of another medical device malfunction. He was glad he did not have to represent that company.

"Okay, let's get started," Vitaly said entering the boardroom.

His team was already seated.

Vitaly shut the door and sat down at the head of the table. He hated that position but it was the only chair they had left open for him.

He sat and slid the chair a little to the right.

"Maiwen, anything new?"

"Not much. The docs just aren't there."

This raised a few eyebrows.

"I went down to archives last week. They don't understand either," she continued.

"They did tell me something interesting though," she added. "The database has been accessed by many people who normally rarely use it. The weird part was that Donald's username kept coming up. I figured it was Donald's secretary but she denies having logged in as him. The techies verified that."

"Okay, what's next?"

"Well, short of masquerading as an investor, I'm not sure how to get into LAM."

"Keep that as an idea," said Brian.

"Okay, what's next? Paul and Derek? Anything."

"Not a lot," began Paul.

"We called that guy in Costa Rica again," said Derek.

"Henry Wade," chimed in Paul.

"This time his brother picked up. Paul had the idea of spoofing a line from LAM."

"Wait, spoofing?" said Vitaly.

"Faking a number so it looks like you're someone else," said Derek.

"I pretended to be a clerk checking some information, making up some excuse. He fell for it. I now have an address."

"So, you've his phone number and address. So what?" said Vitaly.

"Well, I know we don't have the budget to go down. We Googled his place. It's remote, hidden like."

"Think you can get him to talk?"

"I sent a request for an interview. Silence."

"Keep on it. If he moved that far away, maybe he's got something to hide. Brian, think we can share our concerns with him? Appeal to his sense of right and wrong."

"I don't know. Maybe he moved for the climate. Maybe there's no love lost. Worth a try though. He may even want to get something off his chest."

"Paul, draft something, show it to me and we'll send it."

"Okay boss. On it."

"Brian," said Vitaly, "what's next?"

"Still can't track down Graham Kent."

"All we have is hearsay of a ghost. He corroborated the allegation against LAM, but he's gone."

"Any thing more on the accident?" asked Maiwen.

"The forensics have come back. It's not conclusive but in talking the cops I trust, it doesn't look like a single MVA. The reporting officer insists it is," Brian noted.

"The accident is just not consistent. In forty years of driving, Hooshang hadn't had a single moving violation. Remarkable for anyone."

Even more so for a cabbie," said Paul. "I drove in undergrad for my uncle. I got like three tickets a week."

"Anyhow, back to the subject at hand. Kent wasn't at the scene nor has he been seen since. I spoke with his wife yesterday. She has no idea where he might be either." Paul added.

"He is clearly henpecked but it's totally out of character for him not to go home."

"So our best lead has vanished and my dad's best friend is dead," said Vitaly emptily.

Nobody said a word for a few moments before Brian continued.

"The other weird part. At Hooshang's internment in Richmond Hill, who shows up to pay his respects? Lister."

"No shit," said Paul.

"Apparently, he's a client of H&N."

"Okay guys, lots to do," said Vitaly.

"Maiwen keep scouring, something will come up." He added.

"Paul track down Wade. Get him to talk."

"We'll continue to monitor LAM but we need to get on the other dockets. There are two on the go right now where we'll need to give testimony next week."

"As fascinating as Lister is," Vitaly added, "Donald wants us to move forward with other cases too. The next ones are slam-dunks if we stay on top of them."

Vitaly turned to the gathering and concluded the meeting: "Okay on your way. Brian, stay a sec."

"What's up?" Brian asked as he shut the door.

"You know there's more here."

"It's obvious that John is involved. Did he cause the crash? I don't know. The missing electronic files are weird. The paranoid side of me assumes that the network is compromised. Might be just the records related stuff. Might be more. This place is not the easiest place to hack into but if you did..."

"Or might be from inside."

"That's a far scarier prospect."

"Why not? Lister's hands are everywhere. I'd be careful what we post on the network, notes, calendars, that sort of thing. The group needs a dummy calendar to protect itself. Do you trust your secretary?"

"Dunno."

"Adriana did," continued Brian, "I would too."

"Get her to keep a fake calendar," he added. "No working on the network. Laptops over a VPN. I'll talk to one of my buddies at RCMP. He can set one up in a night."

"Do we need to worry about safety... I mean John, will he...?"

"There always a risk..." Brian fell silent for a moment.

"As a cop, for now, I don't think so. We're not the ones betraying secrets."

24

"Yay, it's you," screamed Olga, greeting Mila with open arms as she stood on her front stoop. "It's been so long."

Olga took Mila's bag and welcomed her inside.

"What's up?"

"Not sure yet. Creeped out. Thanks for letting me crash."

"Of course. Here. Let me take your coat. Make yourself at home. The place is a mess but it's my mess," Olga said.

Mila had had Mike to drop her off at the student housing residence where she had booked a room for her stay. She entered the lobby, checked-in, went up to her dorm and then waited, just sitting on the bed, replying to messages on her phone. After twenty minutes, she was sure that Mike would have driven off. Surely he would report back to John and convey her message. Mila turned off "Tatiana's" email, put her phone away and left the building by the rear exit, walking across campus and into the surrounding neighbourhood, all the while checking to see if she was being followed. By the time she got to Olga's, she was frozen and tired but the precaution had given her a chance to have a smoke and calm her frayed nerves.

"So, why are you in town?"

"I'm doing some research for a prof back in the 6. I have a bunch of interviews to conduct. It's gonna be kinda intense."

"Why's that?"

"I'm meeting drug addicts who are weaning themselves off heroin and morphine."

"Aye! There's a lot of that shit going around. Tons at the pub."

"Never, ever touch it. Not even once. Leaves a residue you apparently never forget."

"I gotta work tonight. When you are done prepping, come by. It's just around the corner. I'll pour you a few."

"I'm glad you're out, you know of the..."

"It's better this way. Mushrooms grow on shit. I do miss the cash though. You're out too, no?"

"Couldn't juggle research, school and the bar," Mila lied. "Way too much. Did my time!"

"Good. Still dancing?"

"Yup. You?"

"Tomorrow morning. I'm working a piece. You can help me."

"Me, help you? I always tried to copy you, your hand movements. Not sure I could add anything."

"You always knew how to bring passion. Bring that."

****

She was two hours early and as the taxi took her downtown. She was elated. Zablon was pleased with the notes from the five interviews she had sent off and he had complemented her on the detail and her initial conclusions. She had checked her mark on-line for the revised paper. It hadn't yet been posted.

Having spent a few days with Olga, Mila was sure that she was on a secure path. Mila felt uncomfortable with her lie and that she was still active. From the look Olga gave her on the first night, she knew she did not believe her. Gratefully, she did not press.

As she rode into the city's core, her giddy mood receded. The concrete offices and condos that filled Calgary's centre blocked most of the western setting sun. Yellow shards of light pierced through towers, stabbing her eyes as the taxi rolled forward.

"Sir, instead of Le Germain, could you leave me a few blocks away? Need a walk and a smoke."

The cabbie dropped her off. Finding a sandstone wall still lit as the sun set, her back was warmed as it radiated the warmth of the day. She grabbed her lighter and fished her cigarettes out of her shoulder bag. She knew John hated the taste of smoke on her lips. She considered a Nicorette but left it in its package. She took a deep drag, exhaling slowly through her nose, enjoying being bathed in the smoke. The air was still. She lit a second with the ember of the first as the shadows reached across the street and lapped at her feet. Mila stood a little taller, moving back into the sun but the dark was relentless. She took her last puff and crushed the butt with the ball of her boot.

Her apprehension grew as she walked down the street to the hotel. Two black Escalades were parked at the corner. The window of the further SUV was open and Mila could see Mike's face in the side view mirror. As she approached, he hopped out. Mila caught a glimpse of a blonde woman as the tinted window rolled up.

"Ms. Tatiana, I trust you've had a few good days."

"Mike, what happened to your eye?"

Mike turned away for a moment.

"Slipped in the shower. Walked into a door. Nothing serious."

He reached into his jacket pocket. Mila flinched. A reassuring smile crossed his face.

"Mr. Lister asked me to give you this."

In his hand was a small envelope. Mila took it from him, holding his finger for a moment as she kept his gaze.

"Mike, be more careful, okay?"

She could feel a card key and the envelope indicated room 1014. She pocketed the key and turned to head for the door.

"Please have a good night, Ms. Tatiana."

His voice made her stop. His face was genuine, nearly mournful. She faced him, rose up on her toes, placed her hands on his broad shoulders and pulled him down to her, bringing him to her level.

"Thank you Mike," she whispered, "you're sweet."

She kissed him under the assaulted eye and patted his cheek gently with the palm of her hand.

"Why are you with him? With John?" she asked.

"I could ask the same of you."

"Two people who know better, right?"

"Uh, huh."

"Good night Mike."

"See you soon I hope, Miss."

"Me too Mike."

Mila walked through the door held open by the bellman and went to the tenth floor. She entered the room quietly, uncertain if John would be waiting. The room was a one bedroom suite and both the sitting room and the bedroom were empty. The only sign that anyone had been there was a single white Calla Lily in a crystal vase on the bedside table, a note at its base.

I have a surprise for you! See you at 7 p.m..

Mila hung up her coat. She unpacked her suitcase and left her evening clothes on the bed; a maroon corset, black lace thong and matching stockings and garters. She considered the two pairs of shoes she had brought, new black suede platforms or black stilettos. Either would be an erotic surprise. She took a small, intricately carved ironwood box with a brass clasp about the size of a paperback novel that contained her toys and protection and put it in the drawer of the bedside table.

She considered having another smoke but there were signs everywhere thanking her for not doing so. She popped a piece of Nicorette into her mouth. It was acrid and she spat it out immediately. She stepped out of her street clothes, folding them in the dresser drawer. She turned the shower to its hottest setting and let the water beat down on her, ruining the little make-up she had on. The tension that had built up in her shoulders began to dissipate. She took some soap and brought it to her face to breathe in its scent. It was sandalwood and reminded her of Hooshang. He was forever offering perfume and oils he knew from Persia: sandalwood, myrtle and orange blossom. She closed her eyes and wished away the image of him wrapped in the shroud slowly being covered by handfuls of earth. She was ashamed of how she had behaved.

She stepped out of the shower and wrapped herself in a heavy white terrycloth robe and attended to her damp hair and make-up. She made her eyes more dramatic than usual, painting them dark and lengthening her lashes. It made her lids feel heavy but she loved the visual. She dried her hair and put it into a braid that trailed off to the side. She was eager to show off the additional work she had done on her Phoenix. She put on the clothes John had requested. The stockings were easy and she enjoyed the feeling of the tight fish nets against her skin. The corset took longer, the cinching of the laces more difficult than she remembered. The last thing she did was place a black silk choker around her neck. She admired herself in the mirror, the epitome of the courtesan, prepared for her client.

She rewrapped herself in the robe and lay down on the bed, the pillow gently cradling her head. It was 5:15 p.m and she shut her eyes.

It was a soft knock on the door that woke her. The lights of the city shone through the sheers. There was a second knock on the door, tentative but more insistent. Mila got up, adjusted the robe so that a glimpse of the crimson lace was visible. She walked as quietly as she could to the door ready to fling it open for John.

"Is that you, Hun?" she asked.

The clock on the bedside table read 8:32 p.m.

"You're late. How shall I punish you, you bad boy?"

There was no answer.

On her tip toes, she peered through the peep hole and saw a comely young woman, about her age, looking back at her, her face bulging in the fish eye lens. Mila covered herself and opened the door a crack, leaving the safety chain on.

"May I help you?"

"Hi... Uh... Oh, this is awkward. Are you uh... Are you Tatiana?"

"I am. Who are you?"

"Uh... Well, uh, John, he sent me. He sends his regrets."

"Sorry, you know John?"

"Yes, he's my... my dad, my father. I'm Lily. He had to leave. I live around the corner. He asked me to come by. May I come in?"

"Yes... No... Wait downstairs... .In the lobby. Gimme five."

Mila shut the door and grabbed her phone from the bedside table. She was going to check Tatiana's email but saw a text was waiting for her. It was sent at 5:53 p.m.

Had to run. Emergency. Needed to leave the country. Wheels up at 6 p.m. Someone will see you with the envelope. So sorry.

She knew he was already in the air and but she replied anyhow.

Your fucking daughter! RU Serious? You bastard!

She dressed in her street clothes, her lingerie and stockings thrown in a pile on the floor next to the dresser. Mila slid her feet into her boots, not bothering to put on her socks. She crudely wiped the rouge off of her cheeks and the crimson from her mouth. She left her eye makeup alone. It would take too long to remove. She untied her braid and left her hair loose, concealing her tattoo. She slipped on her pea coat, wrapped Caroline's scarf around her neck, and donned a black longshoreman's cap to keep her hair out of her eyes. Mila grabbed a hundred in twenties from her wallet, stuffed them along with her card-key deep inside her coat pocket and headed for the elevator.

She found Lily in the lounge area at a small round cocktail table with a glass of water in front of her, a twist of lime submerged beneath the two inches of ice. Her red wool overcoat was unbuttoned but still on her shoulders, her hands on her knees, legs tucked under the chair, back rigid. She was looking at her drink, swirling the ice with a stir stick, trying to fish the lime to the surface, trying to act calm. Her hands trembled she picked up the glass and put it down with taking a sip. Mila strode over but did not sit down.

"Hello, again," said Mila.

"Hello," said Lily.

"Let's go for a walk. We can talk."

"Okay... Yes."

They left through the main entrance. Only one of the Escalades was still there. As they walked by, Mila could see the two silhouetted heads, obscured by tinted glass. The forms followed them. Mila was sure that if Mike were in there, he would have rolled down the window.

"Don't worry," said Lily. "They're not his. Some other hotshot's around."

Mila fell into step with Lily but remained silent. She had no idea where to begin. She reached into her pocket and took out two of the maple candies and offered one to Lily. They sucked on them as they walked in silence. After four blocks, Lily spoke.

"I came here to get away, you know," she said, her choked voice just above a whisper. "He promised to leave me alone, that they would. That I wouldn't have to see him. He lied."

"Most men do."

"You're not the first. You're older than the others. I mean, there's a smaller age gap between you."

Mila nodded. To her, the gap was a chasm. Lily could have been her kid sister by a year or two.

"I've known your Dad for about three, four years I guess."

"Don't call him that. He's just John to me."

"Sorry."

"He talks about you sometimes. You're pretty. Sorry, that was random."

Mila did not reply.

"Don't worry, I know who you are. It's okay. I have money but I've done the same as you."

"You're an escort?"

"Okay. No. I'm not, but I tolerate his shit because he's a means to an end. I know I sound spoiled, but I need to cut... to cut it all off."

"You need your independence. I get it."

"My parents have this bizarre arrangement. John has you and Mom has Ernesto or Federico, whoever, in Miami. At social functions where they wield influence, we present the traditional happy family. You know, Brooks Brothers' LBD, satin pumps and string of pearls. I try not to embarrass them but don't often succeed. They spend the evening working the room, sucking up to people from whom they want something or making sure anyone under their thumb doesn't squirm away. Everyone's chattel."

"He's dependent upon Mom, you know. He may have gone to UCC and Queen's but his real success is because of her at the Yacht Club. No way a punk like him ever would have made it off the clerk's desk if Mom hadn't slept with him after some Christmas party. He was better looking then and ambitious. Mom was bored with the North Toronto puffs chasing her at the racquet club."

"He got Mom pregnant and to make matters right, he proposed. My grandpa tried to dissuade her. He described her choice as a life-limiting move. He said her problem could be fixed. Thanks Grandpa."

"The wedding was a joke. I saw the photos. They got married in a grand ceremony at the Timothy Eaton Memorial Church. His side was vacant save for a single pew. Hers was filled to beyond capacity, spilling over at the back over to his. Four months later, me and Alison were welcomed into this world..." Lily trailed off. "Great start, eh? Tatiana. That's not your real name, is it?"

"No, it's not," replied Mila.

"Didn't think so. They never are."

Mila kept quiet.

"I'll call you Ana. Tatiana makes me think of some doomed aristocrat."

Lily looked at Mila.

"Are you doomed?"

"I hope not," said Mila half laughing.

"I'm not sure yet. Don't get me wrong. Please don't think of me as a trust fund bitch too stupid to realize the plenty that's been provided. I worry for nothing. Still, I need to get away."

"You need to own your life."

"Yeah, I've had everything given to me and yet I've nothing. I'm lost. I'm managing... poorly. I need something else. Why do you see him?"

The question caught Mila off guard.

"Like you, he's a means to an end. That end is much the same as yours; freedom to do what I choose, how I choose."

"Ana," she said looking down the street, "John's a bad person. He's done things. He doesn't know I know, but I do. I've seen papers, contracts with names of people he doesn't know... whispered phone calls with Tim and Val."

"I've heard of them."

"I've caught fleeting images of text messages when I've barged into his study. He's not fast enough to shut down the mail when I come 'round his desk."

"Really?"

"I suspect you've been to my house. I caught him once with someone else. You've been there, haven't you?"

Mila nodded.

"I used to care, but I don't anymore. At least you're over eighteen."

Mila's stomach churned.

"I snuck into his office once go on YouTube and check out some movies my friends had posted. My computer wasn't working, the wireless connection was fried or something. He'd left the house just after his cell phone rang. Probably one of his..."

"Prostitutes?" said Mila.

"Companions," said Lily as if it did not apply to Mila. "He has access to sites he shouldn't. Government stuff."

"I've seen that too."

"I heard the chirp as the front door opened. Usually, I'd hear the car and the garage door and I'd have time to run. He must have left the car in the driveway. I tried to shut down the computer and hide. You know the office. There's nowhere but the closet. I got in just as he opened the office door. His chair was pushed back. In my haste, I forgot to tuck it in as he always did. He sat down at the computer. Typed a few strokes and cursed. He walked over to the closet and he punched through the veneer. His hand was over my head, blood dripping. He pulled back and light came through the jagged circle he had made. He stood in front of the door, silent. I was paralyzed."

"He stood there, just breathing. Underneath the bottom of the door, I could see his shoes and blood. He crouched down on his haunches. I heard his knees crack. He whispered, 'Never again, Lil', never again.' Then he walked out. I could hear the water running in the bathroom and then the tearing of towels that he must have used as a bandage. He walked back into the office and grabbed something from his desk. I heard the door slam followed by the electronic charm. I opened the door and the room was empty. The computer was gone. He didn't come back for three days. I left for boarding school the next week. It was planned anyhow but I persuaded my mom to go earlier."

Mila corralled Lily back to the hotel. They had been walking for almost two hours and she was feeling the strain of the evening. The SUV was gone.

"Goodnight then, I guess?" said Mila.

Mila turned to enter the hotel. Lily grabbed her arm.

"Ana, wait. I forgot. He wanted you to have this."

Lily reached into her coat and handed a thick envelope to Mila. She knew it was her usual fee for an overnight outside of Toronto.

Lily stepped forward and gave Mila a tight hug, the kind teenage girls give to their best friends. Mila stood rigid, gradually reciprocating, her hands resting lightly on Lily's back.

"I know this is weird," whispered Lily not letting go.

"You should never have met me. No daughter should. No daughter should ever know their father like this."

"He ceased being my father years ago." Lily paused "Ana, be careful."

Mila let her go to look at her.

"I will. You're going to be okay?"

"I think... I'll be fine."

"Just be yourself."

"Like you."

"No Lily, like you."

"I'll be fine, Ana" Lily said.

"Lily, My name is... my name's Mila."

"Thank you, Mila."

"Goodnight Lily."

Mila entered the hotel. There was no sign of Mike or any of John's other guys. The elevator took her directly to her floor without having to push a selection.

She entered her room. It was untouched. Her clothes were still in the same pile. The pillow was still creased from where she had lain while waiting for John.

She bolted the lock but she still felt uncomfortable. She struggled with the sofa but was able to push it in front of the door, snug against the jam. No one was getting in. No more surprises tonight.

Mila checked her phone. There was no text nor email from John.

Mila set the alarm on her phone for 4:45 a.m. and then she called the front desk to ask for a wake-up call at the same time should she sleep through it. She reckoned she could get the first plane on standby.

Exhausted, she quickly packed her bags.

She pulled a plastic laundry bag from the closet from a hanger and picked up the garments she had worn for John's benefit, feeling the darts of the corset through the plastic.

She went to the bedside table, opened the drawer and emptied the contents of the box as well before pulling the drawstring tight. She slid it all under the sink too big to fit into the garbage can.

Mila stripped naked and slid under the covers, enjoying the coolness of the soft sheets against her skin. She shut her eyes.

Her mind screamed to know more but her body demanded rest. A minute later, her breathing was heavy and even, her sub-conscience processing the evening's events.

In what seemed like seconds, Mila was jarred awake by the ringing of the telephone. Her alarm rang seconds later. Her mind began to race. Was last night real?

She turned on the bedside lamp. The couch still propped up against the door.

Mila contemplated a shower but skipped it. She had little time before she needed to find a cab to take her to the airport.

She removed the eye make-up she had neglected the night before, staring into the mirror. She was unsure of what to think of the woman who was looking back. She barely recognized herself without the make-up. She dressed in the same clothes she had worn the previous night.

Mila heaved the sofa out of the way, not quite returning it to its original spot. Its lightness surprised her.

She grabbed her luggage, thought of the plastic bag and its contents for a moment and made her way downstairs.

The street was deserted save for a waiting cab which she hailed with a curt whistle. There were no SUVs, no Mike to offer a hand. She had an hour-and-a-half to make the first flight back to Toronto. She might even be able to catch her evening class.

25

Vitaly put on his coat and sheepishly informed his secretary that he was heading off to lunch. It was a white lie. It was a quiet day in the office for a change and he knew he needed to chase away the paper tigers.

The two dockets before the court this week were ready. Maiwen was doing research on one of the new cases. Brian was out at some training course. Paul had called in sick. The Leafs had played the night before and Paul had attended it with a buddy from Kingston. Derek had taken the day off to look a china patterns with his fiancee.

He went downstairs and walked briskly through the PATH. He was amazed at the number of people passing through the underground warren.

"Shouldn't they be at work?" he thought to himself. "This is what life looks like."

It took him ten minutes to reach his athletic club. He had five minutes to make the spinning class.

While confident in his strength, Vitaly was unsure of his endurance. He opened his locker and took out his gear. It was all covered in a fine layer of dust. Sheepishly, he shook them out.

As he dressed, the triathlon group boasted about their 200 kilometers weekend rides. This hour-long class would be a mere sprint for them.

He joined them, heading upstairs, filling his water bottle on the way. Hip hop was already blaring from the speakers. It was Mila's music. He hated it then and he hated it now.

The room was almost full with people either adjusting their bikes or rolling along already at a leisurely pace.

Three tiers of bikes were arranged in a semicircle around the leader's and oversized fans were already moving air with such force that Vitaly was relieved it was not a real headwind.

He made his way to one of the few remaining bikes in the back of the room. There were empty saddles in the front row but he dared not go there, not wanting anyone to see him flagging as the hour wore on. There was a guy to his left and a free bike on the other side. He took a few minutes to adjust the bike.

An enthusiastic instructor bounded into the class, headset already on, and she spoke over the cacophony of whirling wheels and jarring music. She encouraged people to introduce themselves to their neighbours.

Vitaly turned left and greeted a guy named James and then he turned right. The bike was now occupied. The woman was tall and slim, a brunette. She was still talking to the woman next to her. Vitaly waited as the instructor began to give the details of the ride. The woman finally turned to Vitaly and over the instructor's voice, said with a smile that disappeared instantly.

"Hi, I'm Isabella, and I'm not interested."

"Okay... Hi, I'm Vitaly," he said, "and who said I was?"

Vitaly turned back to face the instructor, wishing he had headphones to drown out the world around him.

For 45 minutes, the instructor took them up and down imaginary hills and until they finally reached the warm down. The music softened somewhat and he heard a voice from his right.

"I'm sorry for being so rude earlier. I saw you make a beeline for the bike. I just assumed that you were like all the guys here."

"I'm not like any of the guys here. I'm too embarrassed about being seen as dogging it, so I wanted to hide at the back."

"Me too," Isabella laughed.

The instructor had everyone cool down and in a few minutes they dismounted. Isabella left as most of the class emptied the room. Vitaly stayed behind with a few diehards to do core strength work. Mats were rolled out and in 15 minutes, the instructor had everyone begging for mercy.

Vitaly was the last to leave, helping the instructor put everything away, and then following her out.

Isabella was waiting, white towel around her neck, looking at him through the window in the door.

She handed him a fresh towel.

"Again, my apologies. Can I buy you lunch? I'll see you at the reception desk in 15."

"Okay, yes," said Vitaly a little stunned.

Vitaly waited a few moments, figuring out what just happened and bounded downstairs to shower.

When he met her in the lobby, she had two plastic containers with sandwich wraps. A juice and chocolate milk were balanced on top of each. Her hair was still wet, pulled back across her skull and ending in a tight braid. Vitaly wondered what her hair would look like in the evening.

"Tuna or tuna?" she asked.

"Hmm... the fish, thanks."

She handed him the carton of chocolate milk. "Follow-me."

They rode the elevator in silence to the ground floor. Vitaly thought she was going to take him to the food court but instead she led him up some stairs. His legs groaned with each of the thirty steps as he followed her.

"More exercise. Is this a test?"

In heels, she seemed not to notice the steps at all. He'd seen the stainless steel staircase before but never bothered to climb it, his curiosity never piqued, always too pressed to get back to the office.

They led to a large platform with thirty or so freestanding display cases, each containing Inuit soapstone sculpture. They could be viewed from all sides and were illuminated separately with every form and hollow highlighted. Isabella sat down at the bench in the middle of the space. They were alone.

"Do you mind if I take a quick look around?"

"No, not at all."

"I've never seen such a large collection. It's lovely."

"That's why I brought you here."

"To see if I was just interested in money?"

"Kinda."

"I'm pretty shallow, ya know," he said as he walked away. "I could be."

As he examined the glass cases, she had caught him watching her a few times through the glass as she began to eat.

"Courage!" he said to himself quietly. "She's just another person. Just talk. She won't bite."

After a few minutes, he sat down and took out his wrap.

"It's wonderful, isn't it?" she asked.

"Thank you for showing me this."

"I love it here," she said. "Okay, so, who are you?"

She had caught him mid-bite. Vitaly chewed frantically and swallowed.

"I'm...Vitaly... Mirkin."

"Isabella Tournimenko. Everyone calls me Boomer."

His eyes darted over her face. Vitaly was stunned by her beauty but he was uncertain which eye to focus on.

"I know," she said, crinkling up her nose. "My eyes... weird."

"No, just stunning."

She blushed.

"It's easier to look at just one of them."

"Thanks for bringing me here. I never knew it existed."

"This, it's my oasis in an ocean of deceit."

Vitaly had noticed her Blackberry had buzzed five times while they ate. She had not answered a single message but he could see she was becoming antsy.

He considered offering her the opportunity to answer, but didn't, not wanting to lose her to the outside world.

"It's good to have a place to break. So, you're on the street? What are you? Lawyer, trader or Indian chief?"

"Vitaly, that's lame. I'm a tech analyst for a hedge fund. How the Hell I ended up here, I'll never know. You?"

He considered using Benny's made up company when he met Kent. "I am one of the troika, a lawyer involved in capital markets."

"That's only partially true, isn't it, Vitaly? Great photo in the paper by the way."

"Ah, my superhero cover is blown. No more dirty old phone booths."

"Saving the world from Solomon Grundy?"

"Something like that. I work in regulation services."

"That's okay. Somebody has to babysit the children. Who knows what mischief they might get up to otherwise?"

"So I.T. covers I.T."

"Lame but a little cute too."

"I thought everyone grew up wanting to do this," said Vitaly. "It's where the action is."

"No," she said, pointing to herself. "Computer science. Waterloo undergrad, Stanford Masters, doctorate from EPITA in France."

"Wow!"

"My thesis: Algorithmes de routage et transfert dans les réseaux securitaires sans fils aux ressources limitées."

To his ears, her French was unaccented, beautiful and flawless. He did not understand a word.

"Sorry. My Russian is better than my French."

"Расчет машрутизации и передачи данных для беспроводных сетей с ограниченными возможностями.."

"Okay," he said with a laugh. "Now you're bugging me. Let me try...routing and transfer calculations for wireless networks with limited capacity."

"Close enough. Routing with encryption."

"You break encryptions? I mean, while the data routes over WiFi? That'd freak me out."

Isabella paused a moment.

"Do you always look at the dark side of everything?"

"Two sides to every coin, no?"

"My research was focused on the encryption, to ensure security. But yes, I need to test it too. Anything encrypted can be broken it. You just need the password."

"Abracadabra?"

"Something like that. Really, it is about controlling the access point."

"Ah..." he said, "And now I'm just pretending I have the slightest idea of what that means. So, how did you end up here, on the Street?"

Her Blackberry danced for the sixth time and then chimed a Zen like gong.

She picked up the device and read the message. Her lips moved as she read. Vitaly smiled. It was endearing.

She was in her late twenties, clearly brilliant, yet she read like Mila used to when she was small.

Isabella glanced at her watch and got up from the bench, stuffing her device in her bag at the same time.

"I'm sorry. Gotta go. The children are calling."

"Will you tell it to me sometime, your story?"

"Yes. I will see you again Vitaly."

It was a command, not a question.

She bent over and kissed him on the cheek.

Then, She reached into her shoulder bag fished out a card and a pen.

She wrote hastily a number on it and gave it to him. She hurried to the far end of the gallery and down the stairs.

"I hope to see you again ," said Vitaly, as she left.

He turned over the card. It read:

Isabella (I. M.) Tournimenko

Senior Analyst

Lister Asset Management

it@lam.com

"Holy shit," he said to himself, looking around to make sure no one had noticed him. "LAM."

He turned the card over.

it@me.com

Write me!

26

Dear Tatiana:

I really should apologize. You are surely angry with me. It was terrible thing do to you and to Lily. I had to leave the country to try to help someone in need. I'll explain the next time we meet.

I am glad, though, that you met Lily. She's wonderful. I'm so proud of her. She seems so happy in her new city! So free to explore who she is and will be. I'm envious.

In meeting Lily, you know more about me than ever before. I'm a father and a spouse as I'm still married to Lily's mother. Lily surely provided details of our sordid charade. Lily's mother and I manage our relationship poorly. We've found a balance. Our lives are a mockery of our promise. We made choices a long time ago. We live with them daily.

I know that love is not at the base of our relationship. I'm not that naive. I'm hopeful for friendship and compassion, but I'm under no illusions. I do care about you. I do think of your future. I imagine where you will be when you are a girlfriend, wife, mother and grandmother, of how you will live, of what you will live for and of how you will put all of this behind you.

John was jolted by the thud of the blue and yellow Nerf football bouncing off the glass of his office. He looked from his laptop to the trading floor where Tim was balancing in his desk chair. John read Tim's lips.

"Watch this!"

Tim turned and whipped the ball at the US equity trader, Oscar Geistermann. John knew what was next.

Tim and Oscar had been at each other for weeks. The row had started over one of them taking the last doughnut brought in by brokers. Three days ago, Oscar had reprogrammed the speed-dial keys on Tim's phone to call mortuaries around Toronto. It took

Tim's assistant a good part of the morning to re-input his contacts. Tim had missed the opening of the markets and numerous trades.

Yesterday, during the traders meeting, Tim's assistant crazy-glued Oscar's blackberry and the contents of his wallet to the trading desk; his credit cards, his driver's license, photos, including those of his wife and son.

John liked Tim's imagination but was not pleased that he had slipped out of the office early to avoid the consequences. You have to have the guts to be present and take your lumps.

It took Oscar's immediate supervisor two hours and four pitchers of beer to calm him down.

This morning's row was over the allocation of a new stock that had just come to the market that was up 20 per cent. It was a US issue and so naturally should fall under Oscar's purview, but Tim wanted it reflected in his book.

It had gone far enough and the fun was now interfering with business. John knew he needed to intervene today and get them to take it down a peg or five. He'd bring in beer and pizza for lunch.

Tim turned towards Oscar, screaming at the top of his lungs, spittle projecting from his lips, his head crimson. The glass partition did not mute his volume. "Share the trade! Don't be such a fucking..."

"What?" Oscar hollered, "A Jew!"

"You said it. Not me."

Tim ducked just as a stainless steel water bottle sailed past, striking Tim's trading assistant in the face, shattering her glasses and knocking her to the floor. Blood gushed from her forehead.

Tim looked at her and threw his phone back at Oscar.

A second later, Oscar's chair went flying by, narrowly missing Tim but knocking his array of six computer screens off the desk on to the floor.

"Strike!" came a booming voice.

Sparks shot from the screens and they began to smoke.

Instantly Tim and Oscar were on each other, a jumble of arms and legs, fingers scratching, fists missing their targets.

The whole trading floor erupted, half cheering them on and half reaching for their phones to film the fight.

Only Yvonne tended to the bleeding woman.

John knew this would never stay quiet. He stayed in his office for a moment, hovering the cursor over the send button. He took a breath and saved the email as a draft.

27

Caroline was nervous and hopeful as she travelled on the subway to the ballet. She always felt a bit awkward in public transit, dressed too beautifully for the underground sewer.

She got off at Osgoode Station and walked up the stairs to the box office, her heels clicking on the tiled steps. A few patrons were milling about, but the entrance and the lobby were mostly empty.

Caroline stepped outside for a breath of fresh air to calm her nerves and after greeting a few friends distractedly and that went to the box office for the third time.

"Still no one, Caroline," said Felecia from behind the glass partition of the box office.

"You're sure? For Mila Mirkin."

"Let me check."

Felicia leafed through a stack of white envelopes in a box and held one up.

"See, still here," she said, "but it's early. I'm sure she'll come."

"Thanks," said Caroline dejectedly. "Cheers."

"Enjoy the show."

Caroline made her way through the glass-enclosed lobby and started up the beech colored stairs. She loved this building. To her, it was the archetype of what a contemporary ballet house should be.

She moved into a broad amphitheater, that had wide steps that acted as seats for the adult and giant treads for the children, most of whom were too antsy to stay put.

The patrons were beginning to gather for the pre-performance talk. It was usually a banal discussion of the history and meaning of the evening's performance.

From her perch on the steps, Caroline watched for the arrival of the patrons, scanning for her friend. It was 7 p.m., half an hour before curtain.

The gongs rang calling the patrons to their seats and Caroline followed the streaming crowds hoping to see Mila's blue locks. Resigned, she did one last scan of the sidewalk below and walked up the back of the amphitheater to her level, hoping that Mila had slipped past her. When she arrived at her row, the seat was empty.

Caroline sat down and listened with anticipation as the orchestra tuned their instruments and held a pause for what seemed to be longer than normal. Caroline barely felt a velvet glove tentatively slip over her hand, fingers interlacing with her own. Caroline could feel Mila's ring through the fabric. It pinched her as squeezed her hand.

She turned as the last of the lights dimmed. Mila held up her index finger to Caroline's lips and smiled.

"There will be time to talk, my sweet."

They turned toward the stage as the music began, their hands clasped during the whole of the first act. Not a whisper was uttered until the curtain fell at intermission.

"You know here is not the place," said Mila. "Shall we go?"

"Yes. Go."

They gathered their coats and walked down the stairs to the main floor, crossed Queen Street and began to walk up University, still hand in hand.

They both held their free hands at the collars, trying to keep out the evening cold.

The clouds were buzzing overhead and to the south, sheet lightning flashed across the sky followed by an ominous rumble.

Caroline half expected a curtain of water to be moving up University Avenue ready to engulf them.

Mila broke the silence.

"How's Marc?"

"Marc? Ah...We're going through the motions. There's just less and less for us. We're scraping by but the joy...."

Caroline trailed off.

"The joy?"

"The joy is gone."

"I see," said Mila.

She let her words hang.

"He's starting a job in Vancouver in September," continued Caroline. "He asked me to join him."

The air left Mila's lungs. Her grip on Caroline's hand slackened.

"Are you gonna go?"

"Don't know. I'm not sure what's out there for us. Or for me."

With her free hand, Caroline reached into her coat pocket and pulled out the card Mila had left for her months before. It was creased and the kiss smudged.

"Ask away," said Mila.

"I don't know where to begin."

"Then I will. I'm still the Mila you knew when you were my teacher. I still love my family, my parents and brother. I love to dance. And I love you."

"And I..."

"Please, this is hard. I'm still in school and getting straight A's. I have a research internship and I'm going to be published. I'm planning on going to Columbia University in Manhattan to do my Masters and a Doctorate in Psychology. I still dance, more contemporary now than ballet. I know I'm taking on too much, too much to balance. You know me. I'm always doing that."

"You always find an equilibrium where others couldn't."

"You taught me that."

Mila paused and let out a deep breath.

"Okay. I'm an escort, a courtesan if that's more polite. I left home four years ago, not because I was forced but 'cause I needed to. I needed the challenge. I needed to challenge myself."

"You left home to start that?"

"No. I didn't seek this. I never expected it. You know I worked at Ki, right? Pretty boring stuff, slinging drinks, making sure the skirt is short enough. For the most part, it was dreadful. Investment bankers and lawyer types blowing off steam from the week, hitting on me like I was the last woman on earth. They wouldn't even bother trying to hide their rings. One night though, this guy was sitting at the corner of the bar, drinking with his buddies. All night long, I caught him smiling at me but he'd always turned away shyly. After his friends left, he stayed on his stool. It was a bit of a slow night, so we talked. Instead of the usual monosyllabic banter I would give, I responded. It felt natural. He started ordering these increasingly complicated drinks just to piss me off. But you know me, I like a challenge. Near the end of my shift, he suggested he take me home for a nightcap. It was his turn to wait on me he said, he'd quadruple my evening's tips if I did. I never took him seriously. As I said, he was charming and it'd been a long time since I had any...uh...fun. I thought why not."

"We spent the rest of the night on his balcony over looking downtown, listening to the hum of the city and at sunrise we moved to his bedroom. It was good and gentle. In the morning light, we had breakfast on the balcony where we had spent the night. Only then did I realized that I overlooking Vitaly's building. He was two floors lower. As we sat warming ourselves in the morning sun, he slid an envelope across the table and said, 'For your time and for your studies.' He asked me to see him again in a month. I still thought it was a joke. I thanked him and pocketed it, thinking it might be monopoly money. As I rode down in the elevator after leaving him, I opened it up. There were 20 reds."

"A thousand?"

"Yup. I saw him twice more before he was reassigned to London. He flew me over once. It was awkward though, clearly he was moving on in his life. I suspected he had found a real love or at a minimum a local girl. Anyhow, soon he stopped emailing me."

"You didn't love him, did you?"

"Oh God no, but the attention felt good."

"So?"

"Money was tight. Ki was super slow and I didn't want to run home. I read in *Toronto Life* the story of a high end Toronto escort. I contacted an agency the next day. The madam gave me the ridiculous name when I told her my background. Apparently, men like the exotic."

"Mila, you explained the how. But why?"

"It allows me to be free."

"Free?"

"Yes. Free. To do what I want."

"What you have, it's not freedom."

Mila bit her lip and looked down at her feet for a moment.

"Next question."

"When will you get out?

"When I've had enough and can move onto grad school. Two years...for sure by then."

"Are you safe? Is anyone making you do this?"

"No one's making me do this. There's no creepy pimp lurking in the shadows. I choose to do this as a means to an end. My end is freedom, grad school in the US, and a job, a real job, a life, a real life with a partner and, who knows, children. These are all the things you talk about. All the things you want, I want them too."

"Do you carry protection?"

"Birth control or mace?

"Either, I guess?"

"Yes, on both counts. Condoms and a diaphragm. I can't take the pill. Gives me scary high blood pressure. My monthly migraines were like a thousand times more intense and would last days longer. I'd be bed ridden and the slightest amount of light would burn through my skull. Oh, and bear spray. Mace is illegal. It's all in my little black bag."

"Caroline, I never, ever do anything against my will. The men I see, they're not dangerous. They're well-mannered, educated. When I was at the agency, about half were single, young alpha-males with no life but work, tons of money and no one to spend it on but themselves. The married guys mostly only want some companionship. Sometimes, I don't even get physical with them. It's sad. They want someone to talk to. Often, we'd just chill, talk and have a few drinks, never drugs. They would take me under their wings and showing me new things. I listen. I'm their diversion. Right now I'm down to just a few clients. One of them is named John. Kinda funny, no?"

Caroline did not smile.

"How much do you make?"

She couldn't believe she was even asking.

"Pardon?"

"How much to buy your time?"

"At the agency, they charged the client two-hundred-and-fifty an hour for my time. They took a thirty per cent cut for booking. When I started out on my own, I asked for donations of three-fifty to four-fifty an hour, depending upon what they wanted me to do. I could work two shifts at the bar and not make anywhere near that. I now have a few regular clients. For the most part, I'm on retainer. They each pay me two-thousand to five-thousand a month regardless of if I see them. Lately, the numbers have dwindled down further and I'm considering cutting the list to only one. I'm there when he needs me but I can set my schedule and choose when I see him," she lied. "The most I ever made was thirty-thousand over four days."

"Thirty grand! Four days! That's more than I make in half a year. Was it a good weekend?"

"Uh-huh. It was amazing. He was a music exec. We flew in his private jet to Iceland, to Reykjavík, and we partied all weekend. We hiked an active volcano and went whale watching. It was the summer solstice."

"Daisies in your hair and everything?"

"And we danced and danced. I watched the sun never set. I meet Bjork."

"No kidding."

"At the cafe where we grabbed our morning coffee. She was so cool. He said it was a coincidence but I know he'd set it up. It was so understated. It was like a fairy tale."

"Fairy tale!" Caroline shook her head, "More like a nightmare. Is there anything you wouldn't do?"

"I'm not going to answer that. I'm always safe. I have boundaries. Next question."

"Even if a guy is paying you thousands per month?"

"Especially if a guy is paying me that much. Don't you see? I control the relationship. The more they want me, the more I can charge. I'm not just a quick lay."

They were now walking around Queen's Park Circle, still hand in hand.

"Most of them are just looking to connect in a way they can't with other people."

"It's not just physical?"

"Sure, it's physical but that only takes a small part of the time, sometimes not at all."

"Did you ever get attached, to a client I mean?"

"With the really kind ones, I chose not to separate myself fully. It's still a business though."

"What then?"

"Caroline, I know it's artificial, but when they listen, I mean, really listen, it's comforting."

"This isn't *Pretty Woman*."

"Actually, sometimes it can be. A girl at the agency did have that ending. He called on her at first like every other client. He'd just sit and talk and she'd listen. She would make a move to start the usual encounter, but he'd hold her off. He paid attention to her, to everything she said. Soon, he started inviting her to travel with him and she'd have to initiate the sex. It wasn't a fetish thing. There was an odd innocence she said. He wanted a companion who accepted him for how he was. He accepted her thorns. He snipped them off, one by one, till her had his rose. When he asked her, she said yes. They're in Paris with two kids, twin boys."

"I'm not sure what to think. I've images of you, naked, doing...things, pretending to be something your not. Were you never repulsed?"

"At first, when I worked for the agency, some were disgusting, smelly slobs. Now, most times, they're impeccable and treat me really well. Better than most dates I've been on. They would hold doors, make sure I was safe. There'd be unexpected gifts."

"Is that all it takes to have you?"

Mila dropped Caroline's hand for the first time since they left the ballet. She walked on, Caroline half a step behind.

"No. None of them have me, but some of them really listen. They would remember details, ideas I only shared once. My thoughts mean something to them."

"Really. To what end? So they can create an illusion of a bond."

Mila was silent.

"Mila, who knows?"

"What? I haven't made a mistake, have I? I trust you. I trust you not to judge. You...you can't judge me! What do you want to hear? Do you want to say it? Is that it? Somehow if I scream it at the top of my lungs, it be cathartic. That I'd stop?"

She took a deep breath and looked Caroline in the eye. She loved those eyes, their kindness but in the dark of Queen's Park, they had changed.

"What do you want to hear? That I blow 'em and I fuck 'em. Is that what you want? I fuck for money. Does that make you feel better? Does it?"

Mila looked down and stuffed her hands in her pockets.

Caroline did not move. She looked down onto the top of Mila's head. She could see the white of her scalp underneath her dyed raven locks. She followed the blue streak from the top of her head to where it curled under her chin. She allowed her fingers to follow it and rested her palm on Mila's shoulder.

"I don't feel bad about myself ever."

"Can't you see what this is doing to you? These people don't love you. They love themselves. They love themselves so much that they refuse to see the harm they're causing you."

"Sometimes... sometimes they make me feel special."

"You're always special. Can't you see that? They don't care about you. You're a passing fantasy. You're an object to possess and then discard. They treat you like plumbing."

Mila bristled and slapped Caroline hard enough that Caroline turned her face. Caroline stumbled backwards, regained her balance and stood tall in front of Mila.

"Fuck you!" Mila screamed. "Fuck you! You give me this shit. I don't..."

"Mila...I'm sorry..."

"I need you. Can't you see that? I reached out to you at the restaurant but Olive got in the way. Only three other people know. Of course, Papa and Zoya don't know. It'd kill Vitaly and would fuck his career too; *The Prosecutor with the Whore Sister!* Great fuckin' headline."

"I... it's... I love you. I always have."

"I've waited for you."

"You don't need to wait anymore."

Mila lunged forward and kissed Caroline hard, her hands reaching around to the small of her back, their lips closed at first and then they slowly tentatively parted. Their teeth collided. Both smiled, their foreheads resting against one another, their eyes darting back and forth.

After about twenty-seconds, Caroline reached around Mila and pulled her close and embraced her firmly. Mila rested her cheek against Caroline's collarbone, her eyes closed.

"What do we do now?"

"I'm not sure," replied Mila, "but come with me."

Mila took Caroline's hand and they hailed a passing taxi. The lights of the city streamed over their faces in red, yellow and green, the intensity rising and falling as they drove.

Mila took Caroline home.

The apartment was deserted. Mila brought Caroline down the hall, opened the door to her room and turned on the bedside light.

Without a word, she undressed and stood naked, hands at her side, her palms forward. In the dim light, Caroline admired her.

Mila slipped under the covers of her bed facing towards Caroline.

Caroline turned away and undressed. She had never been naked in front of any other woman, at least not with the intention of entering her bed.

Caroline joined Mila under the sheets and pulled them up to her chin.

Mila turned away from Caroline and backed into her until their bodies were spoons.

The contact was soothing, their breathing synchronized.

There were no words.

Caroline lifted Mila's hair and admired her tattoo. She kissed its wings, her tongue flicking across the flames. Caroline placed her hand tentatively on Mila lower back, her fingers reaching forward, caressing the crest of her hip.

Mila guided Caroline's hand up her torso to her breast, her hand cupping Caroline's around it, allowing Caroline to feel its small weight.

Mila brought Caroline's hand to her lips, kissed the base of her wrist and then bit the tips of her finger playfully.

She took Caroline's index and middle fingers deep into her mouth. Caroline let out a soft moan. Mila sucked them, her tongue pressing against the webbing of her fingers.

After a few moments, she directed Caroline to below her navel and let her hand rest against her pubic bone.

Caroline stroked her, her fingers feathering across the smooth, waxed skin.

The light of the lamp illuminated the goosebumps that spread across Mila's shoulders Caroline reached lower, exploring her softness.

Mila gasped and then exhaled slowly. She had been waiting for her touch for years.

28

Mila dreamt that night for the first time in months.

She was at dinner on a patio. On the table were glasses half full, some with wine, others water. A large earthenware salad bowl containing the remnants of the meal that had just been consumed: chicken bones, artichoke leaves, olive pits. Several stacks of plates stood at the far end, utensils piled on top, ready to be removed but everyone was too engrossed in conversation and wine to bother.

Everyone she loved was there: Caroline stroking her back, her parents holding hands, talking to Vitaly. Petr glanced away from the conversation and smiled at Mila, raising his glass in a small toast. She reciprocated and blew a kiss. His eyes showed his happiness at seeing her with Caroline. He returned to listening to Vitaly and Zoya. Her old friend, Olga, and Martha sat on either side of Vitaly, laughing at something Vitaly had said. Martha rested her hand on Vitaly's forearm. Mila felt peace, satisfaction and belonging.

She cradled three empty wine bottles in her arms and went to the kitchen. She opened two more and returned to the table to find one new person seated. Lily was sitting across from Vitaly. No one seemed to have noticed her. She was stone still, her face was drawn and ashen, her shoulders slumped and her hands cradled in her lap. Her long hair was matted against her white cotton blouse. She turned to Mila and opened her mouth. Water and bits of dark seaweed flowed out and down her chin, turning her shirt translucent.

The bottles slipped from Mila's fingers and shattered on the ground. Wine splashed her sandaled feet and broken glass cut into her feet.

The sound of silence rang in Mila's ears. The conversation stopped, frozen, lips parted mid-sentence and mid-laughter. The water that Vitaly was pouring into Martha's cup had turned into an arching, stream of clear glass. Mila ran over as Lily slumped to one side. Her weight was too much and Lily dragged her to the ground.

"Lily, no!" cried Mila as she bent down over her, stroking her hair and the blue-grey skin of her lifeless face.

Her tears fell on Lily's shirt and dissolved into the fabric.

A presence loomed over her. Someone grabbed her wrist and she was wheeled around with such force that she flew off her feet before crashing into the wall of the house, falling hard to the ground. Her lungs screamed for air.

The assailant was in shadow, the head silhouetted by the lamp that hung low over the table. It was a man. He reached down to Mila and caressed her face with the back of his hand, then his fingers slipped around her neck, cupping her larynx, slowly applying more pressure. He turned towards the table.

John.

"They can't hear you. It's just you and me."

Mila could not breathe.

John closed his eyes and leaned forward to kiss her. Mila screamed but no sound came. The glint of metal flashed in John's other hand. He released his grip on her and tore open her shirt, drawing the tip of a blade down her body stopping at her navel. She dared not move. She looked at the table. No one was aware. Everyone was still frozen.

"Just you and me."

The blade pierced her skin. A bead of blood formed around the tip, a thin red rivulet snaked down Mila's abdomen to her groin. John's eyes were wide with delight. Mila struck him again and again, but the blow had no power. Her eyes lost focus.

She clawed at any orifice where her nails could do damage. He did not react as she gouged his eyes, her digits in the sockets. He began to laugh, spat in her face, twisted the knife to its hilt. Now she felt pain, excruciating pain.

He bent forward again and locked his lips on hers, pushing his tongue into her mouth. Mila coughed once. Blood was on his lips.

Caroline was sitting in Mila's lone chair, wrapped in Mila's silk robe, her knees tucked up under her as it was too short for her. She had been watching Mila sleep for half an hour while playing idly with her phone. Something had changed. Mila's mouth opened, her lips pulled back against her teeth, her jaw wide, her back arched and her neck flew up, lifting her torso off the bed for an instant. Mila struck the bed ferociously.

Caroline leapt over onto the bed astride Mila and tried to shake her friend awake, controlling her hands to avoid her strikes.

Mila freed her wrist, lashed out and caught Caroline in the throat. Caroline yelped and regained her grip on Mila's hands.

"Mila, wake up! It's just a dream!"

Caroline slapped her hard.

"Wake up!"

She eyes opened. They were wild. She struggled against Caroline.

"Mila, it's me, your Caroline. You're safe."

Mila eyes darted around the room and settled on Caroline' s face. She forced her breathing to slow, letting out deep breaths through her nose.

Caroline, still astride, let go of her wrists. Mila sat up and threw her arms around Caroline's torso and held her tight, tears streaming down her face, sobs spasming through her body. As they subsided, she lay back on her bed, eyes red and her nose running. She wiped her face with the back of her hand as Caroline held her close.

"Whatever that was...," said Caroline.

"Yeah, it was awful. I'm okay now," Mila said snuggling into her friend, kissing her cheek.

Caroline pushed Mila away and propped herself up on one elbow.

"No, no you're not. Was that the first time?"

"It was scary. It was violent, but it's done. I was alone and I was attacked, but I fought back."

"Do you know who it was? I mean, someone familiar?"

"No."

"Have you had that dream before?"

"That one? No," he had lied again. "Come here. I want to look after you."

Mila pulled Caroline in, wrapping her arm around her mid-section.

"No, it wasn't just a dream. I just want to be sure you make it to where you want to go. What I saw...I wonder if you can handle it."

"Caroline, it was just a dream."

"Was it? Whatever you say to me will always stay with me, you know that, right?"

Mila nodded but said nothing.

"Okay then, I need to know you are safe and I know no other way to do it. I want you to download a peer-to-peer tracking software program called Bonded. Think of me as your angel. I'll be able to see where you are and you can find me when you need me. No-one else can see this."

"But Caroline..."

"No buts. You want me to be part of your life, this is it."

"Do I have a choice?"

"Do you want one?"

"No."

"Good."

29

"Vitaly! Brian!" Paul hollered. "Get in here! Now!"

Vitaly and Brian ran into Paul's office at the same time. Maiwen and Derek were already there.

"Look," said Paul. "On screen. I guess the email worked."

On the computer screen, there was what looked like a balcony with a few chairs and a laptop on a table. The back drop was a verdant canopy that spread into mountains.

"Nice screensaver," said Brian sarcastically.

"What is it?" asked Vitaly.

"Wade! The guy in Costa Rica," said Derek. "He'll be back in a moment. He's getting a beer."

A few moments later a shaggy man with a Toronto Maple Leafs baseball cap sat down in the chair and took a long pull from a bottle.

"Pura Vida!"

"Henry Wade?

"Well, big surprise. You found me," Henry said.

"Mr. Wade, a pleasure to make your..." said Vitaly

"The name's Henry, Vitaly," he interrupted. "Don't bother with the pleasantries or introductions. I know who you all are: Paul, Maiwen, Brian and the newly engaged Derek."

Brian spoke first.

"Do you mind if I record this?"

"Sure thing detective. Knock your socks off."

Brain handed his cellphone to Derek to videotape the screen.

"Great. I need ask you a few preliminaries," Brian began,

"Please state your full name and address?"

"For Christ's sake, Brian, are you serious?"

"We need to do this right. I know this is boring. Please just answer the questions."

"You're pissing me off," he said and taking another long pull from his beer. "Okay, Henry Arnold James Wade, La Fortuna, Costa Rica."

"How long did you work for Lister Asset Management?"

"Seven years, two months for LAM and its predecessor."

"When did you start?"

"January 2003."

"What position did you hold?

"Last role, CCO."

"Chief Compliance Officer. Correct?"

"Yes."

"Before that?"

"Analyst, hired by John, John Lister, CEO of LAM. Covered wireless companies. Did that for two years. We bought RX Wireless based on my recommendation. Later on he wanted me to look at applications in remote upgrading of software for industrials and health care applications. I did that till he hired Boomer."

"Boomer? Who's that?"

"Isabella Tournimenko," said Henry.

"Then you became CCO?" asked Brian.

"Yes, after that she stole my job."

"Stole?"

"You've not met her, have you?"

"I have," said Vitaly.

"Hard to miss? Don't blush Vitaly. She's a hottie."

"Couldn't she simply be better than you?" asked Derek.

"Please ignore Derek," said Brian. "He's a shit-wit."

Henry smiled.

"Yes, Derek, she was in every regard."

"Did you enjoy the job as CCO?"

"It was simple and boring. Follow the rules. Nothing creative. You're the meter maid. Everyone hates you. Is this what you want to ask me?"

"Why'd you leave?"

"At last, an interesting question. In my role, I worked closely with the then CFO, Francis Sequeira."

"Sequeira?" Paul interjected, "the current CFO of Trinity Asset Management?"

"Yes. He and I would compare notes on cash flow and the development of the trading strategies. I had noticed that over time the holdings and weights were vastly different from the sub-advised funds. I got an earful one day from my counterpart at Sunquest, complaining about the performance. Francis told me not to worry about it. The person from Sunquest was fired a couple of weeks later."

Henry took another pull from the bottle before he continued.

"At its inception, LAM was a front-runner. We had better information than everyone else, some public, a lot private, stuff you weren't supposed to trade on," Henry noted.

"John demanded that LAM be the first call on all ideas and that we'd be offered all the large blocks of shares before anyone else. If you screwed us, if you played favourites with anybody else but LAM, you were in the penalty box." Henryadded.

"We'd cut your trading commissions by ninety per cent. Sometimes, we'd cut you off completely. If that happened, you'd better have saved up a few pennies because you'd be the sacrificial lamb. If John was satisfied by your firm's contrition, he'd resume trading."

"He's got that much power?" asked Derek.

"More like he had. That all went when T-plus five died.

"Sorry? T-five?" asked Derek.

"You've never worked in the industry, have you? You're just a baby lawyer," Henry sighed.

"T-five. It would take five days for a trade to settle, trade date plus five. With better technology and faster processing of trades to ensure the cash was exchanged for the shares delivered, the period shrank to three days," he explained.

"Eventually, it went to same day settlement. That meant no more fun and games from John. He could no longer reallocate, keeping the good trades for himself and the bad trades for the other accounts."

"And performance suffered."

"Yup."

"We've already got confirmation of that. We spoke to one of John's stock allocators."

"You spoke to Kent?" Henry asked with a smile.

"Yes, we spoke to him at length."

"Let me guess, he gave you a sob story about being passed over. The guy's a bag of hammers. He strutted around the office like he was important. Let everyone know he went to UCC. Pathetic. Let me guess. You gave him a few drinks, a wee bit of pressure and he spilt. Told you everything."

"Kind of. We wanted to follow up with him, but he disappeared. He was in a car accident on his way home from our meeting and hasn't been seen since."

Henry sat a little more upright.

"Disappeared?"

"We think John's involved," said Brian. "It's a bit of a leap, but yes, I'm certain he is."

"Why?"

"John's getting nervous."

"Nervous, eh?" Henry asked fidgeting in his chair.

Henry clearly was. Brian was pleased.

"Perhaps Kent's information was reliable?"

"Yes and no," said Henry.

"Sorry?"

"Well, any information that Kent provided on John reallocating stocks to favour his fund over the sub-advised funds is correct. But Kent's a fool. When I was at LAM, the in-house lawyer wrote him what he thought was a get out of jail free card, a letter exonerating him from his role in reallocating the bad trades. Even with cursory read of the regulations, you'd know you weren't protected."

"So there's a letter indicating what they were doing?"

"Yes. I was asked to destroy it. I destroyed the paper copy but I scanned it first. I'll forward it if you like."

"Please," said Brian.

"This scam works because they managed funds on behalf of five other companies."

"Five?" said Derek.

"Well, if it works once, run it again was John's philosophy. LAM has sub-advised relationships all over the world. If you dig a little, you'll find the stooges. By Derek's reaction, you've only looked in Canada."

"And Kent did the reallocation for all of them?"

"Yup."

"You will provide me with the names of those companies," Brian stated.

"Yes, I could but what fun would that be? Do some digging."

"The team will."

"Surely that's not all you' re looking for though?"

"No. I do have few more questions."

"Continue."

"The night Vitaly and I spoke with Kent, he intimated that something much more sinister was going on. He was too drunk to continue, so Vitaly put him in a car to go home. We were going to drag him back in the next morning. As I said, there was an accident. Kent was not found at the scene, even though the car was a wreck. Little chance anybody walked away from it. Forensics found hair and blood and a torn seatbelt in the back seat, but nothing more. The driver died from injuries sustained in the crash."

"Interesting," said Henry.

"Why'd he disappear? He's got the same information as you, but you sit there breathing?"

"Interesting, isn't it?"

Henry gulped down the remainder of the bottle and belched.

"It is interesting," Brian parroted. "What was Kent going to tell me? What are you going to tell me?"

"Tell you? John's dirty little secret? Am I now? Well, I think someone should know before it's too late. Before John wins."

"Wins?"

Henry toggled the screen and all they could see were a set of flashing numbers.

"What is that?" asked Brian.

Symbols would appear and disappear, in green and in red for varying amounts of time. It didn't make any sense. Henry toggled the screen back and they could see his face again.

"Miss Maiwen, gentlemen, why do you think I'm here?" asked Henry. "It's not the view... I prefer the concrete jungle over the real one. It's not because I enjoy drinking Imperial. Well, that's not true. I do. But this, gentlemen and lady, this is my last stand. What's it you are looking at? Paul, tell me!"

"Stock symbols?"

"Back of the class Paul. Maiwen, your turn!"

She shook her head.

"Security defence," said Brian.

"Good. Now, what's it protecting?"

"No idea what it is, but it's keeping you alive."

"Correct. Kent is stupid. His insurance policy was a piece of paper, written by the guys he was trying to blackmail. Mine's information. It's locked away but Isabella's helping him get at it. I left LAM with the information so that he'd leave me alone. I wrote myself a little back door program. The computers at LAM continue to dump their trades."

"You've got his secrets?" said Derek.

"We had found a fine balance, or so I thought."

"Something changed. Something's threatening you."

"Not something, someone. Isabella. From a technical standpoint, she's brilliant. In the world of finance, she's an innocent. Hers are not crimes of commission. She doesn't realize what John has asked her to do. She doesn't know about the game John and I are playing. My information is locked behind layers of encryption. Only I have the key while I'm alive. She's helping him crack it through the little projects he gives her. He thinks I don't know. We had an agreement. Leave me alone and everything stay locked up. If I die of unnatural causes, the information gets released to the authorities."

"Oh God no! Not Wikileaks!" said Maiwen.

"No Maiwen, to Detective Cranston's desk of course."

"So, how do you have it set up?"

"It's a Matryoshka Defense. Think of the encryption as a Russian wooden doll. There are layers upon layers of encryption. I thought it was unhackable."

Henry pointed at the screen.

"John just got through level three today."

"Why can't you re-encrypt it?" asked Derek.

"That's how I lost the second level. Before it can be re-encrypted, there is a brief moment when it's open to attack. Well, it's a brief moment to us, but to the computers at LAM, it's like I left the house keys in the front door and headed out on a month long vacation. If John, or more precisely LAM's computers, are looking at the right time, they can see right through one layer to the next and the next. When the attacks started, he spooked me. I flinched."

"So, this computer program of yours is tracking the attacks," said Maiwen. "The red is what, the offence and the green your program's defence? The program is rebuffing the attack."

"John's tweaked the protocol. He's increased the testing rate."

"Sorry?" said Brian.

Paul piped in.

"Testing rate. You encrypted this with 256 bit encryption at numerous levels. Lister began a brute force attack and got lucky. In theory, it should take two to the 200 years to complete, more than the age of the universe."

"Add another 50 or so digits."

"You don't look like an idiot. The first layer he broke was blind luck."

"Continue," said Henry.

"Now there's something else, isn't there? Encryption algorithms are just large matrices. You start out with something simple and then add complexity by transposing rows and shifting columns of numbers. To understand the data you need to re-sequence the numbers in the correct order."

"Continue," Henry said again.

"But there are some vulnerabilities, aren't there?" asked Paul.

"Yes. Vitaly, your boy's smart. Continue Paul."

"A side-channel attack."

"Bingo!" said Henry.

"Side channel?" said Brian.

"Imagine you're a thief breaking into a bank just after closing. You have sixteen hours until the branch manager arrives. You think there's just a single lock on the safe. You drill the first lock, you open the door and there find a second, inside the first safe. You drill the second and by chance the third is left unlocked. What do you do now?" Paul paused, then continued.

"There is a fourth safe inside and maybe more, and you're running out of time. The bank manager will be opening soon and you want to be long gone by then. You change your tactics. The side channel attacks focus not on the underlying lock, but rather they attack the technology that implements the cypher system. What they go after has nothing to do with security. And that is the inherent vulnerability of the system."

Brian still stared at him blankly.

"You think creatively when you're out of time. Since the locks are all magnetic, the easiest way to get in is to demagnetize them. You cut the power. The side channel attacks are like cutting the power to the lock. If you can do that at each layer, you don't have to force your way in. It will open for you."

Henry picked up where Paul had stopped.

"This type of attack was a theoretical concern of mine when I set up Matryoshka. John's watching for weakness and is picking off data about the encryption as the system changes itself."

"It's not impossible, is it?" asked Paul. "You can't protect yourself if someone is looking in the right places."

"Why are you so important? What's John hiding?" asked Brian.

"You don't know," Henry was clapping his hands like a child. "You really don't know."

"Why hasn't he come down here and overpowered you?" asked Brian. "Add a bullet to the equation."

"As I said, if I die, the info gets released. The data is escrowed with my lawyer in San Jose. I check in with her twice a week. If I'm late by twelve hours, she'll release the data and the encryption key to you. As long as I'm breathing, it remains locked."

"He doesn't know that, but he might suspect that you put in a trip wire."

"Yup."

"Mostly, John needs to prove he's smarter, doesn't he?" asked Brian.

"He's toying with me," said Henry. "To him, it's but a game. "You're waiting for the end, then," said Brian. "If you reveal what's inside, you're dead. If he breaks in, you're dead. You won't tell me what's locked away, will you?"

Henry smiled again.

"Why accelerate the inevitable? Give up all this?"

Henry gestured to the surrounding countryside, the beautiful, foreboding forest.

"I hate it here. Tell you what, I'll nudge you in the right direction. Look at the differences in the sources of returns for the fund."

"Asset classes?" said Brian.

"Yes, and the different level of discretion John has in pricing."

"Sorry," said Brian.

"Different assets classes are priced, well, differently. Some are observable and others aren't. The stuff John is investing in, he determines the price based on his own models. There's nothing rigourous about way he comes to the price. He sticks his finger in the air and he decides. The models are flimsy. Focus there."

"We've been trying to get the material but we can't. It's..." said Brian.

"It's been removed from your database. I know," Henry said. "I can help you. I see everything, remember. I believe Maiwen was looking for that information."

"You've known?"

"It's been kind of fun watching you bumble around."

"Why not come in? I can get you into FWPP for your help?"

"The Federal Witness Protection Program?" Henry chuckled, turned the computer around and typed for about thirty seconds. He then turned it around so they could see the screen. Brian recognized it immediately.

"Oh shit!" said Brian.

"Oh shit indeed."

"It's unhackable!" exclaimed Brian.

"I'd thought so too. If I can get in, so can Isabella."

"Right," said Brian. "Henry, I'm going after Lister. You understand, right? I'm gonna put him away. You'll be safe then."

"You're gonna prosecute? You think you can keep me safe?"

"I'll take this as far as I can."

"That's not the same. That's not a promise."

"You're right, it's not. For now, it's the best I can do."

Henry thought for a moment.

"Okay."

Wade ended the call.

"Okay what?" said Vitaly to the blank screen.

"We'll keep digging," said Brain. "Wade told us where."

"There's no paper trail, remember?" said Paul.

"There is now," said Maiwen holding up her Blackberry.

"What?"

"Look."

They gathered around her screen.

"It's from Wade."

There was a web address and a key to a drop box. Paul typed it into his browser of his laptop and entered the password.

There were twelve folders, one each for the past ten years and two extras.

Paul clicked on the first. A 800 pages long file open. There were fifteen files for the first year.

"Motherlode."

"We got Lister."

"Nope," said Brian. "Not yet. But soon."

"Soon?"

"It's the compliance records. It's everything," said Maiwen.

"Every trade, every reallocation. It's even better than what would have ever been stored in our database. I'll need help and I need it now. The case will be super easy to prove with this."

"Paul," said Vitaly, "you're off everything else. You and Maiwen work together. Derek and I will handle the other dockets."

"We got 'em! We got 'em!" Maiwen hummed as she went to her office to get her laptop.

30

Mila's phone buzzed for the fifth time in half an hour and she ignored it again.

She knew it was not Caroline. Mila had given her school schedule and the deadlines she faced. She was patient with Mila and she was still sorting things out with Marc.

Mila was putting the finishing touches on her last assignment for Zablon for the year before the start of her final exams. She wanted to impress him.

She also knew that someday she would have to, no, would *want* to come clean with him.

Mila took a sip of her tepid green tea. Her phone chirped again.

"Oh, for fuck's sake!"

All her messages she received were from John.

She opened the oldest message first. It included an attachment. She clicked on it.

> *Three day trip to Miami. Leave in a week. 2X the usual overnight. Bathing suit and an elegant dress.*

Am I not always elegant?

> *Of course you are. Need your name, the way it appears on your passport and an address for the plane ticket. If you are uncomfortable with that, you could buy your own and I will reimburse you. Please don't say no.*

He already knew her name from the motor vehicle database but there it was only listed as Mila Petrovna since she had dropped "Mirkin" for space.

Her passport read differently and she knew it would be a problem if that document and her ticket did not match. The cash would get her that much closer to leaving her pseudonym behind.

The meeting with Lily had changed the relationship. She knew too much but she wanted to know more.

I accept. I think you know my true name already but in case you've written it wrong, Mila Mirkin Petrovna

She gave her parent's old address in Richmond Hill hoping it would keep a degree of anonymity.

Please buy the ticket and let me know the other arrangements. I am looking forward to it. ;P Tatiana. P.S. And don't bug me anymore. I'm studying for finals!!"

Three minutes later her phone chirped again.

Mila opened the new email message.

Last email for 72 hours, promise! See the two attachments. First is the ticket. Second are the details. Since I now know your full name, may I call you Mila?

She wrote back.

Something wrong with Tatiana? I kind of like it.

Tatiana it is then. Good luck but you won't need it!

John, don't you dare! I need to earn this.

Just kidding. Promise I won't do anything.

At moment later, her phone buzzed that she had a text message. She was annoyed by the disturbance but opened it anyway. It was from Zablon.

Good luck tomorrow. You've done good work this semester.

Z

It was sent from his personal account. Mila shut down her iPhone and turned off the email program on her computer.

She needed to concentrate. The exam material was in her head but it was jumbled. She was excited about Miami — she had never been before.

Mila took three deep breaths, pushed back her chair and stood up.

She slid into the splits, she bent forward at the waist to touch her forehead to her knee. This was her settling position, and it allowed her to erase all thoughts. She spoke to herself.

"Concentrate. Breathe. Focus. Breathe. Prepare. Breathe. Succeed."

It was the mantra Caroline had taught her.

31

Mila was packing for Miami, trying to find appropriate attire, but for what? The need for a bathing suit and an evening dress intrigued her. While he had asked for specific clothing before, his requests had never been so pedestrian.

She had rarely been out in public with John, never in Toronto, and she thought it was odd for him to ask her to do so now. The first time she had travelled with him outside of Toronto, they did not leave the hotel except to go to the opera.

He was being more adventurous. She was concerned: out of country and he had for full name.

Mila pulled her black one-piece bathing suit out of a drawer, looked at it and decided to take her black string bikini instead. The one-piece hid too much of her tattoo and she enjoyed showing it off. Her preferred grooming aids were duly packed and as she was planning on carryon luggage only, she left the incriminating tools of her trade hidden in her bottom drawer.

She reached under her dresser and extracted an envelope, just brushing the mouse trap as she withdrew her hand. The trap snapped shut, the metal bar just missing against her knuckles. She took out a $300 US, replaced the stash and reset the spring in its place.

The last things she packed were her little black dress that showed off her dancer's calves and a simple floor length summer dress with spaghetti straps in a blue and red floral pattern on a white background.

She had bought it recently and thought it would be perfect with wedged sandals. With those shoes she appeared to float over the floor. She might even be taller than John. She liked the idea of that.

Mila packed no additional jewelry. She was wild enough with her piercings and the blue streak in her hair, and she felt that subdued clothing made an arresting contrast. She only wore her grandmother's ring.

"How'd exams go?"

Mila swung around. Caroline was standing in the doorway, holding up a brown paper bag.

"Those aren't from there, are they?" Mila sighed.

She could smell the still warm almond croissants through the paper. She skipped over to Caroline, gave her a quick peck on the lips reached for the bag. Caroline tucked it behind her back.

"A little reward. How'd they go?"

"Aced 'em. It was almost easy."

"Even Stats?"

"Okay, that was brutal, but I got it done. I recognized every trap. Everyone else seemed to be crammed for time."

"Fantastic. You've worked so hard. I knew you had it in you."

Caroline glanced over at Mila's half packed bag.

"Where are you off to?"

Mila lunged for the croissants but Caroline was too fast and her arms too long. She kept the pastries just out of reach.

"You only get one if you tell me where you're going."

Mila smiled, grabbed the middle of Caroline's shirt and pulled her close. She moved up onto her tip toes and kissed Caroline. Caroline was motionless in Mila's embrace, absorbed in the moment.

"You know," Mila said, her tongue grazing her lover's upper lip, "You know, you're the best I've ever had."

She bit Caroline's lower lip and held it tenderly between her teeth for a moment and released. Mila could feel Caroline melt into her. Mila's hands slid to the front of Caroline's waist, her finger tips reaching over the crest of her hips and on to the low of her back and beyond to Caroline's outstretched hands.

"Hold on Br'er Rabbit, not so fast," said Caroline as she swung the bag back over her head, tantalizingly out of reach.

"No fair," Mila pouted.

"You didn't answer my question."

"Miami."

"With him?"

There was a flatness in her voice.

"Who do you think?"

"What I can give you is more than money."

"But you have Marc."

Caroline glared at Mila.

"We're done. You know that. I'm leaving Marc for you."

"But you can't get me to Columbia. After this trip, I'm done. Promise. He's giving me 30 grand for four days. I'll have enough for my Master's. I'll worry about the PhD afterwards. I'll go...We'll go to New York."

Caroline thrust the bag into Mila's hands and slumped down in Mila's desk chair.

Mila stood silent for a moment and sighed. She made her way over Caroline, pulled out a croissant, broke off a piece, and fed it to Caroline. She playfully licked at the little bit of icing sugar that was on the down of Caroline's lip.

"Mila, don't!"

"I'll be back in time for Zoya's birthday. I'll keep the phone on. We're bonded, right? You'll see me wherever I am."

Mila got up from Caroline's lap and crossed the room to the laptop. She hit print on her computer, grabbed the pages and handed them to Caroline.

"Here. My itinerary. When I get back, we'll be together then. I gotta go now. I forgot to call for a car and I need to snag a cab."

"I'll drive you. My car's downstairs."

"Okay, but I gotta go right now."

Mila stuffed the remaining clothes she had pulled out into her suitcase and zipped it shut. Caroline's car was less than a block away. They drove in silence. Caroline was quiet until they were on the highway.

"I'm going to ask you again. You're safe, right?"

"Caroline. I wouldn't go if I wasn't. It's just for four days. It's Miami, not Honduras or Brazil. I'm fine."

"I need you need to be more than fine. I need you to come back. I've... I need you, Mila. I do. How much longer do I need to wait?"

"After this, you'll have all of me. I'm done. I promise."

"And when he offers you fifty grand, what then?"

Mila didn't respond.

"I know it's unfair and confusing. I'd hate if you did it to me. I really would."

They arrived at the airport and pulled-up to US departures. Caroline stayed in the driver's seat, facing forward, her grip tight around the steering wheel. Her emotions alternating between joy, fear and anger.

"Thanks for the lift... You didn't have to," Mila said.

"Mila, don't! Don't go! You don't need to. Fuck the money."

"I hear you Caroline."

"Then don't go!"

"I love you. I'm yours. The best way for me to be with you is to leave Toronto. Start new. I don't want to bump into anyone from my past. I'm not saying I'm going to Miami for us. I'm doing this for myself, for New York. Then, it'll be just the two of us. We can go. We can be free. Next summer, after I graduate from York, come with me to New York. What I do is not who I am."

"I know."

"I love you Caroline. I have since I was seventeen, since you first kissed me under the willow. You first brought out emotions that I've kept bottled up inside because they're too fragile. This is my last trip. The last time I will lay down with anyone but you."

Mila bent over the stick shift and kissed Caroline gently on the cheek.

"I'll be back in four nights," she whispered.

"Should I wait while you fuck him?"

"It's just sex. Nothing more. I feel nothing for him."

Mila got out, grabbed her luggage and shut the door.

Caroline was standing on the other side of the car, her arms folded in front of her on the roof of the car, her chin resting on her forearms.

"I understand your anger. I do."

Caroline didn't betray any emotion at all.

"I gotta go. I'll miss the flight."

Mila moved backwards two or three steps, nearly tripping over the curb. She was not sure Caroline would pick her up if she fell.

Mila turned and walked towards the terminal without looking back.

In the reflection of the glass doors, she saw that Caroline had not moved. She was still watching her.

Each breath was toxic. She couldn't look back.

32

As the plane taxied, Mila relaxed in the business class seat that John had booked for her. She appreciated the gesture. The plane bumped down the taxiway. Mila had yet to switch her phone to airplane mode as she was hoping Caroline would respond to her text message. It had consisted of only three words -

I love you

She watched the lines on the ground, trying to determine how the pilot knew where to go. It made little sense to her. She slipped her headphones on discretely so that the flight attendant would not admonish again for listening to music. She leaned her head against the cool plastic of the window and closed her eyes. She hated what she had done. She brushed her hair in front of her face to hide her tears. She was so close yet she had placed a chasm between them.

Mila awoke as the plane slowed with her cheek still glued to the window. The water below was a brilliant aquamarine. She marveled at how it shimmered. She followed the highway below her, imagining riding her motorcycle without leathers, feeling the warm, humid air on her arms, her hair whipping the back of the tank top. Tucked behind Miami Beach, Mila could see a labyrinth of canals, industrial sites, cranes, warehouses and endless rows of squat bungalows. Yards were strewn with garbage, the gardens unkempt and brown. Rusting cars sat on blocks, many with their doors or hoods removed. She had always thought of Miami as a place where people played. She scolded herself. Where people partied, some prospered and others always got left behind.

She deplaned and collected her bag. Having gone through customs in Toronto, the exit was quick. She passed through the opaque sliding door and there was Mike, holding a sign with her pseudonym.

"Ms. Tatiana, good to see you again. I hope you had a pleasant flight."

"Hello Mike. So you fly south too?"

"All in a day's work, Miss. Please, let me take your bag."

Mila's suit case seemed weightless in his grasp. He started to walk and she followed.

"Will I be seeing John right away?"

"I'm not to say Miss. He's planned a surprise."

And then Mila stopped dead in her tracks.

"A surprise?"

Her voice was flat. Mike continued walking in silence and they got into a black sedan with tinted windows. It drove them to the private departures zone to a small black jet. Mike handed the bags to the steward and guided Mila on board.

"Welcome Miss Nikoleavna. Hello again, Mike. My name is Gillian. Please take a seat. We'll be departing for Nassau in ten."

Mila leaned in towards Mike.

"The Bahamas? No."

Mila was both pissed off and elated.

"Mike, this was not part of the plan."

"Have you ever been to Nassau?"

"No, but..."

"You'll love it. Sorry for the deception. I had no choice."

"Mike, there's always a choice.We're in this together, right? Can I count on you?"

His cheeks flushed.

"You can."

Gillian interrupted.

"There's a washroom in the rear of the cabin if you would like to freshen up before take-off. Would you care for some champagne?"

"Please," said Mila.

"Henriot or Taittinger?" Gillian asked.

"The first one please," replied Mila, not sure of the difference.

"Mike, I presume you will have the usual."

"A double please."

Mike eased into one of the leather chairs and picked up the newspaper that was sitting in a pouch attached to the side. He turned to the Op-ed page and began to read. From her seat, Mila read the headlines.

DEATH TOLL GROWS AMONG BRAINSTIM'S PARKINSON'S PATIENTS

FAULTY COMMUNICATIONS SOFTWARE. FDA INVESTIGATING

PIERRE LAROQUE SOUNDS THE CLOSING BELL

"Mike, when you're done, may I take a look?"

"Of course, let me just finish...Ah here you go. I'll read it later."

Before she could refuse, Mike had handed her the front section and Mila went to the article on Brainstim right away. She had overheard John talk about it back in March. The stock had been crushed, down forty percent in the last three days. Gillian hovered over the two of them.

"Here you are, Miss Tatiana. Henriot 1997. Mike, your usual: tomato juice with two slices of lime, three cubes of ice."

"Thanks Gillian."

"Yes, thank you," said Mila, remembering her manners.

She took a sip from the flute. The liquid was soft yet, lively and fresh. It was not at all like the Asti Martini she had shared with John. She never knew it could be so refined. She felt young.

A minute later the cabin door closed as Gillian returned and asked Mike and Mila to buckle up. She assumed a seat in the galley, behind a small curtain that she had pulled. Mike lifted his feet as the plane taxied down the runaway, and he kept them there until they were in the air. Only then did he set them down.

"I can't stand how planes rattle."

"My Hulk," she smiled, "afraid of flying."

"Ms. Tatiana," said a voice over the intercom, "flight time to Nassau is fifty-five minutes. If you need anything, please ask Gillian. Welcome back aboard Mike."

Mike was asleep in a minute and he dozed until the plane began to descend towards Nassau. The sun was beginning to set. A large illuminated complex stood in contrast to the flatness of the surrounding land.

"Mike, what's that?" Mila asked pointing at a massive resort with sprawling grounds. Everything seemed to gleam in the sun. Mike shifted in his seat to get a better look out of Mila's window.

"That's Atlantis. You'll be staying there."

"Mike, what the Hell am I doing in the Bahamas?"

"It was Mr. Lister's wish that I bring you, so you could relax after your exams. So here you are."

They landed smoothly and the jet taxied to a large hangar where they were greeted by two Bahamian customs and immigration officers who climbed into the plane as soon as Gillian lowered the doorway steps. Mila handed over her passport, but the men barely glimpsed at her photo before stamping her document and left the plane.

"Is that normal?" she asked. "They didn't even ask me how long I would be staying. I feel cheated. Didn't even have to lie."

Mike smiled and guided Mila off the plane to a waiting car. Mike opened the rear door for Mila, but she ignored him, walked to the front passenger door and sat down, closing the door behind her. Mike walked around the front of the sedan and got in, looking a bit serious.

"Mike, I didn't hire you. You don't wait on me. We both work for him."

"Ms. Tatiana, I thank you but I know my role."

He gestured to the rear seat.

"If you please."

Mila sat for a moment, arms crossed. She sighed her acquiescence. Before he could get out, Mila threw her purse over the driver's seat, forcing Mike to duck. She followed the bag, tucking her head down and squeezing between the two front seats, and plopping down into the rear passenger seat. She leaned forward and grabbed a chilled bottle of water from the seat pocket and took a sip. She kicked off her shoes and rested her heels on the leather arm rest.

"Happier now?"

"Much."

It was clear to Mila he had done this before as he navigated amongst the various airport vehicles and small planes, seemingly unconcerned as they were jockeying for the space. The brightly lit buildings she had viewed from the plane were nowhere to be seen. Exiting the airport, Mike drove quickly but carefully through rows of clapboard shacks, each no bigger than 10 by 20 feet, all on low stilts, all in need of repair or, at a minimum, a coat of paint. The yards were unkempt and heavy with overgrown vegetation. Mila was fascinated and uneasy at the same time.

"Mike, I thought you were taking me to some place fancy," she said sarcastically.

She had seen neighbourhoods of Toronto that looked like this, parts where she had volunteered as an assistant social worker, parts no one wants to exist.

"If I'd wanted to see this, I'd have gone to Jane and Finch."

"Miss Tatiana, we'll be at Paradise Island shortly. The contrast will be... well, you'll see."

As they drove, Mila was delighted to see the bougainvillea, and even the occasional banana tree, illuminated by the streetlight. To her surprise, the fruit was vibrant green and pointed upwards. Mila stared through darkened windows at the stream of people standing at the road side under the stark light of a lamppost. Mike slowed the car as the traffic on the road got denser. She lowered her window to get an unobstructed view. The car filled the deep bass of a calypso and the rich, sweet night air. Young teens, thirteen, maybe fourteen years old, in short shorts and halter tops cradled toddlers on their hips as they talked under street lights. The window rolled back up on its own.

"I'm sorry. I know the night air's pleasant but I think it's be better this way. Are you uncomfortable? I can adjust the temperature."

Mila tried the window switch again, but it had been deactivated. She opened her mouth to say something but slumped back in her seat and watched the rough, mangy dogs in small packs that sat along the side of the road barking as the sedan passed. Mike pulled to a stop at dimly lit intersection behind a rusty, white pick-up truck, the back filled with men sitting on its bed. Some young teenage boys in ragged shorts and stained T-shirts ran up beside the car. The smallest one carrying what looked like a water balloon. The two trailing boys were carrying cricket bats. Mike slammed the car in reverse just as the balloon was thrown. The car plowed into a delivery van behind them. Mila was thrown back into the seat, her head banging against the padded frame of the window. The balloon landed on the hood and burst, spreading white paint on the lower right side of the windshield and over the bodywork.

The men in the truck pointed and laughed. Mila looked forward but could not see out the windshield on her side of the car. Mike accelerated hard, squealing the tires, clipping the back of the truck ahead with the left fender and pushing it forward, causing the rear taillights to shatter. A few men toppled in front of Mike. He popped back into reverse and slammed into the van again. The second boy launched the cricket bat. Mila watched as it headed straight for her head. The window shattered, the tinted film preventing the shards of glass from penetrating the interior. Mike lurched forward, veering hard right, missing the men sprawled on the ground. He drove quickly and accurately, accelerating as he could around the traffic. After about ten minutes, he moderated his speed to match the traffic.

"Are you okay?" Mila asked in a quiet voice.

"I should be asking you that."

"Banged my head a little, but I'm fine."

"I'm so sorry. It was careless of me."

"You didn't throw the bat."

She reached forward and patted him on the shoulder and squeezed the back of his neck. His nape was as taut as a bridge cable.

"Thank you for getting me out of there."

The shacks gave way to broad streets and in ten minutes Mike drove up to a massive, oversized brick archway. It was blocked by a gate and two security guards that looked comical in their white Bermuda shorts and Panama hats. Less comical were the holsters on their hips. Mike slowed the sedan to a crawl and stopped as the taller of the two guards looked over the damage to the car.

"Michael Brennan with Tatiana Nikoleavna for John Lister."

"Good evening. Eventful trip tonight, sir? Need I call the police?"

"Thank you, no."

"Thank you and good night, Sir," the man with the clipboard said, allowing them to continue.

The security guard tried to peer over Mike's shoulders to see Mila. Mike rolled up his window and drove forward slowly. Mila sat quietly as they drove to the Royal Towers, twin buildings connected by a bridge. A flurry of bellhops descended upon the car but they all stopped as they saw the paint. They did not know how to react.

"Some entrance you provide," she said. "Only teasing. Thank you again for getting me out of there."

The door of the sedan opened and a brown hand extended into the car to help Mila out.

"Ms. Tatiana, welcome to the Atlantis at Paradise Island. My name is Andrews. Mr. Lister asked me to escort you to your suite."

Mila followed her to the elevator. She had never seen so much gold plating anywhere. The elevator was waiting and Mila entered first. Andrews entered a four digit code and pushed the button for the 23rd floor.

"Spa and salon services are available in the suite, 24 hours a day."

Mila ran the soft pad of her thumb over her nails. Andrews had spotted that Mila had nervously picked at them after the boys and the paint.

"There are 48 shopping opportunities, all of which can be charged. If there's anything I can help you with," Andrews said handing Mila her business card. "Please call me, day or night."

The elevator arrived at the appointed floor and Mila insisted Andrews exit first. The lobby was impressive, flanked as it was by 12-foot floor to ceiling windows. Andrews muttered something about the number of rooms and the pool on the grounds but Mila stood mesmerized by the view. She had read about this suite in the GQ issue she'd thumbed though when she was last at her gynecologist appointment. It was one of the top ten most expensive places to stay in the world; $25,000 per night. From the picture window, the resort glittered as Andrews ushered her to the far end of the hallway.

"These are your quarters. Mr. Lister asked me to prepare them for you. I believe you will find all that you need. Again, if there is anything you desire, please let me know."

Mila followed Andrews into a room that was larger than any bedroom she had ever seen. Six, no seven cartwheels Mila thought to herself. It was clad in embroidered silks. The curtains were white gossamer sheers that flowed in the cooling sea breeze. Mila stepped through them and onto a large balcony. She had an unbroken view of the sea with the moon glistening in the waves.

"I'll leave you to take in the view."

Andrews shut the door. Mila's bag was already on a stand next to the dresser. She had no idea how it had arrived in her room before she had. Her favourite cosmetics and the perfumes she had worn for John were waiting on the counter, including one she had not worn in years. He had left the envelope too. She did not bother to check it. She picked up a bottle of face cream. It was the same brand she used, a brand that Hooshang had brought back the last time he had been in Tehran. Mila left her bag closed and opened the door to her room, startled to find Andrews outside her door, waiting to serve her.

"Mr. Lister is dining with his daughter this evening. They should be returning in forty-five minutes or so. Bernard, the butler, will prepare a meal for you in the bar area, down the hall. Mr. Lister mentioned that you enjoy sushi. Again, if there is anything you require, please let me know."

With that, Andrews left her.

"Lily was here?" Mila thought.

She was apprehensive. She never thought she would never see her again. While Lily had left in good spirits, she was still concerned about the girl. None of what she had talked about was good, and she was in desperate need of counseling.

Mila went back into her room and had a quick shower, unsure of what lay ahead. The air was humid and she twirled her hair into a bun to keep it off her shoulders.

She put on the black dress, mid-heigh pumps and the lightest of makeup, delicate purple eyeshadow highlighting her pale blue eyes. She made her way down the hall in the direction of what she hoped was the bar. Instead, she came across the master bedroom and what was surely Lily's room, given the clothes that had been thrown over the back of the chair at the ornate desk. She retraced her steps, and found Bernard, who escorted her to the balcony. The breeze was gentle and Mila sank into a chair overlooking a series of lagoons that led to the sea. Bernard brought her a delicate plate of sashimi and sushi and a small bottle of chilled, unfiltered sake. As Mila finished her meal, she heard a male talking in strong but hushed tones and a female who was sobbing but defiant.

"How could you?" cried Lily, "First Calgary, and now here! You'd never have done this to Alison. Never. You always loved her more than me. Admit it! Admit it!"

"No Lily. It's not like that."

"She followed you where ever you went like a spaniel and you adored her for it. If she only knew the monster I know."

"I'm..."

A door slammed before John could complete the sentence. There was a silence followed by a long sigh.

"Yes, I loved Alison!" he bellowed. "Lily, I...I've always loved you too. I do. I'm sorry."

Mila stayed seated, unsure of what to do, not wanting to cross paths with him. Somehow, it was right not to move. She heard John walk up behind her as she pretended that the sea held great interest. He kissed the nape of her neck and she caught her breath. He ran his fingers over her hair. Mila suppressed her instinct to move away when his hands touched the bruise on her scalp where her head had struck the window. He slid the strap of the dress off her shoulder and gently replaced it with a kiss. John's right arm reached across her body, cupping her breast. Mila exhaled and turned her head towards him with her eyes closed. John reached forward and took her cup from the table and took a sip without swallowing. His pushed his lips against hers and let the sake seep into her mouth. She swallowed the offering. He pulled his head back, his warm breath caressing her ear.

"Give me your tongue."

Mila opened her mouth against his, slid her tongue forward, her stud between is lips. He melted.

"Come with me."

John took her hand and guided her down the hall towards the elevator. Bernard was waiting for them. He had blue blazer for John and he draped a light, gold embroidered, purple pashmina shawl over Mila's bare shoulders. Bernard summoned the elevator for them and they descended to the ground floor.

"Let me show you something."

John took her hand and they walked in silence along a path to an enormous underground aquarium. It was obvious to Mila that John had been there numerous times, as he led her directly to the centerpiece of the exhibit, a gangplank that took them to the centre of the tank. Eight-foot black tip reef sharks swam by lazily, remoras stuck to their bellies. Amberjacks kept a watchful eye as they swam around the perimeter, remaining out of striking distance. Three large hammerhead sharks lazed over their heads, their anal fins resting on the glass enclosure. Mila sat next to John on the bench in silence, watching the graceful, powerful creatures. Mila felt sad they were constrained, forced into an artificial environment for her pleasure.

"I don't know what to do about Lily. She's all I've got."

John covered his face with his hands. Mila slid a bit closer on the bench, her hip touching his, her hand rubbing the small of his back. He stayed motionless, the glow of the tank reflected in a single tear at the edge of lower eyelid. He wiped it away with his index finger.

"She's all I have. I wasn't born this way. My dad couldn't afford to go to university or even college out of high school. He started working at a small auto parts plant, operating a simple metal stamping machine. Dangerous work. He lost hi pinky on his left hand one day when he wasn't paying attention. Over time, he worked his way up to supervisor when the owner's started to notice his sketches during lunch breaks. He was redesigning parts, overcoming some of the obstacles that engineers faced. The owners sponsored him to go the U of T for mechanical engineering, part-time. It took years and was a challenge."

"He said that was when he started to drink, trying to balance school, work and his young family. He struggled. Later on he started seeing clients on the road, spending more time on the way, more than he needed to I suspect. I lied back in Toronto about my mom. She didn't run away from me. She didn't run away from his drinking. She never had a fuckin' chance. He threw her down the stairs in a fit of rage. She broke her neck in the fall, paralyzed but she was still alive. I came home from the movies with my girlfriend and found her lying there, her head angled against the tread, awake and unable to speak. She could only blink. He sat in the living room in front of her in his favourite chair watching her, drinking four fingers of scotch. She died two days later. I was eighteen."

"Oh God John. I'm so sorry."

"I was out on my own. I worked my way through university. I wriggled into jobs. I got on the trading floor once I finished undergrad. I was a junior peon, a slave to an equity position trader named Donald Wallace. If you wanted to trade oil stocks, you went through him. I'd fetch coffee, lunches and pick up laundry but I learned the trade. He was the master and I his pauper. I worked hard. I did some things that were good, others not so much, moved around to new opportunities and climbed. I made a few enemies and had a more friends and I took on clients I knew I shouldn't have. I did it for them, for Alison and Lily."

John took a deep sigh.

"She's all I have now."

He got up from the bench and walked over to the tank, resting his head against the glass.

"She had a fraternal twin sister," he said in a whisper. "Lily was the second born but she always was the stronger. In grade one, Alison got leukemia. She died just shy of her fourteenth birthday. The treatments back then were not like they are today. The survival rate was low. Three of ten never made it past the first year. We put our faith in God and the staff at the hospital. Both let us down."

Mila walked up from behind, lifted John's arm and hugged him, her arms wrapping around his torso, her face against his chest. Mila looked up at the reflection of John's face in the glass of the tank. Tears were running down his cheeks. She held him closer.

"After we exhausted all venues in Canada, we tried the US, in Miami, but by the time we did, it was too late. Hen—that was Lily's name for Alison because she couldn't say her full name when she was little, fought to the end."

"That's when everything fell apart for Joan. She started drinking again. This time, she added Vicodin and Valium. I couldn't handle it and we drifted apart. She found solace at our cottage on Lake Joseph and a string of relationships, mostly with men. She never engaged with Lily. Nor did I. We sent her to camp for eight weeks that summer while I stayed in the city. I buried myself in my work to forget the pain. I was lonely too, and I missed our Hen so much I forgot about the girl who was still with us. I drank and I sought comfort in the arms of others. That's how I stumbled upon you, Mila."

It was the first time he had ever called her by her real name. She did not care. Mila took his hand in hers and held it. A guide came by and interrupted their quiet conversation.

"Pardon me. The aquarium is closing for the evening," she said with a chuckle, "unless you want to sleep with the fishes."

"Enough of the heavy stuff," said John, wiping his tears away. "We need to have some fun or at least a drink."

John led Mila out of the labyrinth of aquarium, along a path for a few minutes and into the main casino. They meandered through what were obviously the tourist tables. Fat, pink men, sunburnt from a day of spit-roasting on the beach were harassing the cocktail waitresses for another rum and coke. Their spouses and girlfriends were sitting out every other hand of black jack to make their diminishing pile of chips last longer. Mila felt sorry for them.

"Look at them bet," whispered John. "They don't know the odds."

After watching a few hands, John led her to a quieter part of the casino. The biggest bouncer she had ever seen standing by a velvet rope welcomed them.

"Good evening Mr. Lister. This must be Miss Nikoleavna. This way, if you please."

Mila followed John through an archway to a table where a woman in her late sixties was already seated. It was obvious that her black hair was dyed as she had not a hint of grey. She wore a blue satin spaghetti strap dress that showed off her excessively tanned, wrinkled and stooped back. Around her neck was a diamond pendant so large that had Mila seen it anywhere else she would have thought it to be a glass crystal. She nodded at John and invited them to join her.

"Maybe you can change my run, sweetie?" she said to Mila.

"Gertie," asked John, "How's Alasdair?"

"Cheap bastard spotted me three hundred to start tonight. After all I've done for him."

Gertie's face was pulled taut from plastic surgery, her crow's feet now narrow creases at the corners of her eyes. Mila was struck by the apparent effort it took for her to blink. Her eyebrow did not move when she spoke. Gertie looked Mila up and down before turning to John.

"Where's Lily?" she asked with an innocent air.

"She's feeling under the weather," replied John tersely.

"Under the weather? Here? In paradise? John you must've really pissed her off."

Mila smirked as the woman stacked and re-stacked her chips. She wondered to herself how Gertie's luck could be considered bad. 'You've got two hundred grand, for pity's sake,' she wanted to scream.

The woman noticed that Mila was eyeing her stack.

"Ah Sweetie," she said, pausing to take a drag from her cigarette, "I was up two-hundred-and-fifty-thousand or so an hour ago. You know Honey, easy come, easy go!"

Mila fantasized snatching them all. This woman had before her all that Mila was short for her Masters and Phd in New York and this was but this was entertainment to her. Mila's cheeks flushed, as anger and nausea rushed over her.

"Mr. Lister, how many hands tonight?"

"Three please, two for me and one for my friend."

A stack of chips appeared on John's left, brought in silently by a Bahamian woman who had entered the room through a door in the wall beside the table.

"Three hundred thousand, sir. Please sign here and here. Good luck."

John thanked her and slipped a US hundred dollar bill into her hand. He slid fifty-thousand dollars worth of chips in front of Mila and the remainder he kept for himself. A waitress brought them both two Old Fashioneds.

She looked at John as he took a long swig.

"John?"

"Just one. To take the edge off."

Mila fished out the wedge of orange and sucked on it but did not touch her drink.

"Let's begin, shall we?" said John clapping his hands together.

Over the next hour, John built up a small profit and downed three more drinks. Mila played sporadically, watching John the whole time. She sipped her drink, letting it go watery, hoping it would slow him down.

As the dealer reshuffled the six shoe deck, Mila bent in to kiss John on the cheek, taking his hand in hers, her fingers against his palm.

John clearly had a system and she was part of it. Counting cards? Into multiple decks? Could he? She did know a simple system of dividing the cards into three groups: highs, mediums and lows. The objective was to do little betting until you get near the bottom third of the shoe. Then the patterns would start to be revealed. The key to Black Jack she knew, was not to get to 21, the key was deciding when to hold because the next card might push you over 21 and an automatic loss.

"I know what you're doing. I'll play along but don't get caught."

She tapped his palm with her index finger: • •• ••• •••••

"Don't worry," he whispered back, "I never do."

"If you lovebirds are done," rasped Gertie, "can we get back to the cards?"

Mila slowly let the shawl slip off her shoulders so that it hung only off the crook in her arms, bunched across her back. All eyes were on her. Judging by their glances, neither the dealer nor Gertie had ever seen so much ink. Whenever she looked up from her cards, all eyes would dart away.

Two more hours passed and Mila was growing tired. John had hit a string of bad cards and he was down to thirty thousand or so. Mila was even for the night. She snuggled up to John and yawned.

"John, can we go? I'm tired."

"Silly me, you must be bored. Give me a few more minutes to earn your fee. Shouldn't take too long, should it Gertie?"

A pall spread across the table. Gertie looked down at the green felt on the table and stacked and re-stacked her chips, studiously avoiding eye contact. Mila gathered her pashmina, tight across her shoulders, stood up pushing her chair over and poured the remnants of her drink over John's chips.

"Gertie, and pardon me for saying this in front of you..."

She turned to John who had remained seated, looking down like a school boy waiting for his punishment.

"John... You, you... You're not even worthy."

Mila stormed away. John looked up at the dealer, shrugged his shoulder and slid over two one-hundred-dollar chips.

"Don't worry sir, I'll look after your account. Good evening."

"Thanks. Sorry about the table. Gertie."

"Most fun I've had all week," she said with a chuckle while taking a final drag from her cigarette before lighting another from the ember of the stub.

John caught Mila close to the entrance to the aquarium, grabbing her left arm to stop her. Mila swung, pivoting as Vitaly had taught her, her shoulder low and behind the hand. He did not flinch and took the hook square on the jaw. Her next action would have been to snap his knee, drop him to the ground, knee to the nose. She had already turned her hips, prepared for the move but John staggered back a few paces then straightened and offered the other cheek.

"Are you done?" he asked, "Or do you have a few more in ya?"

He rubbed his cheek.

"I'm sorry I embarrassed you."

"You embarrassed yourself. I'm working for you, but I don't take shit from anyone!"

"I'm sorry."

"I'm done for tonight. My agreement's to spend three days with you. I will. If you want me to, I can service you but you may be disappointed by the passion I conjure."

Her voice softened.

"Go back to Gertie and your precious winnings. I'm not a spoil. You may treat others that way, but not me. I'll see you for breakfast tomorrow at nine am. Good night."

Mila hurried away. John did not follow.

In a few minutes, she was back at the suite. Bernard was at the entrance when she got off the elevator. Mila handed him the pashmina and walked down the hall but took a wrong turn again and found herself at the door to the master suite.

She retraced her steps, passing Lily's room. She could hear her sobbing softly. She considered knocking but thought better. She did not need any more drama this evening.

Mila retreated to her room to find the bed turned down and the few things she had not put away herself, tucked neatly in the dresser.

She contemplated barring the door but decided that there was no need.

She sat on the bed and turned on her cell phone. She connected to the Wi-Fi hub in the suite and downloaded her messages. There was one from her mom wondering where she was. She had stopped by her apartment to drop off some baking.

Mila had not told her about her travels. She sent back a vague message about being swamped with work. There was a message from Zablon. He had read her final exam first and she would not be disappointed with the mark. Also, he needed her to go back on the road for more interviews.

There was a terse message from Caroline, wishing her a good night. Nothing else.

Mila's only response was to ensure that the Bonded program was on.

33

The iPhone chirped Mila's favourite alarm at 6 a.m., jolting her awake.

From her bed, the sea was the colour of oranges and soft roses.

The breeze coming through the balcony door was cool but Mila knew that the water would be warmer than the air.

Hurriedly, she put on her bikini, grabbed a towel from the bathroom and headed down the hall. The suite was still quiet.

As she pushed the elevator button, Bernard appeared, holding out a proper beach towel. Mila exchanged hers with his.

"Miss Lily left a few minutes ago," he said.

"She was headed for The Cove. When you exit, turn right and follow the path. If you hurry, you should catch her."

"Thank you Bernard and thanks for making up my room last night."

He smiled politely.

"Not at all, Miss. Breakfast will be served whenever you return. Is there anything else?"

"No. Thank you."

As Mila exited the building, she could see Lily turn around a corner as she followed a paved path that meandered through the hotel property.

Mila hurried along as quickly as she could in her sandals, arriving at the beach shortly after Lily plunged into the water.

Mila quickly shed her sandals and left her towel on a lounge chair and followed Lily, enjoying the sand between her toes as she walked out to chest height before launching herself into the freedom of buoyancy.

"Lily! Lily! Wait!" Mila called out.

Lily did not look back, she seemed to swim even harder.

After ten minutes, Mila had not caught her. She could feel a current carrying her along.

"Lily, stop!"

Lily continued. Mila renewed her swimming, finally tagging her on her heel. Lily whipped around, surprised.

"What are you doing?" Lily said.

"Following you. Come on, Lily, let's go back in."

"I'm not going back."

"What are you going to do, swim to Cuba?"

"Miami, if the current pulls us far enough into the Gulf Stream. It should dump us just north of there."

"What? Come on Lil'. Stop fooling around."

"Unless the sharks get us first."

"Sharks?"

"Did he take you to the aquarium?"

"Yes, why?"

"Those aren't the scary ones. It's the pelagics you need to worry about. They're nasty."

Mila looked down at her feet. It was no longer bright emerald but navy. Her silver rings glinted in the clear water.

"Come Lil'."

"No."

"Lily, I don't know what happened between you and John," Mila gasped between breaths, "but he's not worth it."

"Then why are you here?" she screamed.

"Because of you. Because you are worth it."

"I can't go back. I hate him."

"Lil', don't let him ruin your life. They don't have the right. And you don't have to let them... if you don't want to."

Lily said nothing as she treaded water. The swells were growing larger and Mila could see that she had begun to get nervous.

"I can't make you go in. I'm not strong enough and I'm too tired. If you come, I promise, I can help when we get back."

A small wave washed into Mila's mouth. The salt on her tongue made her cough. She was tiring fast.

"Lily, I need to feel sand under my toes again."

There was concern in Lily's eyes.

"Come, Lil'. Come with me."

Mila began to swim back toward land, angling towards the beach.

She swam five controlled, precise strokes before turning around. She did not see Lily.

Mila rode to the crest of a larger wave. Lily was there, following her. Mila waited for her to catch up and they swam side by side.

Mila's fifteen minute paddle out turned into forty-five minutes of a hard stroking against the current.

They talked to each other along the way, encouraging one another, stopping when a wave unexpectedly washed into the mouth of one or the other.

To Mila's relief, the water turned to green again as they inched closer.

Finally, their feet felt sand.

On wobbly knees, they made it to the shallows of the beach far from where they started.

They both collapsed, exhausted. The water lapped at their bodies.

After some time, Mila rolled onto all fours, sat back on her haunches and stood.

Mila helped Lily to her feet and put her arm around her. They then started back towards the hotel.

"Lily, I'm serious about what I said. When you get back to Calgary, call me. We'll work it out. I can help. I can help you get away. You can do it."

As they reached the cove, John was running down the beach, visibly shaken.

He wrapped his arms around Lily and he sobbed in her hair.

"Bernard told me you went for a swim but you didn't come back. He said you followed her and... and I saw... Lily and you, both swim out... lost you in the sun... Your heads were gone. Oh God Lily, you're safe."

"Nothing to worry about."

Her voice was shaken but cold.

"Here Honey, put this on. You must be exhausted."

John pulled off his navy blue cable-knit sweater and handed it to Lily.

She slipped it on, her damp hair pulled down over her face, and wrapped her arms around herself.

John walked Lily back onto the stone walkway to the residence.

"Just a little swim, Dad," she said looking over at Mila. "Really, it was nothing."

Mila followed behind. The path warmed her feet.

34

"Hello...Vitaly? It's Isabella."

"Isabella?"

"Sorry. I shouldn't have called."

"No, it's fine."

"I'm disturbing you. I can hear it in your voice. I'm sorry."

"Isabella, please don't apologize. What's up?"

"I need to talk."

"Okay."

"I'd rather do it face to face."

"Sure. That's always better."

"I'm just outside your office."

"Where?"

"On the South-East corner of Nathan Philips?"

"Really? Just a sec."

Vitaly went to his office window. "I see you."

"I know."

She waved. "May I come up?"

"No. Stay where you are. I'll be down in a moment."

"Okay."

"Right now." Vitaly hurried to the elevator. They were all on the bottom floor. *"Oh for Pete's sake."*

He ran the stairs, two at a time, and exited the building across the street from her. He motioned to her to walk to the square behind her into a crowd. He caught up to her a moment later.

"Coffee?"

"I'm good."

"Hungry?"

"Vitaly, that's not why I'm here."

"Right. Why then?"

"I need out."

"Out?"

"I need out."

"What do you mean?"

"Out! Now!"

"Why?"

"I've done things, for John, things I shouldn't have."

"What?"

"First I need to know you'll help me. Can you?"

"I can, but I need to know more."

"Just tell me, are you going after John?"

"I am."

"Can you protect me? If I help you."

"I will, but I need to know everything you did."

"Done."

"No Isabella. You need to think about it. Prosecution may have to extend to you too. This could get dangerous. John... I don't know how far he will go."

"Okay," was all she could muster.

"Come to the office now. Talk to my colleague, Brian. He's with the RCMP. He can protect you."

"Okay."

35

"He's late," said Brian.

"I called his secretary," said Maiwen. "He's on his way."

"You saw how slowly he hobbled around he office," said Derek. "He looked horrible."

"I haven't seen him. I've a hearing with a judge in an hour," said Vitaly as he got up to leave. "Tell him I...."

"Tell me what?" said Donald as he opened the door.

Vitaly could not continue. Three weeks earlier, Donald had been a powerful man, walking with purpose. He commanded the attention of every room he entered. His bespoke suits were crisp, his shirts starched. A gold tie clip, though dated, held his Hermes ties in place.

Today, he looked like a paper cutout that had been left out in the rain. He shuffled in, leaning on an ebony cane. He was gaunt, his hair was unkempt and his eyes were watery. He breathed heavily through his mouth and his face was covered in a fine white stubble.

"That I have to see a judge...How are you feeling Donald?" Vitaly asked as he rose to helped him into a chair at the head of the table.

"Fine. The ticker's fine. Enough chit chat."

Donald coughed, wiping his mouth with his handkerchief, and sat down at the head of the table.

"Okay hotshots, who booked my entire morning with you to deal with LAM?"

Donald tapped the file in front of him.

"That would be me, Don," said Brian.

"It's Donald, Constable."

"Yes, Donald, and it's Detective."

Vitaly piped in.

"Allow me to recap," Vitaly said. "A trading compliance complaint was lodged LAM."

"I'm aware of it. Continue."

"We've investigated and uncovered conclusive evidence that points to systemic irregularities at LAM. The complaint is valid. Maiwen and Paul have been working on this for the past two weeks. Detective Cranston and I had the opportunity to interview one of LAM's employees regarding their activities and we've been able to ascertain what has been happening."

"How come there's no mention of a current LAM employee in the file?" he asked holding it aloft.

"The employee in question was Graham Kent," said Vitaly. "He disappeared the night that we had our discussion."

"Disappeared? Did you lose him?" Donald mocked.

"You may recall an accident along Mount Pleasant at Branksome Hall." Vitaly continued.

"You mean the drunk limo driver who plowed through our fence?" said Donald. "Cost us $100,000 to fix. I'm on the Board, you know. We had a special levy to pay for the work."

"There was no evidence of drunkenness," Brian muttered.

"What's that? Speak up Constable!" Donald barked.

"I said, Sir, there is no evidence that alcohol was a factor."

"That's not what the officer on the scene wrote. I have a copy of his report right here."

Donald opened his briefcase and pulled out a narrow, black binder marked Branksome Hall - Board of Trustees. He flipped forward two tabs, clicked open the binder and removed a number of sheets that had been stapled together.

"We're suing the driver's firm for the repairs."

He began to reread the report to himself.

"By the way, there's no mention of a passenger," Donald noted.

He flipped over a few pages, to a sheet that held a chart emblazoned with the logo from the Ontario Centre of Forensic Sciences.

"You shouldn't have that," said Brian. "That's privileged."

"How we got it, I don't know. A blood alcohol level of 2.22, and that was drawn from him while he was at St. Michael's Hospital."

"May I?" Brian asked reaching out for the folder.

"Be my guest," Donald said and slid the papers over to Brian. Within three seconds, he muttered.

"Son of a bitch!"

Brian handed it over to Vitaly, pointing to the name of the officer on the chart.

First Constable Sean L. O'Malley

A wry smile creeped across Donald's face.

"As head of the finance committee," continued Donald, "I spoke to Constable O'Malley. I needed him to sign some papers for the insurance company, to make sure the claim was complete. Pleasant chap. Exceedingly helpful."

Vitaly could see Brian tensing and he continued on.

"While we haven't been able to track Kent down, through some good field work by..."

"I didn't authorize any field work," interjected Donald.

"Paul and Maiwen were able to corroborate the claims. LAM has been diverting strong trades to their own funds and bad ones to their outside advisors. According to Maiwen's calculation, this has added about $432 million in profits to the LAM funds. Given their overall performance, and based on the patterns of returns, that has resulted in more than $85 million in excess performance fees. Fees that have been fraudulently earned by the General Partners. Would you care to see a list of the limited partners?"

Donald's eye widened.

"First there was no mention of Graham Kent. Then you accuse John Lister, one of the city's most generous philanthropists, of embezzlement. Now you're trying to drag in the limited partners of the fund into this. None of this was in the report. What else have you left out? Any other surprises?"

"No, just revelations. Maiwen has done most of the work. I'll let her explain."

"Someone has infiltrated the OSC email and file networks," Maiwen began, her glance flitting between Vitaly and her notes.

Donald just glared at her.

"There's no telling how much is compromised. All the relevant documents were missing. Someone from inside the system is deleting files. It took a while, but they all traced to one account."

"So we've got a sloppy person in the organization," snorted Donald. "Might even be one of those virus, worm things my grandson talks about."

"No," cautioned Vitaly, "that's not it."

Vitaly opened a folder and pulled out a file.

"Donald do you have any affiliations with John Lister?"

"Of course I do and you know it or you wouldn't be asking. John and I sit on numerous boards together including Upper Canada College and St. Margaret's Hospital. He's a fine contributor to the school's bursary program and he's funding projects at the hospital that no one else would. I wish we had more people like him donating their time and money. His foundation has been extremely generous."

"Donald, do you have any financial affiliations with Lister?"

"I'm not a direct investor in his fund if that's what you're implying," Donald retorted. "You know my investments are in a blind trust. For a hotshot, you do pose the most obtuse questions."

"Donald, who administers your trust?"

"I just told you. It's blind."

"Even so, please answer the question."

"It's on the record. Aislin Investments, London, Ontario."

"The problem, Donald, is that your half-brother Perry administers Aislin Investments and that Aislin was set up with your money. As far as we can tell, there are three investors in Aislin: you, Perry and a third party we haven't yet identified. Who is it, the third party?"

Donald did not answer.

"Further complicating matters for you, your half-brother does not seem to like you much. He has provided us with a list of your investments."

Donald blanched.

"What's most interesting, and Paul here is to share the credit for uncovering this, is that Aislin was not a unit-holder in any LAM funds until three years ago."

Vitaly looked over at Paul and nodded.

"Paul, go ahead."

"Thank you. Donald, I mean, Mr. Wallace. I just want to confirm the time frame. Three years, correct?"

"Yes, something like that."

"Good. I was reviewing the history of some of the changes to the settlement policies and procedures. From my research, I believe that is when the new trading rules came in, wasn't it?"

"I don't recall. Yes, probably."

"The new rules shrank settlement from trade date plus five days."

"If you says so," said Donald, turning to Vitaly. "You scheduled this meeting for a history lesson by one of your juniors?"

Donald turned back to Paul.

"Is there a point?"

"Under the new settlement rules, companies could no longer reallocate trades to different funds after the trading date. That was around when the performance began to suffer."

Donald shrugged.

"Now why would you invest in a fund that was suffering performance wise?"

"So my brother made some bad investments. He probably thought they'd turn it around."

"And turn it around they did. What was interesting is that the source of the returns changed after you, sorry, Aislin, invested. There was a huge increase in Level Three Assets."

"So what? All the leading hedge funds have large amounts of them. It's the only part of the market that is still inefficient."

"I'd have thought that a prudent man like yourself would be concerned about the risk of having a fund with so many assets that were valued without observable pricing," continued Paul.

"First, it's in a blind trust, remember? Furthermore, Level Three assets aren't scary."

"With the onus on the manager to provide the pricing," continued Vitaly. "These are best described as marked to model."

"More like magic," Derek piped in.

"They're just agreements between two parties," said Donald, "like swaps or insurance contracts."

"What's truly amazing, there has not been a single loss associated with Level Three assets," said Derek.

"He's lucky, I guess. The ones we've traced are all life insurance policies bought from individuals."

"So, there may have been some problems with pricing. You think they overcharged on performance fees. Audit them!" scoffed Donald.

"Donald, your investment in the LAM fund corresponds to when John started to invest in the insurance policies," Vitaly continued. "Aislin invested in LAM many, many times. Every time Aislin put money in, John bought an insurance contract a week later. You, or your brother have been funding the contracts."

"No...but even so, they're a legitimate asset class and a proper response by a manager facing an efficient market. LAM's not unique in making these buys. I've been reviewing a number of hedge funds and they're all doing it."

"That may be so," continued Maiwen, "but no other fund have paid off so handsomely. Seems like you knew what Lister was doing?"

"Everybody out!" Donald snarled.

36

"Out, out, out!" Donald bellowed, waving his cane over his head. "Everyone but Vitaly."

Paul, Derek and Maiwen gathered up their papers and stepped out of the conference room.

"As you wish, Donald," said Brian. "Vitaly, I'll be outside if you need me."

"I don't think Vitaly will need your brawn, Constable," snarled Donald. "He certainly can't use your brain."

Donald waited till the door was shut.

"Your allegations are just that. That my blind pool breached its obligations, mea fuckin' culpa."

"It's not that simple," said Vitaly.

"Make this go away," Donald continued. "It's embarrassing."

"I don't think so."

"You fucking boy scout!"

He slammed his cane on the table. The crack startled Vitaly.

"You're just try to take the shine off my career, you half-man, you child!" he screamed. "Being a giant killer at such a young age will not win you many friends."

Donald trembled with rage, breathing heavily.

"Let me ask you something," Donald continued, attempting to calm his voice.

"Vitaly, are you a builder? An Atlas, holding society strong for others, or do you suck on its teat like a greedy piglet? What John's doing, is it so wrong? The insurance policies he owned provided people with the means to eke out a few more years of dignity in a world that had forgotten them. Those are the wages of life. John provides an alternative to those people. Should he not benefit? He's entitled to a return for his efforts for what he's provided them."

"Donald, that's not what this is about."

"Sure it is. The medical insurance system decides all the time how much a life is worth. They do it every time they restrict the usage of an expensive drug. The system has decided the value of life. John's doing the same thing. Sure he gets paid out when they die, but he never knows when that is going to be, does he now?"

"Donald, are you equating what the medical profession does with what John is doing?

"Are you obtuse? We do it all the time. John's just buying other people's fate. He gives them a better life before they die."

"No, Donald," Vitaly said carefully. "He determines when they die."

"What?"

"It's circumstantial but I've pieced it together through the work of the team and an insider at LAM. He's involved in their deaths."

Donald's fingers ran back and forth over the handle of the cane lying on the table.

"He is not! Yes, he determines their value of their life through careful analysis of the information they readily give him."

"Donald, you don't understand. Adriana..."

"When she joined us here, she had too much life insurance. The OSC provided her, free of charge I might add, group life equivalent to five times her salary. From what I understand she left it to her nieces. I persuaded her to give up her own term life insurance, to sell it to a life settlements broker rather than let it lapse. Adriana had bought her policy when she was in the US working for the American branch of McDermott in Boston."

"She worked for MacKenzie Walter."

"Yes, that's it. Some charlatan got a large commission for setting her up in a $5 million term life policy. It was costing her a fortune. I'm glad I got her out of that."

"Donald, you've no idea of what you've done."

"What? What've I done? Me? Nothing!"

"The term life policy she sold was put into investment pool set up by Val Kozak at LAM. Your blind trust owns Lister's fund. You profited from her death."

"I did no such thing."

"Yes, you did. When Adriana died, LAM received a payout from an insurance company. The proceeds go to the LAM master trust, of which your trust owns four-point-three per cent."

"Aislin owns that."

"Donald, yes it does. We also know Aislin's not blind. It's directed by you. Aislin put money into John's fund every time they bought more of life insurance contracts. Every time. Please don't tell me it was a coincidence. You and I both know it's not. I've got the proof. Maiwen established it by going through documents we have tracked down."

"Vitaly..."

"I have testimony from an employee of LAM. Don't bother asking for a name. The person is not going to reveal themselves but suffice to say that they were responsible for our understanding of why the insurance policies were bought."

"Vitaly..."

"A few years before the life insurance investments started to ramp up, LAM acquired wireless technology company, RX Wireless. This is a list of the 21 companies that received approval from FDA to include the RX technology in their devices."

Vitaly slid a sheet of paper to Donald. He pushed it back without reading it.

"I have no interest in this shit!"

"We found that as we looked through the pools of term life policies and at obituaries across North America, we were able to match the policies. When we got the securitization documents and drilled down into the individual policies, ninety-seven percent of the people who died, had passed well ahead of their predicted age of death. They all used devices, either implanted or for diagnostics, that licensed technology from RX. All of those people died a month to six after the insurance policy was bought. RX is John's backdoor."

"You're saying that LAM is responsible for their deaths?"

"LAM has been buying the term life policies, looking through to see who is using a wireless device, and hacking into to it. Lister is killing for profit."

What little colour Donald had drained from his face. Vitaly pushed the file back over to Donald.

"I believe Adriana used a device from Glucosure," said Vitaly.

"You're saying... He... The bastard killed my Adriana?"

"Yes, he probably hacked her monitor. The official cause of death for Adriana was an insulin overdose. Donald, how would a Type One diabetic, who had controlled her diabetes since she was a teen, make an error when she was stone cold sober?"

Donald reached across the table and looked at the list of devices. His finger followed down the list and stopped three from the bottom.

"Heartwave. I've a device from them. They just put it in... in my chest!"

"You contributed to the death of Adriana."

Donald, terrified, mumbled to himself incoherently.

"By persuading her to sell the policy, you sealed her fate."

"John recommended the doctor to me. Rudie Gelt. He said he was the best. Gelt pushed the device I just got. He touted the advantages. I wouldn't have to go to his blasted office and wait for monitoring. He could just adjust it wirelessly. I need to go..."

Donald gathered his papers. His hands trembled as he tried to slip them back into the folder. Vitaly reached over to help him.

"Fuck off. I can do it," he snarled, slapping his hand away.

"I'll call 911 for you. Get you to emergency now."

He looked up at Vitaly, his eyes watering.

"No!" he continued, his voice softening, "I'll drive myself... to my old cardiologist at Sunnybrook Hospital. He'll know what to do."

"Okay. When you come back, you'll need to have a lawyer with you. You'll talk to Maiwen. She'll take your deposition so we can protect you."

Vitaly helped Donald to his feet and then held his arm in the crook of his own.

"Not a word to anyone. Understood?"

"Understood."

Donald nodded and opened the door. The team was waiting in the hall, ready to be called back in. He shambled past them to the elevator and went directly to the basement parking lot.

Being the head of the OSC gave him the privilege of a parking spot next to the elevator. Given his state of health, he was thankful that he did not have to walk any further. He unlocked the car and eased his dwindling frame into the front seat. Increasingly, he cursed his Porsche Panamera, his ego having trumped practicality when he had leased it.

He put the key fob in the dash and pushed the ignition button. The car hummed to life. He put the car in reverse and froze. A large man in a poorly fitting, pale grey suit was in his rearview mirror, his hands on the sloping window. His face was fleshy and pink and his nose was crooked. A tall blonde woman in a well tailored blue pinstriped suit knocked on the driver side window and made a motion to lower it. Donald locked the door.

Through the glass, she said, "John says hello."

The woman stepped back and continued towards the elevator. The man in the grey suit quickly caught up to her.

 Donald took a deep breath, put the car in gear and left the parking garage, heading north on Bay Street. The left lane was congested so he drove in the right reserved for buses and taxis.

He accelerated up Bay Street, hitting speeds of up to 70 kilometers per hour between lights. At Gerard Street, he noticed red and blue lights flickering in his rearview mirror. He continued through the light and he slowed at the other side, hoping that the cop would pass him. The cruiser slowed as well and the two came to a stop. Donald could see an officer typing something into his on-board computer. Two minutes later he was at the door. Donald rolled down his window.

"Good morning officer."

He looked up and saw a familiar face behind mirrored sunglasses.

"Oh, O'Malley. Good to see you. I need to get going. Can you help me get to Sunnybrook? I need to see my cardiologist now!"

O'Malley took off his sunglasses and hung them from his shirt pocket.

"Good morning, Sir. Do you know why I pulled you over?"

Donald looked at O'Malley and then glanced in the rearview mirror. He saw a second officer in the car. He understood, O'Malley had to play the game.

"Gee, was I speeding?"

"Yes, Sir, and you were in a restricted lane for five blocks. Any reason for that?" O'Malley asked.

"It's an emergency. I'm on my way to my physician's office. God damn it, O'Malley, I need to get to him. It's urgent."

"You don't look like you're having a medical emergency. Late for an appointment? Never mind. I don't care. License and registration, please."

Donald grunted.

"O'Malley, I need to get going."

"License and registration. Please don't idle, sir. We'll get you on your way as quickly as possible."

Donald turned off the car and reached into the glove box for the registration and removed it from its folder. He reached into his jacket, pulled out his wallet and extracted his license and insurance.

"Here you go. Hurry!"

O'Malley just looked at him, put on his sunglasses and sauntered back to the car. Donald knew that he was enjoying this. O'Malley handed the papers to the other officer, who began to type the information into the on-board computer.

O'Malley stood next to the cruiser and dialed a number on his cell phone. Donald stared into the rearview mirror, willing O'Malley to move faster. He did not.

The screen of the in-dash entertainment system flashed, indicating an incoming call.

Donald spoke to the car.

"Accept."

He glanced in the rearview mirror and saw that O'Malley was now seated in the cruiser, in conversation with the other officer.

"Connecting," said the computerized female voice.

"Yes," Donald said curtly.

John's face appeared on the screen. Palm fronds swayed in the background. Donald pursed his lips.

"Hi Donnie. How's tricks?"

"John, where are you? Never mind. I'm in a bit of a rush right now. Can this wait? I've just been pulled over by O'Malley and he's giving me the gears."

"Yes, Donnie, I know," said John.

"What? How do you..."

"How was your meeting with Vitaly? Did you learn anything shocking?"

"Nothing about LAM or you. The meeting was about another case."

"You've always lied poorly. Kind of surprising, given your past. I saw your agenda on your computer and hacked into the file that Vitaly had sent you for today's meeting."

"How? How? Our security..."

"Security? Oh please. I see everything you read. The file's incomplete. It was fascinating nonetheless."

Donald sat in silence.

"You've failed in protecting our interests. I no longer require your services."

"John, my hands are tied. I tried to..."

"I could say it's been a pleasure but you're a sniveling..."

"You bastard. After all I have done you for. I gave you your first job, funded you when you were nothing. I got you your whales when you needed cash. LAM would be nothing without me!"

"Ancient history," John said calmly.

"I kept the OSC off your ass for so fucking long. You should've been done years ago."

"You got scared, didn't you?"

"I'm not afraid of you."

"Yes, you are. You put Adrianna on the case because you knew she would solve the complaint and uncover so much more.

You knew she would do me in. You S.O.B. She'd never turn on you. She was too loyal. You'd keep the money. You'd be tucked away in your Lake Ontario estate."

He lowered his voice to a whisper. "With Adrianna gone, you put Mirkin on the case."

"I tried to sway him. I tried to get him to see the bigger picture, of where he'd fit in longer term. John, you've got to believe me."

"But Vitaly isn't cooperative. Bit of a boy scout. Always doing the right thing."

"I brought Jargit when you were so fucking strung out you couldn't even remember your dead girl's name."

"Don't mention Alison," John said tersely, his teeth clenched.

"You'd be nothing without me. You and Joannie, you'd still be in that dump in Kensington Market, counting your nickels so you could buy another bag of smack. Well, fuck you John. Fuck you!"

"I've no debts to you. Goodbye. See you in Hell! Oh, Donnie, in about fifteen seconds, you're going to feel a sharp twinge in your chest, maybe some nausea," said John. "You might be short of breath. This is the first time I'm doing this with your brand of defibrillator. Not sure how you'll react. Be a darling and leave the camera on, would you? I wanna watch."

"Fuck you!" screamed Donald, glancing in the rearview mirror at the cruiser behind him.

The first spasm gripped his chest. It was like a troll was ripping his heart out through his back.

"Vitaly knows..." he gasped.

"I know that...as did Adriana. She was getting too close. I couldn't allow that now. Thankfully, she had switched glucose monitors. Otherwise things would have been messier."

"You son of a...She was a daughter to..."

Donald's chest spasmed again. He inhaled sharply. After twenty seconds, the stabbing passed.

"You didn't have to kill her. We could have found a way."

"How's it feel so far?" John asked. "Clutch your chest if you want. I like melodrama."

The pain was excruciating. Each shock was more pronounced in intensity. It seemed that his defibrillator was recharging in shorter intervals. He banged at the screen, trying to turn it off.

"Don't bother. Not much you can do now. In two minutes, you will be slumped over the wheel. You will convulse until the battery is drained."

"Fuck you!"

"Now, now. Such language. Not much of a legacy. You know, you can always try to disconnect it yourself."

John smirked and turned away from the camera.

"Tatiana, babe," John said raising his voice, "Would you be so kind to fetch Bernard and ask him to pour me another drink?"

"Sure. Just a sec John. Finishing a voicemail. What do you want?"

"I need something uplifting. One of those umbrella thingies."

"A margarita?"

"Yes, I feel like celebrating."

John turned back to the screen.

"Farewell Don. I'm just gonna sit here and watch."

Donald started clawing at his chest. He ripped open his shirt and with his right hand, he reached into his armpit and felt the scar where the surgeon had cut him. The wound was still healing and the staples were still in place. They were due to be removed in three days.

He moved his fingers down two centimeters and felt the device through his skin. It was the size of a box of matches. He squeezed it and tried to move it up to the semi-healed opening. It did not budge. He tore at the wound with his finger nails, splitting the fresh scar.

The pain was intense; blood oozed onto his fingers, over the fat of his chest and onto his white cotton shirt.

He gritted his teeth and dug in, his fingers just touching the hard plastic shell of the device, but he could not grab hold of it, his blood and fat making it slippery. He felt the three wires.

His chest convulsed again from another shock. He dug in and tugged at one of the wires.

Donald received another shock and lost control of his hand and his fingers.

He slumped over in his seat, his head on his chest, his seatbelt holding him in place. His body still convulsed with each new shock. O'Malley and his partner walked up to the car.

"Call a bus, now!" O'Malley yelled.

The rookie ran back to the car. O'Malley pulled out his black leather gloves from his pant pocket, put them on, opened the car door and leaned inside. He looked past Donald to John's face on the telephone screen.

"This will make for electrifying news," said John.

"A death most shocking!" O'Malley chuckled.

O'Malley reached across Donald's slumped body.

He looked over his shoulder. His partner was still in the cruiser, talking into the mic of the radio.

O'Malley erased the phone's memory and waited beside the car. The ambulance siren wail could be heard five minutes later, coming across Gerard from the Toronto General.

Of course, it would be too late.

37

"Caroline," pleaded Mila, "Please pick up. Don't let it go to voicemail again. I'll be home soon."

"Tatiana, babe, would you ask Bernard to pour me another drink?" said John in the background.

"Sure. Just a sec John. Finishing a voicemail. What do you want?" Mila continued whispering. "Caroline, I gotta go. I love you."

Mila turned to John.

"Margarita?"

John had been entirely focused on Lily all day.

He had been only stealing away from her side to talk on the phone when she dozed. When he did, Mila noted that he was oddly jovial.

His only interaction with Mila was to ask her to fetch a drink. Of course he had to do that when she was briefly on the phone herself, trying to get in touch with Caroline.

But all her calls went to voicemail.

The door was open for Lily to reach out to her but Mila knew she would have to walk through it herself. No prodding could make her change.

Mila lounged in the sun, keeping her distance at the far end of the balcony some six meters away, watching, to make sure that John treated her well. All thoughts were of Caroline.

38

"Brian Cranston here."

"Detective, it's me, Sean, Constable O'Malley."

"What's up?"

"I thought you'd want to know."

"Know what?"

"I, uh, I stopped Mr. Wallace on the way up Bay Street about an hour ago. I'd been following a car that had been speeding and driving in the express lane for five blocks. If it's just a few blocks, I cut 'em some slack but after five, I pull 'em over."

"And?"

"I had no idea it was him till I walked up to the car. I had a rookie riding shotgun, so for shits and giggles, I ask Mr.Wallace for his license and registration. He tells me he's in a horrible rush to get to his doctor. I go back to the rook to get him to run the L and R and discuss what we should do. We both agree to give him a warning, given Mr. Wallace's position and all.

"O'Malley, is there a point to this?"

"The rook and I get out, walk up to the car and Mr. Wallace was slumped over the steering wheel, convulsing, There's like blood everywhere. I get the rook to call for a bus. They were there in five minutes from Toronto General. I tried CPR. He looked like shit when they took him to emerg. Looked like he dug into the side of his chest. He was pronounced twenty minutes ago."

Brian looked at his watch. Donald had left the meeting less than an hour earlier.

"Thanks O'Malley. Where's the car now?"

He got his answer and hung up and slammed it down four times. The phone base cracked and the handset fell apart in his hand.

Vitaly rushed in from the office next door just as Brian hurled the phone base across the room. It smashed into a wall, splintering into shards.

Without acknowledging Vitaly, Brian reached into his desk, picked up his cellphone and dialed.

"Staff Sergeant Methven please... Detective Brian Cranston... I'll wait. Tracey, Brian... Donald Wallace just died. I need you to get involved and only with guys you trust. The body's at TGH. Keep Sean O'Malley away from everything. Yeah, that O'Malley. I'll call you later, Tracey, thanks."

Brian snapped his clamshell shut.

"Change of plans," he said. "Wallace just died. O'Malley called me too soon after. He should be locked down in paper work."

Vitaly nodded, shut the door and sat down.

39

Near the end of the day, John left Lily sleeping in a chaise lounge and sat down next to Mila.

"Thanks for staying with her out there. She's a good swimmer but sometimes she exceeds her own capabilities."

"She's stronger than you think. We just got caught up in a rip and had to angle back."

"Well, thank you nonetheless. I'll be leaving for Miami tonight. I've given Lily something to relax her. Bernard will take her to her room and she'll sleep 'til morning."

"As for you, you're free to do want you want, but I'll need, I mean, I'd like you to accompany Lily to Miami tomorrow," John continued gently.

"I'm sorry again for my behaviour from last night. If you agree to come, Mike will give you the rest of the information. I know this wasn't part of our original plan but would 15k cover the inconvenience of it all?"

"John, she just needed a little help out there. I was glad I was with her when she got caught in the current. Not sure if I would have made it back it if I was me."

"In any case, thank you again. Will you come, to Miami?"

"I will," she began with a yawn. "I'm tired too from the swim and the sun. I just need a little down time. I had plans for tomorrow but I can change them. Just need to send off a few emails."

He looked at her quizzically.

"I need WiFi access," Mila explained.

"Remember, you said Miami, not the Bahamas. I don't have data down here. Last night, I could access the network but the configuration's changed. Can't seem to find the hotel's anymore. There are a number of access points but all need a password."

"Sorry. Andrews said there were issues. Here, try the port called EPITA1. Andrews said it's their back-up when the Atlantis is down. Apparently it's on a separate system. The password is ITIT."

"Thanks. I just need to send an email to my Mom. It's her birthday today and I was supposed to be in Toronto tomorrow for a lunch. Need to make things right."

He just smiled and left her on the balcony.

Mila lay in the sun for another hour until its warmth began to dissipate and then made her way to her room. Seated on her bed, she could hear John chatting with Bernard.

"Please Bernard, check on her in an hour or so. I need to go to Miami this evening. There are some preparations that I need to attend to. Please have Mike ready with the car in thirty minutes."

A few moments later, the light on the phone on her bedside table lit up. Mila logged on to the network and entered the password. She sent an email to her mom and then checked her inbox. There was no note from Caroline. It was the third day without a word.

Through her door, she could hear John talking loudly on the phone.

"Val... What?... Wallace died today? O'Malley called. No... Found in his car, blood everywhere... Open sutures? Holy Fuck, that must have been a mess! How'd they know it was his pacemaker? I told him not to get the Heartwave product. Well, wonder who will replace him at the OSC... Mirkin?... too junior. It'll never happen... I'm telling you he's too fucking junior! Anyhow, I won't allow it."

Mila froze.

"Won't allow what?" Mila said to herself.

"Val, are all the shorts in place? We're up fifty-three per cent already... yes Val, that's quite a score. Val, What's the kid's number again? Yeah Tom. He's still short of the goal, isn't he? I want to provide a little motivation to him. Okay... Repeat the last four digits... Got it... Thanks. Tim's coming down tomorrow. Hold down the fort 'til I get back, okay?"

The light on the phone in her room went dead for a few seconds and lit up again.

Mila decided to listen more carefully, making notes on her cell phone.

"Tim, what the fuck happened at the office today? Healthcare, uh huh, small cap shorts. Uh huh... they were crushed... How much did we fucking lose? Oh Fuckin' Fuck Fuck. You were supposed to be watching that. Christ... No we don't need to fucking hedge that long... I don't care how many points we're offside... No, you're fucking wrong... No, you're a fucking trader so fucking trade... No, I'm not wrong. Yeah, I heard about Wallace... He was useful but he didn't do what I needed him to... Mirkin... He knows shit... Now you're complaining about bonuses too... Jesus Christ, Tim, when have I ever let you down?... Yes, I promised to look after Boomer but I'll protect you too...Who's gonna pay?... I'll find a fuckin' way... Act like a fuckin' partner, would ya? Can you do that? Don't give me shit about the primes, they have shit for brains... Are you done stating the obvious? Tell Boomer to start something. After the street stops looking at her ass, they listen to her. What the fuck! Do I have to do everything? All right don't snivel... See you tomorrow night, seven p.m. the Mandarin. No, don't bring your wife. She wouldn't approve of the treat I've for you. Similar to last year... Believe me... Much, much better... Good job today and find out where the fuck Boomer is. I don't like it when she's out of my sight."

He hung up and dialed another number.

"Hello... Tom Tournimenko please. Tom, it's John Lister... Hi Tom, Val gave me your personal number... Says you've been avoiding him. I do appreciate all the work you've done thus far. Val tells me you were moving at a quick clip and then everything dropped off. Nothing for the past two weeks. Not even updates... Yes, good... Tom, you know you're still short of the goals Val set out for you... Wally Babiak died... I know... So sudden... It all seems so strange, no? No, the claim should go through... Edna had three good months with Wally. Without the operation, it'd have been much worse... You're right, but I need you to get moving. I am upping the amount of money we're committing to the space... Yes, it's hard but I don't care... Tom, Stop and listen! Do it or you're done... Done... I'm not screwing around. Understood? Good. Thank you and good luck."

John hung up and dialed another number.

Mila sent her notes as an email to Caroline. She was the only person who could understand. She locked her phone and walked into the bathroom and grabbed a small white hand towel.

She padded down the hall in her bare feet towards the living room, shaking out her arms as she went, controlling her breathing. John was on the sectional couch, still on the phone.

Mila sat down in his lap and began stroking his ears and kissing his neck. She had a role to play.

"Boomer, pick up," John said, ignoring her entreaties.

"Oh fuck, just so you're in the loop. I spoke to your brother just now, he's doing an okay job but I need him to move faster. He hasn't hit any stretch goals. I may have to hire another person to chase down leads."

Mila slid off of him and sat on the cushion next to him. She glanced down the hallway and made sure that Lily's door was closed. She was sure she would not see Lily again tonight.

Mila unbuttoned the top of her dress so he could see her lace bra, slipping her hand under the fabric and caressing her flesh. She took his free hand and put it between her legs, rubbing on the outside of her skirt. John stayed on the phone.

"Isabella, tell your brother to get his shit together. This is his final warning. Boomer, let him know."

He hung up and dialed another number.

Mila got on all fours and whispered in his ear.

"John, you sound so stressed. Let me see what I can do to help you."

She blew gently in his ear and nibbled his lobe.

"Get, um, get Beate."

John was silent for a moment.

Mila sat back and laid the towel across his leg.

She loosened his belt and undid his pants, slipping her hand between the waistband of his boxer shorts and his skin, first playing with his pubis and then stroking his member.

"Beate, I need you to find Isabella. She's disappeared. Hasn't been at work for a few days. No, it's not a family trip... I think her loyalty might be... wavering."

He continued his conversation as he swelled in her hand. She bent over and took him in her mouth, flicking her tongue stud over his glans. She felt him engorge and begin to twitch. He slid down the couch, shifting his hips.

"Find her and talk to her and ahhh... Figure out what's going on. Call me back at anytime with anything you know..."

He held the back of her head, as she bobbed slowly. He knew she hated being forced and he resisted at first as she tried to shake him off. He relented, his conversation unbroken as he came.

She wiped her lips on the towel. Mila got up from the couch and smiled with her mouth closed. John nodded, absentmindedly.

"What Beate? Kent's widow came by the office...She returned some papers. Val gave her the cheque, right? Good."

Mila bent over pinned his hand with the phone to the sofa, listening to the tinny voice prattling away.

She pressed her lips to his and inserted her tongue into his mouth, funneling his bitter liquor back to him.

She held the embrace for a few seconds, and then wiped her mouth with the towel. He swallowed and continued his conversation without pause.

"Ah, text me when you know anything. Thanks Beate."

Mila went to her room, shut the door and rinsed her mouth with Listerine.

She ran the shower and stared at herself in the mirror.

A thin film of condensation covered the glass. She knelt down in front of the toilet, and stuck two fingers down her throat and vomited.

John finished the last of his calls and made sure all the preparations for Miami were in place.

He walked from the living room to his makeshift study and sat down at his computer.

There were a few miscellaneous emails from Joan, complaining of the quality of the penthouse in Miami.

John closed his emails and although he had told himself before sitting down that he would not, he opened the resident WiFi screening program, EPITA1, Isabella had developed as part of her PhD; it was what had caught his eye when he had interviewed her.

He had not look at it since he had arrived.

Lily had accessed the hub when she had updated her online diary. John was tempted to read it but resisted the temptation. Mila was a different matter.

The first was a draft, unsent.

Dear Mama:

Sorry I missed your birthday. It was rotten of me not to be there. I'll make it up to you when I return. I love you so much.

Love You

Milaska

John read on.

Caroline: I know you're pissed. I'd be too. I'll be home soon. Then the world will be ours my love. M.

Caroline: I'm attaching a file. I'm not sure what to do with it. Just keep it somewhere safe. It's stuff I overhead. It's important to V. Love you with all my heart. M.

John clicked on the attachment and read what Mila had sent.

He was not sure what incensed himself more; the note or that she loved someone else.

He slammed his fist down three times on the desk.

"Patience," he said to himself.

"It's just some woman she sent it to. No one of consequence. There'll be time enough after Miami."

John packed his laptop into his satchel and headed to the lobby.

Bernard was there with his bag, ready to join John in the elevator.

"I trust you've have had a good stay, Sir."

"Yes, thank you Bernard. Pleasant as always."

"Permit me sir if I may, Miss Tatiana, she's a remarkable young woman. Ms. Lily's fortunate to count her as a friend."

"Indeed, Bernard, remarkable."

40

There was a gentle knock on her door.

"Mila, it's time," said Lily. "Mike's waiting."

Mila was ready, bags packed and closed. She had been admiring the view from the balcony, engraving the contours of the beach and the sea in her mind's eye, trying to find something redeeming about the last few days.

She had snapped a photo for Caroline but had deleted it, the pixels not doing the vista justice. She would not want to see it anyway.

Mila joined Lily downstairs.

The sun was searing. Lily was waiting with her sunglasses on, leaning against a sedan chatting with Mike. She ran over to Mila threw her arms around her as she descended the stairs. It was the first time the two of them had been alone since their morning swim.

"Thanks for not saying anything... to John."

"I meant every word when we were swimming."

Mila's phone rang. She looked at the incoming call.

"Excuse me. It's my brother."

She took a few steps away and cupped her hand around the mouthpiece. Mike was getting antsy.

"Ms. Tatiana. We must leave."

Mila held up her index finger.

"Ladies..."

Mila finished her call and took Lily's arm in hers and walked to the sedan, the door already opened by Mike. They climbed in beside each other, safe in their twisted sisterhood.

The ride to the airport was uneventful. The shantytowns, so foreboding in the dark, were now just pathetic. The shacks were simply poor.

The women, teens really, should have been on their way to school in blue tunics and starched white shirts. Instead, they were carrying toddlers on their hips, their faces devoid of joy.

Boys, who might have been the ones who had assaulted them, lazed in the shade of grand date palms, catcalling after the young mothers.

The contrast Mila's last few days was extreme. Gertie's amusement money would go a long way here. Heck, her own stash would make a real difference.

Mila reached for her purse and tapped it, reassuring herself that the envelope John had left for her was still there. The balance would be waiting for her in Miami.

Mike entered the airport through the regular gates and he turned west toward the helicopters. He parked next to a large navy blue one that was bigger than any Mila had ever seen.

"Uh, Mike, a helicopter?"

"Mr. Lister took the plane last night."

"Oh Mila, come on," said Lily. "No need to be white as a sheet. It's not that bad. October's when the air's choppy."

Mike hopped out of the sedan and opened the door for Mila and Lily.

Gillian appeared at the door with lifejackets that she handed out. Lily gently pushed Mila forward.

Gillian helped Mila into her lifejacket and sat down in her seat. Mila looked at the five-point harness.

"I'll let Lily help you," said Gillian. "She's seen it enough times. She could do my job."

In moments, Lily had Mila buckled in, the straps snug. The cabin closed and the air was suddenly stale. Mila took a deep breath to reassure herself, but her lungs felt empty.

The whirling blades created impenetrable white noise. With a sweeping motion of her hands, Gillian got everyone's attention and motioned to the ceiling of the cabin where the earphones were racked. Mila slipped her's on. There was near silence.

"Can you hear me now?" Lily asked, speaking in the mouthpiece.

Mila gave her a thumbs-up.

"Cause here we go!"

The helicopter rose, the nose tilted down and began to yaw to port before gaining both airspeed and altitude. Mila's headset crackled as the pilot spoke.

"Welcome back Ms. Lily and Mike. I'm Captain Billy Holiday. Yes, my parents had a sense of humour. Ms. Tatiana, I hear from Lily that this is your first time in a whirlybird. I'll bet your knuckles are white from holding the harness tight. You can let go. The vessel still flies."

Mila looked down at her hands. Her knuckles were indeed white. She relaxed her grip.

The helicopter dipped suddenly. Her hands flew to the harness.

"Just kidding. Lily asked me to tease you. I'd never do such a thing on my own."

There were smiles all around the cabin. From Mila too.

"Captain Billy" said Lily rolling her eyes, "remember when you..."

"Now Lily, let bygones be bygones. Sit back and enjoy the flight. Flight time to Miami is about 90 minutes. We'll be touching down at the Bayside Heliport to clear customs. I believe Mike will be taking you to the Mandarin Oriental from there. If Lily wants, though, I could hover over their beach and you both could jump into the pool."

"Thanks Captain," said Lily looking at Mila, "I've swum enough for a few days."

"Suit yourselves, but you haven't lived till you've jump from great heights."

Soon they began their descent as Miami loomed ahead.

They landed gently and the pilot wound down the engines, the decibels dropping as the blades came to a complete stop.

Gillian opened the door and the warmth and humidity of Miami rushed in.

Two customs officers arrived a minute later dressed in blue shorts, white short sleeved shirts, wide brimmed hats and mirrored sunglasses. They looked comical apart from their sidearms.

"Passports please. Any United States citizens?"

"Yes, Sir," said the pilot and copilot unison. The captain continued. "All others are all Canadians, Sir."

Gillian collected the passports and handed them over. The officer looked at each in turn.

"Lily Lister, anything to declare."

"No Sir."

"Michael Brennan. Anything to declare Mr. Brennan?"

"No Sir."

"Thank you. Gillian, good to see you again. Same as always."

"Yup. Bottle of rum. A carton of Marlborough Lights."

Lily looked at Gillian.

"What?" she said with a shrug of her shoulders.

"Ms. Mirkin Petrovna. You must be Mila."

"Yes, Sir."

"Haven't seen you before, have I?"

"No Sir."

He looked her up and down. The blue streaks in her hair, the tattoos, the piercings; she could feel the interrogation starting. It happened at every security check.

"First time in Miami?"

"She was here for a few days ago," said Mike. "She was en route to Nassau."

The officer looked at Mike.

"Mr. Brennan, she can speak, no?"

"Yes officer."

"Ms. Mirkin, what brings you back to Miami?"

"A few days' vacation with Lily. Just finished exams."

"Oh yeah, what's your major?"

"Psychology, focusing on mental health and addiction."

"So did I. Would have done better if I'd gone to classes though. Why were you in Nassau?"

"A bit of beach time and a little swim."

"Anything to declare?"

"No Sir."

"Well, enjoy yourself and stay away from South Beach at night. Unless you're looking to party. Okay, you're good to go."

He handed the passports back. Mike led Mila and Lily to a waiting sedan. The driver got out and handed the keys to Mike.

Gillian stayed with the pilots and went to a second waiting car. The ride over to the hotel took about five minutes. The Mandarin loomed as they crossed a causeway from the mainland, a tall, cream coloured, curved structure built right on the water. The drab exterior did little to indicate what lay inside.

As Mila and Lily entered the main lobby, they walked straight to the large plate glass windows overlooking the water. Both women had spotted the artificial beach that had been set up on Biscayne Bay, replete with day beds, cabanas and white sheers billowing in the soft breeze.

Mike appeared behind Mila and Lily and handed them each their room keys. They compared room numbers. They were on different floors.

"I know, I know," said Mike. "These were the rooms that your father booked."

"I guess I should go see John," Lily said with a resigned voice.

Mila followed Lily to the elevator, checked the envelope again, and pushed the button for the four floor.

"See you later, okay?" asked Mila.

"Yeah, sounds good."

Mila exited the elevator and followed the corridor down to the end of the hall.

She opened the envelope and noticed that there were three room keys. Two were identical. The third had a sticker on it. 1900. Mila waved a card in front of the door handle and listened for the lock to click open.

The room was dark despite the mid-afternoon sun. She felt for a light switch and needed to step halfway down the alcove entrance before finding it.

She hoped that the blackout blinds had been drawn, but they were not. The rooms sole window faced a wall not ten feet away, one floor above the renovation site they had passed when they arrived.

She waved at the construction workers below. The windows trembled as the work crew jack-hammered the concrete. She was not impressed.

Her bags were waiting for her on the folding valet caddy. She unzipped the larger one of the two. On top was the pashmina she had worn in Nassau. There was an envelope tucked inside the fold.

Dear Ms.Tatiana,

I hope you don't mind. It looked perfect draped over your shoulders. It was a pleasure to serve you. I saw what you did for Lily and how she responded to you. You have the character I wish my own daughter had. If you ever need assistance, please call me at the number below.

With kind regards,

Bernard Taylor

bt@bahamatel.com

Mila slid the card back into the envelope and tucked it into a zippered compartment of her purse. She opened the closet to hang her longer items and stood back stunned. There were four dresses, each of a different style, and each supremely elegant. A sign hung from the bar.

These are all for you. J.

Below each was a shoe box marked Jimmy Choo, each in her size. She gathered up all four dresses and lay them on the bed.

Her cell phone rang.

"Thank you so much!" she gushed.

"Uh, Mil... Ms. Tatiana, it's me, Mike. Mr. Lister gave me your phone number. It was faster than calling you through the hotel switchboard. I hope you don't mind."

"Not at all Mike. What's up?"

"Mr. Lister would like you to join him at six p.m. Suite nineteen-hundred."

"Mike, there were four beautiful dresses in the closet but I have no idea which one to wear. I presume you put them in the closet. How'd you get them in there anyhow? You were with me the whole time."

"I arrived in Miami two days before we departed for Nassau. I dropped them with the concierge with instructions. I hope they're to your liking."

"They're too beautiful. But Mike, where am I going tonight?"

Mike was silent.

"Mike?"

"More surprises. Sorry. This evening is the Tenth Annual Fundraiser for *Off the Streets*. It's a charity event to raise money for the homeless of Miami. Mr. and Mrs. Lister host it each year."

"Mrs. Lister?"

"Yes. She will be in attendance along with about three hundred and fifty other people."

"Will Lily be there? Please tell me that I'm sitting with her and not some blue rinse and her lecherous husband."

"I don't know the seating plan but I'll do my best to make sure you are comfortable."

"Thanks. So what should I wear?"

"You always look beautiful. The blue is my favourite. Goes with your hair. Also, the safe code is 2611. In there, you'll find your accessories. I believe that's what they're called."

"Thanks Mike."

"You're welcome... Mila."

41

Vitaly breezed into Biff's, ignored the hostess station and pushed his way through the crowd waiting to be seated. He had stunned himself. He had just accused his boss of complicity in murder and he was running off to lunch with his parents to celebrate his mother's birthday.

As he walked up to the restaurant, he had seen saw Petr and Zoya in their usual spot by the bay window. They had been holding hands across the table, eyes connected, deep in conversation. Vitaly felt a vice-like grip on his elbow.

"I need to talk to you," said Caroline with a strained smile.

"Caroline, good to see you. How's Marc?"

Vitaly leaned in to kiss her but Caroline turned away.

"What's up? My parents are waiting. Can't be late for Petr?"

"Come," she insisted in a low, deep tone.

She still held his elbow firmly. He let her lead him past the dining rooms reserved for lunchtime presentations and out into the courtyard behind the restaurant.

"Caroline, what's so important?"

She handed him her cellphone. There was a map of Florida and the Northern Caribbean. A red dot flashed over Nassau.

"I don't get it."

"Vitaly, Mila's in Nassau."

"What? She's supposed to be here. Ah Christ, she promised."

"She's... she's down there with a... friend."

"Caroline, I can't keep track of her friends."

"Vitaly, she's supposed to be in Miami. Only Miami. That's what she told me. She spent the last two nights in Nassau. She wasn't supposed to. She promised me."

"What? Why are you worried?"

"Vitaly! The friend she's traveling with, he's bad news."

"I don't like any of them either, except for you, of course."

"She wasn't supposed to go to the Bahamas," Caroline repeated slowly.

"She's just blowing off some steam after exams. She'll be fine."

"How can she afford to go? Where'd she get the money?"

"Caroline, I... I don't know. What are you not telling me?

"It's... She shouldn't be there with him. She should be here. She should be here in Toronto."

"You're tracking her?"

"We've a little pact. Watch each other's backs."

"Why wouldn't she be safe?"

"A woman in a man's world."

"You didn't answer my question. Why wouldn't she be safe?"

"I just don't like the guy."

"Don't like the guy? Are you jealous?"

Caroline turned beat red with anger.

"I'll talk to her when she comes back, said Vitaly. "When's that?"

"This morning, in time for lunch. Now, I don't know, couple of days?"

"Okay, I'll talk to her, promise. Hey, don't say anything to Zoya or Petr."

"How stupid do I look?"

"Zoya saw me when you grabbed me. Bring over a bottle of Veuve, and a couple of dozen oysters. It will be our cover."

"Used to lying to your parents?"

"Only to make them happy. You go first. I'll follow."

Caroline hurried back into the restaurant. Vitaly took out his cell phone and dialed.

"Hey V.!"

"Mila, where the Hell are you?"

"Yo Bro, whatta ya know?" she asked casually.

"Where are you?"

"Just chillin'!"

"Mila!"

"South."

"South?"

"You know...ah... Miami."

"Really? You sure? Do you know what day it is?"

"It's today?"

"It's the day after Mom's birthday. I'm at Biff's right now about to sit down with them. Shall I have Caroline remove your place setting?"

"Shit!"

"Yeah shit! Mila, where are you?"

"Nassau."

"So Caroline was right."

"What'd she tell you?" Mila asked

"That you're supposed to be in Miami with some friend. Don't panic. She didn't say much, just that she was concerned, almost like she was jealous. Who's your friend? Do I know him?"

"Nah, he's from school."

"Mila you're lying. I cross exam people for a living. She said he's bad news."

From the phone, Vitaly could hear a man's voice.

"Ms. Tatiana. We must leave. The helicopter's ready for us."

"What? Tatiana? Helicopter? Mila, what the Hell's going on? Why are you in Nassau?"

"Why do you care?"

"Mila... Mila, are you okay?"

"Vitaly, don't be a hard ass."

"Hard ass? Me? You're the one ditchin' Zoya!"

"Think she'll be pissed?"

"I haven't talked to her yet. She'll be disappointed. You promised you'd be here."

"Cover for me, please. Tell her I'm doing research. I'll take her to a spa when I come back. Please Vitaly! Please."

"Okay, I'll make something up, but we need to talk."

"Yeah, yeah. Thanks for covering."

Vitaly hung up. He walked back briskly into the restaurant and found Petr and Zoya, still holding hands.

Caroline accompanied by another waiter, brought the champagne and oysters over moments later. Zoya turned to Vitaly.

"Oh Vitaly. You should not have!" she said.

"Happy Birthday Mama!"

"Yes, Happy Birthday Mrs. Mirkin."

"Caroline, still so formal," Zoya chided. "But Caroline, you forgot someone. There are three flutes. We need four."

"Mama," said Vitaly looking up at Caroline for a moment, "Mila texted me this morning saying that she couldn't make it. I should have told you."

"Why not? She promised!"

"Dr. Simintov asked her at the last minute to work on a new survey group, this one's in Miami. She'll be back in a few days. I'm sure she'll have something wonderful for you then."

Zoya had a half smile, but her face was pained by her daughter's absence. Petr squeezed her hand.

Caroline unwrapped the foil around the bottle's neck and eased out the cork with a gentle pop. She poured the three glasses, offering one to each of them in turn.

Zoya examined the flute and admired the bubbles as they danced to the surface. She lifted her glass and looked to Petr and then to Vitaly.

"To us... To all present in body or in spirit."

42

Mila donned the iridescent steel-blue dress Mike had recommended. After hunting around for the safe, she found it concealed in a nightstand. She passed over the bejeweled pendants and chose a simple black, silk ribbon choker adorned with a rabbit-shaped pendant carved from ivory. She hated the thought of a tuskless elephant, lying somewhere, its body dried and withered by the elements, but the pendant spoke to her. It reminded her of the Durer etching that hung on her mother's side of the bed and of course of Caroline too. It made her feel calm.

She slipped off all of her rings except for her grandmother's. Though battered and scratched, it added an old world elegance, working beautifully with the pendant. Her Babushka would be pleased, though not proud of the circumstances. She looked radiant. She thought it was a pity her Jimmy Choos were hidden under the floor length hem.

Mila turned off the lights and slipped the two rooms key and her lipstick into the blue silk clutch John had provided. She walked down the hall to the elevator and rode up to the nineteenth floor. The doors opened onto a dimly lit vestibule. Mila stood in front of the door, smoothing her dress one last time and feeling nervous, as if were back at her high school prom. Except, tonight her date was not achingly shy. She could scarcely believe only four years had passed since that painful rite. Her thought was broken by a screaming match on the other side of the door.

"John! She's here? You invited her here!"

"Joan, what's the difference? You insisted your man come."

"He's my assistant!"

"Bullshit!"

Something broke against the door, water splashing against the floor. A pitcher? A vase? Mila reconsidered using the room key

John had provided and knocked firmly on the door. The cacophony ceased.

A woman's footsteps approached and Mila stood back from the door. A shadow passed over the peephole and Mila heard a sigh. The doorknob turned slightly, there was a pause and the door opened quickly.

"Yes, oh do come in, dear," said the woman in a saccharine voice. "You must be Lily's new friend. She has spoken so much about you. Come in. Please excuse the mess. I was frightfully careless and knocked over a vase. I'm Joan, Lily's mother."

"Tatiana Nikoleavna. Pleased to meet you Mrs. Lister."

"I insist you call me Joan. Mrs. is so passé.

The rug squished audibly under Mila's heels. She wobbled a bit and Joan held Mila's arm gently, almost warmly, and led her through the foyer and down a hallway. She stopped at the threshold of the living room.

"I believe you've met my scoundrel," Joan said pointing to the balcony.

John was seated on a couch in his tuxedo. A white bow-tie was still loose around his neck. He held a newspaper in his hand, pretending to read it. A martini glass warmed on the side table next to him.

"Mrs. Lister, Joan, I didn't realize you'd be here. Wonderful to put a face to Lily's mom," Mila said bravely.

"Oh no, Tatiana, it's my pleasure to meet you. Lily tells me you're quite the swimmer, that you kept up with her in Nassau. She used to compete, you know. She won the Ontario Independent Schools 400-meter breaststroke in all four years at Branksome."

"It was tough keeping up."

Joan turned to Mila with her head cocked.

"Pardon me for asking, but are you Russian? Your eyes say Baltic to me," said Joan.

"Yes, my mother's Latvian but my dad's Russian. I was born in Canada."

Joan moved in closer. She smelled of gin and it was now Mila who steadied her.

"Did Lily ever tell you I had majored in Slavic Studies," Joan continued. "I earned my Masters and then my Doctorate in 19th century Russian History. Ah, but that feels like a revolution ago."

She laughed to herself.

"My thesis: 'The Decline of Serfdom in Tsarist Russia.' Tatiana Nikoleavna. That's cute. I thought the last Russian aristocrat had died long ago."

"Sorry?"

Joan fingered the pendant hanging from Mila's chocker.

"The jewelry will only protect you for so long from the firing squad, my dear. Eventually, everything cuts to the bone."

"I'm sorry. I don't understand."

"Oh but you do, don't you?" Joan continued. "You're prettier than the last one."

"Excuse me?"

"Honey, Tatiana, don't worry, we both fuck him, just for different purposes."

Mila looked at Joan, not knowing whether to be humiliated, ashamed or brave.

"It's okay dear," Joan continued. "Mine will be along shortly. He's Latin. They never come early. Not like John. Come with me. Let's go see Lily, shall we?"

It was a command. As they walked continued past the living room, Mila gave him a pleading stare but John just sipped his martini as his gaze followed her until Mila was out of sight.

Mila followed Joan down a narrow hall. Joan stopped at the second to last door, knocked, and entered without waiting for a reply.

"Lily" she said in a shrill voice, "John's little friend's here."

Joan let Mila in and shut the door, returning down the hall. Lily was seated on the bed, in a little black dress, facing Biscayne Bay. She wiped her eyes with the back of her hand and sat a little more upright, her shoulders back. Mila rounded the bed. She knew Lily's eyes would be red. She was not expecting was the welt on her left cheek.

"Oh Mila! They're horrible."

Lily threw her arm around Mila's and started sobbing.

"I know. I know Lil'," Mila said as she gently rubbed her neck. "There is nothing you can do about them. But you can change. You can change your life."

Lily slowly relaxed, tension slipping away.

"Give me a sec."

Mila went to the ensuite bathroom, returning with tissues, a wet wash cloth and the few meagre amount of make-up she could find. She handed the tissues to Lily who cleared her nose loudly. Mila applied the cool wash cloth to her cheek and made Lily hold it while she then laid the make-up on the bed on top of a hand towel.

"You want to change?" Mila said, marveling at Lily's beauty. "Give me ten and I'll make you over."

Lily surrendered to Mila's touch, closing her eyes and breathing deeply while Mila to deftly applied the cosmetics.

She began to hum "Popular" from the play, "Wicked," smiling for the first time since Mila had entered the room.

"Stop smiling or I'll make you look like the Joker."

Mila hummed along too.

There was a knock on the door and Joan poked her head in.

"Ladies, come, John and I are heading down. We mustn't... My God Lily, you are the most beautiful creature."

Lily blushed and then she drained of colour, the make-up looking hollow and papery.

She turned away as Joan returned down the hall.

Mila led Lily to a mirror hanging over a dresser.

"There. You like?"

Lily nodded yes.

"Good, but this is not beauty."

"I know."

"Beauty can be revealed only if the soul's good and pure."

"I will show it. I will, you know? I won't keep it in."

"It'll be some of the hardest work you'll ever do. It's hard to be honest. God knows I struggled, but where I've been true, I've been rewarded."

Lily smiled through fresh tears.

"Now you're ruining my work."

Mila caressed Lily's shoulders with the palms of her hands.

"C'mon. There's got to be somewhere to get a drink."

"I'm not twenty-one."

"It's not a problem. Stick with me."

They walked towards the living room. John and Joan were standing, talking with a third person, a man who was holding Joan's hand and listening intently.

"Lily, Tatiana," said Joan, "Allow me to introduce Ernesto de la Sedna. Ernesto, this is John's friend, Ms. Nikoleavna."

Ernesto turned to Joan.

"Juanita?" Ernesto whispered, "I'm Costa."

"De la Sedna," repeated Joan, smiling at Mila. "Lily, you do remember Ernesto?"

"How could I forget?" Lily said with a saccharine smile.

Ernesto kissed Lily on the cheek and he turned to Mila.

"Pleased to meet you, Ms. Tatiana," said Ernesto.

Ernesto took her outstretched hand, bent down and kissed it.

"Likewise I'm sure, Che?" replied Mila.

"Quick girl."

"¿Que? ¿Como? I'm Ernesto!"

Mila released Ernesto's grip, took Lily's hand and headed to the elevator.

The other three followed in haste, slipping through the elevator doors just as they closed. John pushed the button for the mezzanine.

"Good evening Tatiana. We need to talk later. Lovely evening, isn't Lil'?"

Lily turned to her father.

"Why can't you and Mom just be normal?" Lily shouted. "You're sadistic!"

Silence dominated the ride down to the ballroom and all five stared in silence at the numbers as it ticked off their descent.

The elevator stopped and John moved forward, his finger pressed firmly on the door closed button. Music and the commotion of a crowd could be heard on the other side.

"Don't mess this up, Lil'!" John said through his smile. "This is a big night for your mother and me. Best behaviour! Ernesto and Tatiana, you understand, right?"

Lily turned away and made a face in the mirrored wall of the elevator at the same moment as Mila. They burst into laughter.

"Girls!"

John and Joan both reached out and gripped Lily's hands tightly.

"Yes, John," Lily and Mila responded in unison, laughing again. Both stopped as the doors opened.

John and Joan strode forward with Lily struggling to keep up. They turned right and disappeared around the corner.

The doors began to close as Mila stood stock-still.

Ernesto held out his hand to keep the doors open.

"Shall we?"

"I can't move," Mila whispered.

"Sure you can. It's all an act. That's all. Come." Ernesto said, offering his arm and repeated his statement.

"Just an act."

Mila reluctantly accepted and they followed their masters.

They caught up with the Listers as a group of photographers snapped photos. They wore static smiles and they turned to provide various angles of the same image; a happy parents and their ingenue daughter. Ernesto and Mila tried to slip by but Lily reached out and caught Mila's hand and dragged them closer.

"Mr. and Mrs. Lister good to see you," one photographer called out."

"Over there Lily? Please?"

"Who's your friend with the blue streak, Lil'? What's her name? I need it for the caption in the Herald."

Ernesto stood behind Joan, striking a pose. Shutters whirled.

Mila turned her head away, a hand in the air trying to shield her face as she dropped Lily's hand and strode forward, praying the JPEGs will be blurred.

43

Eventually, Lily caught up to Mila playing with the olives in her martini glass.

"Now who's the shy girl!"

"Lily," Mila started with a voice sterner than she wanted. "This is not part of the deal."

"I suppose it's not."

Mila continued, softening. "It's not your fault. It's mine. Anyway, join me. I can't drink alone."

"I'm underage," she whispered.

With a quick nod and smile, Mila turned back to the bar. Lily noticed as Mila worked her charm on the bartender or perhaps it was simply her aura. Whatever it was, he was smitten.

"Freddy, Old Fashioned for my friend here."

"Tatiana, uh, is she..."

"Yes, she is," Mila said.

He paused for a moment, taking in Mila.

"Coming right up, one Old Fashioned."

Freddy turned away.

"How'd you do that?"

Mila fluttered her long lashes like a butterfly.

"Ah!" said Lily, trying to copy her. She looked like she had grit in her eye. Both started laughing.

Drinks in hand, Lily took Mila's arm and led her in the Grand Ball Room. Mila was in awe at the opulence. Each table was festooned with a four foot high ice-sculpture: a mermaid in repose or a unicorn rearing, all slowly melting in the humidity of the Miami night. Rubies and emeralds floated by around leathery necks. Diamond earrings so large and the clarity so pure that Mila could see them across the room that would seat three hundred. It was a roving constellation of stars.

Mila spotted John across the room talking to Joan and Ernesto. A waiter came by offering champagne. Each took a flute. John downed his in a single gulp and picked up a second flute to look social.

For most of the evening, John ignored Mila as he read and re-read his speaking notes. He was more nervous than she had ever seen him. None of the benefactors appeared to understand the irony of raising money for the homeless substance abusers by spending lavishly on themselves. Mila surveyed the crowd with increasing disdain; emerald earrings maybe an inch in diameter, ruby chokers glittering around sagging necks, broad gold arm bands that should have been worn by Nefertiti or Cleopatra held in place by flabby biceps. Stones, gold, platinum. It was bewildering.

The last two seats at their table were occupied by two recent recipients of the evening's largesse, Carlos and Vera Vega. They were a handsome couple, both aged beyond their years. Their once black hair was overrun by grey and their skin creased and wrinkled from exposure. Their dark eyes surveyed the room, unsettled in front of such a large crowd. They sat tall in their chairs. They had never been to such an event.

"Carlos," began John, "what are you are Vera up to now?"

"Well Mr. Lister, I have work as a gardener. Doesn't pay much, but Vera and I are happy."

Vera gripped his hand.

"Don't need much when you clean and sober. Crack's so expensive these days."

"She is only joking. We stick to water. We pray for good."

"We pray for you and Mrs. Lister," said Vera. "And we are grateful for the support for our after care program."

"We live a simple life, but we're happy."

"You're welcome both of you," said Joan. "Seeing you gives John and me such great pleasure."

Mila squirmed in her sumptuous dress and caught herself repeatedly reaching for the ivory pendant around her neck, caressing it, feeling its beauty, ready to tear it from her throat in disgust.

After the main course, John walked over to the podium. He pulled a couple of sheets of paper from the breast pocket and smoothed the papers out on the lectern, patting himself down, his hands probing for some forgotten object.

"Here they are Daddy!" Lily said far too sweetly as she jumped up and handed him the reading glasses he had left on the table, giving him a kiss on the cheek before returning to her chair next to Mila.

"He does that every time," Lily said as returned to her seat.

John began to read his prepared remarks, without inflection or passion. There was a long list of people to thank and solemn promises to keep. His voice rose only at the end.

"The Dade Country Health Network deserves better!" he said, sweeping his hand to the invited guests at his table. "For Carlos and Vera, and the others here tonight brave enough to be in recovery, please open your hearts!"

There was gentle applause.

"Thank you. Thank you. In recognition of their need, Joan and I have decided to make a donation of $10 million dollars to the addiction research center at the University of Miami."

The room erupted. Some of the benefactors even stood. John raised his hands to calm the room.

"Don't be too hasty my friends. This is a challenge grant. You need to match us. Joan and I would like you to rise and join us."

The crowd quieted. John leaned forward on the podium and spoke in low voice into the microphone.

"By join us, I mean tonight."

Mila looked around the room. Eyes of many were suddenly downcast. Hands went to jewels as if they were about to be ripped from their necks. Mila did some quick math. There were 150 couples in the room, each clad in finery she, Carlos and Vera could only dream of. To match John's donation, it was about $70,000 each. To this crowd, this would be the loose change left over after a New York shopping spree.

"There are forms on the table for each of you. In fifteen minutes, the kind volunteers will be circulating to collect your pledges."

A murmur began to grow.

"If you exceed our target tonight, Joan and I will contribute another $5 million. Our largess is for tonight only."

John paused a moment and took a sip of water. He looked over the crowd, relishing their discomfort. His gaze settled on the table in front of the podium.

"Senator Gill, will you meet my challenge? Governor Ortega, how about you? Congresswoman Wyeth, please don't be shy. Surely you will lead the sugar growers of Florida to help combat this scourge."

John continued, baiting the audience.

Mila leaned over to Lily.

"Let's have a little fun."

Mila dropped her napkin on the floor, bent over to pick it up and as she did, placed the flat of her palm on the inside of Ernesto's thigh. He stifled a turn of his head and kept chewing his salad, trying to act nonchalant. Her hand crept towards his groin. Mila sat up and leaned over to whisper in his ear.

"So, Che, tell me," she said in a voice loud enough for Lily to follow, "when you disappoint Joan, how do you make up for it?"

Lily muffled a giggle.

"What? It was only once and I was tired from a day of carrying her bags."

Lily laughed out loud, loud enough that her father stopped, annoyed at the interruption. Joan glared at Lily and then at Mila and Ernesto.

"You three, shut up!" Joan squeezed out between the clenched teeth of her smile. "Ernesto, smile my darling, smile!"

He parted his lips meekly, greenery stuck in his teeth, and then he looked down, poking at his salad. Mila turned back to the lectern. John was shielding his eyes from the lights as he looked over the room.

"Who will join us?" John continued.

"I will," came a clear voice from the rear of the room.

It was the Sikh from the opera in Toronto. Soon, seven or eight other voices followed. After about five minutes, while John was thanking everyone for their generosity, Ernesto dropped his napkin on the floor next to Mila's. He bent over to pick it up and placed his hand on her arm.

"We're really quite similar, me and you. We're both caught up in something we'll not look upon fondly. Do I regret what I do? Of course. My wife's still in Cuba you see and cannot leave. I send her the money so she can eat, so my daughter can have a tutor at school. I understand my actions and they do too. Do you?"

Mila bristled and looked straight forward.

"I'm nothing like you!" she seethed between her teeth.

"No, you're right," he said. "I do this for my family. Tatiana, you or whatever your name is, you do this for you!"

"Che, can you read sign language?

Mila placed her hand flat on the table and bent all of her fingers save her middle finger underneath her palm. She turned her head to him and smiled and looked down at her hand.

"Can you read this?"

The speeches ended and the diamonds floated away to their Bentleys and Ferraris. John caught up to Mila as she was walking alone down the long hallway towards the foyer that lead back to the elevators.

"Tatiana, I've been looking for you. I need you for a moment."

"Oh sorry, John. I presumed that given Joan's presence, my services would not be required this evening."

John led her back into the ballroom. The crowd had for the most part dispersed and there remained a small gaggle of people, mostly men, unadorned by spouses or girlfriends. Lily was there too, talking to a pink, rotund man twice her age and three times her size, smoking a cigar. She was looking anxiously at the other people in the group and caught Mila's eye and waved her over. The Sikh was there as well. As Mila reached Lily's side, she caught the last of a joke.

"Brett Turner, I thought you said bend over," the fat man guffawed.

Lily laughed in a stilted manner at a joke that was surely misogynist or homophobic. The turbaned man looked away, bored as well, waving the smoke drifting amongst them away from his face. John grabbed three flutes of champagne as a waiter walked by, and handed one each to Mila and Lily and kept one for himself.

"Tatiana, permit me to introduce you. This handsome gentleman is Jargit Bhutani Singh. He's the representative of the largest investor in my fund."

Singh took Mila's hand in his and bent over and kissed the back of it on her tattoo. It was so elegant. Mila felt goosebumps.

"John we've met before," said Jargit.

"At the opera, Romeo and Juliet," said Mila. "But I am pleased to meet you formally, Mr. Singh."

"Call me Jargit."

"Jargit," Mila repeated with a subtle curtsy.

"Tatiana, it's a pleasure to meet you properly. John has spoken highly of you."

Mila's stomach tightened.

"He mentioned that you're a good friend of Lily's and that you dance. How wonderful! I love the ballet too."

Jargit turned to John.

"The hour's late and I must get some sleep. My flight departs early in the morning."

"Fly back with us," said John,

"Thank you no. I have a stop in Manhattan along the way."

Singh turned back to Mila.

"I trust you'll have a good evening. Please be safe. You know men and the drink."

With that, Jargit bid each in turn a good night and left. John turned to the fat, pink man.

"This here, Tatiana, is my good man, Tim Fleming. He's the head trader at my firm, the best in the country, maybe the continent."

Tim gave John a punch in the arm and an awe shucks look. Tim turned to Mila.

"Hello," he croaked, sounding nervous.

"This is Tatiana Nikoleavna, the beautiful creature I was telling you about."

Mila gave him an air kiss on both cheeks. He looked at her as something to devoured.

"Mr. Fleming, pleased to meet you."

"Call me Tim. Everybody does."

"Tim," Mila said flatly with a slight nod, and turned to John. "I'm exhausted. It's been a long day. I'm going to go to turn in."

"Stay a while. These people are fun. I've arranged some cars to go to South Beach. C'mon, you'll love it."

With a smile, Mila motioned to John to step away from the crowd.

"I'd rather not," she said. "I want to make sure my mom got my earlier message."

"Just your mother?"

"I suppose I might email a few friends too. They were expecting me to return today. I blew them off to be here. What time's the flight tomorrow?"

"Whenever I want it to be."

"John, really, I'm not feeling well," she said leaning in and, lowering her voice, whispering in his ear. "You know the rules. I told you long ago. I don't care what you pay me. I've been exposed. The photog... I've played the role you wanted and you got to show me off. Enough."

Mila raised her voice back to a normal level.

"I've had too much to drink and too little food."

"Do what you will," said John.

"Good night, then," she said. "Thank you for a lovely evening. Lily good night. Mr. Fleming."

She kissed John on the cheek. He held her hand and pulled her close.

"Tim will escort you to your room," he whispered. "He'll make sure you get tucked in."

"You've bought my time," she replied tersely. "No one else. Ever!"

She wrested her wrist out of his grasp, turned and walked away. John caught her in two steps, grabbed her wrist and whipped her around so that a lock of blue hair stuck to her lips.

"You will do as I say," he hissed. "You're Tim's."

"Daddy... John!" Lily whimpered in disbelief.

Mila and John turned to Lily's grieving voice. John dropped Mila's wrist.

"John. How could you? What have you become?"

Lily ran away, kicking off her heels and sprinted barefoot out of the foyer. John stood fixed in place. Mila saw Lily pass Mike who looked out of sorts standing in his tuxedo, sipping a glass of tomato juice. He turned on his heels watching her go by but he did not follow. Mila made for him.

"Mike, I'll be down from my room in five. I need you to take me to the airport, but go tend to Lily. Now!"

"What?"

"Mike. Now! Please!"

He nodded and ran after Lily down the stairs to the lobby. Mila hurried down the hallway to the elevator and went up to her floor. She was expecting to see Tim waiting for her in the hallway.

The doors opened and Mila made her way to the end as quickly as her dress and heels would allow and entered the room. She took a few steps and found the light switch.

Her room was not empty.

Olga was lying on the bed, shielding her eyes from the overhead light. There was a bottle of rye toppled over on the bedside table.

"Mila?"

"Olga? What the Hell? You're supposed to be in Calgary."

"John invited me down. Sent me a ticket and everything. Left me a few drinks. Told me to wait."

"We gotta go!"

Mila began packing her bags frantically.

"When did you two meet?" asked Mila. I thought you were out."

"About a week after you came to Calgary."

"What? Where?"

"At the bar. He was glum and talked about his daughter non-stop. One of those dads, you know, wrecked the relationship and wanted to make up for it."

"No, Olga, that's not John."

"You're wrong. He's been nothing but sweet."

"Olga..."

"You want to keep him to yourself. Your own sugar daddy," Olga slurred.

"Oh fuck Olga, you're in way over your head."

"You're jealous."

"No, you're stupid."

"We're going to spend tomorrow together in Nassau. He took me to the opera once."

"Romeo and Juliet?"

"No? What?"

"I was there. He was with another blonde. He forced me to the basement at intermission."

"What?"

"To blow him Olga. He's just using us. He just gave me away to some fat asshole. I'm leaving now."

"What?"

"My brother says he's involved in the death of a family friend. Olga, I met his daughter, the one he says he loves so much."

"What? You know her?"

"When I was in Calgary, he sent her to deliver the envelope when he took off somewhere."

"He did? She knows who you are?"

"She knows what I am. Yes, she knows. Did you know I was just in Nassau with John and Lily? She and I have developed a... friendship, an understanding."

"You have?"

"Yes, Olga. Lily tried to commit suicide yesterday. I saved her."

"What? He said she's happy."

"She fucking hates him. He treats her like something stuck to his heel. Her mother doesn't give a shit either."

"Mother? John told me she was dead, that he was a single father."

"Lies. Can't you see? It's all lies. I'm getting the fuck out of here."

"I haven't been paid."

"Paid? Are you fuckin' kidding? Go. Stay. I don't care."

There was a firm knock on the door. Olga started to talk but Mila leapt towards her, landing on the bed and cupping her hand over Olga's mouth to silence her.

"Shut up!" she whispered.

There was another knock, followed by the clearing of a throat. Mila raised her finger to her lips. Olga nodded that she understood. Mila slipped off her shoes and rolled off the bed.

"Security!" she thought.

She picked up the receiver. The line was dead. The wire was missing.

The knock became more insistent. Mila looked to the credenza. There was a large bottle of water. Just like the movies, she thought. Smash the bottle on the head. Use the broken shards to inflict further damage. She rushed across the room. Plastic! Mila's phone rang. It was Mike. She answered.

"Mila, something terrible has happened. I can't drive you."

320

"Mike? What? I need your help now."

"Lily..."

"Lily?"

"Lily just jumped... off the bridge... into the water. I followed her onto the causeway. She stopped and told me to say goodbye to her father. Kissed me on the cheek. I didn't know what she meant. She walked away from me, about ten yards away, waved and then suddenly she straddled the railing."

"Mike, I need..."

"Before I could get to her, she slipped her other leg over and dove into the water. I ran over to the edge but she didn't surface. The impact was hard. The water was dark, murky. Gotta go, Mr. Lister wants... I'll get you a car."

The line went dead.

Mila hit redial. Mike's phone was busy.

"Shit."

Mila moved to the door and peered through the peep hole. Tim was grinning madly, slicking back his hair with his hands and then pulling up his tuxedo pants, sucking in his ample gut. Mila motioned to Olga to stay put.

"C'mon Mila, I can see you're there. Darling, don't keep me waiting."

"Just a second, Hun. Can't wait to see you. I was admiring you all evening."

She went back to bathroom and flushed the toilet and cracked open two bottles of mouthwash.

"C'mon you...you lovely thing. Please let me in," he said in a loud voice. More quietly to himself, he added, "Please, you bitch."

Mila exited the bathroom and motioned to Olga to move closer. Mila opened the door a crack, smiling at Tim with her mouth closed. The Listerine was burning her tongue and cheeks.

Mila undid the chain and pulled Tim into the room. He saw Olga on the bed.

"Alright! Duo!"

Mila put her arms around his neck. Without her heels, she was half a foot shorter than him. She gazed up as she pulled him in for a kiss. Tim tilted his head downward, his eyes open, taking her in. Mila sprayed the contents in a stream at his eyes.

He clawed at his face, his eyes aflame. She took a step back, hiked the dress, turned her hips and kicked his right knee. It gave little resistance as the ligaments snapped. Tim dropped to the ground flat on his back, clutching his knee and howling in pain.

"You Fucker, Tim. You don't get to have me. You fucking don't!"

He roared. Mila kicked him in the gut twice and dropped her knee into his face. His nose crackled and blood flowed. A large bubble formed as he exhaled. Mila dropped elbow after elbow on to the side of Tim's head, his head hitting the carpeted floor with every blow. She stopped when he stopped groaning. His jaw hung loosely. A tooth was lodged in his upper lip, the flesh split, and dark blood seeped out. Olga lay curled on the bed, fixed in place, stunned at her friend.

Mila's dress was torn and flecked with blood. Mila stripped it off and pulled the choker from her neck, breaking the clasp. She threw everything into a corner. She dressed, stuffing into her carry on every item that Bernard had taken the care to fold. Mila found Olga's passport in her handbag, and handed the bag to Olga.

Mila rolled Tim over onto his back and reached inside his tuxedo jacket. She emptied his wallet, pocketing close to three thousand in US cash. In his other pocket, Mila found his passport. She slipped it into her purse. Then she spat on his hand and wrestled his wedding band from his fat finger.

"There," she thought with a sneer. "The image is complete: beaten up and valuables stolen. It could never have been done by a hundred-and-ten-pound girl."

Mila ushered Olga out the room. She was still in shock. Out in the hall, Mila slipped the "Privacy Please" sign onto the door handle and shut the door.

They hurried to the elevator and waited for what felt like an eternity for it to come.

Mila stared down the hall, expecting Tim to explode from the room.

When they finally arrived in the lobby, it was bathed in the strobe of blue, white and red lights.

Mila dragged Olga through a throng of curious onlookers to the parking lot.

There were no taxis.

"Mike!" Mila muttered to herself. "Please."

There was one dark sedan in the parking lot. A Hispanic man was leaning against, taking a drag from a cigarillo. He threw it away when he saw Mila and he nodded in their direction, opening the rear passenger door.

They hurried over and slid into the rear seat after handing the man the bags.

"Good evening. Where to?"

"Airport. International Departures. Hurry."

"Not much leaving this time."

Mila had not considered the hour. It was 11:30 p.m. All the commercial flights would have departed earlier.

"Don't worry, Mila," the driver said.

"Mike asked me to check. There's a charter to Toronto. They have a one-fifteen a.m. flight. You'll get in around five-thirty a.m. Kind of shoulder season, so there might be some seats. I'm Pablo by the way."

"You know my name. This is Olga," said Mila.

"Mike and I go way back. I'll get you there. Stay low. Some shit tonight, no?"

"Yeah, some shit!"

The bridge was clogged with emergency vehicles narrowing access to a single lane.

The traffic moved at a crawl. Through the railing Mila could see a police boat, its search lights reflecting off the green water. John was standing at the edge of the bridge surrounded by police officers.

Mike was at his side. Joan ran up to John, and starting beating on his chest, screaming before collapsing in his arms.

After a few moments, an officer lead her away. John looked up as the sedan passed. A glint of recognition reached his tear-filled eyes as Mila rolled past.

She thrust Olga's head into her lap and eased back into the seat in a panic of concern but could not resist the pull to look at John. She watched as his expression changed from grief to disappointment and to rage. He struck Mike with the back of his hand hard across the jaw.

John followed Mila as she watched out the sedan's rear window until she disappeared as they rounded a corner.

They were at the international terminal in half an hour and were in seated on the charter back to Toronto an hour after that, having used Tim's cash to buy the tickets. As they taxied, she fired off a quick text:

Rabbit needs a warren.

She shut down her cellphone. Olga was asleep before wheels up and Mila dozed off as she tried to piece everything together. How did John find Olga? But Olga had left the business. What had he offered her?

Mila studied Olga's sleeping face before turning away and shutting her eyes. She was swimming with Lily far offshore. A tear trickled down her cheek.

The landing jolted both awake.

Mila dragged Olga over to the Sheraton hotel where she prepaid a room with the last of Tim's cash, but she left her credit card number in case of incidentals. She tucked Olga in, amazed at how quickly she fell asleep.

Mila promised Olga that she would return later in the day and left her card with her phone number on it next to the bed just in case.

Mila exited the hotel and seeing the taxi stand empty, decided on a limousine despite the higher cost. She needed to get home and was too tired, too wired to wait. Her phone buzzed.

The warren is always warm and dry. Come.

She was going home.

****

It was 6:00 am and the first green light of dawn was beginning to light the wispy con trails left by the passing jets. The air was cool and the gulls and terns were beginning to stir.

John and Joan sat next to one another on the balcony overlooking Key Biscayne. John rubbed her back with a tenderness he had not shared since Alison's death. It was the first time in years they had been this close in a setting that was not forced.

They had spent the night reading Lily's on-line journal. Joan never bothered to ask how he had obtained it. She was more interested in its contents.

The first entry was the day Alison's death. Lily had detailed her life in her own words; the first time she had fallen in love, her first joint, her first rave, where she had lost her virginity, her struggles to fit in.

There were nothing but harsh words for her parents. She was stunned by the infidelity, their disregard for each other's feelings, of how she felt like a pawn in their tactical game.

It stung.

After Joan had sobbed herself to a restless sleep beside him, John turned to the last few entries, the first in March:

Dear Diary: I can't believe Dad made me deliver the money to her. She has a name. This one's different. She talked to me as a friend. Wants me to get away. Can I trust her? L.

John skipped a number of entries that just talked about school. He scrolled down to the entries from three days earlier.

Dear Diary:

Arrived in Nassau to see Dad again. Since Calgary he has left me alone but he remembered my birthday. He was early with the present, not because he goofed on the day, but because the Kings of Leon concert was before my actual birthday. He listened and remembered. First time in three years he did not send belated wishes and a thousand bucks. He has a long way to go but I appreciate the effort. Love L.

John opened the next one.

HE FUCKING DID IT AGAIN. He's no longer my father. He's just an ATM. A fuckin' ATM. He invited HER here, to Nassau on our time. I'm done.

John went to the next entry from two days ago.

Dear Diary: I can't do this anymore. I'll go for a long swim. As FAR as I can and then further still. I will slip beneath the waves. Air is toxic. Every word that leaves his mouth is foul. It will be quiet. It will be calm. I'll be in my element. L.

The next entry.

No feeding the crabs. Mila saved me!!!!!!!! There's another way. She'll help. How could we become friends? How could we not? What a massive heart! My protector. John better not do anything to her. He needs to treat her well. HE MUST. I don't know what I would do if he doesn't. She told me I need to get away. That she'd help. She needs to get away too. L.

John deleted the last three entries and stared out at the sea. His phone skittered across the table. He set the laptop down and accepted the call. Joan stirred and lifted her head.

"You're going to answer your phone? Now? John, our baby's gone, she's gone!"

She began to sob.

"Joan," he said, "it might be the detective."

John rose from the sofa and stood at the edge of the balcony, leaning against the railing, He stared had at the concrete walkway 19 floors below. Falling would be easy. He pushed receive on the phone.

"Yes, Beate."

"They've landed."

"Okay."

"The blonde's at the Sheraton Airport. Tatiana dropped her off and got in a limo. There was just me. I couldn't cover both."

"Okay."

"What do you want me to do?"

"Take the blonde. Find a safe place for her under your personal care. I'll call when I need her. Don't worry about Tatiana for now. She'll be easy to lure. I'll...we'll be back soon."

"Sorry for your loss, Sir."

"Thank you Beate."

John walked back to the couch. Joan had fallen asleep, her head resting on the arm of the sofa. He passed over the scotch and picked up one of the bottles of water on the table next to the couch and drank.

44

Vitaly arrived at the office and followed the routine that started his every day, opening the link to his favourite US news aggregator website.

"Holy Shit!" he said out loud.

In bold font, at the top of the page, he read:

LISTER FAMILY TRAGEDY

LISTERS GRIEVE THEIR DAUGHTER'S DISAPPEARANCE IN MIAMI CANAL

Socialite Philanthropist Lily Lister Falls from Bridge

U OF CALGARY STUNNED BY MS. LISTER'S ACCIDENT

There were a series of articles from the Miami Herald; one on the accident, another on the Lister family's philanthropy, and an article on Lily's emotionally devastated parents. Vitaly clicked through the articles.

Brian walked into the office, a clutch of papers in his hand.

"Now here's a good mug of our guy."

Brian set the stack down in front of Vitaly.

"That's Lily," he said pointing to the photo above the story.

"Who's that?" Brian asked, pointing at the blurred image. Vitaly scrutinized the photo. Though the photo was blurred. The woman was clearly trying to avoid having her photo taken, her hand up, her face turned.

"Kind of looks like Mila," Brian said with a laugh. "What would she be doing at a thousand-dollar-a-plate dinner."

"There are plenty of raven-haired girls."

"With blue streaks?"

"Yes, Mila's in Miami, but she's partying in South Beach with some friends. If I could see her tats..." The sleeves of the woman's dress covered her arms down to her wrist and her palm face the camera lens.

"I know, I'm just teasing ya. Is the meeting still on with your girl?"

"You can say her name."

"Loose lips..."

"Yes, I know."

"What time?"

"We'll leave at 9 a.m. 15 minutes to get there."

"Okay, see you then," Brian said, as he paused on the threshold. "You know, with Lily's death, John might make a mistake if we press."

"I'm not hounding a grieving father. No judge would grant me a warrant before the funeral. No way."

"Vitaly, get your priorities straight. You use leverage when you it. No sense in waiting."

"It's all a bit rushed."

"Get use to it. We're on the edge of what you do and what I do. It ain't gonna slow down."

Brian left and Vitaly leafed through the other articles he had printed, seeing if there was anything that he had missed. There was nothing new apart from a Canadian executive assaulted in a Miami hotel room, his wallet and wedding band all stolen. He had seen the name before. Right, Tim Fleming, John's head trader. Weird. Of all nights. What was he doing in Miami?

The last page was a brief press release from LAM.

It is with great sadness that John and Joan (nee Hurst) Lister announce the sudden and loss of their darling daughter, Lily. She was so full of promise. She had an infectious enthusiasm for life and was so looking forward to the future. The family asks for privacy in this time of grief.

Vitaly unlocked his lower desk drawer and took out a file marked 'Lister'. He put all the articles in the folder save one, the Miami Herald photo of the Listers and the mystery woman. He studied the photo. Lily's smile was that of a socialite, lips drawn back in a strained fashion, maintaining the pose for the photographers to take multiple shots. John stood tall and relaxed. But the woman to his right? Raven hair, loose around her shoulders, the blue streak, rare but not unique. The ring or was that rings on her right hand. Vitaly peered more closely at the image. The outstretched hand was not in the depth of field of the lens. Could it be? Vitaly knew the image could be read in a number of ways. He picked up his phone and texted Mila. It was 8:45 a.m.

M. When are you back from Miami?

Vitaly had barely set his phone down when it buzzed.

Back last night late. Had a fight with the travel mates. Need sleep. Call ya later. Hugs :)

Mila, Need to talk. Not meant to harass. Just concerned. Love V

Vitaly stared at his phone. He noticed in the message that Mila was typing but had not yet hit send. He waited. It came a minute later.

Got a bunch of great things going on. I've someone new. It's awesome. Real deal. Appreciate your concern. I do. I fucked up with Mom. I know. But you'll see. I'm changed. I'll fill you in shortly. Now let me sleep!!! Hugs. M

Derek poked his head into Vitaly's office holding up an article he printed off.

"Boss, can you believe it?"

"I saw. Brian and I are heading out. Not sure when we will be back."

"You're meeting the insider, aren't you?"

"Yes. I can't say more."

****

Soft morning light came in through the lace curtains of Caroline's bedroom. Mila lay in bed for a few minutes after Vitaly's message, thinking through what had transpired in the previous 72 hours. It was more than she could ever have imagined, more than she cared for. Mila could hear a deep baritone voice delivering the introduction to the CBC's radio program, "The Current." She had not listened to it in years. Might be part of her new routine, she thought. She could hear the rustling of papers and a man and a woman talking in tones, too quiet for her to make out. She rose, wrapped herself in Caroline's robe and crept down the hall. The floor boards in Caroline's century-old apartment creaked under foot. There was some giggling.

"It's okay Mila," the man said in a clear voice. "Come join us."

"Come, Marc's cool."

Mila walked confidently down the hall to stand in the doorway of the kitchen. The two were sitting at the small kitchen table, each with a notepad. The floor was littered with torn-off sheets.

"Caroline explained everything to me a few days ago. We've reached an understanding. I'm off to the Left Coast and all its beautiful rain. My beloved, my muse, has chosen to stay here. The sky will cry for me as I leave my love. I love her so how can I not set her free?"

He took Caroline's hand in his.

"It's been a good run. We've had our triumphs and our defeats. I regret that this did not last and that the legacy of our love will be but our memories. My life was never as full as it was when you were happy. I can see I'm not alone in providing that happiness. As we promised, if our relationship does not make us truly, happy, then it must change. I know I've changed. You have too. There's no fault. No blame. Truly Mila, I bear you no ill will. I will love you Caroline always."

Mila started, "Marc, I never..."

331

"I know. This was coming."

"Yes," said Caroline, "it was."

"I'll be out in a couple of days," Marc continued. "My brother's traveling and until then and I can't get into his apartment."

"Caroline can stay with me," said Mila.

"No Mila, Marc and I still need to work on a few things."

"Okay, I'll leave then."

Caroline got up, gave Mila a kiss on the lips and a hug.

"I just need a few days, Rabbit," Caroline whispered. "I'll call you when I'm ready."

Mila was out of the house in five minutes. She grabbed a cab to her apartment, dumped her suitcase on her bed and dressed in fresh clothes. Then she called her father, asking if it was all right for her to come and spend some time at home. She felt bad about missing Zoya's birthday and wanted to make it up to her. The ride over was uneventful. It felt good to be back on the Suzuki again.

It was just before 10:30 a.m. when she arrived at her parent's house. Her mother greeted her at the door.

"Milaska!"

"Mama, I'm sorry. I should've been there. How was Biff's?"

"Vitaly said you were in Miami Beach working for Dr. Simintov."

"Mama, I'm..."

Mila could feel the old pattern in their relationship starting up again. The words would soon turn bitter.

"Mama, I don't want to fight. I've no excuse. I'm sorry."

Mila moved forward and hugged Zoya. Her mom barely hugged her back.

"I have meeting all day. You look after yourself."

"Mama, I love you."

"Milaska... I know."

Zoya broke the embrace, pulled on her coat and left Mila standing in the foyer without another word. It was the first time in a long time Zoya hugged her daughter with any affection. Mila climbed the stairs to the second floor and slipped into her old room. Her parents had not changed it much. Her old posters still hung on the wall: Dead Kennedys, DOA, Johnny Cash. The only difference was that she could see the floor that had been forever covered in discarded clothes. She sat on her old bed and began digging through her hand bag. When she finally found her phone, she called the Sheraton and asked for Olga's room.

"Ma'am, that guest checked out this earlier morning," said the woman. "Around nine-thirty a.m."

"What? Who closed the bill?"

"Ms. Komolski did," he said.

"Can you please email me a copy of the bill with the confirmation of a zero balance? I hate to let things hang."

"Most certainly ma'am," the manager said. "Shall I send it to the e-mail on file?"

"Yes, thank you."

Mila set lay down on her bed.

"Olga, where are you? Why'd you check out? Why'd John drag you to Miami?"

Her phone signaled an incoming email. It was from the Sheraton. She opened it and clicked on the attachment and stared in disbelief.

"Olga, you stupid..."

The sole charge on the bill was a call to John's cell phone. The room balance was not charged to her credit card. The signature was illegible but the first letter was definitely a B.

Mila went to the kitchen and poured herself a glass of milk. She scanned the newspaper that her Mom or Dad had thumbed through in the morning over breakfast. There was nothing about Lily.

Zoya's iPad was on the table. On Bourque Newswatch, there were a number of brief four sentence articles about Lily and the devastation her death had caused in the Lister and Hurst Families. The memorial was to be at the Timothy Eaton Chapel on St. Clair seven days hence. She noted the time, unpacked her bags and called Olga's phone. The call went to voice mail.

"Olga. Call me. Same number as always. Okay? You don't know what you're doing! Call."

Mila checked a Google locator service for Olga's cell. Nothing showed up.

"Okay," she said to herself, "calm down. She could have checked out on her own. She's lived here before."

Mila tried to remember if Olga's brother was still in town. Maybe she went there. Why did she call John?

Mila knew the funeral arrangements would take time. He likely would not be back for two days at the earliest. Could he be back in town already? Even if he was in town, he would have to deal with the funeral.

Oh, Lil.

Mila emailed Zablon, and told him that she needed a break and that she would return in August.

She promised to get back to his research in September. She was going through other emails when he replied.

Mila, Congratulations! Your mark on the final exam was the highest of any third year student. I was discussing your success with a colleague and we've decided to nominate you for a Barbara Humer Scholarship. In case you don't know, it's $10,000. Also, I received my funding for next year. I have a paid research position for you if you want it.

I want you to consider studying under me for your Masters. I believe you would be an ideal candidate for the program. There are many here who are impressed with your independent thought. There are many ready to guide you. I know you have your heart set on Columbia. Please consider it. Dr. Z

Mila began to dial, hung up and responded to Zablon by email.

Wow, Zablon, thanks. When do you want me to come up to campus?Are your office hours still the same? M.

A response came a few minutes later.

No. I am traveling for a few days. Let say the 29th of May to be certain. Around 2:00 p.m?

Mila looked at her calendar. That was in five days. She replied that she would be there and hit send.

Her Mom's cigarettes were on the counter. She fished one out, lit it and inhaled.

Her mind drifted, considering the offer: New York or North York. She ached to be in Caroline's arms right now; to smell her scent, to look at her freckled cheeks, to feel the strength of her embrace.

Mila picked up her Mom's iPad and went to the York University website and looked through the courses she could take to complete her degree.

The scholarship would make life easier. The $10,000 a year would half a year's rent for the two of them.

With Caroline's income, what she would earn if she worked a few nights at Ki and the stipend as a TA, their needs covered for an entire year. Zablon had given her a bridge.

Mila spent the rest of the day in her room, going through her old things, thinking about how childish they now seemed.

She made of checklist of what she would want to keep. One thought kept coming back to her.

"Olga, where are you?"

45

She was excited. It was noon and Mila was gathering her things to go see Zablon. She was finding her path and was proud of where she was going. She had shared with her parents her relationship with Caroline. Both were taken aback at first, but Petr embraced his daughter' happiness. Zoya was longer to warm to the thought, but she did. Mila had to hold her tongue a few times over her comments but it was nothing new.

Mila ached for her love. They were supposed to get together a few days after she had left her with Marc, but Caroline' mother in Montreal had fallen ill. She had come back this morning and had gone to Biff's right away. It was okay. Mila planned to pop over after her meeting with Zablon, bringing with her more go news.

Mila had stayed longer at her parents house than she had expected. It was easier there and she felt more secure than being at her place.

John's silence had been unnerving. He had sent not an email nor a text. Mila had followed the proceedings around Lily's funeral in online. Her body was never recovered. The Miami police speculated that the tide may have pulled her out to sea. She might never be found. A service had been held two days prior.

Mila had budgeted plenty of time to get to Zablon's office and wanted to be there before he returned from his lunch, eager to show that she merited his confidence. She packed her shoulder bag and went down to her motorcycle in the garage. Her dad had looked over the work that Mickey had done and had been impressed. He too had spent a few evenings with the bike. The dented chrome shone a little brighter. He had reupholstered the cracked leather of the seat will new blue material that matched the blue of her hair. Mila grumbled to herself when she saw it. She had grown to love the old seat but it was sweet of her dad and she loved him for it. She kicked up the stand and pushed the bike out into the alley.

She headed up St. George to St. Clair and then rode Dufferin north to the Allen, swinging west on the Highway 401 to the 400. On the 400, a red motorcycle flashed by her, leaving her Suzuki far behind. She caught up to it on the off-ramp to Keele, the rider's progress interrupted by a red light. It was her Ducati Monster, purring at rest. She had never seen one in the wild. She admired the simplicity of the design, the complexity of the engineering. It was sleek, compact, powerful. The rider glanced over at her bike and acknowledged her with distain. He clicked the bike into gear and accelerated hard away, popping onto its back wheel through the intersection.

Parking was easy. With exams over, the summer student population had dwindled to about a third of what it was during the regular school year. The demographic had changed. These were the grinders, the students who had to make their own way, the ones who succeeded when there was no family back-up. Her kind of people. Many old Hondas and Hyundais were dotted around the parking lot. A few even looked slept in with sleeping bags in the back and clothes stuffed into unzipped bags.

The only thing that stood out, though, was a black SUV in the lot next hers. She worried that it might be John's guys, but this was such a public place and even in summer, there were still plenty of people around. She headed over to Vari Hall and made her way up to Zablon's office. She caught the elevator, thrusting her hand through the doors just as they closed. There was a gurney and two ambulance attendants who fell silent for a moment as the door reopened.

"No space for you," the shorter barked, stabbing at the close button. "Take next."

His accent was Russian, his meter brusque. Mila spoke back in his language.

"Dude, there's plenty of space. I'll just slide in here. Not in the way. See."

The attendants shifted uneasily in the elevator. Mila noticed that they had already pushed the button for the fifth floor. Zablon's floor. The door closed and the elevator rattled as it made its way upwards. Mila caught both men staring at her and looking at one another repeatedly. Each broke off their gaze whenever she made eye contact. She was used to the unwanted attention with her hair and the tattoo on her hand. She smiled at them and looked at her phone. She was ten minutes early.

The radio on the short man's phone crackled.

"Where are you? We need you here."

Mila thought she recognized the voice but dismissed it. John? That made no sense she said to herself.

"On way now. Student in the elevator with us."

"Understood."

The elevator reached the fifth floor with a jolt and Mila pushed the open door button and held it for the attendants who exited first and started down the hall running.

"Odd," thought Mila. Her instructor from her first aid course had pounded into to her that she was never to run, that she always needed to be aware of their surroundings and face any situation. Mila followed them walking quickly.

The radio crackled again.

"Room 543."

Mila panicked. Zablon's office. She broke into a run, passing the attendants before they could get to the office.

"Zablon!"

The door was open a crack. She burst in. It slammed shut behind her.

"Hello Mila."

She turn to the voice.

"Good to see you again."

"John…"

He was dressed as an ambulance attendant. From behind her, a hand reached over her mouth with a cloth that had been soaked something noxious.

"Hit, bite, kick!" she thought.

She felt herself being lifted her off her feet. She kicked, her riding boots knocked the bowl of candy into the air. Her exertion forced her to breathe and she took the fumes deep into her lungs.

"Fight it. Fight!" she ordered herself.

She felt her body fail her mind. Her eyes remained open as her limbs went limp. John caught her as she collapsed and lifted her unto the gurney. He stroked her hair. A blonde woman in her forties dressed as an orderly hovered over her as she buckled her down with orange straps.

"Beate. How long will she be out?"

"Fifteen minutes tops. In the van, we can give her another dose."

Mila's vision blurred and then she was being rolled down the hall. She heard Zablon's voice.

"What happened? Mila, are you okay?" he asked out of breath. "What's going on?"

She tried to move her eyes, to blink out a message to him, but could not. The overhead pot lights drifted past. Each stabbed her eyes.

Zablon turned to the EMS workers as he continued to follow them down the hall.

"What happened?" he demanded.

"Somebody called it in," John said. "She was found at your door."

"I'll ride with her," said Zablon as they reached the elevator.

The doors opened. Beate pulled the gurney in and John held out his hands to Zablon indicating for him to stop.

"Sorry Professor. You're welcome to follow if you'd like."

"Where are you taking her?"

"Sunnybrook."

"Why not Humber Regional? It's much closer," Zablon asked.

"Better staff in case of a drug overdose."

"Overdose?"

Beate pushed the close door button repeatedly.

"We found these," said John holding up a bottle, "in her bag when we were looking for I.D."

The elevator doors shut.

"Sunnybrook? Drug overdose? Hey you're..."

Zablon ran back to his office as quickly as his bulk allowed and grabbed his car keys out of the top drawer of his desk.

He sprinted back down the hall, jabbed the elevator call button a few times and looked up. Both elevators were on the ground floor.

He started down the stairs stumbling, twisting his ankle badly. His keys and cellphone flew out of his hands, clattering down the stairwell some twenty stairs away.

"Damn it."

He rose to his knees and tried to stand leaving heavily on the railing but toppled over onto his back. Only then did he realize his ankle was fully dislocated.

"Help," he hollered. his voice echoing in the concrete stairwell. "Help! Somebody. Help!"

****

Mila regained consciousness, the rocking of the van jolting her awake.

Her mouth was gagged and her throat was parched.

She opened her eyes but she could not see.

Her arms were bound in front of her, cinched so tight that her fingers were numb. She wriggled them and they began to tingle.

"Beate, get your driver to slow down," said John. "He'll draw attention."

She barked out an order to the front seat.

"Медленный ебут вниз."

Mila felt the van slow immediately.

The blindfold was ripped from her eyes.

"You little bitch. I read Lily's diary. It's your fault she's dead! You twisted her thoughts. You made her want to get away from us, from me."

"I didn't do anything."

John struck her with the back of his hand.

"You gave her bullshit and lies."

Mila felt her lip split and tasted her blood.

"What am I going to do with you?"

"John, I can walk away from all of this."

John laughed.

"You think you can?"

"I know nothing."

"You know everything. I read the email you sent to your beloved Caroline."

His carotid artery pulsed.

"I trusted you. You could have had it all. All. I was going to sever all ties for you. I need you."

"John, I told the police. I told my brother!"

"Lies! You'd be exposed," he said as his voice softened. "You think I don't know who you are? You think you can play your little charade with me? You'd never expose yourself. No way does your brother know what you do. No way do Petr or Zoya know anything about their precious little girl."

"Leave 'em out of this!"

"They'll know soon enough what you are: cheap, common, expendable."

Mila lashed out with her leg, but Beate was immediately on top of her, pinning her against the gurney.

"Give her another dose," she instructed.

John held a cloth over her mouth and nose.

She held her breath as long as she could and gasped.

In seconds, she could move no more.

****

Zablon could hear footfalls coming from below quickly. He remembered the track team sometimes did sprints up the stairs.

"Help!"

A face appeared over top of him.

"Professor Simintov, are you okay?" asked a young woman.

"Christ, of course not."

"Can I help you up? Woah, your ankle's a mess."

"Dislocated."

"Let me help you sit up."

"No, go get my phone. You passed it on the landing below."

The student ran down the stairs and came back.

"I'll call nine-one-one," she said.

"No. Give it to me."

Zablon looked at the phone.

"Crap," he said as he swiped the phone open. "I've been here for nearly two hours."

He went to his contacts and dialed Mila's phone. It went to straight to voicemail.

Zablon opened his contacts and dialed another number.

"Vitaly Mirkin?"

"Yes."

"Zablon Simintov. I'm Mila's academic supervisor."

"Oh, hello Dr. Simintov. She speaks highly of you. Mila always..."

"Mila's been abducted."

"What?"

"She was taken away from my office on a gurney. They told me that she was incoherent and catatonic. That she'd overdosed on pills."

"Mila doesn't do drugs."

"I know. They were going to Sunnybrook, but that makes no sense. Humber Regional is so much closer and has a much better drug trauma centre. I swear one of the attendants was the guy in the paper, the fund manager whose daughter died in Miami."

"Lister?"

"That's him. He was dressed in a uniform."

Vitaly snapped his fingers at Brian who was walking by his office.

"Dr. Simintov, I've put you on speaker phone. An RCMP officer is in the room with me."

"I don't know what happened. It was so fast. Their uniforms looked real. It was odd that the campus police weren't there, but they never are when you need them."

"Dr. Simintov, where are you now?"

"I stairwell in Vari Hall at York. I fell in the stairs and can't walk."

"Are you safe?" asked Brian.

"Fine. Dislocated ankle. I've got a student with me who's calling nine-one-one."

"Good. We'll be there ASAP."

Brian hung up.

"Let's go."

Brian went back to his own office and took a key chain from his pants pocket. He opened the drawer, removed the gun from the safety box and inserted a clip into the grip.

He and Vitaly ran down to the basement parking garage, jumped into Brian's sedan and pulled out on to Bay Street.

He had Vitaly put the red flashing light on his roof.

Brian drove rapidly but confidently to the university thirty minutes away.

"Holy Fuck Brian. He's got Mila."

"Vitaly, I know."

"My sister."

Vitaly was near tears.

Brian kept quiet, concentrating on the traffic ahead of him. He avoided the major thoroughfares and snaked through neighbourhoods at speeds that frightened Vitaly.

Brian was clutching the wheel tightly as well.

They made the campus and parked in front of Vari Hall.

Zablon was in the atrium on a stretcher, the attendants readying to take him.

Vitaly called Caroline but the call went to voicemail.

"Caroline, Mila's missing. Her prof says she's been abducted," he said. "Call me right away. I need that bonded program you two share."

"Vitaly," asked Brian, "where does Caroline work?"

"Biff's."

Brian dialed another number.

"Tracey, Brian here. I need a car at Biff's on Front now. Tell the officer to pick up Caroline..."

"Spencer," said Vitaly.

"Caroline Spencer. Make sure it's not O'Malley. Call me when he has her. Have her driven to York, Vari Hall, and make damn sure she has her phone."

He hung up. Brian made his way to Zablon.

"Dr. Simintov. I'm Detective Brian Cranston, RCMP. I work with Mila's brother. Start from the beginning. Just try to remember everything. No detail's too small."

Vitaly approached the two. Brian held up his hand.

"Vitaly, take a walk."

"Brian..."

"I got it. Vitaly. Go! Now!"

Vitaly hesitated, then stared up at the sky.

It was cloudy and darkening rapidly.

He exhaled loudly before walking away. He felt like punching the plate glass of the atrium.

"Oh Mila! Mila!"

46

Mila's head throbbed and she tasted copper in her mouth. She was lying on her side, her head against the wall, her neck twisted. The blindfold was over her eyes again. The restraint had loosened. She tried to wrench her hands free but could not. Mila moved to lift herself into a sitting position. She felt nauseous. The pain in her head exploded when she moved. The blindfold had shifted. She rubbed her head some more and was able to move it off first one eye and then the other. A crack of light came from around the door. It stabbed her eyes.

She heard the soft scrape of leather-soled shoes on a wooden floor. They approached her and stopped. Mila sat upright with her back against a wall, drew her knees back, and prepared to lash out. Mila heard the squeak of casters rolling against the hardwood floor and the soft sigh of a cushion. Tapping on a keyboard. A drawer opened, some rustling around and the drawer closed. There was silence for thirty seconds and then she heard a soft tapping and some gentle scrapping. A snort. A sigh and then longer snort. The chair squeaked again and the footsteps came closer. There was a knock on the door.

"Come."

Mila heard the door to the office open and the muffled voice of two women. One was strong and confident. The other not.

"Olga, glad you could join me," John said.

"John, when can I go?" she whimpered. "Beate...you promised Mila would be here."

"Oh, she is. She can hear you," said John. "Beate, thank you."

"Yes, Mr. Lister. Will there be anything else?"

"No. I'll handle them from here."

Mila heard a door shut.

"John! What the..." said Olga. "Who's...who's the guy on the floor? What the Hell?"

And then Mila heard a slap. She had seen John deliver one before, but the last time it was Mike and he was 100 pounds heavier and six inches taller than Olga. John was in his forties and he was stronger than he looked. Mila heard heels scraping on the floor. She imagined Olga, supine, scrambling to get her feet underneath her. There was another slap.

"Stop!" she shouted.

"I don't think so."

Mila could hear John grunt as Olga was thrown against the door of the closet. The sliver of light went dark. Olga was just outside, not moving. There was no whimper of fear or moan of pain. Mila could hear the scratch of John's shoes. She presumed that John was hovering over Olga as she heard the sound of tape being ripped. The light reappeared under the door as Olga was pulled away. Mila recognized the wheels of the desk chair as it was dragged across the floor. Then there was the tearing more tape. The footsteps moved back towards the closet. Her head was still spinning. A key was inserted in a lock handle and the cylinder turned. Mila was blinded by light for a moment as the door opened.

"Oh Mila honey, we have company," John said.

John lifted Mila to her feet and pulled her out into the office. A large blue tarp was spread out on the floor up against the wall. On in, Olga was slumped, unconscious in John's office chair. Her wrists were bound to the arm rests and her calves were taped to the chair legs just above the casters. She was naked from the waist up. Her skirt was hiked up as well, her underwear torn away. Olga's head rolled from her chest to an upright position. Grey duct tape crudely covered her mouth. Her eyes went wild as she realized she had been bound. She fought but the tape did not yield. Olga looked from Mila to the corner of the room and muffled something through the tape. Mila saw Mike lying prone, his hands tied behind his back, his feet bound with duct tape and his mouth taped shut.

His eyes were closed, and if not for the large welt on his temple, Mila would have believed him to be sleeping. He looked peaceful.

"Mila," John said. "Look at me. Are you going to behave?

He sniffed and wiped the back of his hand across his runny nose. His nostrils were red. His eyes bloodshot.

"Shit," she said to herself. "He's hopped up."

She nodded yes. John slipped the rope that bound her hands onto the sturdy hook above her head. She was forced onto her tip toes. Mila looked towards Mike.

"Ah, your protector. He showed me his loyalty. You know I don't like to be disappointed."

John walked over to Mike, crouched down on his haunches and whispered into his ear. Mike's body stiffened and he began to struggle against the duct tape. John stood and place his foot on Mike's neck and looked back at Mila.

"Just telling him my plans for the evening. There, there, Mike. I've already paid for her time."

Mike's eyes were pure anger. John stood and kicked Mike in the jaw and then stomped on his temple with the heel of his shoe.

"John! No!" cried Mila.

Mike shuddered for what seemed an eternity. Then he lay still.

"What? Caring about your Mike. You're sentimental too? I knew that already. I saw you crying at the funeral. Yes, when you turned to avoid me. You buried you head in Nico's shoulder. You used him. It was too bad Hooshang had to die. There was no other way I could get to Kent."

John turned back to Mike's unconscious body.

"I'll finish with you later."

Mila noticed that her clothes were folded on the floor by the French doors where John had written her cheque. Her helmet rested on top of her jacket and jeans. Her satchel was there, too, standing unopened, but she was certain John had rifled through it. She had no idea what to do.

John swung the room's two overstuffed armchairs around to face Mila and keeping Olga out of kicking range. Mila wondered if the chairs were the ones that John's father sat in as he watched his helpless wife lying at the bottom of the stairs so long ago. John then went over to his desk. That's when Mila saw the mirror lying on the blotter. John picked up the rolled up dollar bill and inhaled a long line of the white powder. He stood upright, closed his eyes and sighed.

"Like old times. Care to join me Mila?"

From the lower drawer, he grabbed a bottle of scotch, two glasses and a small green, metal box the size of a child's lunchbox. He left the box on top of the desk. He moved to back to the armchairs and sat down in front of Mila and Olga.

"I've been saving this. I always assumed that I would be having it with you: Lagavulin, forty-nine years in a bourbon quarter cask. I picked it up last summer when I went to Scotland. Peaty beyond belief. Beautiful."

"John, is that the chair your dad sat after beating your mother?"

"Do you think I'm that sentimental?"

"John, you don't have to do this."

"I've a choice, do I?"

With the bottle resting on his knee and studying the label, he removed the dull green foil seal. The cork came out with a soft pop. He threw the cork into a corner.

"Oops! Old habits die hard."

John poured two fingers and raised his glass.

"To fine endings!"

He took a sip, paused for a moment and downed the remainder of the glass.

"We could have been something."

He took a long pull from the bottle, not bothering with the glass, swallowing two or three mouthfuls.

"You and me!" Mila began. "You think I've ever had feelings for you?"

John lunged forward out of the chair, pushing her head back, forcing her jaw open, he poured the bottle over her open mouth. She tried not to swallow. He bent forward and kissed her, thrusting his tongue into her mouth. Mila bit down hard. John winced in pain and punched Mila in the temple. She released and gasped for air. John took a step back, spat on the hardwood floor. There was blood mixed with the spittle.

"To the bitter end? How do you wish to pay for your transgressions?"

"Pay you?"

John spat again, the spittle landing on her chest.

"I count that you owe me for two things. First, you breached my trust in the most sacred of my possessions. No one, no one on the outside knows how I make my money, except you. Now, what am I to do about that?"

"Money first? And your daughter?"

"You poisoned her mind."

"You can't even say her name. She hated you. Lily hated you. She found you repugnant. What kind of man forces his daughter to meet his..."

"His companion, lover, courtesan, his mistress."

"HIS WHORE!" she screamed.

"Such an unseemly word. I like the word thief. You and Olga will go down as common girls, but not without means, greedy really, without morals. Selfish. This is how it'll play in the papers. Upon reading about the untimely death of a man's beloved daughter, two escorts decide to burgle the family home. The loving parents would be too preoccupied with grieving their only remaining child. The bereaved father comes home to collect his daughter's mementos to share at a memorial only to find the two ransacking the home. They attack him. In self-defense, he shoots... at least one of them."

John walked over to the French doors of the office, opened the curtains and the doors and looked out over the golf course. He picked up Mila's helmet and weighed it in his hand and smashed the helmet against the pane. The first blow created a spider web in the glass. The second broke it inwards, shards of glass skittering across the hardwood floor. The glass crunched underfoot he walked back, tossed the helmet at Mila, striking her on the chest. Mila gasped for air. He took a pressed, white cotton handkerchief out of his pocket, picked up a handful of shards and threw them at her. Instinctively, Mila tried to push her elbows together to shield her face. The shards had the desired effect. The blood began to trickle down her arms.

John turned away and scoured the ground for a moment, bent down and lifted a larger shard with his thumb and index finger. He wrapped Olga's torn shirt around it, creating a handle.

"So, Mila, shall Olga pay for you?"

"John, Olga's innocent."

"She knows enough thanks to you."

"Let her go. I'll be yours."

"You already are."

John turned to Olga. She was quivering in her chair.

"You dance?'

Olga nodded, clearly terrified.

"Mila, have you seen her?"

"Yes."

"I hope you enjoyed that."

John pushed the shard against the back of her ankle, just piercing the skin. A rivulet of blood snaked to her heel. Olga moaned in pain.

"Shall I cut her Achilles? I ask you again Mila, how will you repay me?

"John. Take me, any way you wish," Mila said.

"How noble! A little late, no? Severing it would be awfully messy. Maybe something else might be in order."

John dropped the shard on the ground, walked over to his desk, took his keys out of his pants pocket and unlocked the green, metal box. He withdrew what Mila thought was a pistol, picked up a clip, made sure the magazine was full and slapped it into place with the palm of his hand. He then removed a silencer and screwed it in place. He lay the weapon flat on the desk.

He went over to Mila, took her head in his hands and kissed her hard on the lips. He stepped back and spat in her face. He walked over to Olga and pushed her chair closer to Mila. The casters crinkled across is the tarp. He sat down in the armchair and looked at his two prizes.

Mila saw John's phone buzz as it sat on the leather blotter on his desk. Her grandmother's ring lay next to it. He rose from the couch and answered it.

"Tim, my brother. Delighted to hear from you."

Mila's eyes widened.

"I'm having a hard time understanding you... Your mouth's wired shut... What happened?... No, she didn't...She did? You'd like to come by? Oh I'm a little busy...Where are you? On my front porch? You don't say."

He covered the mouthpiece and whispered. "He's on the front porch. Should I let him in?"

John bent over his desk and did another line.

"Ring the doorbell for me, would you?"

Mila and Olga's heads both turned towards the door leading down the hallway to the entrance as the chime rang. John left them and hurried down the hall.

"Shit, Olga, that's the guy I kicked the crap out of."

Olga struggled against the tape. The pool of blood coming from Olga reached Mila's feet. She tried to get a foot onto the arm rest of Olga's chair, but her heel pushed Olga away under the pressure. Both turned back to the door as Tim followed John into the room.

Mila half expected him to lunge at her right away. He could not move fast. His right leg was in a brace from his ankle to his groin. He was leaning heavily on a cane. His face was a horrible mess; his eyes purple and yellow. He still squinted from the swelling. Jagged stitches danced across this nose. He smiled when he saw them. His jaw was wired shut.

John gestured over to the desk.

"Tim, a little something before, well, you know."

"I shouldn't with all the meds I'm on. Who knows what it'll do?"

"Wimp."

Tim looked at John and went over to the desk. He licked his index finger and dabbed it on the mirror. He rubbed the small amount of powder caked to it across his upper gums. A small grin crossed his face.

"Good shit," he paused, "next time, okay?"

Tim walked over to Olga and Mila, but he kept his distance.

"So, I get my duo after all."

"Tim, careful now. The short one's feisty."

"Hello Tatiana. Remember me?" Tim snarled.

"The name's Mila!"

Tim balanced himself on his left leg and brought the cane down hard on the front of Mila's right shoulder. Mila gritted her teeth.

"Didn't make a sound? Interesting."

Tim stepped forward, tore open her shirt and ran his hand over her ribs, his fingers pausing over her tattoo. He scratched an X on her skin with his finger nail, drawing blood. The cane struck his mark. Air screamed out of her lungs.

Olga's eyes darted. She saw Mila's resolve and hardened.

Tim hobbled over to Olga. She struggled but was pinned to the chair. Tim tore the tape from her lips and pressed his mouth to Olga's. She spat in his face as Tim moved back. He wiped the spittle with the back of his hand.

"You're pathetic. You call yourself a man," Olga said. "You've never satisfied a woman, have you? Have you?"

Tim struck her hard across the temple. Her head fell limp.

"Tim, easy, my man. They're no fun when they're out."

John turned Mila around so she was facing the wall, still hanging form the hook. She tried lashed out with her feet, but instantly her shoulders were on the edge of dislocation.

He parted her legs with his feet and unzipped his fly. She twisted and tried to kick, but with no purchase on the ground, she could not defend herself. He spat into his hand, moistened his erect glans, held her hips hard and with one brutal thrust, he raped her. Mila refused to make a sound. He thrust hard, over and over, his entire length buried within her.

He finished, stepped back and zipped up his pants. He took hold of her hair in his hand, pull her head back as far as her neck would allow and plowed it into the wall. Her world spun. If not for her arms, she would have crumpled to the ground.

Her head swung to the side and she saw Tim raise his cane. After three blows, he forced the crook of the cane around her neck and jerked hard. She could breathe but she felt the blood throbbing in her brain, screaming to return to her lungs. He laughed.

She heard him unbuckle his belt.

"No sloppy seconds for me, John."

Tim tried pushing himself into her but he could not. With his pot belly and the cast, he could not reach her. He bent in close to her ear, his stale breath on her neck.

He tugged a little harder on the cane, cutting off the air to her lungs, but lightening the pressure on her aorta, bending her neck to its limit. Her vision came back.

"Next time, my bitch."

Tim grabbed Mila's head and rammed it into the drywall. The gypsum yielded, an oval depression cupping her bloody forehead.

"Now, we're even!"

Mila's vision blurred and her left eye went dark.

Tim removed the cane from her neck and hobbled over to the couch. He plopped himself down next to John, who handed him a glass of Lagavulin. They toasted and downed the glasses like shooters.

47

Mila was still facing the wall when she woke up, her face nestled in the indentation her skull had made. She saw she was lucky. She had barely missed the stud behind the drywall, the crew just millimeters from her temple.

Blood ran down her forehead and into her eye. Every breath brought stabbing pain. She turned herself around gingerly, facing away from the wall, surveying the room. Her groin ached horribly. Her legs and nether regions were wiped clean.

The tarp was gone. So was Mike. So was Olga.

There was the faint scent of bleach. There were still shards of glass on the floor, but that would be consistent with a break and enter. She knew John could try, and it would be hard, but he could get away with this. Money could buy anything. She knew she would never stand up to a rape kit. She knew that one would never be administered. Her story would never be told. She would be made to disappear. She had to get away.

The tape on the desk chair had been cut crudely, much of it still attached to the ornate wooden arms and legs. The chair had been jostled slightly closer to her than before. Mila lifted her right leg and curled her toes over the armrest, tape sticking to her feet. The chair resisted at first and threatened to topple over as she struggled to move it closer.

She applied less pressure and the casters gave, squeaking ever so slightly. She got the inch she needed. With the ball of her foot on the middle of the armrest, cursing that it had better support her weight, she rose up just enough to free herself from the hook. Mila stood on the seat of the chair for a moment, finding her balance, tears of pain flooding down her cheeks as she lowered her arms. Her rotator cuffs complained bitterly. Each degree of descent required enormous control. Nausea came over her and she vomited on the hardwood floor. Her eyes went dark for a moment as the pain in her ribs crested.

She raised her bound hands to her collarbone. It was bruised but not broken. She found a path through the splitters of glass to the garden doors and managed to rub the cord that bound her hands against a protruding shards. It frayed and eventually yielded after ten passes. Feeling cold, she slid into her jeans and her tank top, then went over to John's desk and swiped her grandmother's ring from its surface. Her hands trembled as she slipped it onto her third finger. She froze: a muffled shot from the silenced gun.

"Olga!"

Mila opened her satchel and slid her hand in, hoping her riding gloves were still there. With them donned, she carefully walked back to the chair, picking up the shard still wrapped in Olga's shirt. The blood had dried into a carmine syrup.

She padded in silence down the hall, horrified to see a continuous streak of blood on the tiled floor leading to the foyer. Small, bloody hand prints adorned both sides of the moulding around the bathroom door.

Mila arrived near the arch in John's front foyer and stopped. She could see John and Tim in the glass of the picture frames that hung on the wall.

"Time to get our second thief."

"John, I didn't sign up for this. This is way beyond any twisted fantasy. There's blood everywhere. No one will believe. A little bit of fun's okay, but murder. She's cute... even if she did kick the crap out of me. The other girl didn't know shit."

"Losing your nerve are you? Don't worry. Beate will clean everything up once she's dealt with Mike. She makes things disappear."

"And Kent?"

"No one will ever find him. The pigs took care of that in about 10 minutes. Help me get her into the foyer and you can go."

Tim hobbled in front of John back towards the office, leaning heavily on his cane, the loaded gun held casually in his right hand. As he moved through the archway, Mila kicked at Tim's hand, knocking the gun to the ground. The pistol bounced off the wall and skidded to a stop between Mila's feet. She swung the cane out from underneath him and then she kicked into his good leg hard. His knee buckled and he fell writhing in pain on the ground. Mila lunged down on him and buried the jagged glass into his neck, twisted it and broke the shaft before dropping it. Tim grabbed at the wound. In moments, his white shirt was crimson. He twitched on his side, his legs jerking as he tried to sit up, his shoes failing to find purchase on the now slippery tiles. Dark blood seeped between the wires that held his jaw in place.

John ran back to the foyer. Mila calmly picked up the gun and considered dispatching Tim from his misery. She stepped over him and inched forward to edge of the archway.

"Olga!" she called

"Come and get her."

Mila ensured the safety was still off, thankful it was labeled clearly.

"No point in threatening," she said to herself. "Need to hurt."

Her feet did not make a sound as she strode around the corner. John was kneeling behind Olga, his left arm around her neck. Her hands were at her waist, holding her stomach. Blood was seeping out between her fingers. John held the blade of his cane at her throat.

"Let her go," Mila said. "She's done nothing."

"Can't do that."

"Let her go!"

"Stop! No closer!"

A bead of red formed at the point.

"John, there's no way to explain all of this."

"You're right. You're right. You took care of Tim for me. Thank you. He knew too much. Deep down, he didn't have the resolve. Never did. I was going to have to deal with him anyhow.

No loose ends, right? It'll be just you and me, my word against yours, a gentile philanthropist versus a greedy whore."

John pushed the blade hard into Olga's throat to the hilt. It protruded ten inches out the other side, the sharp, silvery point now smeared with blood. Her mouth moved without a sound. He withdrew it and shook the blood off. Crimson poured from the wound as he let Olga fall to the ground.

Mila fired three shots. The first two missed, exploding in the tiles, sending broken porcelain and dust into the air, hitting the rear wall of the foyer. The third hit his right leg. The force of the impact spun John around and he dropped the blade.

"You bitch. You shot me. You bloody shot me."

He breathed through the pain and smiled.

"You've never disappointed me," John said.

He sucked air through his teeth.

"Kill me now and the police will have to think it was a home invasion gone bad. I've instructed Beate to splice the security tapes and to erase the rest."

Mila strode across the floor and stood over John. She raised the gun with shaking hands and pressed the end of the silencer against his temple. John yelped. The heat of the barrel seared his skin. Blood dripped down Mila's forehead and along the bridge of her nose. She wiped it away with the back of her gloved hand. She moved the silencer so it pointed square in the middle of John's forehead.

"This is for Olga," she said.

John eyes darted to the darkened window at the front door. It burst open.

"Mila. Drop it!"

"Detective Cranston! Thank God you're here! She broke in. Her friend attacked me. She stabbed Tim."

Brian looked to his right. Tim was no longer moving.

"She just shot me!"

"Mila," Brian said, "put the gun down. I'm here. It's over."

Vitaly pushed past the officers who had followed Brian in.

"Listen to Brian. It's okay now. Put it down."

"Mila, give Vitaly the gun," Brian said.

"He raped me! He killed Olga!"

"Mila, give me the gun, now!" said Vitaly quietly taking a step forward towards her.

Mila cocked the trigger.

"Stop. No closer. He killed Kent. He killed Hooshang."

John looked Vitaly in the eye. A smirk crept across John's face.

"He raped me. The dead puke tried to sodomize me. Don't you understand. He killed my Lily. He kills everything around him."

Her hands had ceased their tremor.

"Mila," said Vitaly, "you deserve better than this."

She pressed the muzzle of the pistol firmly into John's forehead, pushing his head back before pulling back slightly. A red circle was left behind. With the blood from her brow, she marked on X over the circle with her thumb. John wet himself, a dark shadow growing across his pants.

Mila lowered the barrel, dragging it over his eyebrow, along his nose and to his lips. She pushed the gun forward, forcing the silencer between his teeth. She thrust it into in mouth until it hit the back of his throat. He gagged and vomited, the barrel still in his mouth. Vitaly just watched his sister in disbelief.

"You always were weak. You were never man enough to be a true father to my Lily. Shall I take you out of your misery? Shall you suffer no more?"

John whimpered and nodded yes. His face became serene, closed his eyes and exhaled.

"You're not worth it," Mila said.

She pulled the gun out of his mouth, turned away from everyone and fired a single shot, hitting the vase of Calla lilies that stood on the vestibule table.

Vitaly engulfed his sister in his arms.

Brian kept his sidearm trained on John as he took the gun from Mila's hand now pinned at her side by her brother. Officers rushed forward, all weapons drawn, all pointed at John.

Two officers hauled Vitaly and Mila down the front steps and ushered them to a waiting ambulance.

The attendant wrapped Mila in a gray blanket and sat her down while she began to tend to Mila's wounds.

Vitaly stood over his sister in silence.

48

"Green tea, tall, not too hot."

"Thanks Martha."

"How's Mila?"

"Had breakfast with her this morning. She's ready for today."

"You're her brother, not her lawyer. How is she?"

"Okay. She's healing. The plastic surgeon said that they'd have to wait a while to see how her brow heals."

"And her eye?"

"Well, let's just hope for the best."

"She's a fighter," said Martha.

"She's changed so much. She used to conceal every blemish, always kept every mark hidden. This week she stopped wearing sunglasses."

"Progress?"

"I suppose."

"That's good."

"I'm still concerned about what's going on inside her head. She's still having nightmares."

"I can't imagine going through..."

"There's still a sullenness that she masks when Caroline's looking. Zablon's work should help her to find focus."

Martha reached over the counter and patted Vitaly on the arm.

"Give it time, my love."

Martha pulled him closer and kissed him on the cheek.

"That's for her. This is for you."

She kissed him on the lips.

"Today's just the arraignment, right?

"Yeah, shouldn't take to long. The Crown attorney spoke with Lister's defense. He's gonna plead not guilty. The securities related charges, my stuff, will come later."

"Good luck then, I guess. I don't know what you say."

"Thanks, but luck will have nothing to do with it."

He blew her a final kiss across the counter and walked up Yonge Street sipping his green tea.

He skirted past the office before making his way up the stairs at Old City Hall. There were a number of protestors out front, demanding compensation from Trinity Asset Management for having lost money on their investments.

Vitaly rode the elevator alone up to the sixth floor and fell into a crush of people as the doors opened.

He pushed his way into the court room and sat down next his parents.

Brian and Zablon joined them moments later. Zoya sat stoic, betraying no emotion. Vitaly knew she seethed with rage.

Petr was visibly stressed, rolling and unrolling Mila's victim impact statement. Petr was prepared to read it should the judge allow.

If not, Vitaly knew the press would enjoy every salacious details. Vitaly reached over to his father and placed his hand on his forearm.

"Papa, everything's fine. She's safe now."

Petr nodded and took Zoya's hand in his.

Zablon sat upright, pointing in John's direction.

"Vitaly, I know that woman sitting with him."

"Zablon, anyone at the table has been vetted by the Court. The prosecutors will know her. Who is she anyhow?

"I can't remember but I've a bad feeling about this."

"Brian and I have been gone through this with the Crown. She expects a lengthy battle on every count. Everything will be okay. It doesn't matter who's here today. We're going to trial and he'll be remanded into custody till then."

"I wouldn't be so sure," said a voice from behind them bearing an English accent. All three turned.

"That, John Lister, he's a rascal," said a Sikh gentleman, with a broad orange turban and eyes unnerving black. "He'll find a way."

"Pardon?" asked Vitaly. "And you are?"

"Jargit Bhutani Singh is my name. The family I work for and I are... were large investors in John's fund. Quite happy ones until well..."

"Sir, did you know what he was doing?"

"Of course not!" Jargit lied. "I'd never advocate illegal activity or immoral behaviour, but the markets are riddled with both, aren't they? Granted John went to an extreme. Our world is rife with people who do. It's not right but it's reality."

"Why are you here?"

"Why are any of these people here?" he said as he his arm swept over the gallery. "Schadenfreude of course. My presence won't change matters. I always thought one day I'd see him in court. Just not for this. If you'll excuse me, I have other things to attend to."

"You're not staying?"

"I've seen everyone I need to. I'll wager John has found a way. Good day."

Singh nodded and left.

"Odd," said Vitaly.

"More than odd," said Brian.

Vitaly watched John slouched in his chair, trying to look nonchalant. John tugged at his collar. The ligature marks ringing his neck were plainly visible.

The two other people at the table were arguing between themselves with great fervour.

Vitaly always loved watching defendant counsels in disarray. It usually did not work in their favour. Justices liked simplicity.

"There's Joan," said Brian.

"New boy toy at her side?"

"Maybe. For her, this isn't about John, you know?"

Joan searched around the room for familiar faces. Most turned away when she smiled or waved.

"Ruthless she is," said Brian. "This is about where she lands next. Was she the victim of her spouse or is she a pariah for having stuck around for so long?"

"Don't know," said Vitaly, "frankly, given how she cooperated with the police and turned on John... well she might survive with the ladies who lunch."

A bailiff walked to the front of the dais.

"All rise."

John stood, waving away the cane that was offered to him by the woman.

"Good," said Brian. "The bastard's still in pain."

John faced the judge, leaning over, his fists resting on the table.

"Mr. John Lister. This is a bail hearing. There is a long list of charges here. I would like you to enter a plea of guilty or not-guilty after each charge. Do you understand?

"Yes, Bill."

"Mr. Lister, you will address me as Mr. Justice Hammond or Your Honour. Is that understood?"

"Uh huh."

"Yes?"

"Yes, Your Honour."

"Thank you, all right then," said Hammond. "Bailiff, proceed."

"In the first charge of the murder of Olga Komolski, how you do you plead?"

"Guilty Your Honour."

A stunned murmur spread across the gallery.

John's lawyer stood up, frantic.

"Your Honour, my client's..."

"Mr. Clayton," snarled John, "shut up and sit down, you little shit of a windbag,"

Hammond banged his gavel on the desk.

"Mr. Lister. Such language will not be tolerated in my court. Control yourself or you shall be removed."

"Pardon me, Your Honour. My lawyer and I have but a small disagreement."

The lawyer slunk down into his chair.

"John, what are you doing?"

John just smiled.

"Mr. Lister, did I hear you correctly?"

"Yes, Your Honour. Guilty as charged."

A few cheers came from the gallery overtop of the general murmur that emanated and enveloped the gallery.

"What are you up to?" Brian whispered just loud enough for Zablon and Vitaly to hear.

"I know!" exclaimed Zablon, pointing at the woman at John's desk, snapping his fingers. "I know who that is."

Both turned towards Zablon. His eyes widened.

"We have to stop her! Please Brian, stop her."

"Zablon, you've got no standing. You know that."

"But Vitaly..."

The judge's gavel came down again.

"Silence! Ladies and gentlemen in the gallery, one more outburst and I'll clear the court. You are here at my pleasure. Do I make myself clear?"

Hammond banged his gavel but the clamouring did not quiet down. The judge banged his gavel again and he spoke slowly, drawing out each word.

"Is that understood?"

The crowd quieted.

John started laughing.

"Mr. Lister, these are serious charges. Is there something amusing?"

"Yes, there are many amusing things, Your Honour. At present I can think of two or three, but please continue."

"Why thank you, Mr. Lister, I suppose we shall. Bailiff, since we have Mr. Lister's permission, continue."

"The following relates to activities on the afternoon of May 29th. In the second charge..."

"Guilty. Mr. Justice, this will be very repetitive. Let me save the Court's time. Guilty to all and every charge."

"Madam Prosecutor, will you waive the reading of the charges."

"If it pleases the Court, yes."

"Thank you Mr. Lister for being so cooperative."

John's lawyer stood up, frantic.

"Bail, Your Honour?" he croaked.

Now the judge stifled a laugh.

"Ms. Prosecutor, any comments?"

"Your Honour, considering gravity of these crimes and their aggravated and premeditated nature and Mr. Lister's financial resources and access to and command of personal aviation, I assert that he's both an extreme danger to society and a flight risk. I request that the accused be remanded into the custody of Her Majesty forthwith."

The judge turned to John's counsel who tried to compose himself.

"Your Honour. My client's under extreme stress. His pleas are not what he had indicated to me just minutes before the proceedings. I submit that he is not fit to enter a plea.

The woman sitting at John's table stood up.

"Permission to address the Court, Your Honour?"

"And you are?" asked the Judge.

"Your Honour, assistant to the defense counsel. I'm Dr. Sylvia Tyrie, Head of Forensic Psychiatry at the Dade Country Health Network, Associate Professor of Psychiatry at the University of Miami and visiting scholar in residence at the Department of Psychiatry at University of Toronto, St. George's Campus. Mr. Lister is indeed not fit to stand trial to enter a plea."

"I beg your pardon Madam. He seems lucid to me."

"With respect, Your Honour, Mr. Lister is quite the opposite. He is exhibiting classic characteristics of a Simintov-Mirkin Displacement."

"A what?"

"This is a condition first described by my colleague, Dr. Zablon Simintov and his research assistant Ms. Mila Mirkin Petrovna."

"The victim?" Hammond asked.

"The condition," Dr. Tyrie continued, "describes the displacement of one addiction with another in reaction to a stressor. In Mr. Lister's case, the death of his first daughter Alison some years ago led to Mr. Lister abusing alcohol and prescription medicine. He was in recovery until the stress of his failing business and familial circumstances caused him to seek a new release, the comfort of paid sexual relations."

"The death of his sole remaining daughter Lily last week resulted in the relapse into abusing alcohol and narcotics," Dr. Tyrie added.

"Your Honour, Mr. Lister requires treatment if ever he is to be fit to stand trial. I humbly request Your Honour, that you order that Mr. Lister be remanded in to the care of a psychiatric care facility."

The prosecutor was frantically discussing matters with her colleagues at the table.

"Ms. Hampson? If could have your attention please? Would you accept that Mr. Lister is to be remanded into the medical care of the Crown pending a psychiatric evaluation."

The woman looked up, bewildered by the rapid turn.

"Madam Prosecutor. Would you care to respond or shall I just accept Dr. Tyrie's recommendation?"

"Your Honour, without prejudice to future actions from on the Crown, we agree that Mr. Lister should be remanded into the custody of the Corrections Canada for a psychiatric evaluation."

"So ordered."

The crack of the gavel hitting the desk startled John.

He looked up and stared at the judge.

Petr and Zoya turned to Vitaly.

"Vitaly, what does that mean?"

Vitaly sat stunned, his eyes burning into the back of John's skull. He had been caught off guard.

John turned around and held Vitaly's gaze. His ears burned red. He mouthed: "You bastard."

John smiled, cocked his head to the right and winked.

"Vitaly, it's all right," said Brian stepping in for his mute friend.

"Mr. and Mrs. Mirkin, Mr. Lister is not going to prison, at least not yet. We'll know after the evaluation. It will take some time. Rest assured, he will be behind bars for the rest of his life. He'll never be free again."

The bailiffs approached John. He stood and he held his hands out in front of him and allowed the handcuffs to be applied.

Joan moved forward, placed her scarf over his wrist and her hands on top of his.

"Goodbye, John."

"Please Joannie, please. I'm so sorry."

"I'm not."

She turned and walked away, the young man she'd sat with scurrying after her.

John watched Joan.

Her step was steady and her gait was confident.

John stumbled as the bailiff led him out of the room.

49

"Lister, you have a visitor. Get up."

He hated being called by his last name. All his adult life, unless he had given permission, he was never addressed without a title. Mister would have been agreeable. Lord and Master would have been preferable. The guards all called him Lister.

John raised his head from the thin pillow on the steel bunk in his cell and looked at the guard through the bars. His sheets were from the institution, his blanket made of coarse grey wool issued to all inmates.

The lone item from the outside world was the picture frame of Alison and Lily that had sat on his desk for so many years. The glass had been removed. He had no idea who had sent it.

John swung his feet off the bed, inserted a book mark into his novel and left the book on his bed.

He looked through the heavy mesh screen covering the window towards the offices of downtown Toronto. He could feel the energy flow through them. They hummed. John closed his eyes and he was walking the canyons of Bay and King Streets again, streets where people feared him.

"Lister, you comin' or what?"

"Yes."

"Yes, what?"

"Yes, Sir."

"Thank you."

The guard insisted on being called sir. His back bore the bruises from when he had not complied. John rose from his bed, picked up his cheap, aluminum cane and stood in front of the door and waited. He hated the cane. He wanted the old hickory one that stood in the umbrella bucket in the foyer of his house. It had heft. It had the blade. Then they would treat him respect he deserved.

Two guards stood in front of his cell as the magnetic lock of the cell buzzed and the door slid open. With his feet shoulder width apart and his mouth wide open, the shorter guard shone a flash light into John's mouth.

"Mouth, Clear. Arms, Clear. Torso, Clear. Legs...Legs clear."

John turned and lifted each foot in turn.

"Clear and clear. Alright, good to go."

The larger guard took a step back and indicated with his truncheon in hand in which direction he should walk. John wore a blue shirt and denim work pants, both now too loose for his frame. Food held little appeal for him. On his feet were white tube socks and white canvas sneaker with Velcro closures.

With his leg still in a brace, John was scarcely able to keep pace with the guards as he hobbled down the long hallway passing through two sets of heavy steel doors. At each one, he waited for the click of the lock before moving forward.

He was led into a large room with booths and a glass partition separating him from the outside. This was the second time he'd been here in four months. He sat down at one of the booths, hooking his cane on the edge of the desk.

"There's no one here!" he shouted over his shoulder to the guard. "Sir, you toying with me again?"

A woman in a long trench coat and a broad brimmed black straw hat pulled down over her face walked up, set down a small leather satchel in the table on her side of the booth and sat down.

"Joanie?"

She reached up and lifted the hat from her head, and lay it on the narrow counter in front of her. She picked up the handset on her side of the plate glass window as did John.

"Mila...You look as beautiful as always. I've missed you. I was looking on the internet at a new piece of art, a David Urban... Art therapy is part of my assessment. Perhaps, if I wire you money, you'd buy it for me. Keep it till I get out."

A chill ran up Mila's spine.

"Out?" she said quietly.

John continued to look at her and was silent. She bore a six-inch zipper scar across her forehead that was still purple. Her left eye drooped where Tim had broken her orbital bone when he had rammed her head into the wall. Her eyes were still beautifully blue.

"Did you get the money?" he asked.

"John," Mila said, "you're not well."

"The money?" he said more loudly. "Do you have it."

The guard stepped forward. John turned around and brought his finger to his mouth.

"Okay, okay," John said in a hushed voice. "I'll be quiet, I'll be quiet. Okay, okay."

John leaned forward and spoke in a whisper into the hand set.

"So?"

"Yes, I got it."

"Good, good. Now you can go to New York, to Columbia."

"I turned it over to Vitaly."

"What? It was for you, for you. I promised. $300,000."

"John, you tried to kill me. Do you remember that?"

"Me? No... I love you."

"John. You don't. You don't love me. You don't love anyone."

"But I do! I do! I do! I do!"

"Vitaly..."

John nodded yes. His eyes narrowed.

"Never liked him much."

"He told me where the money came from. That you were killing people for profit. How could I ever accept it?"

John stiffened in his chair, irritated.

"I was just protecting my investment. I accelerated my return. Activist investing."

"No John, it's premeditated murder. The money has being turned over to the families whose lives you've destroyed. They're using it litigate against you and LAM."

"You bitch."

He banged the handset against the desk in the booth. The guard stepped forward and gave John a warning. John put the receiver back to his ear.

"Temper, temper. I'm sorry to disappoint you."

John began to speak but Mila set down the phone on the counter in front of her, the handset turned upwards and oscillating against the tension of the coiled cord.

She reached into her bag, pulled out a brown manila envelope and undid the red string that held it closed. She extracted two pieces of paper. John leaned forward, straining to see what was on them.

Mila held the first one up to the glass.

John noticed her ring. It was on the third finger of her right hand.

He knocked on the window, indicating to her to pick up the handset, holding up his right hand. Mila picked up the receiver.

"I see you kept your promise," he said. "Who's the lucky guy?

His voice was filled with jealously. Mila could not reconcile John's behaviour. He tried to kill her and now he is jealous of not having her.

"We could've had something, you and me," John added.

She did not respond. John's eyes went to the paper. It was a grainy black and white photo from an ultrasound of a fetus.

John's eyes widened and he smiled. A tear came to his eye. He wiped his nose with the back of his hand.

"Mila, I had no idea. How wonderful!"

"It's yours."

"What? I'm going to be a father. Boy or girl? When's it due?"

Mila remained stationary for a moment and lowered her hand. She held up the other paper.

John was confused. The text was too small to read through the distortion of the window as he sat in his chair.

He stood up and leaned forward, his nose pressed against the glass partition.

The guard stepped forward. John waved him off, put his hands behind his back.

The form was a medical chart from Planned Parenthood. There was a procedure date and a note in red ink in the comments box.

PREGNANCY TERMINATED

John fell back into the chair and hung his head, and covering his eyes with his hands, he began to sob. Mila knocked on the glass with the handset John looked up, picked up the receiver.

"Now we're even," she said quietly and she hung up.

She placed the photo of the ultrasound and the termination paper back into the satchel. She stared at the mass sobbing in the chair.

John began to bang his head against the desk, slowly at first, and then with increasing violence. Two guards stepped forward to restrain him and with incredible force he shook them off, sending both to the ground.

John lunged forward and cracked his head off the glass, mere inches from Mila. Blood gushed from his forehead.

He grabbed his cane and began beating against the glass, the pane shaking against the force.

Mila retreated, worried the partition would give way.

Two more guards fell upon John with truncheons and he fell to the ground as others rushed in to subdue him.

The last to enter held out an electrified prod. Mila could not see John beneath the desk but could hear his whimpering cries.

She hurried out of the room towards a guard standing in front of a locked gate.

He held out the clipboard that she had signed on the way in.

She flipped through the sheets which covered weeks of visitors, and she could see that no one else had come to visit John. He was alone.

The guard pushed a button and the magnetic lock of the gate disengaged. The guard slid the gate open and Mila strode past him and continued down the hallway into the lobby and out the front doors.

A black sedan with tinted windows and the letters "H&N" written in large, gold, stylized letters painted on the front passenger door.

Mike was waiting at the front passenger door.

"Not today, Mike. I think I'd rather sit in the back, if you don't mind?"

"But of course, Mila, as you wish."

Mike opened the rear door and Mila accepted Mike's hand as she sat down. She swung her legs in and he shut the door gently.

Caroline was where she had left her a half hour earlier. She held Caroline's hand in her's against the low of her belly.

"You okay?"

"It's done."

"Yes, but are you okay?

"Yes, Caroline, I'm fine. We're fine. We're safe."

About the Author

Vince Fernandez is a financial professional with more than twenty years of experience investing in capital markets.

In zen moments, when he is not typing with two fingers, he enjoys sabre fencing, fishing, and carving wooden kayak paddles.

Vince currently lives in Toronto with his family. *Little Sister* is his first novel.

Vince Fernandez

Manor House
www.manor-house.biz
905-648-2193

Little Sister

Manor House
www.manor-house.biz
905-648-2193

Manor House
www.manor-house.biz
905-648-2193

Little Sister

Manor House
www.manor-house.biz
905-648-2193

Manor House
www.manor-house.biz
905-648-2193

CPSIA information can be obtained
at www.ICGtesting.com
Printed in the USA
LVOW04s2054130916
504425LV00002B/359/P